E.D. Steele,
Sidney Sussex College.
February; 1956.

FRENCH LIBERAL THOUGHT IN THE EIGHTEENTH CENTURY

FRENCH LIBERAL THOUGHT

IN THE

EIGHTEENTH CENTURY

*A STUDY OF POLITICAL IDEAS
FROM BAYLE TO CONDORCET*

By KINGSLEY MARTIN

Edited by J. P. MAYER

TURNSTILE PRESS LTD.

First published in 1929 by
Ernest Benn Ltd.,

Second Edition, Revised,
published in 1954 by
Turnstile Press Ltd.,
10 Great Turnstile, London, W.C.1

Printed in Great Britain by
Lowe & Brydone (Printers) Limited, London, N.W.10

EDITOR'S FOREWORD

The present work, long, established as a text-book in British and American universities, has been out of print for years. Even on the second-hand book market it was difficult to obtain, and the library copies showed signs of strain through over-use. No other book in the English language has superseded it, which is, perhaps, the greatest compliment one can pay to its author. Paul Hazard in France, Ernst Cassirer in Germany, Carl Becker in the United States, Basil Willey in this country, have all in recent years contributed to our deeper understanding of the spirit of the eighteenth century, but none of these writers, eminent as they are, has made Kingsley Martin's volume superfluous.

One reason for the persistent vitality of this book lies in its method. Mr. Martin illustrates it when he writes: " In this inquiry there are three influences to consider: firstly, the inheritance with which the ideas came into the eighteenth century; secondly, the social conditions and political events in which they developed, and thirdly, the individual peculiarities of men whose own experience necessarily affected the shape and the phraseology of the creed they formulated." Thus Mr. Martin uses a combination of three methods: the " great thinker " method, the philosophic and chronological methods (page 19). I believe that it is this methodological insight which has made the author avoid the pitfalls into which so many histories of political ideas have fallen. They neglect, to use Mr. Martin's own words, " the selective power of events, the actual importance of minor writers in forming doctrines which other and more famous men completed."

Another reason why the present book has kept its freshness must undoubtedly be seen in the fact that its author built its foundation on the original sources. His analysis, for instance, of the influence of the *salons* is remarkable. So is his treatment of Bayle, Voltaire, Diderot and Rousseau. His interpretation of Montesquieu is, perhaps, less congenial, though he maps out with accuracy and pertinence the influence of the *Esprit des Lois.* I could mention another point where I differ from him. I feel he underrates the influence of the aristocracy and the *notables* during the preparatory period of the French Revolution, though of course recent research has added much to our knowledge since Mr. Martin wrote his book. His picture of the economic and constitutional framework of pre-revolutionary France is perhaps too much influenced by Taine, whereas I see it more through the eyes of Tocqueville. Yet this or other points cannot change the author's general appreciation.

He admirably elucidates the formative influence of eighteenth century political thought upon the ideas of 1789. He knows that new historical principles grow slowly. Consequently he deals at length with the seventeenth century: it laid the ground for the new ideas of civil and political liberty, scientific humanism and economic liberalism which the eighteenth century perfected and transmitted for good or for worse to the following generations.

Mr. Martin is by no means blind to the limitations of the eighteenth century philosophers: " The mistakes of the *philosophes* " he writes, " were due to their failure to realize that natural law has a changing and developing content. When Montesquieu compared the customs of one country with those of another he distinguished permanent underlying principles from superficial differences due to local circumstances; but he spoke as if the principles themselves were always constant, and as if geography and climate modified their application without any help from the development of social life itself. Voltaire, whose historical perspective was truer, though narrower, could write: ' The empire of custom is vaster than that of nature: it extends over manners, over all usages: it covers the scene of the universe with variety: nature spreads unity there, establishing everywhere a small number of invariable principles: the foundations, therefore, are everywhere the same, and culture produces varying fruits.' Even here the invariable principles seem static, and the idea that the needs of men in primitive society might not prove an adequate guide to those of modern civilization, totally absent.

EDITOR'S FOREWORD

The Aristotelean conception of the natural as the full development of the potentialities rather than as the original constitution of the organism seldom makes its appearance in the
eighteenth century." (*page* 134) These sentences are full of
meaning. The eighteenth century opened man's mind to the
historical nature of our world but it remained the task of the
following century to discover the philosophic implications that
individuum est ineffabile.

I accepted with great pleasure Mr. Martin's invitation to
see his book through the press. As editor of Tocqueville's
Ancien Régime I have had to cover within recent years much
of its ground. Moreover, it is easier to edit the book of a living
friend than the works of the illustrious dead. Needless to say,
I have taken advantage of the fact that the author of the
present book is very much alive. He has seen all my altera-
tions, and he has generously—in the tolerant, humanist
tradition of the eighteenth century—given his approval to
them. Our agreement was not always so readily forthcoming
when we discussed contemporary problems during the long
years of our friendship. . . . Apart from correcting very few
minor errors or misprints, I have added a bibliography which
may help the student to follow up some of the problems
where the author has left off, or where more recent research
will implement Mr. Martin's findings.

I am confident that this volume will keep its place as an
outstanding text-book for a long time to come.

J. P. Mayer

Stoke Poges, Bucks.
August, 1953.

FROM THE PREFACE TO THE FIRST EDITION

In this book I have tried to discover what that social creed which we have since learned to call Liberalism meant to the eighteenth-century thinkers who formulated and popularized it. If this creed is much blown upon to-day, that may be due in part to its intrinsic defects as a system of thought; in part to the inadequacy of a fighting creed made in a comparatively simple agricultural society to meet the needs of a more highly organized industrial one; in part to the acquisition of new scientific and especially psychological knowledge; and in part to our own failure to differentiate between the essential principles and the accidental accretions of a philosophy which for historical rather than logical reasons was passed on to succeeding centuries as a single body of thought. With this in mind I have set out to inquire what words like Liberty, Equality and Fraternity meant to men who believed that the principles they embodied were in themselves solutions for the problems of society, and to discover why the idea of progress came to be related to that of democracy and why both seemed to their exponents to involve a particular political and economic programme.

The clue to the political thought of any period lies in the conflict between various views of human nature. Theories continually change, but the main division between authoritarian and libertarian remains the same at all periods. In the eighteenth century, Church and State were founded on the belief that human nature was essentially bad and capable of regeneration only through the gift of Grace and the exercise of absolute sovereignty. From the Renaissance onwards that view had been challenged by free-thinkers, who held that life was made to be enjoyed, and that men needed not Grace but freedom to develop their faculties, to cultivate the arts and to profit by the pleasures of society. The peculiar interest of the eighteenth century, however, lies in the growth and apparent triumph of a third view, which repudiated clerical discipline and transformed Renaissance hedonism. It substituted knowledge for Grace as the means of salvation, and held that the prospect of

ix

improving men and society could serve as an ideal, sufficient to co-ordinate men's purposes and provide them with a criterion of right and wrong. This effort to give men a secular religion —a religion which is the real basis of Liberalism and the Socialism which is its lineal heir—is the theme of this book.

CONTENTS

CHAPTER I

CONTENTS

CHAPTER II—*continued*

PART TWO

THE CREED AND ITS ENVIRONMENT

CHAPTER III

CONTENTS

CHAPTER IV

PART THREE
THE CREED DEVELOPS

CHAPTER V

CONTENTS

CHAPTER V—*continued*

CHAPTER VI

CHAPTER VII

CONTENTS

CHAPTER VII—*continued*

CHAPTER VIII

CONTENTS

CHAPTER IX

CONTENTS

CHAPTER X

PART FOUR

THE COMPLETION OF THE REVOLUTIONARY CREED

CHAPTER XI

CONTENTS

CHAPTER XI—*continued*

applying scientific knowledge. The beginning of scientific Utopias—Mercier, Volney and Restif de la Bretonne. Condorcet's *Tableau historique* summarizes the whole religion of democracy and progress. Reasons why the two ideas are obviously one to him. The nine epochs of advancing knowledge, freedom and equality.

The future certainly glorious, because natural laws were now mastered and evolution therefore conscious. No limits to the possible improvement of human nature and of society by deliberate change of environment.

Summary. The reasons for loss of faith in the religion of the French Revolution. Its value.

CHAPTER I

INTRODUCTORY—THE RELIGION OF THE FRENCH REVOLUTION

I. LIBERTY, EQUALITY AND FRATERNITY

IN 1685, by an extravagant act of piety and sovereignty, Louis XIV. outlawed his Protestant subjects. There was scarcely a whisper of protest, except from the exiles themselves. The Revocation of the Edict of Nantes marked the summit of the power of the French monarchy. The *ancien régime* had reached its perfect form, a unified nation, under an absolute and conquering monarch, supported by a strong bureaucracy, a courtly aristocracy and an obedient populace. After 1685 the decline of the *ancien régime* visibly began. During the century which elapsed before the French Revolution, ideas which were incompatible with the existing social, religious and political system were gaining steadily in force and coherence. It was no longer possible to prevent the thoughtful and the discontented from discussing those social, political and religious questions which authority always prefers to regard as finally settled. In the reign of Louis XV. an inquiring child had his choice between the old answers, supported by authority, and the new answers, first implicit in the murmurs of malcontents and the curses of heretics, and then increasingly explicit in the writings of the *philosophes*. Many of these ideas were at least as old as Aristotle, St Thomas Aquinas or Rabelais, but they were new in their eighteenth-century application and new in their fusion with seventeenth-century science. By the time of the Revolution they had ceased to be tentative answers to doubtful questions and had become a series of dogmas, articles in a new religion. The Revolution was, therefore, the climax of a long process: a dramatic moment when feudalism, clericalism and divine monarchy collapsed, making way for the era of economic Liberalism, modern science and representative government.

It would, of course, be untrue to suggest that every

Frenchman was a sincere Catholic[1] and an unhesitating believer in the divine monarchy in 1685, or that the theses of popular sovereignty, natural right and secular progress were universally accepted in 1789. Nevertheless, the common and unthinking assumptions of most ordinary men and women in the seventeenth century were that all the doctrines of the miraculous Church were indisputable; that men were born wicked and could be saved only through the Church and her priests; that the King, reigning over France by divine right, was endowed with absolute power; that legal and social inequality, feudal privilege and arbitrary government were part of the permanent order of things and unalterable. By 1789 these instinctive assumptions had been replaced by another system of ideas in the minds of almost all the urban population of France, and its social, though not its religious, aspects were accepted with equal enthusiasm by the peasantry. The old creed, which had been dominant under Louis XIV., was a lost cause at the fall of the Bastille; and the new creed, which had been shaping itself piecemeal in the minds of scientists and men of letters in the seventeenth century, had become a religion to the deputies who met in the States-General. For these revolutionary doctrines in their final form served all the purposes of a religion. Liberty, Equality and Fraternity were the new watchwords which embodied an ancient and continuous social ideal—a community of equal and free citizens, conscious of a common heritage and a common goal. At the Revolution this vision seemed closer to realization than it has at any other moment of history; men believed that they were in fact equal, and needed only to cast off their chains and to proclaim their common brotherhood. Their faith was upheld by a new metaphysic, an ethic, a series of dogmas and a means of grace. Science had substituted a natural for a supernatural explanation of the universe: knowledge, not obedience, was the gate of salvation; the key was held by men of science, the true priesthood, less exclusive intermediaries between man and the hidden

---

[1] Moralists were already deploring the rapid growth of scepticism in Paris even in the mid-seventeenth century. Indifference and heresy, however, have never ceased to be dangerous since they were denounced by St Paul.

mysteries of nature. Finally the doctrine of progress transformed the whole from a philosophy into a working faith :
men could believe in the ultimate success of the causes for
which they worked, since there were natural and historical
forces greater than themselves working with them.

The new religion won its way in the nineteenth century as a
fighting creed, intellectually and spiritually victorious, flaunting
the prestige and the terrors of its revolutionary triumphs. It
was generally accepted in Europe in spite of the continued
resistance of the traditional Church, the ancient monarchies
and the surviving aristocracy. Both democracy and progress—
ideas closely connected in history but not necessarily in logic
—were attacked by numerous critics, and the spokesmen of the
industrial workers in every country objected to the application
of democratic principles in the interests of men of property.
It was not until the twentieth century, however, that the revolutionary creed was widely discredited, that its fundamental
assumptions were shaken, or that any but isolated thinkers
doubted that truth and the future were substantially on its
side.

In the twentieth century, new knowledge and bewildering
experience have once more brought disillusion, scepticism and
a paralysing sense of impotence. Nowhere except in the United
States, where prosperity strangles criticism, do ideas of democracy and progress still command religious respect. The same
causes which undermined the *ancien régime* are again at work
in Europe : a shifting of the balance of economic power, new
answers given by science to physical, biological and psychological questions, the failure of institutions to satisfy not only
the aspirations of idealists but also the plain needs of ordinary
men and women, and, finally, the example of countries where
liberty and democracy are openly scouted—all these have united
to weaken the authority of the nineteenth-century creed. Indeed
it would be strange if a creed, forged in the battle against the
eighteenth-century institutions, a weapon used to secure individual liberty in a comparatively simple agricultural society,
proved adequate as a basis for the organization of a complex
industrial society. Yet, because that creed came into the

nineteenth century as a single system of ideas, to be accepted or rejected as a whole, any failure in practice, or doubt thrown upon its underlying philosophy, seems to threaten the whole. Men are not quick to admit that one article of a creed may be true and another false, that its philosophic basis may not be entirely absurd because dogmatically held or loosely stated. Theory seldom proceeds by quantitative methods, and equilibrium is not easily found in the shock of reaction. The discovery that inheritance plays a larger part than our forefathers have believed, and reason a smaller part than politicians and philosophers have imagined, is supposed to render futile all deliberate effort to improve social behaviour by environmental change. Strangely enough it is not argued that the cause of failure has been our inadequate use of the reason we do possess, but that, since it is weaker than we believed, reason may be neglected in future as a helpless servant of instinct. A misunderstood Freudianism superimposed upon a misapplied Darwinism is a potent weapon of destruction. It becomes easy to dismiss the hope of a free and equal community as an illusion of childhood.

It may nevertheless be worth while to examine the conditions under which the ideas of the Revolution won their way, to discover what were the claims made for them by their eighteenth-century champions, and what philosophic arguments seemed to justify democratic government, equal rights and social progress. Such an investigation may throw light on the nature of this faith and do something not only to explain the cause of failure and disappointment, but also to turn impatience and disgust into critical appraisement. A fuller understanding of the historical perspective might temper the joyful ardour with which men continually throw out the babies with the bath water. The creed of the Revolution is worthy of a closer examination than its champions or its enemies are usually willing to accord it.

Equality, Liberty and Fraternity are ideals for which men still strive, even though their attainment now seems a more difficult matter than it did a century and a half ago. We no longer expect to build a science of government on first principles, and we are not able to believe that men, whatever their race, class or colour, are naturally equal in capacity. It no longer seems obvious that liberty consists in the exercise of certain fixed and definable rights and that universal brotherhood will be the inevitable result of destroying national and class barriers. It may nevertheless be worth while to diminish, as far as may be, the social inequalities which destroy the hope of communal life, and natural rights may still have significance even though they demand a new interpretation in an age which analyses human nature more thoroughly and less confidently. Even the idea of a peaceful world-federation is not necessarily futile because we can no longer assume its automatic arrival through the operation of free trade and natural harmony.

The positive doctrines which sprang from these ideals are naturally inadequate to twentieth-century discontents. It is well to admit their inadequacy but not to forget their value. Personal liberty still needs champions in an age which has learned that release from stone walls does not make freedom. Equality of rights, even in the limited and legal sense, is a cause for which men must fight no less strenuously when they have discovered that the right of property needs drastic modification if they are to enjoy the substance, and not only prate of the shadow, of liberty and equality. Indeed the rights which the eighteenth-century *philosophes* demanded were not on a par : unlike thought and free speech, property is limited in amount, and one man's right of ownership restricts the rights of another. This was not so obviously true in an agricultural society in which landed property was widely distributed, and in which the outcry against inequality was directed against legal privilege rather than against the irresponsible power of money. The principle of legal equality remains valuable, however, in spite of the fact that the poor can never be really equal with the rich before the law, or in any other way. Similarly the political interpretation of democracy has disappointed the hopes of enthusiasts, but the conception of responsible and even of representative government may survive the failure of some of the usual methods of enforcing responsibility and organizing representation.

2. ARTICLES OF FAITH

In 1789 the National Assembly of France summarized the principles of the Revolution. In the Declaration of the Rights of Man, " the representatives of the people of France, considering ignorance, neglect or contempt of the rights of man to be the sole cause of public misfortunes and the corruption of government," set forth, as they believed, for all time, " these natural, sacred and inalienable rights." [1] These were the rights of "Liberty, Property, Security and Resistance to Oppression." The Declaration proceeded to define liberty as the right to act without any restraint except that imposed by law, and to assume that, in a country where the law was " an expression of the will of the community," all actions would be legally permitted to the citizen except those which injured the equal exercise of rights by other persons. The right of property, it further explained, meant that the State would not interfere with the free enjoyment of ownership or confiscate property " except in cases of evident public necessity, and then after payment of a just indemnity." " Security " would result from the existence of a single legal system, equally applicable to all, administered by courts which presumed innocence until guilt was proved. The right to resist oppression implied that any government could be legitimately overthrown which trampled upon individual liberty. In order that these rights might be for ever guaranteed, they were to be embodied in

---

[1] Thirteen years earlier the American colonies had anticipated this Declaration, explaining their reasons for assuming "among the powers of the earth the separate and equal station to which the laws of nature and nature's God entitled them. . . . We hold these things to be self-evident, that all men are created equal, that they are endowed by their Creator with certain inalienable Rights, that these are Life, Liberty, and the pursuit of Happiness." The authority of governments was justified only if it secured these rights for every individual, and it was justly forfeited where the rights of men were violated. In the year of the French Revolution the thirteen American States formed a federal Constitution, resting on a basis of popular consent and guaranteeing individual rights by the mechanism of the separation of powers. Some years later they added a Bill of Rights, which was intended to summarize the gains of the past and to secure individual liberty from infringement by the wills of peoples or governments.

a written Constitution, which could not be changed by any ordinary legislative procedure.

In England, where no sudden revolution took place, Jeremy Bentham analysed the French Declaration of Rights and declared it to be mere "bawling on paper." He had himself found a more stable if less absolute philosophy of liberty in contemporary French literature; it was in Helvétius that he had first found the greatest-happiness principle explicitly stated. Why could not the French deputies base their demands on sound utilitarian arguments instead of indulging in vague declamations about eternal and inalienable rights? Why could they not say that, in their opinion, the greatest happiness of the greatest number would be promoted if certain rights were, under present circumstances, legally bestowed upon every individual? Starting from this basis, he proceeded to justify on grounds of utility the very rights which the French were claiming on grounds of nature. Men should be treated equally, because they were all susceptible to pain and pleasure, and had equal needs; they should be given civil and political liberty, because a man's happiness depends on his opportunity to follow his own interest without interference; they should be allowed property, because without it there is no incentive to produce nor harmony between private interests and public welfare. Security is essential if men are to know how to promote their own good, and as for the right to resist oppression, men are always justified in overthrowing corrupt and arbitrary governments if they can. Thus the substance of the Utilitarian creed, for the time at least, coincided with the Revolutionary doctrine : utility and natural law agreed because they were weapons against the same evils, and in every European country middle-class persons, who were neither theoretical exponents of natural law nor systematic Utilitarians, but who resented bad government and thought they could govern better themselves, were found to be making similar demands and advocating the same changes. They strove to abolish all monopolies and privileges; they looked forward to a new age of equality, when they should have liberty to trade, to speak, and to worship or not, as they chose.

The French Revolution was so great a release of the human

spirit, and its grandiose phrases cloaked needs so urgently felt everywhere, that their satisfaction seemed to offer men permanent happiness. The same optimism was to be found wherever the principles of the Revolution prevailed. Bentham himself was not less confident than Jefferson ; and if it was a French deputy who asked for a constitution equally valid for all times and all places, and Sièyes who declared that he had completed the science of government, it was Bentham's most intimate disciple, James Mill, who remarked, when explaining the virtues of democracy, that if his arguments were not valid, the task of finding a good government must be for ever abandoned. For the time being, then, the two great trends of Liberal thought were in practical agreement : the Utilitarian and the exponent of natural rights both wanted the same things, made the same fundamental assumptions about the nature of man and society, and were equally confident that the recognition of their principles would render men happy and virtuous.

The substance of their common creed may be expressed in a series of propositions. The only justification for the State is the promotion of the happiness of its citizens. Men are rational : they are, that is, able to perceive the good, to discover means of attaining it, and to direct their lives by their knowledge and experience. This ability to seek rational ends by rational means is shared by all normal men, who are, generally speaking, equal not only in their elementary needs but also in their natural capacities. To attain happiness, therefore, men need and are equally entitled to liberty : the function of the State is to preserve men's rights, not supervise their use of them. Since rational beings best know their own interests, no conqueror, autocrat or aristocracy can have the right or capacity to govern : the laws, therefore, should accord with popular wishes, and must be administered by an executive which is responsible to the people or their representatives. Finally, since men learn by experience, it follows that with the destruction of ancient forms of government, the inauguration of an era of equality, and the advance of scientific knowledge, men can constantly improve their society, achieve greater happiness and ultimately perfection.

8

3. THE DEVELOPMENT OF THE REVOLUTIONARY CREED

These propositions were stated with new significance in eighteenth-century France. They were, of course, not new in themselves. It would be convenient if ideas were born like Athene, fully armed from the head of Zeus, or arrived less aggressively like Aphrodite, perfectly shaped from the foam of the sea. In fact, it is otherwise. They are born, like other children of this earth, trailing clouds of glory and of shame, heirs and victims of an historic past, bearing the stamp of their progenitors, misshapen by the accidental circumstances of birth, compelled to fight for existence, developing as best they may in the stress of conflict. Their development is surprising and their maturity unlike that expected by those who first nourished them, not only because every idea is a compound of past associations, and charged with hidden explosives, but also because the social *milieu* exercises a rigorous selective and transmuting influence. Established institutions—the Church, the State and the Law—have everything to lose and nothing to gain by change, while at most times the inertia of ordinary citizens increases the astonishing capacity which any society has for slowly digesting the most unassimilative of matter and remaining apparently unaffected by the process. New facts and new ideas are imperceptibly incorporated, not deliberately substituted; somehow or other they are reconciled with the most incompatible views until suddenly, it seems, the work is done and everyone unites in declaring that a new age has arrived.

To describe the origin and growth of the individual tenets of the new creed would therefore be a complex and unlikely story, which would begin at least as early as fifth-century Greece. It would not be an account of a tidy or logical evolution. In the history of ideas logical relations may be unrelated in fact and actual relations may leap centuries. The new doctrines had appeared in earlier generations, and had served in their time a variety of causes ; they had been frequently in opposition to each other and been advanced by groups which seemed, in general, their enemies. Some of the ideas of the

Revolution could be traced to ancient Sparta, others to Athens ; in one form or another they were all discussed by Plato and Aristotle. They appeared in the Roman Republic and in the Empire ; in Mediæval Christendom they fought for and against the Papacy. They gained new vitality in the Renaissance, and in the Reformation the national king was often their champion. For the time, at least, the prince, not the common man, profited by their success, and, although the cause of mental freedom was advanced by the humiliation of the priesthood, political liberty seemed farther off under national monarchs than it had been in the Middle Ages.

The conception of natural law which served the cause of liberty in the seventeenth and eighteenth centuries was of Stoic origin ; it had been transformed by its combination with the *jus gentium* of Roman Law ; it had flowed on, an undercurrent beneath the main stream of mediæval thought ; it had emerged at the Renaissance, and was used to support tyranny as well as to overthrow it. The claim to toleration, which was commonly based upon an appeal to natural law before it was supported by Utilitarian arguments, was at length accepted, not because men recognized its social value or respected one another's opinions, but because, after many attempts to found states upon a single religion had failed, the religious wearily accepted the view of the sceptics that the extermination of neighbours who differed from you was too troublesome, uneconomic and dangerous a business. The scientist and freethinker indeed had often found most toleration under despots, who were not so slow as their subjects to realize that political unity and national peace were preferable to religious conformity and civil war.

There has been no single line of development with liberty, equality and fraternity on one side, and tyranny and oppression on the other. The idea of equality has sometimes meant that all the children of God are to be of equal spiritual value; has sometimes been a plea for freedom by natural inheritance; and sometimes an argument for the opposite idea, that all goods should be equally shared amongst weak and strong alike. Similarly the demand for liberty, though at times expressed in universal language, has commonly been made by a particular group desiring a specific reform. Indeed until the French Revolution itself liberty meant, as a rule, religious and civil liberty, which was more likely to be secured under an enlightened monarch than under a popular government where, as in some of the American colonies, a fanatical group might be as intolerant as the Papacy itself. As for the theory of popular sovereignty, its principal champions had been lawyers, who derived the Mediæval Empire from the free vote of the Roman Assembly, and sixteenth-century Jesuits, who eloquently explained that it was the duty of the faithful to overthrow kings who failed in zeal for the Pope or the Society of Jesus.

Such words as Liberty, Equality and Fraternity are catchwords which deceive the historians as well as the populace. Analysis shows that they have commonly been the battle-cry of groups suffering from oppression, ready to become oppressors in their turn ; anxious to overthrow privilege in order themselves to exercise a more rigorous monopoly, and proclaiming the brotherhood of man within their own ranks in order more effectively to tyrannize over their neighbours. Those who have made revolutions have usually known what they meant by liberty and equality with a fair degree of accuracy : they have invoked the goddess of freedom in their struggle against specific forms of oppression. They have not been worshippers of vague abstractions. It is the philosophers and historians in search of systems and universal explanations who have supposed the concrete demands of the moment to be conscious aspirations after the eternal good. But it is also easy to make the opposite mistake. The realist who analyses social discontent, and finds that philosophic ideas are merely rationalizations for subjective desires, misses the mark even more widely than his idealistic colleagues. It is true that the idea of a liberty, an equality and a brotherhood which would include every class, colour and nation has been only the rare dream of isolated individuals, yet the universal element has persisted and grown in spite of partial interpretations and frequent betrayals.

The Christian slave in ancient Rome or modern America was comforted by the thought that earthly inequalities would be remedied in heaven, where the last would be first and the first would be last. The peasantry who rose to demand the rights of Adam in the fourteenth century, and the Anabaptists who demanded the restoration of Christ's Church on earth in the sixteenth, the Diggers and Levellers who thought that the land was equally the property of every man in the seventeenth, the Parisian shopkeeper who, inspired by Rousseau and 'Mably, claimed the rights of man in the eighteenth, and the Trade Unionist who asked that each should be rewarded according to his needs in the nineteenth century—each of these and many other groups were moved directly by the pricking of particular grievances. But the historian is right in seeing their struggles as all part of a single movement. In each period there have been men who related their own wants to those of their neighbours, who were not satisfied with the filling of their own stomachs, and were in search of a society where the hunger neither of the body nor of the mind should go unsatisfied. The vision of such a society has haunted the ages; in the eighteenth century it became conscious, and seemed closer to realization than at any other period in history.

The Liberal application of the historic phrases of democracy first appears in modern history when the sovereignty of the Renaissance monarch ceased to appear an advantage and grew to be an oppression to the middle class. At the end of the Middle Ages the supreme need was for order and protection against lawless feudalism, but the class of men who had been prepared to support tyranny for the sake of security began to fret against the tyrant's interference with their trade, their thought and their religion. In the case of Holland this revolt took a national form. The Dutch asserted their national and religious independence, while Althusius, profiting by Jesuit example, revived the doctrine of popular sovereignty to justify revolt against a legitimate king. A little later the English, accounted by all contemporaries the least stable and most disorderly of peoples, executed one king, deposed another, and, in the course of the struggle, united the ancient theories of natural law and individual rights with the conception of responsible government and popular sovereignty. The British settlement of 1689 became, therefore, the pattern of free government for European Liberals.

The chief theorist of 1689 was John Locke, in whose writings democratic ideas first became associated with the scientific movement which had been growing since the Renaissance. For Locke was not only an exponent of natural law, toleration and government by consent, but was also a doctor, a scientist and a rationalistic philosopher. Above all, he was the originator of a psychology which provided democratic government with a scientific basis. After Locke, it was possible to give reasons for holding that men were rational beings, with equal needs and capacities, almost all able under free government to develop, to learn, and to build on the basis of experience. Pascal had been wrong: men were not born in sin and destined for destruction, but born in ignorance and destined through reason to work out their own salvation.

Locke's scientific and political conclusions were the logical outcome of tendencies already far advanced in contemporary science and philosophy. The attack on the Ptolemaic cosmogony usually connected with the names of Copernicus and Galileo, the determination of Descartes to begin metaphysics with the known and to accept only deductions made from axiomatic premises, the insistence of Bacon upon the experimental and inductive method—all these shook the metaphysical basis upon which political and also religious authority were founded. The ground was cleared for a new scientific treatment of the universe, in which the human race abandonod its claims to preferential treatment. At the same time the individual's responsibility was increased by the substitution of human inquiry and human will for supernatural revelation and providential guidance. Protestantism had overthrown the priesthood and —in its ideal, if not in its organized forms—claimed for every individual direct access to the Almighty, or, at least, the Almighty's own account of Himself in the Bible. The scientists were also individualists, and were also sure that their approach to truth was the only reliable one. Leaving ultimate philosophic problems unexplored, they set out to build solely upon the basis of external and measurable experience. Their assumptions, which only gradually became conscious and acknowledged, were that all problems were ultimately soluble by the methods they had found useful, and that the concepts of matter and energy which led to such surprising immediate results in the early days of modern science provided a satisfactory and even a final explanation of the physical universe.

The success of seventeenth-century scientists, culminating in the unequalled achievements of Newton, silenced remaining doubts, and seemed, to the eighteenth century, to establish for ever the validity of what Newton had regarded only as a hypothesis. Even the unanswered and perhaps unanswerable criticisms of David Hume were neglected by his contemporaries, who naturally preferred to work at the open task before them rather than speculate upon its possible limitations. Eighteenth-century writers neglected at least half of their Cartesian inheritance. The great philosophers and scientists of the seventeenth century were not under the delusion that they had escaped from dualism, nor did they lay down a materialistic dogma about the ultimate nature of reality. They were as much " vitalists " as materialists, and in different circumstances—if, for instance, the Catholic Church in the eighteenth century had been true to its spiritualist philosophy—much of the clerical rigidity and intolerance associated with the scientific spirit might have been avoided.

In the eighteenth century, however, the mechanical assumptions which Newton and his predecessors laid down as a basis for research invaded other spheres of thought to which they were inapplicable.[1]

The study of individual psychology, which was the great feature of the age of La Rochefoucauld and La Bruyère, was

---

[1] Professor Whitehead says that the seventeenth and the two succeeding centuries were dominated by physical concepts very unsuited to biology ; they " set for it an insoluble problem of matter and life and organism with which biologists are now wrestling " (*Science and the Modern World*, p. 51). This is just to the eighteenth century but not to the seventeenth. The unmechanical aspects of the work of Descartes, Spinoza and Leibniz seemed to the eighteenth merely to prove that they had feared the Church or failed in logic. There was enough truth in this view to make it easy for the Encyclopædists to neglect the difficulties which the Cartesians had failed to overcome.

continued in the succeeding century by only a few comparatively obscure writers.[1] Moreover the same mechanical assumptions, based in this case upon the sensationalist empiricism of Locke, affected political and economic as well as purely scientific thought, and the social speculations of the eighteenth and nineteenth centuries also suffered from a tendency to apply these mechanical assumptions to problems of social organization to which they were altogether unsuitable. Even analogies drawn from mechanics were misleading in political thought. The form in which democratic ideas were passed on from the seventeenth to the eighteenth century was already influenced by the study of physics. For Locke, whose political ideas dominated the eighteenth century, approached politics from the point of view of a seventeenth-century physicist, and made it possible for his followers to treat problems of individual and social psychology exactly as if they were set to dam rivers or to build bridges. A mechanical psychology is at the root of all eighteenth-century thought : empiricism and democracy developed side by side, not only because they were two aspects of the revolt against the spiritual and political authority of the *ancien régime*, but because they were logically connected, and based upon similar concepts. The religion of the Revolution was thus founded on the belief that all men and all societies were capable of improvement by deliberate and scientific adjustment of their environment.

From the beginning of the eighteenth century, therefore, there were two strands of thought, both subversive of orthodoxy. In the first place there were the sceptics, who did not accept the philosophic assumptions upon which society was founded and who remained without delusions about the past or hope for the future. It is to this eighteenth century that the twentieth returns with such empty satisfaction. In the second place there were

---

[1] Perhaps Vauvenargues is the most interesting of them. Although Voltaire expressed a boundless admiration for him, his intuitive psychology and literary manner were so exceptional in the eighteenth century that his contemporaries completely failed to understand him. For an excellent account of Vauvenargues and an appreciation of his effort to find a more satisfactory psychological theory see *Luc de Clapiers, Marquis de Vauvenargues*, by May Wallas.

the apostles of progress, who were not content with repudiating existing creeds and who found in science and history grounds for believing in the indefinite improvement of the human race. Religious scepticism was a stage on the route to a new faith in human perfectibility.

By the reign of Louis XV. most educated French people had ceased to accept the philosophic assumptions upon which society was founded, and had lost confidence in the economic and political institutions of the *ancien régime*. Almost all of them were sceptics in matters of religion. Even such officials of the Church as defended Catholicism were inspired not by faith but by fear; institutionalists, they naturally assumed that moral laxity would result from the decay of religious authority. They gave, as Condorcet said, a "half-submission," remaining "free to believe what they liked, provided that they believed something incomprehensible." In the same way, existing political and economic systems were seldom championed on the ground that they were good, but were supported because social disruption seemed their only alternative. Where there is no coherent faith, no commonly accepted scale of values, no ideals at which the intellect does not scoff, no confident sense that anything in particular is worth while, there is not likely to be great art or literature on the one hand, or striking material achievement on the other. The cultured aristocracy of the eighteenth century was acutely conscious that a great epoch had passed, and it remained under the spell of Louis XIV. and of Racine, outwardly satisfied with its own sterility. It had no confidence in the future and no understanding of current intellectual movements, which appeared to be merely uncouth, Gothic and in the worst of taste. God, immortality and the Divine Monarch were natural subjects for witticisms, while democracy, until the period of the American revolution, was a somewhat remote topic which arose in discussions of ancient history. If they had considered the matter seriously at all, Madame du Deffand and her friends would certainly have agreed with the Abbé Coignard in repudiating the Declaration of the Rights of Man "because of the excessive and unfair separation it establishes between man and the gorilla." The sceptical eighteenth century is, therefore, not wholly a twentieth-century invention. Yet it was only a restricted social circle which was as sceptical of the goodness of man as it was of the goodness of God.

The main trend of eighteenth-century thought was all in the opposite direction. Beyond the circle of those who clung to the dead forms, and could conceive of no freer society, a new philosophy, confident and assertive, was in process of formation. Scepticism was an aristocratic attitude. The middle class was sceptical of Catholicism and Divine Right, but altogether free from that paralysing scepticism which leads men to doubt whether they are capable of any conscious control over their social life or future. The new philosophy, which was to be completed at the Revolution, was a blend of many elements which had one thing in common. They were all assertions in different forms of what the *ancien régime* denied, that ordinary men and women were able by the exercise of their own will and reason to form a society in which they would be happy and in which they could develop and realize all their natural faculties. This conception of equality, the basic notion of democracy, had been undermining feudalism and steadily transforming conceptions of art, literature and politics since the later Middle Ages. The eighteenth-century thinkers who advanced this democratic movement were few of them democrats in the political sense, but in their long battle with an authoritarian church, a feudal aristocracy and an arbitrary government they made a new synthesis and passed their diverse and loosely connected doctrines of revolt on to the nineteenth century as the simple, final and indubitable truth. At the Revolution itself the conclusions of science seemed to justify the most fervent declarations of popular orators. It was a moment of extraordinary agreement, in which politicians, scientists, poets and business men all held the same view. It was only gradually that the superficial unity disappeared and underlying disagreements became apparent. For the moment, it seemed scientifically sensible, as well as politically sound, to trust the intelligence and good will of the people, even though in practice one drew the line somewhere. It was certainly easier not to ask whom

" the people " were and with what they were to be trusted. In any case, the lowly were exalted and the mighty cast down. The people themselves, as Heine said, could "wield their own sceptre and crown with which the monkeys had played."

The literature dealing with the philosophic doctrines of the eighteenth century is immense. A large part of it is concerned with a single controversy—the degree of influence exercised by the *philosophes* upon the French Revolution. That fundamental problem is unavoidable, and is briefly discussed in the third chapter of this book. My main object, which has already been indicated and may now be conveniently summarized, is a different one. I have traced the gradual formation of the creed of the Revolution from the critical point of view of the twentieth century and attempted to show to what extent the democratic and progressive principles which dominated nineteenth-century politics were conditioned by the temporary and local circumstances of the French *ancien régime*. The *philosophes* of the eighteenth century popularized not only a faith in humanity and an ideal of a free and equal society, but also specific economic and political doctrines and a psychological and biological theory. Their followers accepted the ideal, the programme and the scientific basis with equal enthusiasm. If we would understand how that creed stands to-day the first necessity is to discover the relationship between these entirely separable but commonly connected aspects of the Revolutionary principles and so build an historical foundation upon which modern criticism may proceed with less danger of confusing essential elements with the accidental products of particular conditions and personalities.

In this inquiry there are three influences to consider : firstly, the inheritance with which the ideas came into the eighteenth century ; secondly, the social conditions and political events in which they developed, and thirdly, the individual peculiarities of men whose own experience necessarily affected the shape and the phraseology of the creed they formulated. If personality alone were important it would be possible to adopt the convenient method, commonly favoured by historians of political thought, of devoting a chapter to each great writer or school of writers. This method would have the advantage of explaining how certain arguments and phrases which have survived their time originated in the genius of men like Montesquieu and Rousseau. And writers so influential and dominant as these can be (and are in this book) treated separately. The exclusive use of this method, however, has disastrous consequences : it neglects the selective power of events, the actual importance of minor writers in forming doctrines which other and more famous men completed, and it leads to the writing of almost valueless histories, in which each famous writer continues the work of his predecessor with a pleasing but quite unhistorical continuity. Whatever history is, it does not consist in the biographies of great men, and whatever the influences which affect the evolution of thought they cannot be explained by cataloguing the theories of famous writers. An exclusively logical treatment of ideas, apart from their social environment, is scarcely more likely to succeed than a purely personal one, while a method which deals with ideas in the chronological order of their appearance would be useful to no one except a compiler of bibliographies.

Each of these methods—the " great thinker " method, the philosophic method and the chronological method—has grave defects. Yet simplification is unavoidable. The plan adopted in this book is that combination of all three which seems most suited to its particular object. Since that object is to show how far the evolution of a particular set of ideas was influenced by the conditions of the eighteenth century, I have dealt with the lives and personalities of writers only when their individual peculiarities—the most obvious example is Rousseau—have given their doctrines a permanent stamp which would otherwise be unexplained. Writers whose importance was predominantly literary and whose works do not enter into the main current of revolutionary philosophy are omitted, or referred to only by way of illustration. Emphasis throughout the book is upon the relation of the ideas to eighteenth-century conditions, and to the selective as well as the formative influence of that environment upon the dominant ideas of 1789.

In pursuance of these principles, Part One deals with the emergence of all the Revolutionary doctrines during the reign of Louis XIV., and thus explains the form in which ideas of civil and political liberty, scientific humanism and economic liberalism came into the eighteenth century.

Part Two describes the conditions and events which enabled them to spread and conquer during the reigns of Louis' successors. It shows how the economic structure of society created a Revolutionary class ready for subversive doctrines, how the constitutional struggle between the monarchy, the religious parties and the *Parlements* increasingly discredited, from the middle of the century onwards, both the Crown and the Church, and gave rise to the revival of the legal theory of natural law. Chapter III. then deals with the economic and political environment. Chapter IV is concerned with the conditions of intellectual co-operation in the century—with the effects of persecution and censorship upon the doctrines of the *philosophes* and with the subtler but no less powerful influence of *salon* patronage, upon which depended academic and literary success as well as the hope of effective propaganda.

Having sketched in this background it becomes possible in Part Three to examine the development of the ideas themselves, and to explain in more detail how far they were the product of that environment. Chapter V. explains the importance of Lockean psychology and Newtonian physics to the Revolutionary outlook, and shows how an initial position was reached by Voltaire which was potent as a weapon against clerical absolutism and irresponsible government but inadequate as a basis for a new régime. Voltaire's politics were no more satisfactory than his metaphysics. He fought for liberty but did not analyse its meaning. We see in Chapter VI. how Montesquieu evolved a new method of political philosophy, and how an extremely influential theory of free government was built on his interpretation of the British Constitution. Chapter VII. traces the way in which the less compromising Encyclopædists pushed Voltaire's premises to more logical conclusions, reaching, in some cases, a complete materialism and a rigid utilitarianism. The search for liberty, moreover, seemed to them to necessitate representative government as well as the safeguarding of civil rights. With the advent of Rousseau, to whose philosophy Chapter VIII. is devoted, a sentimental belief in the sovereignty of the people takes the place of this utilitarian argument, and political democracy finds its most powerful advocate. The theory of liberty in the eighteenth century has thus completed its evolution and is left with two rival defences, which are only with difficulty reconciled at the Revolution.

So far the philosophic basis of the Revolutionary creed has been examined, and the particular meaning of liberty in the eighteenth century analysed. Chapter IX. deals with the idea of equality and explains how it came about that the nineteenth century inherited a doctrine which made the free ownership of private property seem equivalent to social equality, and neglected, until the industrial worker became strong enough to champion it, the alternative conception, also widely stated in the eighteenth century, that social equality was possible only where communism, or at least a large measure of socialism, was in operation.

There remains the Revolutionary conception of fraternity, and Chapter X. explains how the theory of universal harmony, the growing conception of international law and the revolt from the dynastic wars of the eighteenth century led to a belief that international brotherhood was possible. The problem of establishing perpetual peace was fully discussed by economic theorists and by Rousseau and Kant.

The eighteenth-century conceptions of liberty, equality and fraternity have thus been analysed, and their relation to the conditions of their growth defined. In the final chapter we see how all the ideas of the century are summarized and given life and religious power by their alliance with the doctrine of progress, stated in comprehensive form by Condorcet. Here we have a theory which rests on the psychology of Locke and the physics of Newton, which utilizes the view which had long been growing that history is a story not of the degradation but of the continuous improvement of man, which has reasons for believing that with the advance of science, and the establishment of liberty, equality and fraternity, there are no limits to the possible improvement of society and of human nature itself. The problem to which this book offers no answer, but perhaps supplies some material for an answer, is the extent to which this theory is really discredited in a disappointed age.

CHAPTER II

THE LEVIATHAN STATE

I. SILENCE—THE THEORY OF ABSOLUTISM

"Le peuple entra dans le sanctuaire: il leva le voile qui doit toujours couvrir tout ce que l'on peut dire, tout ce que l'on peut croire du droit des peuples et de celui des rois, qui ne s'accordent jamais si bien ensemble que dans le silence" (*Mémoires du Cardinal de Retz*).

IN the seventeenth century the English and the French monarchies were both engaged in a struggle to secure their sovereignty. In both countries the absolute power of Pope and Emperor had passed to the national King; in France sixteenth-century lawyers had made Henry IV. the residuary legatee of the Roman Empire and, in England, Hobbes, with even greater assurance, had justified the irresponsible sovereignty of the Stuarts on a Utilitarian basis. In England Divine Right was effectively countered by the doctrine of fundamental law; behind all human laws, Coke held, there existed a law of nature, a moral law, which no Government was entitled to violate. Its practical expression was to be found not only in Biblical precepts but also in the Common Law of England; English kings had recognized its final authority, embodied in the Coronation Oath and the provisions of Magna Charta. The Puritan House of Commons willingly utilized Coke's theory in its struggle with Charles I., but the revolutionary settlement of 1689 resulted not in the recognition of a fundamental Constitution but in the doctrine of government by consent and the assumption by Parliament of the sovereignty wrested from the Stuarts. "The divine right of the Whig landowner" took the place of the divine right of the monarchy.[1]

In France the seventeenth-century contest ended in the complete triumph of the monarchy. The Bourbons were stronger than the Stuarts for many reasons. The power of the French monarchy, like that of the English, was founded on national

---

[1] It was left to the United States of America to revert to Coke's theory and to attempt to embody the political certainties of mankind in a fundamental Constitution, superior to any regular legislative body, and capable of interpretation only by an independent judiciary.

opposition to the Papacy and the desire of the trading middle class and populace for the destruction of the lawless power of the feudal aristocracy. But the humiliation of the aristocracy had been of a different kind in the two countries : in France, as Tocqueville said, the aristocracy had lost their powers and kept their privileges, while in England they had lost their privileges and kept their power. The new English aristocracy, created by the Tudors and employed by them in local and central government, itself led the rebellion against the monarchy which had called it into existence. Religious and economic grievances also united a large section of the middle class against the Stuarts.

In France the monarchy made no attempt to extract money from the aristocracy, seldom even called upon it for military service, and entrusted the administration of the country to *intendants*, directly responsible to the central Government. Moreover the middle class was far less formidable ; the reformed Church had won only a precarious foothold, and was loyal to a king who tolerated its existence. The States-General, having no control over taxation, was easily dispensed with, and was not called again after its presentation of grievances in 1614. The only constitutional check upon the royal power was the right of the legal *Parlements* to register the King's edicts, but their resistance or criticism could always be overruled by a ceremonial *lit de justice*.

The *Fronde*, therefore, could never reach the dimensions of the English rebellion. Without disinterested leadership, religious enthusiasm or constitutional machinery through which to work, the movement quickly degenerated into a series of Court intrigues, and was crushed. Yet it was not insignificant. Its theory closely resembled that of the early stages of the contemporary rebellion in England. The spokesmen of the *Fronde* relied on the same principles as the English Puritans, admitting the legitimacy of royal authority as long as it was exercised in accordance with a fundamental law embodied in French custom and tradition. The King's edicts, they insisted, could be constitutionally enforced only after free registration by the *Parlements*. Pamphleteers, like Claude Joly, went further, and talked of popular sovereignty and natural rights.[1]

Some observers expected the *Fronde* to lead to other rebellions, and finally to a limitation of the King's authority. Cardinal de Retz, who played so prominent a part himself in the revolt, believed that it marked the awakening of public opinion, the beginning of an era of criticism in which men would demand constitutional safeguards against arbitrary government. "The people entered the sanctuary and raised the veil which ought always to hide all that can be said or believed about the rights of peoples and kings, who never agree so well as in a relationship of silence. *La Salle du Palais* violated these mysteries."[2]

The *Fronde*, however, did not mark the beginning of an age of criticism, but paved the way for the despotism of Louis XIV. For the time, at least, the people were the more firmly excluded from the shrine. Between 1651 and 1680 the relationship of silence, which de Retz judged the only safe one between absolute monarch and subject, was more completely established than at any other time in modern history. Louis never forgot the *Fronde*, and after Mazarin's death in 1661 never appointed another Prime Minister. He left little room for the critic. The right of printing was reduced to a minimum; the censorship was increased and the periodic Press disappeared. The Paris *Parlement* became merely a court of justice, and between 1673 and the death of Louis in 1715 its right of remonstrance was only once exercised.[3] The rule of the *intendants* and the

---

[1] A good summary of the political theory of the *Fronde* is contained in Sée, *Les Idées politiques en France au XVIIᵉ Siècle.*

[2] "L'on chercha en s'éveillant, comme à tâtons, les lois : l'on ne les trouva plus ; l'on s'effara, l'on cria, l'on se les demanda ; et, dans cette agitation, les questions que leurs explications firent naître, d'obscures qu'elles étaient et vénérables par leur obscurité, devinrent problématiques, et dès là, a l'égard de la moitié du monde, odieuses. La peuple entra dans le sanctuaire ; il leva le voile qui doit toujours couvrir tout ce que l'on peut dire, tout ce que l'on peut croire du droit des peuples et de celui des rois, qui ne s'accordent jamais si bien ensemble que dans le silence. La Salle du Palais profana ces mystères" (*Mémoires du Cardinal de Retz,* ed. Feillet, t. i., p. 294).

[3] The *Parlement* protested on the occasion of the registration of the Bull *Unigenitus* in 1713.

use of royal councils were extended, and the old provincial assemblies were deprived of their functions. "It was God's will," said Louis, "that the subject should obey without discrimination."

In the *Mémoires* of Louis XIV. the three great arguments for sovereign kingship were for the first time completely blended. Louis inherited the *suprema potestas* of the Roman Emperor, rediscovered by sixteenth-century lawyers for the benefit of Renaissance kings; his, too, was the *dominium* of the feudal overlord, with the ultimate right to dispose at will of all land usually considered private property, but actually only held in usufruct; finally, as Christian Prince, elect of God and deputy of Christ, his authority over the minds, bodies and consciences of his subjects was proven both by Old Testament example and New Testament precept.

In Louis the Renaissance State and the Sovereign Monarchy had reached their apogee. The Crown, the State and the Nation were but three words for the same thing. The interests and the will of the Monarch were those of the State, and assumed to be also those of the Nation. In all things they were final and admitted neither limit nor responsibility. In external relations the State was its own justification; it recognized no obligations except those it cared to impose on itself and no responsibility except its own expansion. The maxims of Rome were at Louis' disposal. "What the King wills is law" and "*salus reipublicæ suprema lex*" are one and the same thing in a state where the people's will is presumed to be included in that of the King. Royal caprice and *raison d'état* are indistinguishable. In his *Politique* Bossuet painted an ideal portrait of his King; he was indeed the Leviathan; "a great people united in a single person, *une raison secrète* shut within a single head and governing all the body of the State." Louis always regarded himself as free from any international obligations, and informed the Dauphin that expressions of permanent friendship and alliance in treaties were useful only as diplomatic courtesies.[1] Throughout his

---

[1] Cp. *Louis XIV. Œuvres* (ed. Grouvelle), i. 64. It is interesting to compare this passage with the Machiavellian precept: "Quelques clauses specieuses qu'on y mette d'union, d'amitié, de se procurer respectivement toutes sortes d'avantages."

reign he treated the conception of international law, which found its first expression in European politics in the Treaty of Westphalia in 1648, as the Renaissance " Prince " was bidden to do, apologizing from time to time when it seemed convenient but never being deterred from following his own interests. Machiavelli was always denounced and always obeyed. God, no doubt, remained the final judge, but, except for questions of religious dogma, the State, not the Church, was His interpreter. The King, supreme head of the State, was himself divine, declared Bossuet on behalf of Louis, and of his interpretation of " *raison d'état* " God was the only arbiter. And even God's judgment did not seem always very sound : at least it is reported that Louis, in the midst of the defeats of the War of the Spanish Succession, cried : " The Lord might have remembered what I have done for Him ! " [1] Apparently Louis and his God differed as to the true " *raison d'état*."

In the second place, as feudal overlord of France, he was, he declared, the ultimate owner and disposer of all the property held by his subjects. In an edict of 1692 he claimed that there was " no right better established nor more inseparably attached to our crown " than that of universal control and disposal " over all the lands of the Kingdom." [2] Finally as God's chosen ruler and father of his people, the King's actions were altogether above criticism. No one had the right to offer him advice or

---

[1] Quoted by Delaisi, *Political Myths and Economic Realities*, p. 60. Louis had been trained to believe himself divine from boyhood—and his later flatterers were no less gross. There were priests who called him "immortal" and declared that in Louis "one could see the lineaments of the Holy Trinity itself," "that he was a prodigy of God's grace whose wisdom is an argument which by itself suffices to convince atheists." A society preacher on the occasion of the birth of the Dauphin compared the King with God Himself and his son with Jesus Christ—*vide* Puaux, *L'Évolution des Théories politiques du Protestantisme français*, 67, and Ogg, *Europe in the Seventeenth Century*, 283.

[2] The doctrine of state socialism implicit in this remark led to no immediate results, though believers in "natural right," like Jurieu, considered Louis' autocracy as menacing to property as to religious freedom. The later struggles between the lower and the privileged orders upon the question of taxation are foreshadowed in Louis' doctrine that in comparison with the Crown all subjects are equal.

to demand explanation. To make a king responsible to his subjects was, in Louis' view, to pervert the order God gave to the world. "*Raison d'état*" he defined in words which embody the perennial defence of irresponsible government. State policy is necessarily "unknown and obscure to all those who do not govern." In his secret and lonely wisdom the sovereign is compelled to conduct a foreign and domestic policy which may perhaps result in apparent disaster: if it appears so, it is because the ways of the sovereign, like those of Providence, are past finding out. If, like God, we could view our sufferings from the point of view of eternity, the death and devastation resulting from a monarch's wars might be as justifiable as the destruction caused by a providential earthquake. The Jesuit Bouhours expressed Louis' view emphatically: "As the Prince is the most living image of God on earth, he ought to be like God, who governs the world by methods unknown to men and who makes us always feel the effects of his kindness and justice without showing us the designs of his wisdom."[1] And Louis himself told the Dauphin that, "holding, as it were, the place of God, we seem to participate in His wisdom, as in His authority; for instance, in what concerns discernment of human character, allocation of employments and distribution of rewards."[2]

Irresponsible to men, Louis acknowledged himself responsible to God. As a father, the King must not be criticized, but he must protect his children, seek their welfare, lead the docile and punish the disobedient. His domestic policy was accordingly one of paternal protection. Kingship was an exacting profession, and Louis' days were spent in the exact routine of official detail. If his nights were spent with Mademoiselle de la Vallière and her successors, that, he explained, was permitted by his conscience on the condition that the affairs of his heart were never permitted to interfere with the affairs of state.

Colbert's economic policy was an attempt to increase the political and military power of France by extending its Colonial Empire, adding to its treasure and encouraging its industries. He was not a complete mercantilist, but he hoped that taxing

---

[1] Bouhours, S.J., *Entretiens d'Ariste et d'Eugène*, 181.
[2] *Œuvres*, ii. 283.

the foreigner and restricting the export of grain would add to the strength and independence of France. This theory involved constant State supervision. Louis' cultural policy was similar in theory, and practically more successful. Versailles became the centre of European culture and the graveyard of the French aristocracy. A great school of classical authors wrote for an aristocracy now finally reduced to a glittering and expensive impotence.

Such a complete arrogation of irresponsible sovereignty was novel. Hitherto it had been generally assumed that the monarch, though supreme, was bound by the fundamental laws of France. Bodin, the first French thinker to construct the theory of royal sovereignty, assumed that the King would obey the Salic Law of succession and adhere to the ancient Constitution and customs of France. To conform to these was in the nature of the French monarchy, even though, Bodin held, nothing but harm could come of any popular machinery to enforce royal responsibility. Even Bossuet, Louis' most thorough apologist, drew a careful distinction between absolute and arbitrary power. The royal authority, he declared, was " divine, paternal and absolute," but this did not mean that it would be exercised " unreasonably." Absolute and arbitrary government, he said, were different things. The King's power is absolute " in the sense that it is independent of all human authority. But it does not follow that it may be arbitrary." The King would not destroy his kingdom or violate the rights of property : the persons of loyal subjects would not be wilfully interfered with, and custom, divine in origin, would act as a useful guide for the monarch. Louis, however, paid no more heed to these limitations in practice than he had in theory. He even argued that he could alienate French soil for his private advantage ; he disregarded the Salic Law and totally ignored the ancient French Constitution. As Madame de Staël explained later : " In France it is liberty which is old and despotism which is new." Arbitrary government began with Louis XIV.

2. THE RIGHTS OF ORDINARY MEN—THE PROTESTANTS AND THE EDICT OF NANTES

During the first thirty years of Louis' reign the gods showed no sign of envying his success. According to their wont they waited till his own infatuation brought him disaster; and Nemesis, with her usual wilfulness, reserved her final visitation for his great-grandson. There are, however, practical limits to all power, however extravagantly justified. The rule of the Bourbons rested primarily on the instinctive obedience called forth by the royal divinity. But it rested also upon the services which they rendered to France. Henry IV. and Richelieu had given the French people order and unity instead of civil war, had enforced toleration at the expense of fanaticism. Their foreign policy had been moderate; it had given France more power and some " glory " in Europe; their home government had been strong, centralized and not generally oppressive. This was the policy which Louis inherited and finally discarded.

There was a contradiction in Louis' policy. As a true Renaissance Prince he should have preserved at least the semblance of constitutional government, his foreign wars should have stopped short of extravagance and, above all, his religious policy should have been always politic and national, and never sincere or Roman. As it was, he undermined the power of the monarchy in all three ways: firstly, by the revocation of the Edict of Nantes he drove out his most industrious subjects and united Protestant Europe against him; secondly, by ceaseless war he involved himself in bankruptcy and the mass of his peasant subjects in penury; thirdly, by adopting a Jesuit instead of a national religious policy he divided his country into warring camps.

The silence was broken and criticism, though whispered till his death, grew daily more bitter and more penetrating. It was Louis XIV., not the *frondeurs*, who brought the people into the shrine of government. The story of France from the revocation of the Edict of Nantes in 1685 until the meeting of the States-General, more than a century later, is the story of the gradual breakdown of the religious and political absolutism of the *ancien régime* and the gradual construction of a religion based on secular and libertarian assumptions. The foundation of the new creed was laid under Louis XIV.

Louis' religious policy was mainly responsible for the interruption of the mystic silence. Since the accession of Henry IV. the Pope's authority in France had been restricted to questions of doctrine, the French Church had become predominantly Gallican, and royal policy was dictated by secular considerations. The Pope had little more direct influence than in a Protestant country. In 1682, when Louis was involved in a dispute with the Pope concerning his right to make ecclesiastical appointments without Papal sanction, the bishops, inspired by Bossuet, proclaimed themselves uncompromisingly Gallican. Their resolutions rested on the theory that even on matters of doctrine the Pope was ultimately subject to a united Council of the Church, and that he had no right to any part in the internal government of the French Church.[1] Religious controversy might rage in France : Molinist and Thomist might abuse each other. Pascal might expose Escobar and the casuistry of Jesuit practice, and the stricter Catholics might recommend the forcible conversion of Protestants, but as long as the King put the unity and security of France first he had nothing to fear from any section of the Church.

The revocation of the Edict of Nantes showed that the King had finally turned his back upon a secular and national policy. The Protestants had been consistently loyal ; they had taken no hand in the *Fronde*, and in 1652 had reminded the King that they were " Frenchmen as well as members of the Reformed Church." "We only ask," they declared, " to be able to live and die in the service of your Majesty in the just liberties which have been granted us, above all in those of our consciences and in the exercise of our religion ; without which life is not only indifferent to us but bitter, and death desirable." Louis, however, hated dissent of any description, political or religious. He readily paid heed when he was told that the

---

[1] *Vide* Loyson, *L'Assemblée de Clergé de France de 1682*, for a documented and honest account of a curious and commonly misrepresented chapter in ecclesiastical history.

Protestants could be "converted" if the interpretation of the Edict was "strict" and if the missionaries were not too gentle and were adequately aided by dragoons.[1] In 1685 he decided that the process of "conversion," the full horrors of which he may not have understood, was complete. The Edict of Nantes, therefore, which alone gave Protestantism a legal footing in France, was revoked as "unnecessary." Claude protested in vain that it was a "jest which suited ill the dignity of so great a King to say that he revoked the Edict only because it had become useless. It was much as if a father who had cut his children's throats with his own hands boasted of being thereby quit of the duty of nourishing and protecting them."[2] Perhaps one day the King would realize what he was doing. His mask would be torn away and everyone would see that the King's great qualities were reducible to "sovereign self-love, to a pride without equal, to an extreme love for great reputation, to a conscience which was intimidated by the magnitude of his sins, fornications, adulteries and acts of violence, and which was therefore attempting to appease God by external observance of religion and a deceptive display of zeal."

The results of the revocation were far-reaching. Du Bosc's [3] solemn warning, uttered as early as 1668, that "it would depopulate his kingdom by more than a million persons, whose flight would inflict a striking injury to business, to manufacturers, to labour, to art and crafts, and indeed in every way to the well-being of the State," was exactly justified in the event. Its effects were not only disastrous in themselves but they also contributed directly to the national bankruptcy. Blenheim and Ramillies were the practical reply to the revocation. Moreover, Louis had opened the way for criticism. Exiled Protestants refurbished the weapons of their sixteenth-century predecessors, laid aside since the time of Henry IV. In addition they borrowed from the well-stocked armoury of

---

[1] Strict interpretation, which meant, in fact, constant persecution, began as early as 1655, and "conversion bureaux" were instituted in 1676.

[2] Quoted by Puaux, *op. cit.*, 38.

[3] *Vide* Puaux, *op. cit.*, 42 ff.

English Parliamentarians whom they met in Holland. Through their medium France and all educated Europe learned the philosophy of the Revolution of 1688.

In the year after James' flight from England an anonymous writer published *Les Soupirs de la France esclave*.[1] " I look with compassion," began the author, " upon the cruel tempest with which my country is threatened. I weep for the desolation of its towns and the ruin of what the tyranny of its government has allowed to remain." He proceeded to recount the ancient liberties destroyed by Louis, the venality of the law under his régime, the destruction of the *noblesse*, once " the most illustrious in the world," and now turned into a " parcel of beggars," a system of taxation which reduced the peasants to the condition of " African slaves." " To-day a thousand channels are open through which the blood of the people is drawn to run into the abyss of the insatiable greed and immeasurable ambition of the Prince." Louis, finding the Louvre, Saint-Germains and Fontainebleau insufficient, must needs expend the taxation wrung from the poor upon a new palace at Versailles. Was it a Christian or a Turkish prince who drove millions into battle for his own ends, who made himself all and the people nothing, who recognized no law, and committed the final crime of driving out loyal and industrious subjects because of their fidelity to their consciences? " Who would not shed tears to see so many millions of men reduced to such a profound misery to satisfy the whims of a single man? "

Jurieu, the Protestant pastor, was not content with denunciations. His spirit was that of the Scottish Covenanters ; like them, he argued that a king whose life was ungodly, who persecuted the saints and destroyed their spiritual liberty, immediately ceased to be legitimate. He pushed the argument further, anticipating Locke's vindication of the recent English revolutions. The King is a magistrate appointed to safeguard the liberty of his subjects, whose duty it is to depose him if he violates their rights. Every relationship, even that of husband and wife or father and child, involves mutual obligations ; whenever

---

[1] A pamphlet attributed to Michel Lavassor.

power is arbitrarily exercised an implicit contract is revoked. Above all comes the duty of worshipping in accordance with conscience. Even if the people were now as foolish as Hobbes thought them once to have been, and attempted to surrender all their rights to the King, it would be impossible for them to do so. For a man's religion was the sole affair of himself and God, and the attempt to coerce conscience was not only wicked but necessarily futile. Thus there were obvious limits to royal power: "Every citizen governed by a king has the right to depose him as soon as he exceeds the limits of his authority."[1] The people were ultimately sovereign: they "alone have no need to be right in order that their acts may be valid." The responsibility was ultimately theirs, and God was their only judge.

Jurieu's attack was not left unanswered. Bossuet undertook the task of refutation.[2] He upheld Louis' claim to Divine Right, using both the patriarchal arguments of Filmer and the Utilitarian ones of Hobbes. Kings, as the Old Testament proved, were directly instituted by God, but they were to be obeyed by subjects not only because it was the duty of children to obey their father but also because division of authority meant misery. To talk of men possessing rights of any kind before the foundation of government seemed as absurd to Bossuet as it had to Hobbes. There were no natural rights: rights were the result, not the cause, of government; against the sovereign there could be no rights, and without his authority the life of man was necessarily intolerable.

Jurieu had asked what reason subjects could possibly have for promising obedience to a single irresponsible individual who could tyrannize over them at will. Bossuet answered by comparing society to an army. Why do soldiers obey without question or contract? Because each one knows that destruction

---

[1] Quoted by Dedieu, *Le Rôle politique des Protestants français*, 66.

[2] Bossuet published his *Variations des Protestants* in 1688. For the controversy it provoked *vide* Rébelliau, *Bossuet*. Jurieu's *Histoire critique des Dogmes et des Cultes* (1704) emphasized changes of Catholic doctrine, pointing out that even the Fathers of the Church were heretics judged by existing orthodoxy. Bossuet denounced the suggestion as blasphemy, but scarcely refuted his opponent.

necessarily follows disobedience. Discipline is maintained not only by the sanction of punishment but also because the rank and file recognize its necessity. To allow discussion or admit any rights of conscience is to make way for anarchy, to encourage every individual to set up his own puny judgment against constituted authority and to make way for disunion, heresy and damnation.

Bossuet did not see the danger of this argument. By appealing to utility he weakened the claim to divine right, and to call the atheist Hobbes to his support was to offer his opponents the most valuable of hostages.[1] The appeal to an unalterable contract in Hobbes is, in fact, negligible—his strength lies in the argument, borrowed by Bossuet, that sovereignty alone brings union, greatness and prosperity. But at the root of this argument is the idea of consent, and the suggestion of possible rebellion. If the strongest reason for obedience is the danger of anarchy, men who find tyranny intolerable will some time prefer to run the risk of disobedience. Bossuet talked of kings " like gods," and Hobbes described them as " mortal gods," but both had undermined divine right. A mortal god is, after all, a contradiction in terms ; the time will come when the bold will be tempted to throw him from his pedestal and put his mortality to the test.

3. SCEPTICISM AND SCIENCE—BAYLE AND HIS CONTEMPORARIES

Though Louis' persecution of the Protestants was economically disastrous, it did not divide France internally. Some writers did indeed contrast the pious lives of the heretics with the loose morals of their persecutors, but Gallicans and Jesuits alike supported the royal policy, and the theories of Jurieu and his fellows found no immediate response, except within

---

[1] Other writers of the same period were ready to use Hobbes to justify Louis' absolutism. *Cp.* Francis Bonneau, 1660, *Eléments de la politique de M. Hobbes.* More striking is the *Traité du pouvoir absolu du Souverain,* by Elie Merlat, written in the year of the revocation, denouncing the notion of popular sovereignty and basing his vindication of royal absolutism on the arguments of Hobbes.

the Protestant community. Louis' decision to side with the Jesuits against the Jansenists, however, had immediate effects within the kingdom itself; it divided France into hostile camps and contributed to the growth of scepticism. The *Parlements* were roused to make their single protest against Louis' policy; they constituted themselves champions of Gallicanism against both Jesuits and monarch, and so began a long battle with absolutism, which lasted till the eve of the Revolution itself. Moreover, France was immediately involved in a general religious controversy in which *libertinisme* steadily gained ground. Nothing could have served the free-thinking disciples of Descartes better than a division in the Church. They held that reason, not revelation, was the key to truth, and the orthodox furthered their thesis by an effective demonstration that, whatever truth was, the Church was not agreed upon it. Once again Louis had released forces which led to Revolution.

The doctrinal differences between Jansenists and Jesuits had long troubled France. What was the true interpretation of the doctrine of grace in Paul and Augustine? Was the Calvinist view, which denied the possibility of salvation except to the elect, orthodox, as the priests of Port Royal held, or had the Jesuit Molina been right in stating that the efficacy of grace can be affected by the exercise of the individual will? The Pope long seemed doubtful, and at one time had been on the brink of censuring the Molinist view. And now that it was decided that the doctrine of grace which the Jesuits found in Jansen's *Augustinus* was heretical, were not the Jansenists still entitled to argue that the heretical doctrines were not, in fact, to be found in Jansen? Might they not discuss the question of " *fact* " while they submitted in the question of " *right* "? In any case, were Jesuit priests justified in refusing the sacraments to Jansenists who maintained a " respectful silence " on the question of fact? A more important question was really involved. What was the position of the Jesuits and of Rome in France? The strength of the Jansenists lay in the popular dislike of the Society of Jesus and of Papal influence. The asceticism of Saint-Cyran and Arnauld was a constant reproach to the comforts of Jesuit wisdom. The Jansenists emphasized the steepness of the narrow way to heaven : the Jesuits, as a free-thinking Abbé put it, " lengthened the creed and shortened the Decalogue," that the broad and worldly path might be the smoother.

Arnauld's *Frequent Confession* was an attack upon the Jesuit fathers, who, as the same critic said, changed the name of the sacrament from Penitence to Confession because they thought it sufficient to avow their sins without correcting them. Frequent confession was a pleasant way of combining a worldly life of gaiety with the certainty of eternal bliss. Balzac's " Prince " remarked : "We have now a more easy and agreeable theology ; one that can be better adjusted to suit the humours of the great, which can accommodate its precepts with their interests and is not so rustic and harsh as the old theology. . . . To-day we have invented expedients which enable the thief to salve his conscience." [1]

Everyone knew the nature of these expedients, since Pascal's *Lettres provinciales*. Escobar's casuistry suggested to common men that every Jesuit was a hypocrite, who undermined the integrity of morals, and since every Jesuit was an Ultramontane, and presumably an intriguer, it seemed probable that he was also undermining the integrity of the State and ready, when the occasion arose, once again to shout for the League and Ravaillac.[2] The controversy, therefore, was concerned with power rather than with doctrine. In 1705 a Papal Bull finally condemned " respectful silence " and closed the last loophole of the Jansenists. In 1709-1710 Port Royal was razed. In 1713 the Bull *Unigenitus* denounced Quesnel's *Moral Reflections*, which contained, it seemed, one hundred and one heretical propositions, hitherto unsuspected, and all the more dangerous since they were so difficult to perceive. Each of these steps was opposed by the Paris *Parlement*, by many

---

[1] Quoted by Ogg, *op. cit.*, 344.

[2] The unpopularity of the Jesuits among the French middle class is one of the most important factors in the development of seventeenth and eighteenth century thought. A century later, in 1761, when a public trial went against the Jesuits, it was said that " the joy of the public was as if everyone had had a private fortune left him."

of the clergy, and by the mass of middle-class persons. The populace supported the Jansenists because they hated Rome, not because they had strong views about the efficacy of grace.[1]

The " Constitution," as the Bull was called, roused an immediate storm. The ninety-first of the condemned propositions seemed to imply that the Pope was infallible.[2] Cardinal de Noailles, and fourteen bishops with him, refused to accept the Bull. All the forces of Gallicanism rallied to their side; the Sorbonne rejected the Bull, and the *Parlement* of Paris was forced to accept it only by a special exercise of royal authority. *Moral Reflections* and all books in its defence were officially suppressed, and its more resolute supporters suffered exile or imprisonment. But Louis could not calm the storm he had aroused. For the first time in his long reign he met with real opposition, and he died with the knowledge that he had destroyed the unity of the Church and undermined the authority of the monarchy. Louis had forgotten that unquestioning allegiance

---

[1] The facts in brief were these. The new edition of Quesnel's *Moral Reflections upon the New Testament* was published with a dedication to Cardinal de Noailles, the Archbishop of Paris. No book, it might have been thought, could have begun its career with more unexceptionable testimonials. It had been specially commended by Clement XI., and Father La Chaise, confessor to Louis, had constantly sought spiritual refreshment in the work, which, he said, was always edifying at whatsoever page it was opened. La Chaise's successor, Le Tellier, however, had different views; the Society of Jesus was in bad odour at the moment in France and he felt that a Bull denouncing Quesnel's book as full of Jansenist heresies would restore the Society's prestige, re-establish the orthodoxy of Molinist at the expense of Thomist, increase the power of Jesuitism in France, and, not least, discredit somewhat Cardinal de Noailles, his Gallican rival for the King's favour. Louis, whose piety grew as old age decreased the will and power to sin, was prevailed upon by Le Tellier to request the Pope to ban *Moral Reflections*. Clement seems to have hesitated before condemning a book he had previously praised so highly, and it was only after a scene in which Cardinal Fabroni, Le Tellier's friend at the Vatican, had called the Holy Father "childish," to his face, that he gave way. A courier was dispatched the same day to Le Tellier, who personally obtained Louis' consent and immediately published the Bull. The agency of Le Tellier and the atmosphere of Jesuit intrigue surrounding the Bull accounted for much of the Gallican opposition.

[2] This proposition stated that "an unjust excommunication ought never to prevent our doing our duty." To condemn this as heretical was thought to imply that an unjust excommunication was impossible.

would in France be offered only to a king whose policy was wholly French.

The battle between *acceptants* and *recusants* did not provide an edifying spectacle.[1] The French Church divided into factions, engaged in a bitter struggle nominally over minutiæ of dogma, while the real cause, which excited universal interest, was a rivalry for political ascendancy. The most famous French ecclesiastics called each other names and gave one another the lie for motives which did not seem free from a political and personal taint.[2]

. The opportunity was a good one for sceptics and there seems little doubt that their influence increased in the latter part of Louis' reign. Fénelon and Bossuet were united in deploring the danger to the Church : Fénelon complained that " instruction increases and faith diminishes," while Bossuet threw the whole of his energy into combating the spirit of unbelief. The Church seemed beset with enemies. The *libertins* were stronger than ever. Saint-Evrémond, their wittiest representative, had employed his congenial exile at the Court of Charles II. to popularize a philosophy which had troubled bishops since the later Middle Ages. He argued that the understanding could not submit to authority, that religion, after all, was a matter of temperament and that the one really odious vice was hypocrisy. He disliked violence and was no propagandist, but a sceptic and a true follower of Montaigne, holding that it was setting a high value on your own opinions to roast neighbours who did not agree with you. Life, he felt, was hard enough in any case : why not let people enjoy themselves in this world, if they chose to run the risk of damnation in the next? Like Molière, he thought Nature the finest guide, and the Epicureans her most faithful interpreters. Moderation was the key to happiness, and happiness

---

[1] The *recusants* were those who refused to accept the " Constitution" "purely and simply." On their side were ranged Jansenists, Gallicans, the *Parlements*, and the mass of citizens. On the other was the King, the Jesuits, and a number of Ultramontane bishops.

[2] The persecution of the Quietists, though far less important, gave the same impression. For the effect of the controversy between Bossuet and Fénelon and the growth of scepticism during Louis' reign *vide* Brunetiere, " *Etudes crit. sur l'histoire de la Litt. Française*," 5ᵉ series, *La Formation de l'Idée du Progrès*.

was, after all, the important thing. Austerity and excess were both bad : a good life could be found in freedom of mind and manners. "Let us not flee from the world, nor hide ourselves in the desert," he wrote. Why not be tolerant, accept each other quietly, and realize that we are, after all, very small, very fallible and with but one life we can be sure about? Wasn't it just as well to make the best of it?

The Renaissance hedonism of Saint-Evrémond, however, was no longer the Church's most serious enemy. The scientific conception of an order of nature, of a world governed by inevitable law, was gaining ground and, as it grew, the position of the Christian God seemed increasingly precarious. The scientific heresy was a more menacing restatement of the heresy of Jansenism and Calvinism : its doctrine of predestination seemed to restrict the liberty of God Himself and make Him as helpless before His own decrees as the gods of Greece had been in the hands of inexorable Fate.

Descartes had greatly increased the difficulty. He had himself remained in the Church and his disciples had striven to show that the rule of law in the physical world did not limit the free will of God or man. "Occasionalism" had been accepted by the orthodox and Father Malebranche was a good Catholic. Pascal, however, had seen the danger of scientific inquiry. "Cartesianism," he had said, "made one well-directed flick from God send the world spinning on its axis for all time."

All the thinkers of the next generation encountered the same difficulty. Fénelon's mind wrestled with the problem and found refuge in Pantheism—a cure for all difficulties, since, if, as he said, "God is all that is," the problems of finding out what He does or does not do and whether we have free will or not seem scarcely to arise. In a less mystical mood he wrote : "Two conceptions of Godhead lie before you—the one of a Ruler, good and vigilant and wise, who will be loved and feared by men, the other a First Cause, so high that he cares nothing for souls he made, for their virtue or their vices, their disobedience or their love. Examine well these two conceptions. I defy you to prefer the second to the first."

The danger had been fully exemplified in Spinoza. "If a

phenomenon were produced in the universe," he wrote, "which was contrary to the general laws of nature, it would be equally contrary to the decree of God, and if God Himself acted against the laws of nature He would be acting in a manner contrary to His own essence, which is the height of absurdity. I conclude then that nothing happens in nature which is contrary to its universal laws, nothing which is not therefore in accord with these laws and which does not result from them."

The mediævalists had believed God's attributes to be discoverable by reason: God was a father whose powers were limitless, but whose ways were reasonable even if they appeared sometimes arbitrary to the small view of individual men. The mediæval theologian had confidence in " the intelligible rationality of a personal being." No doubt, as Professor Whitehead has argued, faith in the possibility of science, in the scrutable and ordered nature of the universe, was " generated antecedently to the development of modern scientific theory." But perhaps it is too much to say that it was " an unconscious derivative from mediæval theology." [1]

For the ways of the personal God of Christianity always remained uncertain to the ordinary man, even if they were presumed to be ultimately rational. The same, it may be argued, could be said of the ways of nature, since the individual who is overtaken by an avalanche or an earthquake receives no help from the knowledge that his death is due, not to a miracle, but to natural causes. Nevertheless the change from a personal Providence to an impersonal law did involve a reaction as well as a transference from a religious to a secular state of mind. Philosophers might argue that God ruled the universe in a rational manner and that He was fulfilling a rational process when He lost His temper with the creatures He had created and drowned them in the Flood, when He permitted the sun to stand still in the heavens at the request of His servant or converted His unfaithful subjects by an occasional miracle. The Second Coming might prove rational enough, when it came, but, since it might occur at any time, its expectation left the

---

[1] *Science and the Modern World*, p. 16.

mediævalist in a precarious and awestruck state of mind. It is impossible to dissociate the notion of arbitrary and irrational behaviour from the idea of personality. A universal and an impersonal law may seem a less friendly conception; it may, at first, appear even more inscrutable and equally unaccountable in its effects upon individuals. But it leaves the way clear for thought, for experiment, for discovery and, above all, it permits men's minds to travel freely in a limitless future which they may learn in time to control. This scientific conception, therefore, was at least as much a reaction against the arbitrary and restricted element in mediæval theology as it was a derivative from its rationality. It was in this development that Bossuet saw the greatest danger to the Church. He saw that the personal and direct intervention of God in human affairs was altogether essential to Catholicism. A Creator of eternal laws with which He never interfered was no God, and could never have founded an apostolic Church. What became of miracles, of original sin, of grace, what was the place of Christ Himself in a universe governed by inexorable and unchanging laws to which even God always adhered?[1] Science might be permitted in its own sphere, but it must be fought to the end if it interfered with revelation, if it encouraged sinful men to behave as if God were not ever-present, ever-vigilant, noting every sin and graciously permitting the fall of each one of His sparrows. "The *libertins*," he declared, "hoped to shake off the yoke

---

[1] *Cp.* Dante, *Purgatorio*, iii. 34-39 :

> " Matto è chi spera che nostra ragione
> Possa trascorrer la infinita via,
> Che tiene una sustanzia in tre persone.
> State contenti, umana gente, al *quia* ;
> Chè, se potuto aveste veder tutto,
> Mestier non era partorir Maria."

> " Mad is he who hopes that our reason may
> compass that infinitude which one substance
> in three persons fills.
> Be ye content, O human race, with the *quia* !
> For if ye had been able to see the whole, no
> need was there for Mary to give birth."
> > *Translation*, Temple Classics.

of this Providence which watches over us, so that they may independently maintain an unruly liberty which lets them live according to their fancy, without fear, without restraint, without discipline." He accepted the challenge boldly. It was his task to re-create the mediæval God in the minds of men. God, he declared, has made abiding laws, and has therefore the power to make or unmake them as He pleases: "He gives nature laws; He overturns them when He wills." God's Providence is an ever-present, an immediate thing; His inscrutable purpose is furthered not only by the common working of His laws but also by the intervention of miracles and special revelations. The whole works, if we could but see it, to a divine climax, but in the drama the individual has free choice: he may behave well or ill and God will make use both of his righteousness and his wickedness. God's purpose, however, is not altogether inscrutable: revelation and history offer a sufficient guidance to the whole, even if the detailed process cannot always be observed in operation. Bossuet felt himself at least able to illustrate this thesis of a providential guidance in history: "There is nothing more absurd than to say that He does not mingle with the government of peoples, with the establishment or ruin of States, with the manner in which they are governed, by what princes and by what laws; if all of these, while being carried out by men's liberty, are not guided by the hand of God so that He has sure means of directing them as He pleases, it follows that God has no part in these events and that this part of the world is entirely independent." [1] Actually the eye of faith can trace the hand of God through history: choosing the Jewish people as His instrument, He prepared the way for the greatest event, the coming of Christ, and since then has guided His Church towards its ultimate triumph.

In this historical perspective the individual can find the solution of the mystery of his temporal sufferings. He can transcend the personal outlook; see that his own good or evil fortune is a tiny and unimportant part of a great eternal purpose. Without this understanding, the free-thinker's blasphemy is

---

[1] For all this see Brunetiere, op cit. 5ᵉ series, *La Philosophie de Bossuet*.

plausible. "The *libertins* declare war on divine Providence and they find nothing stronger against it than the distribution of goods and evils which appears unjust, irregular, without any distinction between good and evil. This is where the impious entrench themselves as if in an impregnable fortress."[1] To the impious, however, the *Universal History* was surely a final answer. If we could only see clearly we should know there was, in fact, no such thing as chance. There is a point, a moment which is beyond men's sight, where God acts, where He brings all things together for good; the eye of faith can detect the purposes of Providence where the scoffer sees the blind accidents of clashing forces.

Bossuet struggled vainly to stop the current. The idea of inevitable law, once stated, gradually undermined the conception of a personal Providence. Rationalism steadily gained ground. Among the thinkers who hastened its progress, de Maistre was right in linking Bayle and Fontenelle together as the most influential, "the fathers of modern incredulity."

Bayle, of Protestant family, exiled in Holland, fought consciously and openly to destroy faith. He invented the technique which his eighteenth-century successors adopted, and passed on to them an inexhaustible stock of arguments, pointed, erudite and unanswerable. Fontenelle, on the other hand, who was perpetual secretary to the Academy of Science, lived peacefully and long in the best society. His attack was necessarily more cautious. Throughout his work, however, alike in his *belles lettres*, his *éloges* and his specifically scientific books, there is the idea that nature is a single unity, working by fixed and ascertainable laws, and that all apparent exceptions are due to ignorance or misunderstanding. The implications of these doctrines—the certainty of natural laws and the solidarity of the sciences—were disastrous to the Catholicism of the seventeenth century. In his early work, Fontenelle, a master of " good form " and the social graces, passed over the dangerous points with a touch that was too gay to be shocking. Even in his later and more outspoken work, when his reputation and age

---

[1] Quoted by Brunetière, *op. cit.*, 61.

permitted him greater freedom, he disguised his meaning and professed orthodoxy. He was a timid but useful apostle of science and rationalism.

His first and most signal service was to begin the popular- (a.) ization of science. With him science ceased to be the monopoly of experts and became part of the subject-matter of literature. And it was not merely the conception of law that he popularized. He hastened the transition from Descartes to Newton. When he renounced prejudices, and sought to build only upon " evident " or axiomatic propositions, Descartes was laying down a mathematical rather than a scientific foundation. The " evidence " upon which Newton had built was not the result of immediate perception but of long labour and exact observation. Science needed both induction and deduction. By these means, Fontenelle declared in his *éloge* upon Newton, " he had at length reached conclusions which destroyed the vortices of Descartes and overturned that immense celestial edifice which we might have thought immovable." [1]

Fontenelle's second achievement was to raise the literary (b.) controversy between the " ancients " and " moderns " from the level of pedantry to that of philosophy. He saw that its tedious disputes really involved the great question whether men were progressing towards some higher form or were inferior to the heroes of antiquity. "Were the ancient trees larger than the modern ones?" Was the stuff of nature being gradually used up and mankind approaching an "old age" of feebleness? There was no reason to hold so pessimistic a doctrine. "Nature," he wrote, unconscious that he was contributing to a philosophy both of progress and of materialism, " has between its hands a certain paste which is always the same, which it unceasingly shapes and reshapes in a thousand ways, and of which it makes animals, plants and men."

---

[1] Fontenelle anticipated Voltaire in appreciating English science and in directly connecting its achievements with English liberty. Toleration was the necessary condition of intellectual life and scientific advance. Newton, he pointed out, had been knighted in England. " His name had reached the throne, where the most celebrated names do not always arrive." There was no need to draw the contrast with France more directly.

Fontenelle also stated the doctrine of the unity of knowledge. All the sciences, he declared in the preface to his *History of the Academy of the Sciences*, had so far taken nature in " little bits " (*parcelles*). But the time would come when the connection between the results of different sciences would be seen, when "we shall join together in a regular body these scattered members." "Various separate truths, of which there are so many, show their relations and mutual dependence so forcibly to the mind that it seems that, after having been detached from one another by a kind of violence, they naturally seek to re-unite." It was this unity which the Encyclopædists set out to prove. Science was the key not only to particular truths but to truth itself.

Men were slow to grasp the significance of this doctrine. They were always retarded by their credulity ; they tended, Fontenelle remarked, to believe first and collect their evidence afterwards. Yet his indirect attack had its effect. His readers were inevitably driven to contrast the evidence for the Christian cosmogony with the evidence for Newtonian physics. Nor could a student of Fontenelle fail to see that there might be less reputable explanations of miracles than the orthodox ones : in his *History of Oracles* he described the trickery by which pagan priests established the reputation of their oracles with simple and uncritical folk, and left the reader to wonder if the liquefaction of St Januarius' blood might be similarly explained.

Fontenelle led men gently from faith in Christianity to religious scepticism and from religious scepticism to a new faith in science. Pierre Bayle was a still more potent influence. To give a full account of his achievements would be to recount the history of eighteenth-century thought. Referring to him, Diderot remarked that the Encyclopædists had "their contemporaries under Louis XIV." If he had said their master he would not have exaggerated. The form, the method and the inspiration, as well as much of the contents of the *Encyclopædia*, originated in Bayle. Voltaire's shafts flew more directly to their mark than Bayle's, but they were borrowed from him. The critical examination of historical sources, which made Voltaire

46

the most workmanlike of eighteenth-century French historians, came from Bayle. The habit of treating the Bible as an inaccurate source-book, placing its contradicting accounts side by side, and submitting Jehovah or the Mother of God to the same kind of criticism as Jupiter or Venus, came from Bayle.[1] Too much has been claimed for the English deists as an influence upon eighteenth-century France ; for Bayle was a deist before Tindal or Toland ; he provided the arguments for natural religion before Bolingbroke or Shaftesbury, and Voltaire learned more from the *Dictionnaire* than from Clarke. As a champion of toleration Bayle preceded Locke, and nothing substantial was added to his argument until John Stuart Mill's *Liberty*, a century and three-quarters later.[2]

Bayle, the son of a Protestant minister, had been converted to Catholicism, reconverted to Protestantism, and finally become equally doubtful of all religions. Finding the condition of a relapsed heretic a dangerous one in most countries, he settled in Rotterdam, where he became Professor of Philosophy in 1681. In 1684 he began his *Nouvelles de la République de Lettres*, one of the earliest critical periodicals. The revocation of the Edict of Nantes directly affected him : in 1685 his brother died a victim to the persecution of Louis. His constant advocacy of free-thought in the *République de Lettres* was supplemented by his *Ce que c'est la France toute Catholique*, his *Commentaire philosophique* and his *Dictionnaire historique et critique*. His arguments, however, were scarcely more pleasing to the Huguenots than to their Catholic persecutors. For toleration with Bayle meant the right to err and the duty to doubt, not the permission to believe in the Reformed Church and the duty to reciprocate persecution if the opportunity arose. From the beginning his works were attacked by Protestants as well as burned by Catholics, and in 1693 he lost the Chair of

---

[1] Biblical criticism, beginning in England about the same time, was greatly aided by Bayle's contemporary, Richard Simon ; like Malebranche, he argued that miracles should be tested by the ordinary rules of evidence and thought it unlikely that God would break His own eternal laws.

[2] Locke's *Essay on Toleration* appeared in 1689 and Bayle's *Commentaire philosophique* in 1686.

Philosophy through Protestant animosity. But he continued to write, and his *Dictionnaire*, a unique compilation of improper information, appeared four years later.

Bayle's work was the application of Cartesian principles to every branch of thought; he began, like Descartes, by ridding himself of current prejudices, but, unlike Descartes, he pressed on to the most dangerous conclusions. There were, he said,[1] three main rules to observe. The first was not to attack your opponents until you had made sure of your facts. He had frequent opportunity of illustrating the dangers of forgetting this principle at the expense of his opponents. The second was to realize that "proofs of feeling conclude nothing": if your object is to discover what is true, passion should be banished from discussion. The reason why Bayle's influence was so lasting, and also so unobtrusive, was because he obeyed this maxim and left the enjoyable task of turning his facts and arguments into diatribes to his successors. The third rule was that nothing should be accepted without evidence which amounted to proof. Nothing should be taken for granted, nothing considered too sacred or too obvious to be examined. Thus Bayle's own task was, above all, to submit the whole scheme of ideas, assumptions and dogmas to an equal and unceremonious examination: all the certainties of society became doubts when he handled them, all the authorities seemed foolish dogmatists, and the fundamental truths resolved themselves into myths and fairy stories, invented to amuse or terrify children and save their parents the trouble of more rational discipline.

If Bayle is not always a sound critic it is not for lack of digging to the roots and discovering flaws that others missed. His weakness was that in the natural enjoyment of scandalizing the orthodox and putting the solemn to ridicule he lost his sense of proportion. He has rightly been considered diffuse, and criticized for writing page after page about obscure and trivial thinkers to the neglect of the more significant and profound. His eighteenth-century followers certainly inherited these characteristics as well as his habit of assuming that the

---

[1] In his *Dictionnaire*, article *Bellarmin*.

value of an argument or doctrine is altogether destroyed by the discovery that its logical foundation is weak. But in fact his method was admirable for its purpose. Men must laugh before they can think, discover their ignorance before they can doubt, doubt before they can know what is true. Nothing could be more effective for the production of laughter, thought and doubt than Bayle's method of carefully stating an orthodox view in such a way that the least critical could not miss its absurdity. His irreverent comment upon everything—sacred, profane, remote and familiar alike—had a similar effect. His readers, led to smile at the follies of their ancestors in one sentence, discovered in the next similar peculiarities in their own generation ; they were astonished to find that the doctrines of Christianity were often similar to those of pagan religions, and that Nero's reasons for persecuting the Saints were those advanced by Louis the Great. Bayle, as Madame de Lambert suggested in 1715, did more than any other to " shake the yoke of authority and opinion." Voltaire's judgment was similar. "He sets forth things with such an odious fidelity, and places the argument on both sides before our eyes with so mean an impartiality and is so intolerably intelligible that he puts even those of the most meagre understanding in a position to judge and even to doubt what is told them."

The idea of toleration has found support from various sources. Humanitarian feeling, political common sense, a belief in the ultimate rights of the individual conscience, a trust in reason and a scepticism about its possibilities—all these have been its ingredients. In Bayle we find them united. No doubt it is logically possible to hold with John Stuart Mill that the truth is always the gainer by the statement of falsehood. But those who have believed their own doctrine eternally true have seldom been willing to risk the perdition of their friends by permitting the advocacy of heresy. Historically speaking, scepticism has been the forerunner of a genuinely tolerant spirit. The Protestant's respect for conscience, the horror of cruelty, the sensible statesmanship of the *Politiques*, confidence in the methods of reason, whether in the mediæval theologian or the scientist who took his place—all these have failed on occasion to guard the freedom of thought which they have generally promoted. Unless there is an element of scepticism, unless, like Montaigne and Benjamin Franklin, men "doubt a little of their own infallibility" they may always become persecutors; the exceptional moment comes when 'they can be persuaded that it is sometimes cruel to be kind, that it is expedient that one man should die for the people or that conscience is wrong-headed. Even the apostles of reason have occasionally been intolerant in moments of enthusiastic certainty.

Bayle's argument is singularly complete. Few have more eloquently condemned the political folly of sacrificing the reality of national harmony for the dream of religious unity, or more forcibly pointed to the cruelty of persecution and the contradiction it involved between the teaching of Christ and the actions of those who called themselves Christians. What could be more ridiculous or unworthy than to take a single phrase, "Compel them to come in," which occurs in one of Christ's parables as a pressing invitation to dinner, as an excuse for compelling men to enter a Church whose doctrines they did not share? To compel conscience was in itself a crime and an absurdity. Persecution might compel people to be hypocrites, but conscience remained its own master by its very nature. "*To compel them to come in* means to ravage, hang, kill, devastate till the individual dare not refuse to join so kindly and true a religion." What indeed could be less likely to convince either Protestants or pagans of the truth of Christianity than the cruelty, the quarrels, the unfaithfulness to their own Master, displayed by the Catholics? Hell, he remarked, must certainly contain many Catholics or its tortures would be incomplete. But Protestants were almost as bad. Nero persecuting Christians, Calvin burning Servetus and Louis murdering his subjects were all guilty of the same folly and the same crime. In his "Dialogue between a Burgomaster of Rotterdam and Jurieu," the latter is made to suggest that such unbelievers as Bayle should be silenced. "Do you consider the consequences of what you demand?" asks the Burgomaster. "You are asking for an Inquisition." "I abhor the Inquisition," says

Jurieu. "Yes, the Popish one. But do you disclaim an Inquisition of your own or an Inquisition on behalf of your own religion? We are not lukewarm. We act upon the principle of Christianity by tolerating all religions and by not suffering any Christian to hurt any other." After all, Bayle asks, " is it not true that to fight errors with blows is the same absurdity as to fight against fortresses with speeches and syllogisms?"

Three basic propositions support Bayle's plea for toleration. First, that all religious and philosophic conclusions are at best doubtful. Second, since morality is not dependent upon any brand of religion, we should take cognizance of men's behaviour, not of their nominal creed. Thirdly, Bayle held that spiritual coercion was always unwise and unjust, since God has given men an intuitive knowledge of His moral law and left it to their individual interpretation : men do not apprehend it perfectly, but it appears in some form or other in all societies, and it is frequently in active conflict with the orthodox and accepted codes which religious systems attempt to enforce.

In the first place, every religion is doubtful since there is insufficient evidence of any doctrines of sin, grace or immortality. Any doctrines not founded on verified evidence can have but a tinsel authority, " fragile as glass." In view of this uncertainty, any coercion of opinion was an unmitigated evil. The truth, if it could be found, could be discovered only by the free play of reason and science. In any case, it was none of the State's business. Bayle anticipated Locke in his purely secular view of the State. The Reformation had given birth to kings who put the material interests of their country before its religious orthodoxy. Henry IV. had consummated the political unity of France at the expense of a measure of toleration : Richelieu and Mazarin had conducted a foreign and domestic policy dictated solely by secular considerations. But Louis had returned to mediævalism and placed religious uniformity above national interest. The result was a definite enunciation of the doctrine that State policy has nothing to do with religion. The State should take no notice of opinion as such : its duty is to safeguard individual rights, and to consider religious questions only if they threaten public safety.

In the second place, Bayle pointed out that a man's sect or creed was not an index to his behaviour. Christianity was a religion of meekness, and to fight was incompatible with the teaching of the Gospel : yet Christians made good soldiers, persecuted heretics and even fought crusades in the name of the Prince of Peace. Mohammedans, on the other hand, were taught the duty of persecution, but were often tolerant. The Church had strict views about sexual morality, but Christians were not specially continent, and many courtesans were amongst the most orthodox Catholics. Atheists, who believed in no supernatural sanctions, often lived the most correct lives. Moralists like Bossuet and Father Rapin had declared that a decline in morals must accompany a decline in faith. The evidence, Bayle thought, pointed in the opposite direction. The manners of society had little or nothing to do with religion, and the chances were that a society of atheists would be as moral as a society of Catholics or other idolaters.

Finally, Bayle's Protestant faith in his own conscience and his study of various religions made him oppose every kind of spiritual coercion. In all religions there were certain universal elements, the teaching of " natural reason " : in all men there was a capacity for distinguishing between good and evil, " a certain persuasion in the soul." And the natural reason and conscience of men, the supreme tribunal, were frequently in opposition to the doctrines and commands of states and churches. Reason suggests that there is a God who created the world and it everywhere approves of the morality taught in the New Testament and in the sayings of Buddha and Confucius. But it also establishes certain axioms : it is impossible to believe such contradictions as that a part is greater than the whole or that a good God establishes a natural order and then interferes to reward some individuals with temporal happiness and to punish others with an eternity of torment. Bossuet had noticed that the free-thinkers had found their strongest argument in the apparently arbitrary distribution of earthly pains and pleasures. In Bayle's view this inequality was neither arbitrary nor Providential. There was no relationship between sin and suffering, unless sin were interpreted as neglect of the teaching of nature. Why, asked Bayle, should a man's misconduct be paid for in ill-health unless he acted in such a way as to damage his body? A stone breaks a piece of glass when it strikes it: the glass remains whole if the stone misses it. We must accept the natural order as it is and not expect God to interfere. The conception of Providence is absurd. The world is in many respects obviously bad: it follows either that God does not interfere with it or that He is not good. How can we reconcile the conception of a good God with our human experience? "Would a perfect Being amuse Himself with raising a creature to the highest point of glory in order to cast him down again to the lowest degree of ignominy? Would this not be the action of a child who has scarcely built a card-house before it knocks it over?" Is God really to be conceived of as a Father who showers favours upon men and then, when they enjoy them in their own way, punishes them for insolence as an example and a lesson to others? If so, God's method of instruction is a singularly inefficient one: for "the utility of these examples is not noticeable: every generation up to this one has needed this lesson, and there is no sign that the generations to come will be more free from such vicissitudes than earlier ones." [1]

While Bayle was advancing the arguments for natural religion in Holland, English churchmen were approaching the same position with more cautious steps. [2] Bayle's criticisms of the Church, his plea for free-thought and his individualist philosophy passed on into the main stream of eighteenth-century thought. His politics, however, were less advanced than his religious views. He believed in the "natural reason" of the average man but not much in his natural intelligence. He combined a tremendous faith in men's right to their own opinions with a consistent scepticism about their ability to improve their social and political organization. He declared that the evil of absolutism was its tendency to inflict wars upon mankind, but even so he thought a strong government better than a weak one. For the most part he concerned himself with religion and free-thought: he left

---

[1] *Dictionnaire*, article *Lucrèce*.
[2] *Vide infra*, pp. 123 ff.

the solution of economic and political problems to others who were less sceptical of the possibility of social improvement.

4. REFORM—FÉNELON, SAINT-PIERRE, VAUBAN AND THE ECONOMISTS

During Louis' reign the stringency of official censorship and the mystical prestige of the monarchy made open political criticism rare and dangerous. But as his wars became more predatory and less successful, as the burden of debt increased and taxation became correspondingly oppressive, as the stagnation of trade and the misery of the peasants grew less easy to ignore, grumbling began in all articulate classes of society. The military policy of Louvois excited anger everywhere, and though Louis was seldom directly attacked he was warned that a king has moral responsibility towards his people. The great preachers thundered against the iniquity of the Court, and dared to tell the exalted that God imposed obligations upon those to whom He gave power and opportunity. Massillon, Bourdaloue and Bossuet were not afraid to remind aristocratic audiences that Christ had thought it difficult for the rich to enter the kingdom of heaven, where the last would be first and the first last. Did not Christ cry, "Woe to the rich !" and offer eternal blessedness to Lazarus? "Oh, ye poor," Bossuet cried, in his sermon upon the dignity of poverty, "how rich you are ! But oh, ye rich, how poor you are ! . . . If you do not carry the burdens of the poor, yours will crush you, the weight of your ill-spent wealth will carry you into the pit ; but if you share with the poor the burden of their poverty, taking part in their misery, you will deserve altogether to share in their privileges." It is not enough, he declared, "to open the eyes of the flesh upon the poor, it is necessary to consider them with the eyes of the intellect. Blessed is he who understands. The man who truly understands the mystery of charity is the one who considers the poor as the first children of the Church : who, honouring their position, thinks himself obliged to serve them : who only hopes to share in the blessings of the Church by means of charity and brotherly intercourse." He calls upon Louis to taste the joys of a " truly royal pleasure " by assuaging the sufferings of the poor. But the world is not regenerated in court chapels. The beggars who daily waited outside the chapel at Versailles, or on the steps at St Sulpice, may have fed better because of Bossuet's eloquence, but the peasant still paid away eighty per cent. of his livelihood to his king and his lord.[1]

In the later part of Louis' reign there were individual thinkers and political groups inside the kingdom bold enough to criticize the policy of the government and to suggest projects of reform. Their criticism and their suggestions followed two main lines : first, they deplored the degradation of the ancient Constitution of France and demanded that " the Orders " once again should share in government ; second, they began to question the necessity of France's economic misery, to call attention to the evils of Louis' aggressive wars and to demand the reform of the whole system of excessive and arbitrary taxation.

The most influential of the reformers was Fénelon. His controversy with Bossuet, his plain speaking to the King, his championship of the shrill Quietism of Madame Guyon, brought him into disgrace, and his later years were spent as Archbishop of Cambrai and not, as he and his supporters had expected, as Archbishop of Paris. Before his exile, as tutor to the young Duke of Burgundy and later as adviser to the Opposition group whose hopes for France were centred in the Duke, Fénelon made numerous suggestions for the better government of France. His *Fables*, his *Dialogues des Morts*, his *Examen de Conscience pour un Roi* and *Télémaque* were written primarily for the Duke's instruction. All of them contained indirect political criticism, while *Télémaque* began the fashion of combining travellers' stories with Utopia-building.[2] The young Prince Télémaque, under the guidance of Mentor, visits one kingdom after another, discovers the principles of good government and finally establishes them in perfect form at Salente. Télémaque sees countries where all land is held in common, where the simple life has never been banished by tyranny, where war is unknown

---

[1] Bourdaloue's warnings to the rich were equally emphatic, *vide* his sermons, " Sur la restitution " and " Sur la richesse."

[2] For the influence of *Télémaque*, *vide* Cherel, *Fénelon au XVIIIe Siècle*.

and men's instinctive happiness finds natural opportunity without conventional restraint. In Salente itself the Platonic State is to be realized: each class does its appropriate work in harmony with the others, the children are educated and trained by the State for their special occupations, and all property is utilized for the public good, allotted in accordance with the needs of each class, and never engrossed or alienated in the interests of individuals.

Fénelon's criticism became more direct. Though he doubted the sacred character of the monarchy no more than Bossuet himself, he was far bolder in reminding the King of his duty to God and his subjects. The fundamental laws anciently observed in France could never lose their authority.[1] In a letter possibly meant for the King's eyes [2] Fénelon complained that during the last thirty years the principal Ministers of State had " overturned all the ancient maxims of State ": " *On n'a plus parlé de l'Etat ni des règles: on n'a parlé que du Roi et de son bon plaisir. On a poussé vos revenus et vos dépenses à l'infini. On vous a élevé jusqu'au ciel, pour avoir effacé, disait-on, la grandeur de tous vos prédécesseurs ensemble, c'est-à-dire pour avoir approuvé la France entière, afin d'introduire à la cour un luxe monstrueux et incurable. Ils ont voulu vous élever sur les ruines de toutes les conditions de l'Etat, comme si vous pouviez être grand en ruinant tous vos sujets, sur qui votre grandeur est fondée.*" In 1710 Fénelon even declared that, if he could judge by observation of his own diocese, the first shock would break down the worn-out machine: the soldiers were unpaid and uncared for; it was surprising that they did not mutiny; the *intendants* and their tax-collectors were everywhere swindling and ravaging the people; bankruptcy would result if peace were not made. Taxation, he suggested, should be certain, not arbitrary: it was wrong to collect money in order to "uphold claims which did not interest the King's subjects, who would not be any the happier for an

---

[1] *Vide* more especially his *Examen de Conscience pour un Roi* (1734), his *Plans de Gouvernement* (1711), and *Mémoires sur la Guerre de Succession d'Espagne* (1710).

[2] *Remontrances à Louis XIV.* (about 1694).

added province." Finally he wrote to the King: "You love only your own glory and convenience. You bring everything back to yourself, as if you were the God of the Earth and all the rest were only created to be sacrificed for you. It is on the contrary you whom God has put into the world for your people."[1]

These were the evils of despotism. What was the remedy? To revive the ancient Constitution of France, to persuade the King to respect the fundamental laws and listen to the advice of the Estates. Formerly the King had not collected taxes on his sole authority. The representatives of the nation granted him funds for his extraordinary needs. In each area a local assembly should once again assess the taxes and in each province deputies from all three Orders should proportion the levies in accordance with the wealth of the district and supervise their collection. *Intendants* would then be superfluous and, with just administration by the deputies, taxation would become so much more profitable that the *gabelle* and other extraordinary taxes would become unnecessary. Above all, every three years the States-General, representing the Church, the *Noblesse* and the Third Estate, would be called for a session of indefinite length, would advise in matters of taxation, peace and war, and remedy and prevent abuses by keeping watch over *seigneurs* who oppressed the people or allowed their territory to go out of cultivation.

In all this Fénelon had in mind the ruined peasantry of France. But when he goes on to consider his administrative proposals in detail it is clear that his main concern was to restore the influence of the aristocracy. The old nobility and the Opposition group which gathered round the Duke of Burgundy during the later part of Louis' reign no doubt objected to the system of government because it was bad, but they objected still more because, as the Comte de Boulain-villiers put it, under Louis all Orders were " equally crushed, destroyed and annihilated."[2] Nobles like Saint-Simon resented the power of bourgeois administrators, and welcomed Fénelon's

---

[1] *Remontrances à Louis XIV. sur divers points de son Administration*, 1694.
[2] Quoted. Sée, *op. cit.*, p. 272.

proposal to reduce the King's secretaries from two hundred and eighty to forty and to establish aristocratic councils to share in the task of government.

To weaken the bureaucracy and to strengthen the power of the ancient *noblesse* were reforms which the outraged aristocracy could grasp. Nor were they averse from the historical doctrine of Boulainvilliers,[1] who declared despotism an evil innovation, individual rights sacred and *raison d'état* a screen for the individual ambition of the King. But his economic proposals were less pleasing to the aristocracy. He criticized the whole system of taxation, denounced the *gabelle* especially, proposed to redeem the national debt—mainly at the expense of the upper classes—and to establish a system of taxation in which the national expenditure should be met, at least in part, by the rich as well as by the poor.

Two contemporaries of Boulainvilliers were also remarkable as economists : Vauban, the military engineer, was a statistician and a practical critic; Boisguillebert was more original, and may indeed be considered the earliest of the Physiocrats. Vauban's approach to economics arose from his direct experience of the provinces, whose resources it was his business to know and utilize. A tenth of the population, he calculated, was reduced to beggary, half of it was on the border-line of starvation and only a tenth could be accounted comfortable. The existing system of taxation was the central evil. In spite of Colbert's reforms in the methods of collection, at least a quarter of the *taille* collected never reached the Treasury, while the customs duties and extraordinary *aides* crushed the peasantry and fed only an idle aristocracy. The general " capitation " levy of 1694 offered the example of a more equitable system. Vauban suggested that at the end of the war

---

[1] *Vide* Boulainvilliers' *Lettres sur les anciens Parlements de France que l'on nomine Etats Généraux, Etat de la France, Histoire de l'ancien Gouvernement de la France*, and *Essais sur la Noblesse de France*, which are careful historical studies in which he maintains the thesis that the conquering Franks were the ancestors of the existing *noblesse*, and that the King, being really elected by the aristocracy, had no right to legislate by edict or to govern without the support of the Estates.

a single tax should be made on all property. For this purpose there should be a complete census of the population and of wealth. Having himself made a survey of the agricultural produce, real estate, industrial profits and luxury trades in the districts of Rouen and Vézelay, Vauban was able to explain his plan in detail. He argued that the adoption of his system without fear or favour would make the King solvent and restore national prosperity. Great fortunes would be less conspicuous, but so would poverty. Financiers, tax-farmers, lawyers, clergy and aristocracy would of course resist, but the vast mass of the poor, whose "only possessions were their limbs," whose labour enriched the community which made them so little return, would joyfully support the monarch against the forces of privilege.

Vauban's imagination did not go further. He remained in general an orthodox follower of Colbert, accepting the mercantilist view that the prosperity of France could best be attained at the expense of other nations. Inside France there should be free trade; famines would then cease and free interchange of produce at home would create national strength.[1]

As a theorist Boisguillebert was far in advance of Vauban.[2] A forerunner of the Physiocrats and of Adam Smith, it seemed to him that just as there are laws in the physical world so there must be laws in the social world. If we want our water pure we arrange for it to circulate: in the same way, if we want to keep our economic system from stagnation we must arrange for a natural flow of goods. In his dissertation on the nature of riches he goes to the heart of the matter. "Nature establishes an equal need of buying and selling in all kinds of traffic, so that the single desire of profit may be the soul of all sales, as much in the seller as in the buyer, and it is in aid

---

[1] Vauban regarded imports of luxuries as "useless and very harmful"; all importation of manufactured goods caused money to flow from the country, and should be prohibited.

[2] He also differed from Vauban on financial reform. Equal collection of the *taille* was his remedy. "The only way," he wrote, "to avoid ruin is to suppress privilege, and make powerful persons contribute to the taxes, as they do in England."

of this equilibrium, or this balance, that both are equally compelled to understand reason and to submit to it." According
to this law, Boisguillebert believed that there is a fundamental
agreement of interests in society: " If the rich understood
their interests, they would entirely exempt the poor from taxation. Moreover, it is not only inside any particular nation that
there is this harmony of interests. States do not grow rich by
making their neighbours poor. Riches consist in the supply of
wants. Money is only a means of exchange and is intrinsic-
ally worthless. A country may be rich without much money
and the country which has only money very wretched, if it
finds it difficult to exchange it for goods." Wealth, therefore,
depends on exchange, and money is useful only in so far as it
facilitates exchange. If we are to be rich, money must circulate
quickly, and not only among a few but among the whole
population. If there were no hindrances to the process of
exchange there would be no poverty.

Freedom of exchange should be international. If corn were
allowed to circulate freely, not only in France but also between
nations, French agriculture would gain, not lose. The result
would not be famine, as some feared, but plenty. Agriculturists
would produce more than enough for French needs, and if on
some occasion there was scarcity in France, as a result of excessive exportation or failure of harvest, foreign corn would be
imported in response to the new demand.

Boisguillebert was not always consistent in his belief in
freedom, but his philosophy opens a new era in economics.
The Liberal theory of the harmony of natural interests, with
its logical deduction of *laissez-faire*, is implicit in his writing.
Nature, as the Physiocrats were later to explain in detail, was
man's Providence, not his enemy. To adjust our ways to hers
is to be reasonable. Boisguillebert was the first economist to
hold the optimistic view that the interests of man and Nature
are identical. It followed that nations should co-operate, not
contest: they should work with natural tendencies, not against
them. The only beneficial legislation is that which enables men
more freely to enjoy the wealth that Nature offers them. To
do this they must study her ways, and realize that " neither

authority nor favour releases anyone from the duty of obeying
the laws of justice and reason."

Boisguillebert died in 1714 without any heed from the Government or the public. Louis defeated his critics by outliving them.
Only one, the Abbé de Saint-Pierre, survived to continue his
self-imposed task of finding remedies for every evil in the State.
The Abbé, indeed, was the most industrious, the most honest
and fearless, as well as the most prolix, writer of his age. Yet
the French Academy regarded his critical spirit with smiling
tolerance for twenty-four years, and it was not until 1718 that
it decided upon his exclusion. Indeed Saint-Pierre's countless
projects seemed to be of the kind which may easily be neglected.
There was no tinge of democracy in his proposals. Even the
" Polysynodies " were only Councils of the kind suggested by
Fénelon, composed of the *noblesse* and the magistrates. But
his *Projet pour perfectionner le Gouvernement des États* contained
at least one significant idea. He thought that there might be a
" science of government." Boulainvilliers, who had also used
the phrase,[1] was almost exclusively concerned with a science of
wealth, and Vauban, who had understood the value of statistics,
had imagined a government which would regulate its financial
system scientifically. Saint-Pierre, however, applied the idea
to government as a whole, and suggested the foundation of a
Political Academy, consisting of forty experts, to advise and
co-operate with the monarchy.

Saint-Pierre was not content to assume that even an enlightened and scientific administration would govern well unless
it had clear principles to guide it. He was perhaps the first
systematic Utilitarian.[2] He stated the principle of utility with a
precision equal to Bentham's. "The value," he wrote, " of a book,
of a regulation, of an institution, or of any public work is propor-
tioned to the number and grandeur of the actual pleasures which
it procures and of the future pleasures which it is calculated
to procure for the greatest number of men." If he anticipated
the principle of which Helvétius and Bentham are usually

---

[1] Boulainvilliers, *Etats de la France* (Preface).
[2] *Vide* G. Lowes Dickinson's introduction to Miss Nuttall's translation of
Saint-Pierre's *Perpetual Peace.*

believed to be the inventors, he was even more advanced in the application he made of " the greatest-happiness principle." Writing before the industrial revolution had predisposed men to *laissez-faire*, he tended to over-estimate rather than to minimize the part which the State could play in promoting happiness. His aim was to transform the irresponsible bureaucracy of Louis XIV. into an efficient and benevolent system of State socialism. He proposed that the poor should be supported by the rich and that public money should be used to promote social welfare : taxation of wealth should provide for free education, highways and canals, a central postal service and public works of all kinds.

In his belief that men were perfectible, and that good laws based upon a scientific understanding of natural principles would be sufficient to remedy all social evils, Saint-Pierre stood alone in his generation, and anticipated both the utilitarianism and the optimistic radicalism of Condorcet and the later Encyclopædists. His contemporaries thought him a harmless oddity. But the succeeding generation admitted their debt to Saint-Pierre. His deliberate and conscious utilitarianism, his complete Erastianism, and his near approach to an historical and philosophical doctrine of progress all directly influenced the *philosophes*. Of his writings, his *Project for Perpetual Peace*, edited and indeed rewritten by Rousseau, has alone survived to be read and discussed two centuries later.[1]

In 1712 Europe was preparing for the Treaty of Utrecht, and the Abbé de Saint-Pierre, who was present at the Congress, hoped that the long war might end in something more than the usual armed peace. The famous proposal attributed by Sully to Henry IV. provided a basis for Saint-Pierre's project. It finally appeared in two immense volumes, which few were likely to read and which no statesman would have dreamed of taking seriously. To outlaw war by a League of Nations, each pledged to support the others in the event of any member-state proving aggressive, certainly seemed chimerical.

There were others, more eloquent but less ceaselessly con-

---

[1] *Vide infra*, Chapter X.

structive than the Abbé, who expressed the common hatred of war and the revolt against the futile waste of Louis' policy. Fénelon wrote : " There never was a war, even a successful war, which did not cause more harm than good to the State : we have only to consider how many families it ruins, how many men it kills, how it lays waste and depopulates all countries and how it authorizes licence." Twenty years earlier he had told Louis that his " subjects were dying of hunger ; the cultivation of the soil is practically abandoned, all business is at a standstill, commerce is entirely ruined. France has become a huge hospital. The magistrates are discredited and harassed. . . . You alone have brought all this trouble upon yourself ; for, the whole kingdom having been ruined, you now hold everything in your own hands, and no one can so much as live save by your bounty." [1]

The death of the King in 1715 was the signal for an outbreak of rejoicing, in which, as Saint-Simon remarked, most of his subjects except the valets of his household shared. The great barrier was down, and, though the letter of the law might remain as repressive as ever, the superstitious awe which made its strict administration possible was immediately diminished. Under Louis there had been groups of malcontents : each group was destined to expand and play its part in the spectacular overthrow of the Leviathan. First there was the remnant of the *frondeurs*, nobles who had set their hopes upon the Duke of Burgundy and looked forward to reasserting the political rights of their order. The bourgeoisie, too, hated both the Jesuits and arbitrary government, and took the part of the Jansenists and the Gallican

---

[1] *Vide* also Massillon's sermons against war, upon which Voltaire commented in the *Dic. Phil.*, art. *Guerre*. Amongst thousands of sermons upon theological absurdities and trivial religious observances " there are three or four at most, by a Frenchman named Massillon, which an honest man can read without disgust . . . you will at least find two where the orator dares say some words against this plague and crime of war which includes all plagues and crimes. The wretched spouters unceasingly talk against love, which is the only consolation of humanity and the only way of improving it : they say nothing of the abominable efforts we make to destroy it."

Parlements. The *libertins* had grown bolder during the reign and had even begun to turn their ironical attention to government as well as to religion. The ruined peasantry could not speak for themselves, but the degradation of French agriculture and the helpless misery of the bulk of Louis' subjects had already made a few intelligent men aware of new aspects of the economic problem, and aroused humanitarians to bitter criticism and imaginative speculation.

From these social divisions, first clearly marked under Louis XIV., arose the three main conceptions of government which were to struggle for acceptance in the eighteenth century. An absolute monarchy in alliance with an absolute Church, claiming divine origin and divine sanction, admitted no corporate or individual rights except those which it had itself bestowed, and repudiated every practical as well as theoretical limitation of its authority. To check this new and irresponsible sovereignty, dating only from the Renaissance, conservatism sought to restore the ancient French Constitution. Louis was reminded of his obligations to his people, of the rights of the Estates, the contractual nature of his kingship and the fundamental law of France, itself an expression of an underlying law of nature. A third philosophy was taking shape, opposed both to the revival of feudalism, and to the arbitrary development of the Renaissance monarchy.

The new philosophy, most conveniently called Liberalism, was concerned above all with the preservation of individual rights. It set men on a legal equality in opposition to feudalism, which grouped them in social strata. It challenged the right of the monarch to govern except in the interests of his subjects; it defended their rights both by an appeal to natural law and upon grounds of utility. It could ally itself for the time with the monarchy against feudalism, and with feudalism against the monarchy. On the one hand, it made use of the conception of contract, which was implicit in feudalism and as old as Stoic philosophy, to attack despotism; on the other, it looked to the monarchy as the one power strong enough to oppose the Church and to abolish the system of privilege which was all that remained of the corporate life of the Middle Ages. In the light of historical analysis it is now clear that of the three conceptions the feudal was, in any case, doomed; it was opposed to the whole trend of economic and psychological development. An absolute Church and an absolute monarch could not long maintain their position when the bourgeoisie became educated and rich, and the peasantry conscious of its degradation. The triumph of the Liberal conception of society may seem to have been unavoidable. But the form which that philosophy took was the result of actual events and the work of particular individuals in the eighteenth century.

CHAPTER III

THE FAILURE OF THE *ANCIEN RÉGIME*

I. THE INFLUENCE OF THE *PHILOSOPHES*

" La maladresse du son gouvernement a précipité cette révolution, la philosophie en a dirigé les principes, la force populaire a détruit les obstacles qui pouvaient arrêter les mouvements " (Condorcet, *Esquisse d'un tableau historique* .., 9th epoch).

" Under Louis XIV. one dared not say anything ; under Louis XV. one spoke low ; under your Majesty one speaks aloud " (Marshal Richelieu to Louis XVI.).

THE controversy about the part played by philosophy in producing the French Revolution began with the Revolution itself, still continues, and is not likely to end so long as there are historians and philosophers to discuss it. For the Revolution is the chosen battle-ground of the idealists and materialists in history. Is the French Revolution — and by implication any similar historical event — to be explained by economic changes over which individuals have little control or by the influence of ideas which moved men to dissatisfaction with their institutions? Put thus baldly, both extreme views are a little absurd. It is impossible to deny that ideas have influence. Karl Marx himself admitted their importance and his followers assume that their own ideas at least have effects. On the other hand, it seems scarcely worth while to refute those idealists who speak as if ideas were controlling factors in history apart from the economic and social circumstances in which they work. But we do not escape the problem by pointing out that both factors are always present and that the same forces are of varying importance in different periods of history. This is the beginning, not the end of an inquiry. The problem is to find the relationship between numerous factors, roughly and unsatisfactorily classified as economic and psychological. During the Revolution itself the two points of view were explicitly stated by Mallet du Pan and Mounier. The writers of the Catholic reaction, de Maistre and Bonald, naturally felt, like Professor Babbitt [1] in America to-day, that when the world goes wrong someone must be to blame. They therefore decided that Rousseau, Voltaire and

---

[1] *Vide* Irving Babbitt, *Rousseau and Romanticism.*

the Encyclopædists were responsible for the destruction of the *ancien régime*. Later the same thesis was majestically and paradoxically expounded by Taine. He described France as a healthy individual who fell upon the ground foaming at the mouth after drinking a cup of poison. The poison, in his view, was the philosophic doctrine. Having thus attributed the Revolution to the *philosophes*, he proceeded with incomparable skill and with great erudition to show that no part of the French Constitution was in fact healthy. The real difficulty was to explain how such outworn institutions contrived to last so long.[1]

Taine's researches have always provided ammunition for his adversaries. The most forcible exponent of the opposite doctrine was Rocquain, who argued that the Revolution arose out of the struggle between King and *Parlements* rather than out of any abstract ideas.[2] Aubertin sustained a thesis similar to Rocquain's in an elaborate study of the memoir-writers of the century.[3] M. Champion supported the view that the Philosophic doctrine was unimportant by demonstrating that the *cahiers* of 1789 were almost wholly confined to a statement of economic grievances and were for the most part unconcerned with any abstract ideas.[4] M. Faguet greeted M. Champion's researches with enthusiasm, showed that the so-called revolutionary philosophy was at least as old as Bayle and, for the most part, much older; that the *philosophes* themselves did not want and would not have liked revolution, being in general enthusiastic and loyal monarchists, and that the Revolution was therefore the outcome, not of ideas, but of a breakdown in government.[5]

Under M. Lanson's guidance, however, a more just appreciation of the *philosophes* came into fashion, and M. Roustan's *Philosophes et la Société française* marked another turn of

---

[1] Taine, *Les Origines de la France contemporaine*, i. (1876-1894) ; *cp.* also Morley's review of Taine in *Miscellanies*.

[2] Rocquain, *L'Esprit révolutionnaire avant la Révolution*, 1878,

[3] Aubertin, *L'Esprit publie au XVIIIᵉ Siècle*, 1872.

[4] Champion, *Esprit de la Révolution française* (1887), *La France d'après les Cahiers de 1789*.

[5] Faguet, *Questions politiques*.

the tide.[1] M. Roustan made two instructive mistakes in his brilliant analysis. In the first place, when championing the *philosophes* he sometimes overstated his own thesis and went so far as to say that " the Revolution remains the work of the *philosophes* whatever M. Rocquain and M. Faguet may have thought about it." His book in fact supports a more interesting and subtle thesis than this. In the second place, M. Roustan would have clarified the issue if he had been more careful to divide it into two distinct problems. For throughout the controversy there has been a confusion, natural enough in a country so sharply divided into Liberals and Clericals. The problems of discovering what the *philosophes* taught, whether it was new or old, whether (to mention M. Faguet's patriotic preoccupation) it was " French " or not in character, and whether its intention was good or evil—these are problems of one type, and their solution does not answer for us the second problem of estimating their actual influence. M. Roustan has not altogether dissociated himself from this confusion. In studying the influence of thinkers it is far more important to know what people thought they said, what people quoted from them and attributed to them, than to know what, in fact, they did teach. M. Roustan, however, has for the most part concentrated on the second question, and has found the balance more accurately than any of his predecessors. His view is that the economic collapse of France and the actual breakdown of government had occurred long before the Revolution, and that the part of the *philosophes* was to bring the situation to a head by expressing the grievances of the dispossessed and even converting a large part of the *noblesse* itself. In 1753 d'Argenson thought a revolution imminent. There was no revolution. Why not? Because, insists M. Roustan, the *philosophes* had scarcely begun their propaganda. 1789 is in fact different from 1753, not because the peasants were more miserable or the town proletariat nearer starvation, but because during the intervening generation the doctrine of the *philosophes* had made known the grievances of all the unprivileged, encouraged the bourgeoisie in its hatred of the Church and in its

---

[1] M. Roustan's book has been translated by Frederic Whyte as *Pioneers of the French Revolution*, with an introduction by Harold J. Laski.

68

hopes of freedom of trade and of thought, had won the favour of great financiers and impregnated the whole *noblesse*, and even found a fluctuating support at the Court itself.

This controversy establishes three facts about the development of Liberal opinion in the eighteenth century. The first is that the economic and social conflict predisposed all the unprivileged to listen to revolutionary ideas; the second, that the constitutional and religious struggle, involving King, *Parlements*, Jansenists and Jesuits, was itself sufficient to stimulate "a revolutionary spirit"; the third that the particular form of revolutionary teaching was the work of the *philosophes*. Though " that conglomeration of disturbance and sedition " out of which the Revolution was to take shape was not the work of the *philosophes*, and though the economic forces in France and the actual breakdown in government must, in any case, have produced some such upheaval, the propaganda of the *philosophes* was necessary to destroy the aristocracy's faith in itself and to imbue the Third, and at times even the Fourth, Estate with ideas of liberty, equality and fraternity.

If this summary is any approximation to the truth, the task of the *philosophes* was at once to state in general form the grievances of the unprivileged and to place before the disillusioned a conception of a freer and happier society. In doing so they enlarged and improved ideas which had already appeared in the seventeenth century. For the most part they wrote for the discontented bourgeoisie; where their doctrines were agreeable to the mental habits of their readers and seemed to promise a fulfilment of popular social and economic aspirations, they were readily accepted and became the basis of Revolutionary change. The further implications of the new philosophy were neglected until later schools of thinkers and groups of the dispossessed realized their utility for their own purposes.

Economically, the *ancien régime* was rapidly disintegrating, and the conflict between an old and a new system of production gave rise to a social struggle between the beneficiaries of the two systems. "The world is changing," remarks the eighteenth-century Jew; "once a man's worth was determined by rank and birth, now it is determined by money." This

struggle between the privileged and the unprivileged under-
lay all other conflicts. Politically the country, governed by
unusually incompetent persons, was convulsed by a long constitutional battle, which lowered the prestige of the established
Church and State. This conflict itself undermined religious
and political authority, revived the legal doctrine of natural
law, and led to an attack upon royal sovereignty. Finally, an
able group of thinkers attacked the intellectual and moral
assumptions upon which society was based, and offered a
complete set of alternative doctrines.

2. THE CONFLICT OF CLASSES—THE REVOLT OF THE BOURGEOISIE

Socially and legally eighteenth-century France was still
feudal in structure. Feudalism had once rested upon a series
of contracts in which property and privilege were a return for
some form of service. The property and privileges commonly
remained, while the services had been either commuted or
forgotten, to be performed, if at all, by others who were outside
the feudal structure. The *noblesse*, exempt not only from the
military service which had once been demanded of it, but also
from regular taxation, still owned about a third of France,
while the clergy, who were also great landowners, drew their
principal revenue from tithes.[1] Most of the peasantry had long

---

[1] Many of the poorer *noblesse* were unable to leave their estates, and lived a
life not very different from that of the peasantry. The upper *noblesse*, however,
flocked to the capital, and, in spite of a passing fashion which popularized
agriculture as a hobby in the second half of the century, the great landowners
seldom visited the land from which they drew their wealth. They had none
of the incentives to end feudal conditions and to adopt the new methods of
agriculture which were changing eighteenth-century England from a country
of small proprietors into one of great estates and landless labourers. Pasturage
did not offer wealth to the French *noblesse*. In any case, caste stood in the way:
to make money by any other method than that of extortion was beneath the
dignity of a gentleman. It is the peculiar curse of such an aristocracy that they
draw upon an unknown reservoir of peasant labour and are always tempted to
regard it as illimitable. Their main occupation was discovering and displaying
expensive and novel luxuries, for which they were frequently unable to pay.
The Marquis de Mirabeau declared that " by the life which they led in their
châteaux the *grand seigneurs* ruined the peasants and themselves."
    The higher clergy had also become a privileged class, spending a vast pro-

before succeeded in commuting personal services for money payments, and the courts were busy throughout the century with litigation between peasants and nobles about property rights. But seigniorial dues and clerical tithes[1] remained, even when the land was the property of the peasant. On the whole the French peasantry was in a far superior position to that of the serfs in most European countries, but the fact of legal freedom only made the surviving badges of servitude more intolerable.[2]

The hardships of the peasantry were increased by royal taxation, which grew always more onerous and more arbitrary. It was estimated that the most common type of peasant, the *métayer*, who owed half the produce of his land to his lord, paid a further thirty or forty per cent. to the Government, and could perhaps rely on retaining from ten to twenty per cent. for his own use. This system produced famine rather than crops. Yet rebellion was rare. In the early part of the reign

---

portion of the tithes and produce from church lands in the capital. Several eighteenth-century bishops are known to have lived in their dioceses and to have concerned themselves with religious and charitable offices, but it was said that there were always twenty bishops living in Paris, and often forty. The poorer clergy, like the poorer nobles, shared the poverty of the country.

[1] The resentment against tithes as well as against the gaming rights of the *seigneurs* is well illustrated by the famous story of a peasant who was asked, in 1789, what he hoped from the States-General. "The suppression of pigeons, rabbits and monks," he answered. "Surely this is a strange way of classifying them?" "Nay, sir, it is clear; the first devour us in the seed, the second in the blade, the third in the sheaf."

[2] The weight of feudal obligations was frequently crushing in extent as well as vexatious and arbitrary, while constant parcelling-out had so much reduced the peasants' holdings that in order to live at all most of them were forced to work as labourers for their lords and cultivate their own land when they could. Justice in many districts and in matters arising from their status was still feudal justice; the peasant could look for redress only in the lord's court when, to take a concrete instance, the lord had himself decided arbitrarily to increase the size of the measure by which his feudal dues were calculated. The lord's right to *corvée*, or forced labour, his hunting and game rights, and his right to demand that the peasants should grind their corn at his mill, amounted in some parts of the country to intolerable grievances. Ancient and humiliating rights like that of *jus primæ noctis*, made famous by Beaumarchais, had never been formally abolished. There were, of course, some prosperous peasants—a fact which Arthur Young did not fail to notice.

of Louis XIV., when war taxes added a new burden, there had been peasant risings which recalled the horrors of the " Jacqueries." But the last six years of the reign of Louis XIV., perhaps the worst ever experienced by the peasantry, passed over the ruined countryside with the calmness of death. In the reign of Louis XV. their condition improved. Later in the century, however, the bankruptcy of the Crown led to increasing royal taxation. Money was extorted even from the *noblesse*, who often attempted to recoup themselves by a stricter levy of their feudal dues and even by the revival of dues that had long been neglected. Here at last were the conditions which breed revolutionary feeling : an economic improvement followed by the fear of a relapse and the belief that new impositions were to be made. In the years immediately preceding the Revolution it needed no propaganda to incite the peasantry to demand that all feudal dues should be abolished, all classes equally taxed, and that the clerical tithes, once consecrated to the purposes of education and the relief of the poor, should be " given back to their original purpose." Upon these points all the rural *cahiers*, which were for the most part practical statements of grievances, not philosophical demands based on natural rights, were unanimous.

By 1789, therefore, the peasantry had become a great revolutionary force which only waited for a signal to abolish at a stroke all that remained of the feudal system of land tenure. In the towns there had also gathered an element which played a part in overthrowing the established order. The mediæval organization of industry had been rapidly breaking down : the ancient corporations of masters, rarely recruited from the ranks of workmen, whose own corporations were scarcely less exclusive, had long been bankrupt and were finally suppressed during Turgot's administration. With the collapse of the corporations, numbers of workmen belonging to no organization swelled the crowd of town paupers. After the treaty with England in 1776 the upward movement of prices was sharply accentuated, and the value of wages decreased. The town workers, however, were actuated by hunger, not by any realization of their interests as a class. Their rôle in the Revolution, therefore, was not in any way comparable to that of the peasantry, who knew what they wanted. They were important to the course of the Revolution only in so far as they strengthened the city mob. Their point of view seldom appears in the *cahiers*, and was neglected by the National Assembly. It was not until modern industry had created a working-class population conscious of collective interests and grievances that the town workman could become effectively revolutionary.[1]

The land revolution then was the work of the peasantry: the political revolution was at times influenced by the populace of Paris. But it was led and directed by members of the urban middle class. They had economic power as well as grievances; they were educated, and they were inspired by an idea. Their economic position had constantly improved throughout the century, and they increasingly resented the legal and social barriers which hampered their advance and reminded them of their social inferiority to a functionless and often less wealthy privileged class. The educated middle class supplied the Crown with administrators and with money; it patronized art and science; it read and appreciated the new philosophy, which was for the most part written by men who had come from its own ranks.

Not all the numerous elements which composed the middle class were equally revolutionary, though all shared in varying degree a constant grudge against the privileged aristocracy. The official class of course profited handsomely by the economic chaos. Only a comparatively small proportion of the money which came into the hands of the King's tax-collectors, estate agents, and controllers of water or forests, actually reached the Treasury. The Farmers-General, who headed this bureaucratic hierarchy and whose opportunity of enriching themselves

---

[1] Industrialism had of course begun in France long before the Revolution: there were silk mills in Lyons early in the century, and after 1775 English inventions began to transform the cotton industry. Strikes of workmen were not uncommon, but the spasmodic efforts of the *compagnons* were easily defeated. The State took the part of the masters, and in 1749 letters-patent forbade workers, under penalty of one hundred livres fine, to leave their masters without written permission, or to assemble, strike or conspire in any way to restrict the employers' freedom in the choice of workmen.

and their friends was unlimited, were perhaps the most un-
popular class in France. When Louis XV. remarked that they
were the support of the State, a courtier is said to have replied:
" Yes, Sire ; they support it just as a rope supports a corpse
hanging from the gallows."[1]

The financiers too, who lived on the deficiencies of the
Royal Exchequer and made profitable contracts with the King
in time of war, had little reason to complain. The Crown had
borrowed so heavily from them that they were the virtual
owners of the State. Living in similar style were retired men
of fortune who had contrived to buy land and who tried to the
best of their ability to ape the life of the old *noblesse*. They
were able to buy titles of nobility and even noble husbands for
their daughters, but they could not buy freedom from the
contemptuous toleration of the aristocracy, nor could they
fail to repay it with the hatred that accompanies a fawn-
ing assumption of equality. Their interests, however, were
naturally identified with those of the *noblesse*, and it is not
surprising that the middle-class electors in 1789 wished to
exclude the *anoblis* from representing them in the National
Assembly.

There is abundant evidence that even these, the most fortunate elements in the middle class, were tainted with revolutionary doctrines before the Revolution.[2] Men like Poupelinière,
the financier, were the greatest patrons of the *philosophes*, and
it was in their salons that Voltaire and Marmontel, and even
Rousseau, felt most at home.[3] They all hated the aristocracy
and the Church, and resented the failure and inefficiency of the
Government. These sentiments were shared with far greater
vehemence by the mass of the middle class, who did not profit
by an antiquated and chaotic economic system, but existed as
best they could in spite of it, and who were untroubled by any

---

[1] It is related that once at Voltaire's table, after several stories of robbers and
highwaymen had been related, Voltaire was thought to have capped them all
by merely saying : " There was once a Farmer-General . . ."

[2] *Cp.* Roustan, *op. cit.*, esp. chap. v.

[3] *Vide* Marmontel's *Mémoires* for the best contemporary account of the
financiers' patronage of the new philosophy.

complicated connections with the aristocracy.[1] It was the business class, therefore, which most urgently demanded legal and social equality and formed the stubborn bulk of the Third Estate which refused to submit to the King and the *noblesse* when at length their opportunity arrived in 1789.

The social aspect of the Revolution becomes clear. The *cahiers* revealed the unanimous opposition of the peasantry and unprivileged middle class to the privileged *noblesse* and clergy. All the *cahiers* of the Third Estate demanded equality of rights, equal justice, free speech, the abolition of feudal dues and of the old trading corporations; they agreed in asking for a responsible executive and an elected Assembly, with full legislative power. When the *cahiers* spoke of equality they meant the abolition of privilege; when they spoke of liberty they were demanding civil rights and finally political power; when they spoke of fraternity they meant the national unity of citizens as opposed to the feudal division of classes. They spoke for the mass of the people. A powerful and wealthy trading class was everywhere growing restive of arbitrary taxation, hampering feudal and State restrictions, tariffs which benefited none but those who collected them, and private monopolies which prevented trade from further expansion. It had economic power, education, intelligence and a vision of a free State in which equality before the law would allow its virtues and activities a fitting reward. Everywhere it was hampered by those who had none of these things and whose power depended upon the accident of birth. Figaro's complaint was on behalf of the whole Third Estate: "Nobility, fortune, rank, office, how proud we are of them: what have you done to procure such blessings? You have taken the trouble to be born, no more! Otherwise an ordinary man! Whereas I, an insignificant unit in the crowd, have had to employ more science and calculation merely to gain my living than has been devoted in the last hundred years to the government of all the Spains."

Common grievances united the Third Estate. Yet its final

---

[1] France was of course still almost wholly an agricultural country, but industrialism was beginning and French commerce increasing throughout the century. Arnould calculates that it was quadrupled between 1716 and 1788.

victory over privilege was postponed until the bankruptcy of the monarchy delivered the State into its hands. The King could tax without consulting his subjects : he could not borrow from them and remain absolute. Fleury had struggled to pay off the load of debt accumulated by Louis XIV., but after his retirement no further effort was made to balance the national budget. The three great wars which Louis XV. undertook necessitated more severe taxation, and his attempts to raise money by unusual means brought him into conflict with every section of the nation.[1] The monarchy lived on loans, and administrators like d'Argenson and Bernis complained that they had almost daily to wait on the doorsteps of great financiers to beg on the Government's behalf. It was not until the administration of Turgot that any attempt was made to restore the national credit. But the efforts of Turgot and sub-sequent controllers failed because the principle that the very rich should live upon taxes collected from the very poor was inherent in the social structure of France. There is a limit to this process, and the State, by long borrowing, had in fact become the property of the middle class : the States-General, it has been well said, was not so much a revolutionary assembly as a meeting of the Government's creditors, called to liquidate the estate of a client whom they regarded as a fraudulent bankrupt.

3. THE CROWN AND THE *PARLEMENTS*—SOVEREIGNTY AND NATURAL LAW

The social conflict within the *ancien régime* was the under-lying cause of its collapse, and the bankruptcy of the Government was its immediate occasion. Many other factors had contributed to diminish authority and to predispose the

---

[1] Attempts to tax the privileged naturally led to protests. *Parlements* even spoke of instituting a "civil list" after the English model, and demanded that Ministers should submit their accounts to public audit. The Church Assembly resisted the King's demand for a free gift, declaring that it would never "permit what had hitherto been the gift of our love to become the tribute of our obedience."

unprivileged to listen to Liberal doctrines. Indeed there were several occasions earlier in the century when Revolution seemed imminent : the degradation and failure of the monarchy and the long constitutional struggle had threatened to destroy the régime many years before the final catastrophe.

Louis XIV. had remained great even in his failure. He lost battles, but not dignity : he ruined France, but the lustre of earlier glory still hung about his head. After his death the dignity as well as the competence of the monarchy decayed. France, it is true, remained obstinately monarchical even in 1790,[1] and the cry of reformers had always been " if only the King knew." Attacks were directed, as usually happens in the prelude to a revolution, not against the monarchy, or even against the King, but against his Ministers. Nevertheless a knowledge of the "Well-beloved " led inevitably to contempt. It was not only that he lost France an Empire—and French monarchs have been forgiven everything before military defeat —but that he did so meanly and ingloriously. The revenge taken upon England in America came too late to save his credit and served only to spread subversive doctrines. The memoirs and journals of the period agree that Louis, at his accession a handsome boy, enthusiastically acclaimed amid the rejoicings at his grandfather's funeral, gradually sank in popular esteem, until during his last illness few people minded whether he lived or died.[2]

To speak of the divine nature of the monarchy when Louis XV. was king was to strain credulity. What could be said for a monarch who officially " did nothing to-day," while his armies were defeated, his administration became increasingly corrupt and incompetent and his Treasury drifted into bankruptcy? His government became " a despotism tempered by epigrams "—epigrams which displayed him as a libertine who

---

[1] *Vide* Aulard, *History of the French Revolution,* vol. i., chap. i.

[2] Compare the oft-quoted story of a canon of Nôtre-Dame that in 1744 six thousand masses were voluntarily subscribed for Louis' recovery on the occasion of his first serious illness ; that in 1757, when Damiens attempted to assassinate him, the number was six hundred, and during his final illness only three.

did not enjoy his sensuality and a weakling who persecuted from inertia rather than from faith. Louis XIV. could afford to be the master of a series of mistresses, Louis XV., moving from one low-born woman to another, was despised as the slave of an even larger number.[1]

His funeral was a national *fête*, and placards, ribald songs and insulting epithets followed his body to the grave. The unintentional jest of the Abbé who remarked that "Louis XV. was loved by his people as tenderly as he loved them" was repeated with shouts of laughter, while common opinion seems to have been summarized in the bitter gibe thrown at his passing coffin, "vas-t'en salir l'histoire."

Louis XIV. had disregarded the ancient French Constitution and angered lawyers and churchmen by his refusal to recognize their immemorial right to offer him advice. Louis XV. was no less arrogant, but he was neither able enough nor powerful enough to prevent their protests from troubling his throne. He fought a long war with the *Parlements*, and finally took the drastic step of totally abolishing them. He never departed from the most absolute pretensions. "In my person alone," he declared in 1760, "resides the sovereign power. To me alone belongs the legislative power, independently and indivisibly. All public order emanates from me."

To state one's own supremacy, however, is not necessarily to enforce silence on others; and during the constitutional struggle the King's royal sovereignty was widely challenged. The conflict with the *Parlements* and with powerful sections of the Church prepared the way for revolution in three ways. Firstly, it brought the populace into politics and accustomed Paris to the spectacle of rebellion; secondly, it led to the revival of the ancient doctrine of fundamental law, which has always

---

[1] Louis' amours have been the subject of many dull books. He was doing nothing shocking in taking mistresses, the position of royal mistresses being a recognized one. On the contrary, complaints were made at his slowness of choice as a young man and his lengthy fidelity to the Queen. But he angered the aristocracy by choosing a *bourgeoise* like Madame de Pompadour. Madame du Barry's origin was still less reputable. The aristocracy complained that with their daughters at the King's disposal it was surely an insult for him to choose from the lower orders.

threatened absolutist pretensions; thirdly, since its climax was the complete destruction of the French Constitution, reform without the calling of the States-General was rendered almost impossible.

Louis' support of the Jesuits, fluctuating though it was, brought him into violent conflict, not only with the Jansenists and the *Parlements*, but also with the whole mass of Gallican feeling. The attempt to enforce the Bull *Unigenitus* led to a struggle in which the whole country took part. "The *acceptants*," said Voltaire, "were the hundred bishops who had adhered under Louis XIV., and with them the Jesuits and the Capuchins : the *recusants* were fifteen bishops and the entire natioh."

The struggle undermined Church and State authority as well as religious belief. The notary Barbier gleefully records in his journal that the battle over the Constitution was discrediting the Ultramontanes, and he remarks in 1731 that the " good town of Paris is Jansenist from top to bottom." D'Argenson adds that it was dangerous to appear in the street in a cassock. Many memoirs refer to the mockery bred by the affair of the Abbé Pâris.[1] When the Jesuits were dethroned the rejoicing seemed to Bachaumont positively indecent. Gallicanism was old enough, but the political criticism which now accompanied it was new. Hatred of the priesthood led to hatred of the Government which supported the Jesuits. "With reform in religion," remarks d'Argenson, "will come reform in government ; profane tyranny is married to ecclesiastical tyranny." The security of the monarchy itself was threatened by its subservience to the Jesuits.

As early as 1720 the Regent had been doubtful of the loyalty

---

[1] The Abbé Pâris died in 1727. His tomb became a sacred shrine, where the sick were miraculously healed and where women had convulsions, " rolling on the ground half naked, foaming at the mouth like sibyls." When the Government forcibly closed the gates of the cemetery, Voltaire made a characteristic comment :

> " De par le roi, défense à Dieu
> De faire miracles en ce lieu."

The Jesuits claimed God as their exclusive possession, and turned Him out like any other defaulting party leader when he deserted to the Opposition.

of his troops in the likely event of a Parisian rising on behalf of the *recusants*. In 1752 the order denying extreme unction to dying Jansenists had raised opinion to such a pitch of fury that d'Argenson, at least, feared a "national revolution," and the President of the *Parlement* of Paris warned Louis that "schism dethrones Kings more easily than whole armies can uphold them." In 1754 d'Argenson's prophecy seemed about to be fulfilled and a "Grand Remonstrance," reminiscent of that which preceded the rebellion against Charles I., was drawn up by the Paris *Parlement*. Troops armed with muskets and *lettres de cachet* were sent to overawe the *Parlement*, and both upper and lower houses of magistrates were exiled from Paris. The Remonstrance, however, was published. It protested against the action of the King in upholding the refusal of the sacrament to Jansenists, and while, as always, reiterating that nothing but zeal for the monarchy dictated the protest of the *Parlements*, it went so far as to say that "if subjects owe obedience to Kings, Kings on their side owe obedience to the laws," and added that, by disregarding the ancient liberties and traditional Constitution of France, Louis was preparing the way for a revolution. The King made concessions which averted danger and the *Parlements* returned in triumph.

Encouraging though their victory in 1754 was, the most optimistic Gallican could scarcely have hoped for the success which awaited his party. The Jesuits never seemed stronger: they dominated Catholic Europe, they ruled the Vatican and the courts of Kings. In France the Jesuit confessors of the King, the Queen and the Dauphin seemed all-powerful, while the education of the nation was still largely in their hands. But in 1761 a series of blows fell upon the Society. Their dismissal from Portugal encouraged their enemies: their trade with Martinique suffered in the war between England and France, and the litigation which arose from a consequent debt of 3,000,000 livres finally reached the upper chamber of the Paris *Parlement*. The *Parlement* did not waste its chance. It insisted on examining Jesuit doctrines, and declared them "murderous and abominable, not only in respect to the lives of citizens, but also in regard to the sacred persons of

Sovereigns." The Jesuits were prohibited from teaching in French schools.

No help came from the Crown. Choiseul and Madame de Pompadour—the reigning influences at the moment—had personal reasons for disliking the Jesuits, and Louis had been induced to believe that they were implicated in the recent attempt on his life. In 1764 the Society of Jesus was suppressed in France and during the next decade suffered indignities in almost every European country. An extraordinary outburst of rejoicing followed its fall, and the philosophic party regarded this as a sign that the Crown had left bigotry and embraced enlightenment. " I seem," said Diderot, " to see Voltaire raising his hands and eyes to heaven, as he repeats the *Nunc Dimittis*."

The destruction of the Jesuits increased the power of the *Parlements*; so too did the military disasters, which compelled Louis frequently to introduce new edicts of taxation. The *Parlements*, though forced to sanction them, had recourse to decrees setting forth that such compulsory registration of edicts " tended to the subversion of the fundamental laws of the kingdom "; that " to sustain a government by force was to teach the people that force would overthrow it." In his diary Barbier made a discerning note : " If the Government," he wrote, " succeeds in diminishing the authority and accepted rights of the *Parlements*, there will no longer be any obstacle in the way of assured despotism. If, on the contrary, the *Parlements* unite to oppose this move with strong measures, nothing can follow but a general revolution."

In 1770 the struggle came to a head. The Duc d'Aiguillon, Governor of Brittany, had come into violent conflict with the *Parlement* of his province, and was accused of participation in a Jesuit plot. He was arraigned before the Paris *Parlement*. The inquiry had already lasted two months when the King intervened and gave d'Aiguillon a complete discharge. Encouraged by Chancellor Maupeou, the King refused to listen to any protests against this arbitrary procedure, and the *Parlement* resigned. In 1771 Maupeou carried out a *coup d'état*. One hundred and sixty-eight magistrates who refused to submit were exiled from Paris, their seats confiscated and the Grand Council induced to take over the title and powers of the exiled *Parlement*. Maupeou then set up new courts of justice, entitled "Superior Councils," suppressed the *Cours des Aides,* which refused to recognize the appointed Councils, and exiled its President, Malesherbes, who had suggested the calling of the States-General. The *Châtelet* itself protested and was suppressed. Thus the whole of the ancient Constitution of France had been wiped out. It seemed that the first of Barbier's alternatives was to take place : that revolution was to be averted by the complete victory of absolutism.

This bureaucratic revolution, however, was achieved only at a price. The *Parlements* had been growing in popularity during the struggle. The lawyers found themselves in the odd position of a body of privileged aristocrats, totally hostile to all Liberal reform, upholding the Constitution of France against the Monarch amid the enthusiastic applause of a populace who looked upon them as the champions of liberty and described them as "true Romans and Fathers of their country." Their exile was the signal for another burst of popular agitation. Maupeou, now ruling almost unchecked in France, was subjected to a prolonged attack in papers and pamphlets which censured his policy and mingled prophecies of revolution with personal abuse and abstract discussions of popular sovereignty.

At every stage of this protracted conflict with the monarchy the lawyers had been compelled to base their opposition to the Crown on some basis of theory : as time went on their theory had grown less selfish and more universal. At first their anxiety had been to regain the ancient privileges upon which Louis XIV. had so often trampled. In 1715 they had asserted their traditional right to act on behalf of the nation in default of an heir to the throne and had co-operated with the Duke of Orleans in setting aside the will of Louis XIV. Thus strengthened they were able to exercise their second constitutional right of discussing royal edicts before registering them. In protesting against attempts to enforce the Bull *Unigenitus* they described themselves as guardians of the

the *Parlements* are the senate of the nation, while the King is merely the chief of the nation," and described the royal edicts as dependent upon the will of the assembled Estates, and even added that "laws are real conventions between those who govern and those who are governed." The Council of State naturally declared that this maxim was "absolutely intolerable in a monarchy, since, in depriving the Sovereign of his most august office, that of legislation, he is reduced to treat with his subjects on terms of equality by form of contract, and is consequently subject to receive the law from those to whom he ought to give it." The *Parlement* of Paris itself seemed to be approaching this point of view before it was exiled in 1763. We may trace the influence of Montesquieu's *L'Esprit des Lois*[1] in their declaration that "Your authority, Sire, is the strongest support of the legitimate liberty of Your subjects, a liberty which subjects them to You more certainly than compulsion, which binds them by ties more powerful than those of force, a liberty which, equally opposed to licence and to slavery, characterizes monarchical government. The King, the State and the Law form an inseparable whole, united in a sacred knot"; by observation of the laws the King strengthens his throne, preserves the subordination of his subjects, ensures their rights and their liberty.[2]

In 1759 the *Parlement* of Besançon added that all the King's subjects were "under the immediate protection of the laws; it is the right of a nation which your *Parlement* claims and has never ceased to claim," while the *Parlement* of Rouen spoke of "the respective rights of Sovereign and peoples," and protested against novel forms of taxation as arbitrary infringements of the "immutable" laws which form the only bond between King and people. Thus the *Parlements*, which had begun as a purely feudal body, defending their privileges, had gone on to claim that the King must obey the fundamental laws of France and of nature, and that they themselves were the guardians of these rights. Finally they spoke of a contract between King and people and hinted that the people had a right to revolt if the King violated their rights.

---

[1] Published 1748. [2] Flammermont, t. i. 407.

When Louis XVI. came to the throne, therefore, the situation was novel. The theory which held that the King's power was legitimately exercised only within the limits of fundamental law, and that the people had the right to overthrow an arbitrary government, had found wide popular acceptance. At the same time the only corporations with any right to criticize or question the Crown had been abolished. The old Constitution of France, disregarded by Louis XIV., had been formally destroyed by his successor. A return to the old type of monarchical government supported by aristocratic corporations was in any case out of the question. Turgot, therefore, hoped to save France and the monarchy by establishing new local federations instead of the ancient feudal ones. Having refused this suggestion, Louis XVI. had only two possibilities before him : either to make unlimited despotism succeed or to admit the thesis of democracy. Revolution had been instituted from above, not below : it was the work of the monarchy, not the *philosophes*.

The *philosophes*, indeed, had supported the King against the *Parlements*. They favoured " enlightened despotism " and criticized Louis, not for his despotism but for his lack of enlightenment. The accession of Louis XVI., the enlightened Monarch in person, and the appointment of Turgot as Controller-General, marked the culminating point of Voltairean influence. The abolition of the *Parlements*, resented by the mass of the middle class, had been applauded by almost all the Philosophic group, who believed in an absolute Monarch enlightened by themselves, not in a restoration of an ancient Constitution. Louis XV. had destroyed the last obstacles to the completion of an enlightened despotism. Enlightenment was forced upon Louis XVI. ; he could not avoid financial reform and he could not suppress propaganda. But a resolute policy might have prevented the Revolution, or at least mitigated its violence. " Events," as Sorel puts it, " had reached the point at which there had to be either a great King or a great revolution."

Louis had then a choice of two policies. In the absence of all constitutional resistance, he could have appointed a few able administrators and attempted by his own authority to institute necessary reforms in the teeth of the aristocracy. On the other hand, he could have made a bid for popularity by dismissing Maupeou and appealing to the *Parlements*, and then to the States-General, for support in the economic crisis. The monarchy was still the centre of men's hopes, the Queen had not yet become identified with privilege and reaction, and either policy might have gained popular support. But a combination of the two was fatal. Louis attempted the policy of enlightened despotism but had not the strength of purpose necessary to defy the party of privilege or sufficient intelligence to avoid ruining any hope of success by combining it with the second incompatible policy. When at length he called the States-General, opinion had gone too far for a constitutional revolution to succeed, and the King, who was not even then faithful to the democratic principle he had invoked, was swept away to make room for less amiable despots.

Louis' counsels were divided from the beginning. The appointment of Turgot and Malesherbes in place of Maupeou and the Abbé Terray was his most certain step. But he yielded to opposite advice when he recalled the banished *Parlements* and restored the *Châtelet* and the *Cour des Aides*. Turgot warned him that the magistrates would oppose every genuine reform, and Voltaire expressed amazement that the King should sacrifice the new *Parlements* which "had always known how to obey to the old ones which had done nothing but defy him." The *Parlements* immediately justified Turgot's fears. Their triumph made them proportionately bold. For eighteen months the King supported Turgot in his battle with privilege. His policy of free trade in France, the suppression of the *maîtrises*, the abolition of the *corvée*, and the gradual transference of the burden of taxation to the shoulders of the wealthy, brought him at once into conflict with the clergy, the Court, the newly recalled *Parlements* and the financiers. Finally the Paris mob, which attributed the scarcity of bread to his reforms, demanded his dismissal. Turgot's outspoken letters warned Louis of his danger : " Remember, Sire," he wrote, " that it was weakness that brought Charles I. to the block." By yielding to a Court intrigue and dismissing Turgot, Louis threw away his greatest opportunity : Necker, more plausible, had even less chance of success.

The ministries of Turgot and Necker in fact hastened the Revolution. The education of the public was proceeding apace. For the first time the Monarchy argued with the nation. The preambles to Turgot's edicts, setting forth the reasons for reform, were worth many philosophic pamphlets, and Necker's *comptes rendus*, disingenuous though they were, let the public still further into the secrets of the Government's failure. In this final period before the Revolution the idea of " enlightened despotism " was superseded by the conception of democracy. Even in 1778, when Voltaire, paying his last visit to Paris, was greeted, as one observer declared, with " an inconceivable idolatry," the generation which worshipped him as a patriarch had already found a new prophet. Rousseau's influence had taken the place of that of the Encyclopædists and the example of the American Revolution had stimulated democratic sentiment.[1] Two hopes were everywhere discussed—the recall of the Protestants and the summoning of the States-General. Even the Paris *Parlement* had become infected with the democratic idea. Younger lawyers, trained in a generation whose inspiration was Montesquieu rather than d'Aguesseau, began to admit that the *Parlements* did not adequately represent the nation. As early as 1782 they suggested that the States-General should be summoned ; five years later they laid down the principle of " no taxes without representation " ; by 1788 they had altogether forgotten " privilege " and were ready to

---

[1] *Cp.* Condorcet, *Tableau Historique*, 9ᵉ époque : " Mais dans la guerre qui s'élevait entre deux peuples éclairés, dont l'un défendait les droits naturels de l'humanité, dont l'autre leur opposait la doctrine impie qui soumet ces droits à la prescription, aux intérêts politiques, aux conventions écrites ; cette grande cause fut plaidée au tribunal de l'opinion, en présence de l'Europe entière ; les droits des hommes furent hautement soutenus et développés sans restriction, sans réserve, dans des écrits qui circulaient avec liberté des bords de la Néva à ceux du Guadalquivir. Ces discussions pénétrèrent dans les contrées les plus asservies, dans les bourgades les plus reculées, et les hommes qui les habitaient furent étonnés d'entendre qu'ils avaient des droits ; ils apprirent à les connaître ; ils surent que d'autres hommes osaient les reconquérir ou les défendre."

ridicule all monarchs who attempted to rule without the help of their subjects.[1]

The relief to the Protestants in 1782, the free-trade treaty with England in 1786, and the final summoning of the States-General were all admissions that the policy initiated by Louis XIV. had failed. Toleration, the rights of man and the sovereignty of the people had taken the place of clerical absolutism, feudal privilege and royal despotism. In the ten years before the Revolution there was no intellectual resistance to the new religion. Balloons, mesmerism, scientific discovery, a vague humanitarianism and the "simple life" had become the vogue among the aristocracy. "They were ingenuously discussing amongst themselves the virtues of the populace, its gentleness, devotion, its innocent pleasures, when already '93 was upon them."

If the aristocracy were blind, there were many who were not. Few historical errors have been so often repeated as that the French Revolution came without warning. Social critics had frequently prophesied it throughout the preceding century, and their prophecies were the common gossip under Louis XVI.[2] The *ancien régime* had lost confidence in itself. It lasted until Calonne could no longer borrow money. Calonne himself pronounced its obsequies when he met the Notables with a statement that the ancient formula, "What the King wills, the law wills," would henceforth be abandoned for the novel preamble, "What the happiness of the people demands, the King wills." The calling of the States-General was more than a confession that the Government needed popular support; it was also an acknowledgment of the people's right to give or withhold it.

---

[1] *Vide* Sée, *op. cit.* 326.

[2] Lord Chesterfield's prophecy is well known. Other anticipations of the Revolution are referred to later, in Chapter IX.

In 1774 Rousseau wrote : "I see all the States of Europe rushing headlong to ruin ; monarchies, republics, all those nations whose origins are so glorious and whose governments were built up with so much wisdom, are falling into decay and are threatened by an imminent death. All the great nations are moaning, crushed by their own weight."

CHAPTER IV

PHILOSOPHY AND PROPAGANDA

Louis XIV. was a grand and tyrannous figure, an overpowering myth who subdued criticism even when he did not convince reason. At his death it was as though a spring were released and the first effect of that release was laughter. And laughter, at first a trivial gaiety in the social life of the Regency, made way for thought. The hushed circulation of sceptical comment was followed by open raillery, raillery by considered criticism, and out of criticism came visions of a better social order. In 1721 Montesquieu published the *Persian Letters*. Almost for the first time since Rabelais a book had appeared in which nothing was sacred. The attack upon French society contained in the letters of Usbec and Rica is barely disguised, though, to be sure, Persian travellers, commenting on the morals and manners prevalent in Europe, can make remarks which would be unseemly from a Frenchman, but which may nevertheless be true. The reader is imperceptibly led to the conclusion that the institutions he has revered, and the authorities he has obeyed, are perhaps unworthy of his reverence and obedience. The King, these observant Persians notice, is " a magician," who persuades men to kill one another though they have no quarrel. What else but magic could make them so irrational? Again self-constituted legislators pretend " their own wills are the laws of nature." Judges condemn " by the light within, without concerning themselves with useless knowledge." The highest aristocrat they visited was a little man who lost no " opportunity of making all who came near him sensible of his superiority, who took snuff with so much dignity, blew his nose so unmercifully, spat with so much phlegm, and caressed his dog in a manner so offensive to the company that I could not but wonder at him. Ah! I said to myself, if when I was at the Court of Persia I had behaved so I should have been considered a great fool." The religious authorities were not treated with more respect. If the King was a magician,

hypnotizing men into obedience, what was the Pope himself
but "an old idol"? As for the Spanish Inquisitors, they were
a "cheery species of dervishes" who burnt those who differed
from them about obscure trivialities. And what reason was
there for believing that Christianity embodied the final truth,
when there were so many religions, each claiming universal
validity? It was grievous for a kindly Persian to have to entertain the idea that all these Christians who had never worshipped
in a mosque would end miserably in hell. Surely, he thinks, we
can all agree about certain moral principles, and leave doubtful
questions of dogma to the varying judgments of the sects?
It is man who has made God in his own image, and if triangles
had to construct a God, the new deity would certainly consist
of three sides rather than three persons. In these circumstances,
was not Louis XIV. unwise in thinking to "increase the number
of the faithful by diminishing the number of his subjects"?
Questions, hints and criticisms of this kind are everywhere
spread among the one hundred and sixty *Persian Letters*.
But the correspondence of Usbec and Rica is not solely concerned with philosophy or politics, for Usbec, in seeking
wisdom abroad, has abandoned the joys of a well-stocked harem
from which he receives a constant stream of letters dealing with
love, hatred, strife and death. Even this side of the correspondence has a certain philosophical bearing. It provides an
example of the revenge of outraged nature which can be denied
no more in the seraglio than in the convent. The chief object of
these passages however was to please the ladies who frequented
Madame de Tencin's *salon*, where Montesquieu was a constant
visitor. His friends there were only likely to listen to appeals
for toleration or social reform when spiced with more appetizing
ingredients; social criticism is, therefore, intermingled with
descriptions of the sufferings of beautiful women and the pathos
of thwarted desire in the eunuchs who assisted at their more
intimate adornment.

These two characteristics, the trivial libertinism and the thin
disguise of an indirect satire, were used throughout eighteenth-
century literature to cover the most savage and subversive
attacks. They reflect the two main conditions under which the

philosophes wrote. It was essential to please a *salon* audience, which could enjoy an artistic and ironical attack upon social evils, but had no notion of practical and inconvenient remedies. It was also necessary to circumvent a censorship which would not permit any direct criticism of the political or religious authorities. Eighteenth-century *philosophes* made no pretence of being detached seekers after truth, and had the greatest contempt for most of what is usually called philosophy. The *philosophes* were humanists and journalists with a common object of propaganda. They wanted publicity and, unlike their Renaissance predecessors, they sought not for immortality in the praise of posterity, but for tangible and immediate influence. " Our philosopher," wrote Diderot, " does not count himself an exile in the world ; he does not suppose himself in the enemy's country, he would fain find pleasure with others, and to find it he must give it ; he is a worthy man who wishes to please and to make himself useful. The ordinary philosophers, who meditate too much, or rather who meditate to wrong purpose, are as surly and arrogant to all the world as great people are to those whom they do not think their equals ; they flee men, and men avoid them. But our philosopher who knows how to divide himself between retreat and the commerce of men is full of humanity. Civil society is, so to say, a divinity for him on the earth ; he honours it by his probity, by an exact attention to his duties, and by a sincere desire not to be a useless or an embarrassing member of it. The sage has the leaven of order and rule ; he is full of ideas connected with the good of civil society. What experience shows us every day is that the more reason and light people have, the better fitted they are and the more to be relied on for the common intercourse of life."

Men who regarded civil society as a divinity on earth, and wished to enlist its support in practical reforms, were likely to busy themselves with metaphysical problems only in so far as their free treatment would cause amusement by annoy- ing the ecclesiastical authorities. In any case, all systems of philosophy seemed remote and scholastic to a generation which believed that science could build a new heaven and a new earth.

Almost all the *philosophes* began by studying some branch of science. Voltaire talked of devoting his life to the study of chemistry and worked with enthusiasm both to understand and expound Newtonian physics. D'Alembert was a physicist as well as a mathematician. Montesquieu's first publications were scientific. Diderot dabbled in all the sciences, and even Rousseau wrote a botanical dictionary. In spite of all their differences the party of the *philosophes* was united by their faith in science, their acceptance of Locke and Newton, and their hatred of the Catholic Church.

Writing in 1765, Horace Walpole asked: "Do you know who the *philosophes* are or what the term means here? In the first place it comprehends almost everybody, and, in the next, means men who are avowing war against Popery and aim, many of them, at the subversion of religion." A few years later, Bachaumont noted in his journal that there had been in France for some years "a sect of bold philosophers who seemed to have had a deliberate plan of carrying a fatal clarity into men's minds, of disturbing all belief, of upsetting religion and sapping her very foundations. Some of these, the light troops of the party, armed with sarcasm and irony, began by using transparent allegories and ingenious fictions as a method of covering with ineffaceable ridicule her liturgy and even her code of morals; others, profound speculative thinkers, armed with learning and bristling with metaphysics, stood out openly attacking her by force. . . . These, being unable to find worthy opponents, have unhappily retained the mastery of the battle-field. To-day, when these unbelievers consider their work to be well advanced . . . they are attacking their adversaries in their last strongholds. They claim to prove that politics has not the least need of religion for the maintenance and government of States."[1]

In the sixties Walpole and Bachaumont could write of the *philosophes* as a united party, engaged in a combined assault on the Church. This unity among the critics of orthodoxy dated only from the middle of the century. During the twenty-seven

---

[1] Bachaumont, *Mémoires secrets*, 22nd September 1768.

years which elapsed between the *Persian Letters* and *The Spirit of the Laws* only Voltaire's *Letters on the English*, published in 1734, was comparable with Montesquieu's work in ability, or in audacity. The other political books of the period— Utopias, for instance, like Morelly's metrical *Basiliade*, or the ceaseless imitations of *Télémaque* by the Abbé Ramsay [1]—were not the kind of books which disturb administrations. Fleury was indeed surprisingly successful in maintaining the relationship of silence between monarch and subject, and even forbade the private meetings of the Entresol club where Saint-Pierre and his friends discussed political principles. In 1748 both Church and State seemed as secure as they had been fifty years earlier; the King was still popular after a successful war, the Jansenists and the *Parlements* were at the ebb of their fortunes in their long struggle with Jesuitism, and the *philosophes* and *libertins* were still disunited, individual critics, apparently as impotent as their predecessors under Louis XIV.

This was the last respite permitted to the champions of the *ancien régime*. *The Spirit of the Laws* appeared in 1748 and the first volumes of the *Encyclopædia* in 1751. The *Encyclopædia*, at first approved by the authorities as a mere bookseller's project, became in the hands of Diderot a central arsenal from which all the apostles of enlightenment could borrow weapons for their combined attack. Against the united forces of the *philosophes* the official attempts to preserve silence were turned to ridicule, and before the death of Louis XV. the Encyclopædic literature had penetrated into all educated sections of society.[2]

---

[1] For the Abbé Ramsay *vide* Cherel's *Fénelon au XVIIIe Siècle*.

[2] From 1750 onwards, Bachaumont's diary bears constant testimony to the "furious epidemic" of Voltairean literature, while Barbier notes with some alarm that all the public had these dangerous books in their hands and were even talking of carrying out the projects suggested in them. D'Argenson declared that though people in the provinces were ignorant and misguided about politics, even they were occupied in discussing philosophy. There is abundant proof that the Philosophic literature was widely discussed outside Paris. The *Encyclopædia* was subscribed for in every part of France, both by aristocrats and bourgeoisie. A striking proof of the influence of the *philosophes* upon the public is to be found in a comparison of the diaries and journals of the period. Men like Marais and Buvat, at the beginning of the century,

2. THE CENSORSHIP—ITS EFFECT ON THE *PHILOSOPHES*

The regulations of the publishing trade remained substantially as Francis I. had laid them down in the sixteenth century. No work could be legally published without the permission of the Director of Publications, and all books were supposed to be submitted to him for examination. In practice, however, the authorities rarely took notice of uncensored books unless they caused offence to someone of importance at Court or among the clergy. In such a case the book would be suppressed, a raid carried out upon the *colporteurs*, and the author imprisoned. If, on the other hand, the author obeyed the law and secured permission to publish, his security was scarcely greater. The Director's permission might always be reversed even after the expense of publication had been incurred, if the clergy or the *Parlement* of Paris or the Sorbonne or the *Châtelet* cared to demand the book's suppression. Finally, it was no uncommon thing for a royal *lettre de cachet* to intervene at the last moment, and condemn an author to the Bastille and his book to the flames. Indeed, remarks Figaro, "Provided I did not write about the Government, religion, politics, morality, officials, or anyone who has any claim to anything, I was at liberty to print what I chose—under the inspection of two or three censors."

In these circumstances most of the bolder books were published under pseudonyms and printed abroad, usually in Holland, and an elaborate secret organization grew up for the distribution of banned or illegally published works. Thus the publishing trade became a game in which the whole of literary France joined. The object of the game was to ensure the circulation of the books of your party, and though hundreds of books were censored all the important Philosophic publications found an excellent market. This constant struggle with authority had two immediate effects upon the Philosophic writing of the century. In the first place the Encyclopædists became a clique.

---

concern themselves only with the gossip of the Court and with external political events. In Barbier's journal public opinion is a recognized force and the determining factor in every political struggle.

They lost the capacity to laugh at themselves, and were enraged beyond measure or reason when a satirical attack like Moreau's *Les Cacouacs* or a feeble lampoon like Palissot's *Les Philosophe* passed the censorship. They learned to regard every critic as an accomplice of the powers of darkness. In their quarrel with Rousseau, Grimm, Madame D'Epinay and the rest pursued him with the venom of a secret society against a deserter. They lied about his work and his character; they forged documents to discredit him with posterity. Their inventions were the more remarkable since the truth about Rousseau offered the most bitter opponent ample scope for detraction. The Church itself could scarcely have shown more intolerance or waged more unscrupulous warfare than the *philosophes*. In their long battle with Fréron they treated *L'Année litéraire* and its editor with a contempt and bitterness which often seem quite undeserved. Fréron's defence of the *ancien régime* was based on principles which were implicit in Montesquieu; and the same principles in Burke's *Reflections on the French Revolution* afterwards proved the most powerful challenge to the Liberalism of the *philosophes*. "Ancient abuses," Fréron wrote, "in the process of growth have become implicated in so many small matters, and are so bound up with the course of affairs, and their roots, in brief, are now so deep and so extensive that to touch them would provoke a serious upheaval. An observer often thinks only of the benefits of the remedy he imagines already applied: and he does not foresee the inconveniences attending their application at the time." "Is not the fanaticism of your irreligion," he asked, "more absurd and more dangerous than the fanaticism of superstition? Begin by tolerating the faith of your fathers. You talk of nothing but tolerance and never was a sect more intolerant." [1] The *philosophes* usually replied by calling him a scoundrel and a bigot. There was a certain dignity in his declaration: "Pour moi, je ne tiens à aucune cabale de bel-esprit, à aucun parti, si n'est à celui de la religion, des mœurs et de l'honnêteté." Unfortunately, he added, no such party existed in his day.

---

[1] F. Cornou, *Elie Fréron*, 365.

Turgot, perhaps the very greatest of the *philosophes*, contributed to the *Encyclopædia* and did more to advance the ideas of economic Liberalism than Quesnay himself. But he complained that the *Encyclopædia* was " the book of a sect," and always refused to call himself a Physiocrat because he disliked cliques and party labels. There were others, such as d'Alembert, who sought to be above the battle. D'Alembert's desertion from the joint editorship of the *Encyclopædia*, which left Diderot alone to cope with contributors, publishers and authorities, was not due to fear of the Bastille, but to the shrinking of a timid and thoughtful man from a struggle in which science was confounded with politics and personal and party rancour seemed as likely to interfere with truth as religious intolerance itself.

The censorship had a second no less disastrous effect : the *philosophes* were forced to adopt subterfuges harmful both to the reader and to the writer. Outward conformity to a despised creed is not in the long run compatible with clear thought and intellectual integrity, however conscious the inward reservations. When Voltaire criticized the *Encyclopædia*, d'Alembert replied : " No doubt we have bad articles in theology and metaphysics, but since we publish by favour, and have theologians for censors, I defy you to make them any better. There are other articles that are less exposed to the daylight, and in them all is repaired. Time will enable people to distinguish what we have thought from what we have said." [1]

Voltaire's own recipe for evading the censorship was one which he was certainly incapable of following himself. He thought it wise to live on the borders of Switzerland, and amused his friends and annoyed his enemies by attending Mass in his village church. He might publish anonymously or under a false name, but the authorship of his books was always apparent however sturdy his lies. He did not disguise his style. Every new subterfuge only brought more laughter and more readers, since no one else could have written *Candide* or the *Histoire du Docteur Akakia*. Nevertheless it was Voltaire who wrote to d'Alembert to try " if you can, to weaken your style, write

---

[1] D'Alembert to Voltaire, 21st July 1757.

dully, certainly no one will then guess your identity. One can say good things in a heavy way. You will have the pleasure of enlightening the world without compromising yourself; that would be a fine action and you would be an apostle without being a martyr."

The method of disguise adopted in the *Persian Letters* remained one of the most popular. To describe a foreign country possessing all the freedom and good government which France lacked involved no weakening of style and was compatible with the highest literary standards. Sometimes the *philosophes* described the happier conditions of primitive people, who presumably obeyed the laws of nature by instinct or natural reason, unimpeded by the artifices and barriers erected by priests and kings. Sometimes they talked of China, where a benevolent monarch was supposed to rule in the full light of philosophic knowledge; or, again, of a Utopia, where everything suited everybody, including Plato and Sir Thomas More; more often still, the sober freedom of English constitutional government provided a satisfactory foil to the arbitrary ignorance of Louis' ministers.

There were other methods of baffling and teasing the authorities. Ever since the later Middle Ages, men who wished to avoid making up their minds, who disliked committing themselves or who feared punishment, had adopted the doctrine of " double truth." If reason, science and historical evidence came to one conclusion and the unchallengeable authority of Scripture to another, it was safest, and also most effective as propaganda, not to attempt a reconciliation. Bayle had been fond of explaining in a footnote how unlikely the Bible story would have appeared had not we known that with God all things, even contradictions and absurdities, are possible. So an article in the *Encyclopædia* proves with some ease that the cubical capacity of the Ark was insufficient to contain the full bulk of the enumerated inhabitants — another case in which reason would lead astray without the help of revelation. The New Testament story is treated in much the same way. The evidence for the Resurrection is such that it carries proof of the truth of Christianity " to a geometrical demonstration."

Similarly Voltaire adds, after a solemn examination of contemporary evidence of the life and death of Christ, that the reason why none but Biblical authorities record that the world was plunged into darkness for the space of three hours, or that the innocents were massacred by the orders of Herod, is no doubt that "God did not desire divine things to be written by profane hands."

Buffon attempted to escape censorship by the same device in his *Histoire naturelle*. The inadequacy of the biological theory, hitherto accepted on the authority of Genesis, by which each species of animals was created in its original and eternal form at one stroke without relation to any other, became increasingly obvious to him. After a consideration of evidence which led him to formulate an early evolutionary hypothesis, he wrote : " if we regard the matter thus, not only the ass and the horse but even man himself, the apes, the quadrupeds, and all animals might be regarded as forming members of one and the same family . . . if we once admit that there are families of plants and animals, so that the ass may be of the family of the horse, and that one might only differ from another by degeneration from a common ancestor (even as the ass and the horse differ), we might be driven to admit that the ape is of the family of man, that he is but a degenerate man, and that he and man have had a common ancestor, even as the ass and horse have had. . . . The naturalists who are so ready to establish families among animals and vegetables do not seem sufficiently to have considered the consequences which should follow from their premises, for that would limit direct creation to as small a number of forms as anyone should think fit. For . . . if the point were once gained that among animals and vegetables there had been, I do not say several species, but even a single one, which had been produced in the course of direct descent from another species—if for instance it could be once shown that the ass was but a degeneration from the horse—then there is no further limit to be set to the power of Nature, and we should not be wrong in supposing that with sufficient time she could have evolved all other organic forms from one primordial type. But no! It is certain from divine

99

revelation that all animals have alike been favoured with the grace of an act of direct creation, and that the first pair of every species issued full-formed from the hands of the creator."

It was not surprising that the Sorbonne condemned fourteen subversive propositions in the *Histoire naturelle*. Buffon, who was botanist to the King, and anxious not to lose his position nor to have the result of many years' labour destroyed, promptly renounced everything in his book " that might be contrary to the narrative of Moses."

In 1750 Malesherbes was appointed Director of the publishing trade, with the delicate task of steering a course among these conflicting forces. He was himself the most moderate of men and shared many of the sceptical views of the *philosophes*. They overwhelmed him with requests for support. For thirteen years he struggled amid philosophic pique, legal bigotry, court arrogance and religious intolerance. His best efforts did not prevent an extraordinary confusion and constant fluctuations of policy. Savage, and necessarily inoperative, decrees were frequently issued. In 1754, when the attempt on Louis' life by Damiens had frightened the Government, blame was thrown first on the Jesuits, then upon the Jansenists and their supporters in the *Parlements*, and finally upon the *philosophes*. Many arrests were made, and a royal decree was passed announcing that death was the penalty for " all those who shall be convicted of having composed, or caused to be composed and printed, writings intended to attack religion, to assail our authority, or to disturb the ordered tranquillity of our realm." Not only were authors and publishers threatened with execution but also " all those who print the aforesaid works, all booksellers, *colporteurs*, and other persons who shall circulate them among the public."

A decree of this kind was calculated to rouse only laughter, except among a number of obscure men and women who were sent to the galleys for selling books " contrary to good manners and religion." [1] The *Encyclopædia*, which contained all the

---

[1] This occurred comparatively often. *Vide*, for instance, Bachaumont's entry for 2nd October 1768 : Two men and a woman, condemned for "selling books contrary to good manners and to religion" were sentenced "au carcan

subversive doctrines of the century, was at that very moment being published under royal sanction. Arbitrary and uncertain persecution had its usual effect in rendering authority ridiculous and criticism both more subtle in its methods and more effective in its attacks. The propagandist is most blessed when ineffectively persecuted.

Though this was at times realized by the *philosophes* themselves, they bitterly resented their position. They lived in an atmosphere of constant anxiety, and were never certain from day to day whether they would be courted or imprisoned. Rousseau's *Emile*, which was largely devoted to an exposition of an educational method and which was the most genuinely religious book of the century, was censored by the Archbishop of Paris and burnt by the *Parlement* of Paris. The case of Marmontel, who was at best but a second-rate writer and comparatively orthodox in his views, provides an instructive example of the uncertainty of literary life. Having succeeded with great difficulty in piloting his *Belisarius* through the censorship, nine thousand copies were quickly circulated before the Sorbonne discovered that it advocated the theory of toleration and questioned " the right of the sword to exterminate heresy, irreligion and impiety, and to bring the whole world under the yoke of the true faith." " The thing for me," he remarked while the Sorbonne was considering its verdict, "was to appear neither timid nor rebellious, and to gain time till the editions of my book were multiplied and spread over Europe." In spite of his caution, Marmontel found himself confined in the Bastille. His imprisonment lasted only eleven days. The governor was extremely polite and supplied him with an excellent dinner from his own table. Marmontel gained an adventure with which to amuse the more advanced among his hostesses and friends, but lost both the editorship of the official *Mercure* and his bride, who preferred to marry a man who had not incurred the King's displeasure.[1]

---

pendant trois jours consécutifs," and in the case of the men to the galleys for periods of nine and five years. The woman was confined in the *Hôpital-Général* for five years. The books included Holbach's *Le Christianisme dévoilé* and Voltaire's *L'Homme aux quarante écus.*

[1] The full story is in Marmontel's *Mémoires.*

Prison archives show that most of the Philosophic party spent short periods in the Bastille, and the poorer among them may have found it less comfortable than did Marmontel. Diderot had been imprisoned after the publication of his *Letters on the Blind*, which contained a phrase derogatory to a Minister's mistress. During his editorship of the *Encyclopædia* he was never free from the interference of the Government and the Jesuits, and never knew how long he would be at liberty. When the significance of the first volumes of the *Encyclopædia* was appreciated the Jesuits succeeded in obtaining an order for their suppression. It was typical of the régime, however, that no order was issued forbidding its circulation, and that Diderot was requested by the Government to continue the editorship. The Jesuits indeed confiscated his papers, notes and plates, but, being, as he remarked, unable to confiscate his brains at the same time, they waited for the appearance of the next volumes before again interfering. In 1757, when the struggle between the *Parlements* and Jesuits was at its height, d'Alembert's article on Geneva, indirectly critical of the lives and dogmas of Catholic priests, roused once more a furious opposition. The publication of Helvétius' *De l'Esprit*, in the next year, led to the suppression by the Council of State of numerous Philosophic works, and the sale of past numbers of the *Encyclopædia* was prohibited. No steps however were taken to prevent their circulation, which continued without the least interruption.

On the whole it may be said that during the ascendancy of Madame de Pompadour the royal policy, in spite of many fluctuations, tended rather to flirt with philosophy than to oppose it. Voltaire described the Pompadour as "one of us," and though she was not a very faithful devotee at the shrine of reason, and though her opposition to Jesuitism may have been due rather to personal than to philosophical causes, the Encyclopædists had reason to be grateful to her. After the banishment of the Jesuits the *Parlements* emulated their zeal in banning and burning the work of the *philosophes*; but in the later years of Louis' reign an official ban was most effective as an advertisement.

was due to Madame Lambert, who, said d'Argenson, had at one time created half the living Academicians. D'Alembert owed his Secretaryship of the Academy to Madame du Deffand. A few years later Madame Geoffrin and Mademoiselle de Lespinasse were close rivals for the honour of dispensing the greatest number of Academic Chairs.

"Women," said Diderot, "accustom us to discuss with charm and clarity the driest and thorniest subjects. We talk to them unceasingly; we wish them to listen; we are afraid of tiring or boring them; hence we develop a particular method of explaining ourselves easily, and this passes from conversation into style." This is an admirable summary of the benefits of the *salons*. They had ceased to be pedantic, and they demanded not preciosity but good journalism. But the *salon* had its disadvantages. Montesquieu once remarked that "the society of women corrupts the morals and forms the taste." If morals include intellectual sincerity and the society of women meant the dictatorship of the *salon*, Montesquieu was right. The patronage of literary women did corrupt the philosopher: he was compelled to adjust his style according to the intellectual fashion; he had always to be alert to please his hostess, to write so that she could talk about his book without having read the part which cost the greatest effort and which would constitute its permanent value. He had to adapt himself to the social atmosphere, to sigh over the *effroyable ton* of the Bible and the deplorable lack of taste displayed by the Holy Ghost. If one wished to be caustic about society and manners it was wise to retain the conventions of classical style, and even Mademoiselle de Lespinasse was disgusted when Buffon, whom she had long wished to meet, made use of a word not to be found in the vocabulary of Racine. A judicious philosopher was discreet in phrasing his criticisms, chose a butt who was universally ridiculed, or, if he was bold enough to use his dagger nearer home, stabbed so delicately that each victim, enjoying the treatment of his friend, failed to notice that his friend was secretly delighting in what he believed to be his neighbour's wound.

In this brilliant and restricted society, in which everyone

knew everyone else, and the same people met night after night at each other's houses and contrived, somehow or other, not to be bored, wit, both in conversation and writing, was the key to success. Great reputations were founded on quickness of wit. Duclos, made a member of the Academy before he had published anything, owed his friends and reputation to his turn for *bons mots*. The Abbé Galiani was a leading figure during the ten years in which he was stationed in Paris as Neapolitan ambassador. He had much to commend him; though he was only four feet six inches in height, he was a considerable economist with a European reputation for wit. Everyone enjoyed the story of how he had sought preferment by sending a collection of volcanic remains from Mount Vesuvius to Benedict XIV. with the request, "Holy Father, command these stones to be made bread," and how, as if to prove that the days of the Renaissance were not wholly over, the Pope had laughingly taken the hint and promoted the jester.

In one of the Persian letters Montesquieu describes how two men, complaining that everyone out-talked them, made a compact to ensure their own fame. What was the good, the first asked, of preparing witticisms only to have them lie like old lumber in his head because there was no opportunity of repeating them? If they arranged reciprocal openings, however, they could both shine. "I see that in less than six months we shall be able to maintain a conversation of an hour long composed entirely of witticisms, but we must be very careful to support our good fortune : it is not enough to say a good thing, it must be spread abroad and dispersed everywhere, or else it will be lost. I must confess that there is nothing so mortifying as to have said a smart thing and have it expire in the ear of the fool who heard it. It is true that this is sometimes compensated by having a good many foolish things we say passed over in silence : that is our only consolation. Act as I have directed you, and I promise you a seat in the Academy in less than six months your labour will soon be over, for you may then give up your art, since you will be a man of wit in spite of yourself."

The society of the *salon* could not have survived had it permitted itself to be solemn. But if solemnity was impossible sincerity and seriousness were also difficult. A small circle of persons meeting almost daily in one another's houses, without social obligations or public responsibilities, could avoid both tragedy and tedium only by keeping close to the surface, and strictly regulating the social game which was their exclusive occupation. An old friend of Madame Lambert complained that at the age of sixty she had set up a *Bureau d'Esprit*: "*Bel Esprit* was a disease which struck her suddenly and of which she died incurable." If the conversation in her *salon* had been too serious the-less intelligent would have felt slighted. Real differences of opinion would have appeared, and the smooth plane of social life have been ruffled. Where an emotion is genuine there is always danger; wherever public evils are faced, consciences may play havoc with easy lives and the barren amusements of social intercourse fail to hide their futility. The most popular amusements, therefore, were games which encouraged a superficial treatment of matters in which the players were secretly furiously interested. A favourite pastime was to compose elegant character sketches of oneself or others; these were passed round the circle for comment and emendation. To read these productions to-day is to obtain an intimate picture of *salon* society, but never to learn anything of significance about the individual described. The convention by which physical characteristics were related to mental ones and good and bad qualities placed side by side in antithesis excellently served the purpose of those who wanted an intellectual exercise, and needed a method of wasting time in perfect French. Almost all the *philosophes* at one time or another trained their wit in some such manner and threw off trifles of the moment lest they should be thought unsociable and serious.[1]

Grimm once remarked in his *Mémoires* that it was a good thing there were half-a-dozen people serious enough to discover

---

[1] It is worth while to compare these *tours de force* with the *Mémoire* of Mademoiselle de Lespinasse which d'Alembert wrote after her death. The woman to whom he had been devoted for many years, and whom he believed to be devoted to him, had died leaving him as a parting gift the passionate letters which she had written to two rivals. Technically d'Alembert's performance is similar to the usual *salon* sketch.

their own ignorance. The really important work of the century was done away from the *salons*, though even the greatest books were affected by the irrelevant trivialities which Vauvenargues described as the disease of the age. Montesquieu wrote : " My great work now advances with gigantic strides since I am no longer harassed with Parisian invitations to toilsome dinners and fatiguing suppers." Voltaire's best books were written away from Paris, when the Court patronage for which he had always hankered had been definitely refused him, and he had ceased to need further self-advertisement. D'Alembert was certainly right when he explained to Voltaire that he would merely waste his time in Paris, since he had both fame and the opportunity for serious work in his home on the frontier.

In view of the restrictions and artificiality of *salon* life, it is not surprising that the *philosophes* formed a new type of *salon* of their own. They continued to call on Mademoiselle de Lespinasse until her death, but they began to find a more lively pleasure in a society where literary tradition was not so strict, where the social graces played a smaller part and where discussion ranged over all topics. Rich men, like Dupin and Poupelinière, had become interested in philosophy ; they welcomed Marmontel and other *philosophes*, accepted the new doctrines, permitted freedom of conversation, and themselves provided good dinners and good music. The financier, execrated and ridiculed in plays and lampoons in the twenties and thirties, had become the valued friend of philosophy by the sixties. Best of all, from the point of view of the *philosophe*, however, were Holbach's dinner-parties. It was there that Diderot, unkempt, indecorous, pouring out a stream of exuberant and blasphemous eloquence, was really at home. At Holbach's, too, one might meet others who seldom frequented the Paris drawing-rooms : Turgot and the young Condorcet, and foreign celebrities like Hume, Wilkes, Shelburne, Garrick, Franklin and Priestley all from time to time enjoyed the hospitality of the "Maître d'Hôtel of Philosophy " in the house that was nicknamed the "Café de l'Europe."

In the sixties, therefore, the Philosophic audience had widened, and the opportunity of conversation and the variety

of social experience from which fertile ideas are apt to spring
had greatly increased. If you were a *philosophe* you would be
wise to maintain your reputation in an older world at Madame
Geoffrin's on Monday or Wednesday, you would certainly call
on Mademoiselle de Lespinasse (who received almost every
evening between five and nine), you could discuss Helvétius'
books (for he always wrote them in public) with their author on
Tuesday; on Friday you could visit Madame Necker, and you
would miss the best part of the week's entertainment if you
did not dine with Holbach on Sunday or Thursday.

Holbach's was an excellent retreat for the philosopher, but
not for the less intellectual persons who were tired of the
artificiality of the *salons* and uninterested in the scientific
pursuits of the Encyclopædists. By the late sixties Paris was
ready for any novelty. Voltaire and his followers had completed
their destructive work, and since the positive implications of
their attack on the Church were as yet seldom understood,
the audiences which had once been thrilled by the *Lettres
philosophiques*, and still found *Candide* infinitely diverting, as
yet remained without any substitute for religion. Into this void
Rousseau stepped.

Rousseau was a *petit bourgeois* whose upbringing and habits
of mind were utterly alien from the conventions and traditions
of the *salons*. Though his entrance into Parisian society brought
him personally nothing but misery, it gave the *salons* new
interest, a new cult, and even in some cases a genuine life. He
was already more than thirty years old when he was first introduced to Diderot and his friends, and his earlier career had
been unusual rather than distinguished. He had left his birthplace, Geneva, an orphan child with a taste for romances; he
had tried his hand in a notary's office, been apprenticed to an
engraver, been ill-treated and revenged himself by pilfering, had
become a wanderer, had temporarily renounced Protestantism
in order to gain the charity of Catholics, had turned lackey,
roamed Savoy as a tramp, taught music "without knowing
how to decipher an air," and discovered, by failing to teach it,
that he had a genuine talent for composition; he had been a
luckless teacher of luckless boys, had acted competently as

secretary to a dishonest French ambassador at Venice, returned to Paris, and, after numerous humiliating experiences with women, whose ideal companionship was his constant dream, but whose more intimate favours he could neither resist nor enjoy without terror and a sense of guilt, had settled down with some contentment and a half-witted mistress to earn a precarious livelihood by copying music.

Rousseau was first received as a neophyte of the Encyclopædists, an interesting novelty, whom Diderot and Madame d'Epinay had adopted. Few things require so much social experience, so much poise and self-reliance, as to enter a clique of clever people who share a common experience, laugh at the same things, know each other just well enough and suspect the newcomer of being a bore or a disturbance. Rousseau had none of the necessary qualifications for a *philosophe*. The subversive views of Holbach's circle disgusted him as much as the formalism of the older *salon*. Vain and sensitive, earnest and sentimental, with no sense of proportion and no capacity for trifling, devoid of wit and contemptuous of a smooth society which did not recognize his latent genius, the goodness of his heart and the purity of his intentions, he could do nothing right. Retarded by a morbid inferiority, he was the more eager to be recognized as the central figure; jealous of his independence, but furious at every hint of patronage; every word of encouragement led him to assert himself and every slighting glance led him to withdraw precipitately.[1] In excitement he rushed to the centre of the picture, only to retire within him-

---

[1] Rousseau's feeling of inferiority was always increased by his poverty, and it was not as easy to be poor and independent as he imagined. When invited to the houses of the wealthy, and received with cordiality, he assumed that he would be always wanted, and repeated his visits with unwise frequency. Some service would be demanded and his pride would revolt at the thought of his dependence. His replies to those who sent him presents reveal much. *Cp.* his answer to Madame d'Houdetot, when she sent him chickens: "O, Madame, had you only given me news of yourself without sending me anything else, you would have made me rich and grateful. Instead of that the pullets are eaten, and the best thing I can do is to forget them. Let us say no more of them. You see what is gained by sending me presents." And to the Maréchale de Luxemburg he wrote: "Thank you for the butter you sent me. I have willingly received your present, Madame, but I cannot bring myself to touch

self bitterly humiliated. He could not speak his mind or keep silent ; " instead of knowing how to hold my tongue," he wrote, "when I have nothing to say, I have a rage for wishing to speak, in order to pay my debt the sooner. I promptly hasten to babble words without ideas, very happy when they do not mean anything. In the wish to overcome and hide my ineptitude, I seldom fail to show it." He was always at a disadvantage. He had none of the easy currency of daily intercourse, and could not " comprehend how anyone could converse in a circle." Neither could he discuss serious matters without the disturbance of personal emotion. Like other men whose puritanism is reinforced by a sense of their own private sensuality he could not tolerate licentiousness in others. He was genuinely religious, convinced by emotional experiences, not by arguments, and altogether unable to let the scoffer go without rebuke. " If it is, a fault," he broke out one day when the *salon* was discussing the defects of the Deity, " to allow evil to be spoken of an absent friend, it is a crime to allow anyone to speak evil of his God who is present. And for my part, gentlemen, I believe in God."

The reasons which made Rousseau a social failure also made the friendship he craved impossible. " I have never known," he wrote, "how to preserve a medium in my attachments and simply fulfil the duties of society. I have always been

---

it. I should think that I took communion unworthily ; I should think that I ate damnation to myself."

Rousseau has provided posterity with more material for psychoanalysis than any other great writer. His *Confessions* are designed to give a complete story of his spiritual and intellectual development, and they are determinedly frank in detail. The praise and blame, the explanations and justifications, which he gives for his conduct, are, however, even more revealing than his conscious avowals. A medical diagnosis of Rousseau would not be in place here, but his approach to society is the better understood if one remembers several facts which his biographers usually choose to refer to only obliquely. His first sexual experience, he tells us, was an enjoyment of being whipped by a governess of whom he was fond, and he remained throughout his life a masochist, prostrating himself before women and finding terror rather than satisfaction in adult sexual experience. He was never free from a sense of guilt in relation to any of his several forms of sexuality. In later life his embarrassments were greatly increased by a weakness of the bladder which caused him constant social difficulty, and his adoption of an Armenian costume was a sensible method of disguising this complaint.

everything or nothing." Social ineptitudes would have mattered little if he could have retained any balance in his personal relationships. But he never saw his friends objectively. He was always preoccupied with dramatizing himself before them : he desired desperately to produce some special impression—usually that of an affectionate and natural person who was too independent to mind what others thought of him. A friendly word in response to an advance was enough to convince him that he had begun a lifelong companionship, and that reserve was henceforth unnecessary. It was his fate to pass his life in rushing into intimacy with those who were merely prepared for amicable relations : he strove to break down every barrier in a society which achieved its social success by a nice discrimination in erecting barriers. He was, as he said, "the most sociable and loving of human beings . . . but the truly sociable man is more difficult in his relationships than another ; those which only consist in unreal show could not suit him. . . . He will hate ordinary society, where the rule is a superficial intimacy and an actual reserve."

Humour or even wit might have saved him, but he had none. Voltaire was as sensitive to criticism as Rousseau himself, but he could always work off his spleen in an epigram or a lampoon. Grimm tells a story of a friend who visited Voltaire, and mentioned that he had lately seen Haller, the German scientist. Voltaire broke in with expressions of warm admiration for Haller. " I am glad," said his friend, " that you have so high an opinion of him. Unfortunately, he has not a high opinion of you." "Indeed?" replied Voltaire modestly. "*Then perhaps we are both mistaken.*" In a similar case, if Rousseau had discovered that a man he admired had no corresponding admiration for him, he would have at once been convinced that his friends had been intriguing against him and that he was the victim of malice, ingratitude and treachery. He would have poured out his resentment in passionate language and then, conscious that he had made a fool of himself, have retired to brood upon social corruption, to think out retorts which would have withered if they had occurred to him at the right time,[1]

---

[1] As he explains in the *Confessions*.

and to purge his impotent wrath in vehement letters which only brought him further humiliation. Such incidents were frequent, and Rousseau was driven more and more to seek comfort in the stolid placidity of his Theresa, who never laughed at him, and to seek peace in the wooded countryside, where, after long brooding in solitude, his humiliations lost their intolerable bitterness, mingled in the main stream of his thoughts and reappeared, transmuted into literature.

"A genuine sentiment," wrote a contemporary, "is so rare that when I leave Versailles I sometimes stand still in the street to see a dog gnaw a bone." It was this fact, the extreme artificiality of social life, which gave Rousseau his power with the men and women of the eighteenth century. He brought, it is true, a romantic insincerity even more distasteful to later generations than the polished show of the cultured *salon*. But he also brought something that was simple, and something that was genuine. His roots were deep, alive in a country soil whilst his contemporaries sought an easy popularity by exploiting a dead tradition. His personal relationships might be usually destructive, and always a little ridiculous, but their failure only brought into relief the hidden desire of most men and women for a deeper and more sincere relationship. His ideal of asexual friendship was perhaps largely mythical, and when he described love in the *Nouvelle Héloïse* the result is to-day neither attractive nor convincing ; but the sorrows of Julie took society by storm, because they did express in romantic fashion the emotions of which most women were conscious and had been trained to inhibit.

Rousseau's imaginative writing was a novelty to his generation. He could create because he had never been taught to compose. Although writing was a long torture to him, he could not rest until the images which obsessed him had taken an artistic shape. The natural tendencies of his mind were unmodified by any youthful discipline.[1] His ideas came to him,

---

[1] Some of the difficulties of Rousseau's work are explained by his method of study—a method which is usually that of the poet rather than the philosopher. He read philosophy, he tells us, in just the way that he had once read romances as a child, forgetting everything while sharing the emotions and experiences

as he said, unbidden and undesired, flooding him with intense emotion which, after long brooding, could be transmuted into a form which swept away literary conventions, social prohibitions and logical difficulties. In one passage he describes the birth of the *Nouvelle Héloise*. As the conception of the novel grew in his mind, he realized the inconsistency he showed in writing a book "which breathed nothing but effeminacy and love" when he had publicly declaimed against the immoral effects of such novels. "I felt this incoherence in all its extent, I reproached myself with it, I blushed at it and was vexed ; but all this could not bring me back to reason. Completely overcóme, I was obliged willy-nilly to submit, and to resolve to brave the *what will the world say of it ?*—except only that I deliberated afterwards whether or no I should show my work, for I did not yet suppose I should ever decide to publish it. This resolution taken, I entirely abandoned myself to my reveries, and by frequently resolving these in my mind, formed with them the kind of plan of which the execution has been seen."

In general, no one was more dependent upon the opinions of others than Rousseau. But he forgot them when he began to write. He wrote without heed of criticism, alike neglectful of orthodox models and of the conventions of the unconventional. He did not tack to meet the winds of fashion ; nor, after his

---

offered him, accepting or rejecting as a whole, making no objective examination or detailed criticism, content with whatever he found of emotional significance to himself.

He composed with extraordinary difficulty. He thus describes his intellectual method : "Two things, very opposite, unite in me in a manner which I cannot myself understand. My disposition is extremely ardent, my passions lively and impetuous, yet my ideas are produced only with much embarrassment and with much after-thought. It might be said that my heart and understanding do not belong to the same individual. A sentiment takes possession of my mind with the rapidity of lightning, but instead of illuminating it dazzles and confounds me ; I feel all but see nothing, I am heated but stupid ; to think I must be cool. . . . When I write my ideas are arranged with the utmost difficulty. They glance on my imagination and ferment. . . . During this state of agitation I see nothing properly, cannot write a single word and must wait until it is over. Insensibly the agitation subsides, the chaos acquires form and each circumstance takes its proper place. . . . Had I always waited till that confusion passed few ¦authors would have surpassed me."

early essays, was his writing a superficial revolt against existing
society. His imagination was powerful enough to take him into
a world of his own, and he was therefore the most creative
thinker of the century. Voltaire and the Encyclopædists led
their generation by expressing clearly what men were already
beginning to think dimly : Rousseau changed his age by so
describing old things that they became new. He was not the
first to notice that the grass was green, that common men were
capable of passion and the aristocrat of common feelings. He
did contrive, however, to make such matters seem interesting
to Parisian society, and was largely responsible for the decline
in the influence of " philosophy " and the growth of that
sentimentalism which is the response of the ignorant and the
trivial when an appeal is made to their imaginations.

The constant stream of English visitors who crossed and
recrossed the Channel during the last twenty years before the
Revolution found the social atmosphere of the *ancien régime*
greatly changed. A few of the older *salons* survived ; Madame
du Deffand lived on until 1780 and philosophical discussion
continued at Holbach's until the eve of the Revolution. Both
types, however, had gone out of fashion : sentimentalism and
politics were taking the place of scepticism and philosophy.
For at the moment that Rousseau was leading a movement
against rationalism and sophistication a parallel development
was taking place. The reaction against a life of social futility
led to a " return to nature " cult ; with the more serious it also
prepared the way for a genuine interest in politics. If the attack
on the Church could so far succeed that the censorship failed
to prevent the appearance of the most scurrilous blasphemies,
was it not possible that philosophy might rule the State as well
as destroy the Church ? Such hopes took tangible form during
the long constitutional struggle which led to the exile of the
Parlement of Paris and the hated dictatorship of Maupeou.
The appointment of Turgot as Controller seemed to justify
the most sanguine prophecies, and his speedy downfall,
devastating for the moment, only prepared the way for more
revolutionary aspirations. For with the advent of the American
Revolution the *Contrat Social* became intelligible as well as the

Emile; democracy now seemed a possible alternative to philosophic despotism and politics became, at least for the time, the fashionable topic of drawing-room conversation.

It was the end of the *ancien régime*. Horace Walpole had once complained that the *philosophes* were spoiling Paris. How much worse when the eighteenth-century *salon* had completed its evolution; it had first been converted by Mr Hume's troublesome *protégé* to all kinds of extravagances and sentimentalism, and then, not content with Rousseauism, it had given up its cultured and aristocratic interests and taken to politics, the most boring and bourgeois of all occupations!

CHAPTER V

THE PHILOSOPHY OF COMMON SENSE

I. THE NEW PSYCHOLOGY—RATIONAL MAN

THE eighteenth-century Church offered men a metaphysic, an ethic, a physical and biological theory, a psychological and a political doctrine, which came from the Middle Ages. Voltaire and the men who shared his philosophy are commonly called sceptics because they expressed the doubts which almost everyone, including most of the ecclesiastics themselves, felt about religious dogma. Yet their work was indirectly constructive; they built a new set of religious and social assumptions upon which a new society was founded.

The form in which the new philosophy was stated was influenced, as we have seen, by the constant necessity of dissembling to escape the censorship and by the requirements of the *salons*. The classical tradition of French literature and a philosophic method inherited from Descartes further limited the *philosophes* to an abstract method of presentation : few of them had patience for induction, and, in spite of their enthusiasm and their experience of science, Montesquieu was almost the only one who tried to apply a scientific technique to social problems. But they were never remote from fact and abstract in argument, in the sense suggested by Taine. Experience played the largest part in the formulation of their theories. They were often dogmatic, because the philosophy they were refuting was dogmatic. Moreover their simple theory of human nature seemed to render detailed social analysis superfluous. Reason—or should we say, common sense—solved all problems.

It is true that the *philosophes* delighted in using abstract terms, such as liberty and equality, reason, nature and humanity. But until the Revolution had transformed them into battle-cries the demand for liberty and equality was generally understood to apply to certain concrete changes, while reason, nature and humanity had more definite significance than has usually been supposed. The *philosophes*, like the mediæval schoolmen, relied on reason to produce valid conclusions from given premises : but whereas mediævalists accepted premises authoritatively provided by the Church, the *philosophes* followed Descartes in repudiating all authoritarian premises and attempting to found their logical structure upon undeniable axioms. Confusion arose from the fact that the *philosophes* used reason to denote the faculty by which these axioms were apprehended. Reason covered both reasoning and intuition. They assumed that reason as driver in the Platonic chariot both controlled the horses and knew exactly in what direction to go. By "natural reason," therefore, men could apprehend the initial certainties and build upon them a firm structure of natural religion and universal ethics. It was also natural reason which led every man to judge of values—to tell good from evil and justice from iniquity. In general, reason stood for a non-authoritarian method of discovering truth of fact or of value.

The *philosophes* were also in general agreement about the use of the word nature, though they differed about what was natural. They all believed that just as examination of physical phenomena showed the existence of certain general laws or principles, so a full understanding of economics and politics would discover natural laws of society. "To follow nature" meant to adjust human conduct to these natural laws, and by positive legislation which harmonized with nature's principles to produce a happy society instead of an unnatural and therefore unhappy one. That they must follow nature's teaching was agreed: unfortunately, it was not always obvious just what nature taught. Some held that men lived "naturally" if left to develop in accordance with instinct; the American Indian was said to be happy without organization or coercion. Others followed Aristotle in believing that the true nature of man could be developed only in a political and civilized society. Natural, therefore, meant both the primitive and the ideal, the condition before misgovernment had perverted nature as well as the perfect social development which might be the result of good government. Confusions were unavoidable; both private property and communism, for instance, could be logically defended as natural. All the *philosophes*, however, agreed that eighteenth-century France was unnatural, and that reason could discover the just and ideal order which the law of nature demanded.

Humanity was a simpler conception—an undeveloped form of the principle of utility. The apostles of humanity refused to admit that tyranny, intolerance and persecution could ever be justified : human happiness, therefore, was by implication the supreme value, and the greatest happiness the test of good and evil. To say exactly whose happiness was intended, or in what happiness consisted, or how it was to be attained, was the task of the conscious Utilitarian. But the initial stages were carried out by the " philosophers of humanity."

If reason, tolerance and liberty were to take the place of authority, obedience and asceticism, a new metaphysic and a new psychology were a necessary basis. The *philosophes* had first to substitute a natural for a revealed religion. If men learned to accept Newtonian physics they would cease to be dependent on an authoritarian creed and an inspired priesthood.

In the second place, living in accordance with nature could be defended only if human nature was held to be good and men supposed to be capable of reasonable conduct. If human beings were born in sin, or so foolish that they could not learn how to attain happiness, an authoritarian creed and coercive government were justified.

The *philosophes*, therefore, required an optimistic theory of human nature. They constructed it with materials gathered from several sources. From the Renaissance onwards the *libertins* had. always rejected the doctrine of original sin, and in the eighteenth century there was a natural reaction against the gloom of Pascal and a tendency to trust men rather than to shackle them. This optimism was reinforced by science : a pleasing view of human nature seemed to be justified by new observation, by anthropology and by the study of Locke. The *philosophes* were delighted to ask with Bayle whether, in fact, the religious orders lived more moral lives than professed sceptics. Diderot's *La Religieuse* is mainly a declaration that the effect of asceticism is to prevent the natural satisfaction of desire and pervert it into unhealthy channels. In support of the theory of free development the *philosophes* relied far more than has usually been supposed upon travellers' evidence about natural man.[1] "Each fresh start," says Dr Myres, "on the never-ending quest of man as he ought to be, has been the response of theory to fresh facts about man as he is."[2] It is at any rate certain that fresh facts about man as he is have given new impetus and encouragement to political thinkers in quest of man as he ought to be. From the sixteenth century onwards, as Dr Myres shows, current accounts of negroes, of West Indians and North American Indians have influenced European thought. Bodin found support for his theory of political obedience in newly discovered America as well as in classical literature. Hobbes had travellers' evidence for his view that the state of nature was nasty, brutish and short. Locke, who wrote an introduction to Churchill's *Collection of Voyages* in 1704, based his reply to Filmer and Hobbes upon the knowledge that moral principles existed among peoples who had no authorized government. His "state of nature" was in accordance with contemporary accounts of the hunting and food gathering, non-agricultural aborigines of New England, where the Indian's only property was said to be the labour of his body and the deer which he killed. Similarly, when the natural man first "mixed his labour with the earth," it was his by an equally obvious natural law. Presumably there was plenty of land to go round, just as there were plenty of wild animals to hunt. Jesuit accounts of Hurons and Iroquois reinforced the current picture of the amiable Man Friday in *Robinson Crusoe*. Lafitau's comparison of American savages with the primitive man depicted in classical literature lays special stress upon the religious and moral sense everywhere inherent in natural man.[3] Pope's *Essay on Man*,

---

[1] *Vide* G. Atkinson, *Les Relations de Voyages du xviiie siècle et l'Evolution des Idées* (1924) and *The Influence of Anthropology on the Course of Political Science*, by J. L. Myres (1914).

[2] Dr Myres does not discuss the opposite aspect—the extent to which political thinkers neglected all anthropological evidence which did not suit their general theory. In the eighteenth century de Brosses' remarkable researches into totemism and fetishism were unnoticed by the *philosophes* perhaps because they threw doubt on natural rationality. *Vide* C. de Brosses, *Le Culte des Dieux fétiches* (1760).

[3] *Vide* Lafitau, Le P., *Mœurs des Sauvages Américains comparées aux mœurs des premiers temps* (1723).

one of the most popular books of the century, is based on the same discovery. In eighteenth-century literature Hurons and Iroquois everywhere share a place of honour side by side with the communistic Spartans and Cretans, while the good manners and mild temper of the natural man, when actually brought from America and displayed in the Courts of Europe, were the object of comment in numerous journals and letters. "Wild Peter," declared by Linnæus to be a natural man, found in a Hanoverian forest, excited the interest of Buffon and all his contemporaries. Rousseau and the school which followed him read and made use of many flattering accounts of primitive peoples, which included, curiously enough, not only the attractive races of North America, but also the Caribs —a tribe of cannibals, who certainly neglected the arts of peace at the time when the attention of Rousseau was called to them. In the latter part of the century, accounts of the peaceful Australasians reinforced the current picture. Polynesia was represented as a Garden of Eden, and the South Sea Islander, who could quickly learn English and chess, seemed to prove that Rousseau had been no dreamer. Hobbes and Bossuet were both discredited : natural man everywhere possessed an innate moral sense or natural reason which enabled him to co-operate freely in society without the aid of an arbitrary despot or of the Catholic Church.

Finally, the *philosophes* found another even more powerful support for the view that man was not naturally evil. The psychology of Locke seemed to furnish a scientific basis for putting trust in humanity. Locke had denied the existence of innate ideas : even axioms such as that " the whole is greater than the part " or that God exists (also thought to be an innate conviction)were the results of reflection and experience. All knowledge, opinions and behaviour, derived from the senses. This doctrine was pushed to its extreme form by Condillac, who argued that even the power of reflection itself was nothing but transformed sensation.[1] He pictured a statue gradually coming to life, and showed how the addition of each sense would increase

---

[1] Condillac, *Traité des Sensations* (1754).

its experience and so at length enable it to build up a complete conception of the external world and to formulate beliefs about its nature. The acceptance of the view implied in this illustration constituted a revolution in human thought.

"Can there be anything more splendid," asked Voltaire with reference to Locke, "than to put the whole world into commotion by a few arguments?" The commotion, indeed, was only comparable to that created by Darwin's evolutionary theory. In the latter case men were offered an intelligible explanation of biological development in which the traditional teaching of religion had no share, and with which the current conception of God was incompatible. Similarly in the case of sensational psychology, men were offered an intelligible explanation of the development of ideas from which it followed that all doctrines, even those of the Church, were the fallible and accidental results of a limited experience, and could be tested by the same scientific process. Men, according to the new psychology, were born neither good nor bad, but neutral : blank sheets upon which experience made its individual impression. The divine gift of "grace" henceforth counted for nothing, and human methods of education for everything. The problem no longer was to restrain intractable passions, but to provide knowledge. Ignorance was man's only limitation and science offered unlimited possibilities. Newton had demonstrated that the world was ordered by natural laws, Locke that men were reasonable beings who could utilize their knowledge for their own happiness. As the implications of the new psychology dawned on men's minds there was a new hope and a new feeling of mastery. The Abbé de Saint-Pierre had assumed that reason and science could perfect society. Condillac seemed to have proved it.

It was the new psychology that really separated the eighteenth-century *philosophes* from their predecessors under Louis XIV. They were no longer sceptics in the manner of Bayle. Bayle, as Voltaire said, had been ignorant of Newton, and, he might have added, had thought of Locke as the protagonist of toleration rather than as the author of the *Essay on the Human Understanding*. Thanks to Locke and Newton, the *philosophes* had a positive doctrine to substitute for the orthodox creed. They believed they could demonstrate scientifically that knowledge was the key to happiness, and that it sufficed to enlighten men to make them perfect.

2. DEISM AND NATURAL RELIGION——VOLTAIRE AND ENGLISH RATIONALISM

It is appropriate to date the Age of Reason from Voltaire's visit to England.[1] Until the publication of his *Lettres philosophiques* the new philosophy was confined to a small group of *libertins* and scientists. The works of Newton and Locke had already been translated into French, but Voltaire made it his business to declare the practical implications of these books to everyone. "The example of England," Condorcet wrote, "showed him that truth is not made to remain a secret in the hands of a few philosophers and a limited number of men of the world instructed, or rather indoctrinated, by philosophers: men who smile with them at the errors of which the people are the victims, but who nevertheless uphold these very errors when their rank or position gives them a real or chimerical interest in them, and are quite ready to permit the proscription, or even persecution, of their teachers if they should venture to say what in secret they themselves actually think. From the moment of his return, Voltaire felt himself called upon to destroy every kind of prejudice which enslaved his country."

Voltaire's *Lettres philosophiques* was itself an effective blow at current prejudices. He succeeded in making many thousands of readers see England as he had done—as a land of freedom and opportunity, where common sense reigned. Driven out of France because he had been wronged by a member of the *noblesse*, he had been accepted on his merits in England. He might laugh at its solemn comfort, and declare that suicide was naturally habitual in a country where the wind was always in the east. But the wind of freedom seemed to him a still more

---

[1] Voltaire landed in England in May 1726. His *Lettres philosophiques* appeared in French in 1734. The English version, *Letters on the English*, had been published in the previous year.

potent influence upon the English character. An introduction from the British ambassador in Paris had given him a pass into cultivated society. He had found not only a governing and hunting aristocracy, but a flourishing middle class, a section of which was genuinely interested in scientific, literary and religious discussion. In England the intellect was granted a large measure of both freedom and respect. Although only one form of religious observance was officially favoured, numerous sects existed and, in general, remained unmolested. Religious thinkers were furiously discussing the historical bases of Christianity, and Voltaire was surprised to find that in England God had become so unimportant that one could worship Him and still remain a scientist.[1]

The final bulwark of any orthodox faith is the fear that morality will be undermined and habits of social restraint destroyed if religious authority be impaired. The example of England seemed to Voltaire a refutation of this doctrine. Bayle had shocked his contemporaries by arguing that a society of atheists might exist and even thrive. England seemed at least to prove the less daring thesis that to permit diversity of belief and discussion of the existence of God was not to prevent prosperity or damage morality.

Religion had got to the dangerous point of trying to rebuild its foundations on a basis of reason. Latitudinarian divines, still intent on attacking Catholicism, had ceased to use scriptural texts as weapons, and were arguing that papal doctrines were unreasonable. It was sufficient, as Leslie Stephen remarks,[2] " to substitute Revelation for Rome to make the attack upon Catholicism available for an attack upon all supernatural authority." By this simple process of substitution a number of thinkers now called themselves deists, while others remained unitarian members of the English Church. When once revelation had been discarded a transition from orthodoxy to unitarianism, from unitarianism to deism, and finally from deism to atheism, was

---

[1] Newton's method of reconciling his science and his Anglicanism was not altogether reassuring. Höffding, *History of Modern Philosophy*, i., p. 412, summarizes his position.

[2] *History of English Thought in the Eighteenth Century*, vol. i., p. 77.

unavoidable. Voltaire himself arrived and remained, somewhat precariously, at the deistic stage.

Amongst English rationalists three main positions were in debate. In the first place there was the view held by Chillingworth, and adopted with little variation by Locke, that the Creator had endowed man with a reasoning faculty by which he could discover truth and reject falsehood. Reason everywhere taught him a "natural religion"; he knew that God existed and that it was His will that men should love their neighbours and tell the truth. Reason also showed that God ruled by law and not by caprice. Having established unalterable laws of nature and endowed man with reason, the main part of His work was accomplished. God was a constitutional Monarch who, having made laws, Himself agreed to abide by them. In these circumstances, no revelation which was not in conformity with reason could be accepted, but revelation, if reasonable, might well supplement reason. Locke, and many with him, accepted the main body of New Testament revelation, considered Christ's teaching the perfect expression of natural religion, and were able to remain inside the Church. The next step was taken by Toland, who angered Locke by basing less orthodox conclusions upon the same premises. He declared that for revelation to be merely not unreasonable was insufficient grounds for accepting it. Proof, not probability, was necessary for the scientist. From the secure respectability of All Souls, Tindal went even further; he thought that the scriptural account of a God who redeemed His creatures by permitting them to crucify His Son was scarcely credible. Any personal interposition by the Deity was repugnant to his scientific outlook. "Tindal," said Leland, "makes rewards and punishments the inseparable attendants of virtuous and vicious actions"; so that "I do not see that he leaves God anything to do in the matter at all." When Bishop Butler demonstrated that an argument analogous to Tindal's would lead to atheism, he forced infidelity upon those whose logic was stronger than their fear. Christian deism in fact was no longer Christian and only formally deism.

A century before Voltaire's visit to England, Herbert of Cherbury had reduced the articles necessary for natural religion to five. He was the founder of the third school, the optimistic deists. It was reasonable to believe in a just and omnipotent God Who would some day reward the righteous and punish the wicked, Who had created the world and was fulfilling a good purpose which men in the midst of their sufferings and with their finite outlook were unable to understand. In the early eighteenth century Shaftesbury was the best exponent of this convenient theory. Bolingbroke, more brilliant, and less consistent, supported a similar thesis. Bolingbroke, however, was always haunted by disturbing questions. Why, if God is good and omnipotent, does evil exist in the world? Might it not be man who had created God in his own image? Goodness, Bolingbroke sometimes suggested, is a human conception, which may have no objective existence in heaven. It seemed clear that wisdom and power were attributes of the Being Who had made the world and set the forces of nature in orderly progress, but of other attributes of God men were wholly ignorant. "God is in their notion of Him nothing but an infinite man."

Voltaire never surmounted the difficulties suggested by Bolingbroke. He did not doubt that a creation implies a Creator : even savages, he gathered, all believed in some god, and this, strangely enough, seemed to him, as it has to many since, a further proof of His existence. The argument from design convinced him, as it convinced most of his generation. The fact that nature worked according to certain fixed principles seemed to argue that an intelligent Being was responsible for them. Anticipating Paley, Voltaire wrote : " I shall always be convinced that a watch proves a watchmaker, and the universe proves a God." This argument always seemed conclusive until the evolutionary idea had found its place in men's minds. It was the discovery that there is maladjustment as well as harmony in the natural world, that decay proceeds side by side with growth, that the appearance of design is rather the result of an elimination of the unfit than a deliberate creation of the fit, that discredited the doctrine that " cork-trees had been created in order to stop beer barrels." Above all, geology, long hampered by the story of the Flood, had not yet given men the idea of development through a vast period of time. A single act of creation was still conceivable, and the eighteenth century had not ceased to think of a law of nature on the analogy of human law—the sole difference being that God's laws were certain and men's arbitrary in their application. It is only in modern times that it has become common to regard a law as a generalization made by men who have observed a regular sequence of events, and therefore assume, until further knowledge disturbs them, that this sequence is universal.[1] In the eighteenth century, therefore, God was necessary as a First Cause, a Being who created the world in six days and had rested ever since.[2] The doctrine of an immanent Deity, a continually active and creative force, was antagonistic to the accepted mechanical explanation of the universe. Rousseau, however, was soon to revive the idea of a living God, and the Catholic revival which followed the Revolution was a natural reaction from philosophic materialism. In England, too, the Methodist revival was a

---

[1] Dealing with the often exposed confusion in the use of the word "law," Bentham compares the laws of men with such a "law" of Optics as that the angle of reflection is equal to the angle of incidence. "We now understand how this matter was brought about. Hark ye (said the author of nature once upon a time), hark ye, you rays. There are some surfaces you will meet with in your travels that when you strike upon them, will send you packing ; now when in such case, this is what I would have you do : keep the same slope in *going* that you did in coming. Mind and do what I say : if you don't, as sure as you are rays it will be the worse for you : upon this the rays (finding they should get into bad bread else) made their bows, shrugged up their shoulders and went and did so " (*A Comment on the Commentaries,* p. 32). This, the first of Bentham's attacks upon Blackstone, has been edited by Charles Warren Everett and published for the first time in 1928.

[2] Diderot, like Buffon, at times approached a more modern conception. With reference to the doctrine that a watch implies a watchmaker, he puts up an atheist to argue that there is no real parallel and no reason to think that such " an infinite piece of complexity whose beginnings, whose present condition, and whose end are all alike unknown, and about whose Author you have nothing better than guesses " is in fact a perfect order. "Who told you that the order you admire here belies itself nowhere else ? Are you allowed to conclude from a point in space to infinite space ? You litter a vast piece of ground with earth-heaps thrown here or there by chance, but among which the worm and the ant find convenient dwelling-places enough. What would you think of these insects if, reasoning after your fashion, they fell into raptures over the intelligence of the gardener who had arranged all these materials so delightfully for their convenience ?"

protest against the inertia of the Church, which had become a purely social institution without any distinctive philosophy. Among scientists there was also a reaction against mechanistic theories, which found expression in the biological theory of Lamarck.

Beyond the view that God exists, Voltaire came to no very definite metaphysical conclusions. Like most of the Encyclopædists, he was proud to admit that there were many things about which he knew nothing. His incursions into metaphysical discussion suggest that its vanity was the more obvious to him because he had little aptitude for it. In one of his satires he describes how a " thousand schoolmen arose, such as the unanswerable doctor, the subtle doctor, the angelic doctor, the seraphic doctor and the cherubic doctor, who were all sure that they had a clear and a precise knowledge of the soul, and yet wrote in such a manner that one would conclude that they were resolved that no one should understand a word of their writing. . . . Such a multitude of reasoners having written the romance of the soul, a sage at last arose who gave, with an air of great modesty, a history of it. Mr Locke has displayed the human soul in the same manner as an excellent anatomist explains the springs of the human body. . . . He sometimes presumes to speak affirmatively, but then he sometimes presumes also to doubt."

Plato, Aristotle, Descartes, Spinoza, Malebranche, Leibniz had all of them wasted their time. " I am a body and I think that is all I know of the matter," wrote Voltaire. " I am naturally ignorant what matter is : I guess but imperfectly some properties of it, but I absolutely cannot tell whether these properties may be joined to the capacity of thinking." The problem of reconciling free-will with unalterable law was equally insoluble. He was satisfied with the common-sense reply that men had some liberty, unlike other creatures of God. " I believe," he wrote, " that the Supreme Being has given us a little of His liberty as He has given us a little of His power of thought." Whenever Voltaire ventures further than this into metaphysics he is as inept as Doctor Johnson refuting Berkeley by stubbing his foot against a stone.

The older generation of Encyclopædists remained content with this practical deism. It supported the conception of unalterable law and permitted free scientific inquiry ; it repudiated all supernatural interference and gave social morality a tangible sanction. It offered a rational explanation of good and evil and made rewards and punishments the inevitable results of behaviour, not the arbitrary fiats of an external deity. Men shared a common religion—" the universal law," as Diderot called it, "which the finger of God has engraved on every heart." A simple belief in God and a consciousness of good and evil appeared to be common to the whole human race, and all the dogmas of faith and elaborate codes of religious observance were the later inventions of interested priestcraft. Voltaire constantly compared the simple savage, possessing an unclouded knowledge of eternal truths, with the missionary who tried vainly to confuse his mind with subtle questions about the nature and attributes of God, the efficacy of the sacraments, and the history and constitution of the angelic hosts. "What," asked Voltaire, " is a true deist? One who says to God I adore and love you, one who says to a Turk, a Chinaman, an Indian and a Russian, I love you." The untutored savages " take the existence of God for granted and think it natural to adore the Creator Who is the cause of their being, and to offer Him prayers and thanksgivings without being so foolish as to request Him for fine weather when their neighbours are asking for rain." God's will was clear enough to the unsophisticated mind. " I think that whatever gives you pleasure and does injury to no man is very good and very right " is the maxim attributed to the happy Indian, who may " thereby live to be a hundred." Among Christian sects the Quakers only had preserved the simple and reasonable faith of their Master.

Voltaire could appreciate the social value of natural religion and the beauty of the Christian life of his Quaker friends, but he grew increasingly doubtful if God was in any way responsible or interested in what men believed to be good. Were Pope and Leibniz right in thinking that all was for the best? "My poor Pope," he wrote, " my poor hunchback, who told you that God could not have formed you without a hump?" The doctrine that "whatever is, is right" was not optimism but "desperation —a cruel philosophy under a soothing name." The great Lisbon earthquake of 1755 moved him to question the guidance of a Deity who was prodigal of benefits to His children and then rained evils upon them apparently without any discrimination or thought of their deserts.

Voltaire's poem on the Lisbon earthquake roused Rousseau to an indignant defence of God and His apologists. Pope and Leibniz, he declared, had at least offered men a balm for their misfortunes and taught them resignation; they had represented such calamities as a necessary effect of the divine constitution of the universe, presumably somehow good even if not obviously so to us. Voltaire's scepticism, on the other hand, destroyed faith and led to despair. Voltaire's reply to Rousseau took the form of a novel, published three years later. The doctrine of "the good and sufficient cause" for pain inflicted by a benevolent and omniscient deity has never recovered its prestige since the publication of *Candide*.

Voltaire remained a deist, but by the time he had finished saying what God was not, it was difficult to find any positive attributes left Him. He had derided anthropomorphic conceptions of the Deity, and denounced the sophistries with which men tried to palliate evil by describing it as the goodness of God in disguise. To argue the benevolence, wisdom and power of God from the existence of goodness and order in the world makes it necessary also to argue that God is malevolent, stupid and impotent, in view of the frequent triumph of evil and the prevalence of chaos. Perhaps, then, Candide's friend, Martin, was right, and Manicheism, which leaves it doubtful whether the power of good which one may call God if one likes, or the power of evil which it is then logical to call the Devil, is the more likely to win. "You see," says Candide, when the wicked captain and all the innocent passengers on his ship are drowned, "that crime is sometimes punished?" "Very true," Martin replies, "but why should the passengers be doomed also to destruction? God has punished the rogue, but the Devil has drowned the rest." To the scientist another possibility presented itself; both God and the Devil might be discarded and materialism substituted. In Holbach's *Système de la Nature* the conception of a Creator is discarded, and the view of Lucretius, that the universe is the result of an accidental combination of atoms, resuscitated. It is true that Holbach ended his system with a panegyric to Nature which had insensibly, and in spite of his protests, become personified in the course of his book. Voltaire was nevertheless horrified, for without the idea of a Creator and a final Dispenser of rewards and punishments he feared, as the Church feared, that men would have no incentive for moral behaviour. In the last analysis, Voltaire's view was that of Gibbon, that "all religions were equally true in the eyes of the people, equally false in the eyes of the philosopher, and equally useful to the magistrate." For utilitarian purposes, if God did not exist it would be necessary to invent Him. When the choice between safety and truth was presented to him Voltaire had no trust in ordinary people to save him from apostasy. He was not really willing for frank discussion, and in this he resembled his enemies—who attacked him not because what he said was untrue but because they feared the consequences of free speech.

Voltaire was perhaps the most effective propagandist who ever lived.[1] His defects were not of a kind to interfere with his main task—the destruction of superstitions which men accepted because they had never been permitted to think about them. He exposed the sacrosanct. His wit was the most powerful of weapons : for when he spoke neither cleric nor layman could resist reading, laughing and questioning. It was his unique accomplishment to set a large section of the Church as well as of the laity thinking : since Voltaire, France has been sharply divided into clericals and Voltaireans. If he seems to-day an unsatisfactory and even a shallow thinker that is because he won his battle and forced the Church to

---

[1] There is interesting tangible proof of Voltaire's influence. He amused people so much that everyone who read at all read him. Lanson (*Voltaire*, chap. xi.) cites the booksellers' and publishers' figures of the sale of his works. Between 1778 and 1835 thirty-four complete editions of his works, as well as numerous incomplete ones, were published, and a million and a half copies of his books were sold within one period of seven years.

take its stand on less vulnerable ground than that from which he drove it.

3. CIVIL LIBERTY—NATURAL RIGHTS AND THE ENLIGHTENED DESPOT

The political theory of Voltaire and the older generation of Encyclopædists was, like their religious philosophy, a cautious compromise, based on a common-sense view of immediate social need. When its intellectual foundations were examined it proved far more subversive than its exponents intended. They wished to destroy the superstitions of the Church, not to undermine the religious habits of ordinary men and women. In the same way they hoped to enlighten and to reform the existing State, but were almost as shocked to find their disciples becoming democrats as atheists. The foundation of their politics and their theology had been laid by Locke, whose defence of the English Revolution easily served the turn of more thorough-going revolutionaries, just as his rational Anglicanism proved a step on the way to a rigid materialism.

The demand for civil liberty was supported in the eighteenth century on grounds both of utility and of natural law. Since the time of Bentham the utilitarian argument has proved more fertile than that from nature. To argue that the only justification of the State is its capacity to increase happiness, that happiness consists in the opportunity of freely satisfying desires and developing with the minimum of external interference, and that, therefore, the primary duty of the State is to secure individual liberty—this is a line of approach which made a science of politics a possible aspiration. The conception of utility was valuable because it opened the way for quantitative analysis : men might differ about the things which made for happiness, but utility did offer a more definite basis for argument than the vague and absolute principles which usually prevailed in political controversy. But to condemn the argument from nature as " nonsense on stilts," as Bentham and more modern critics have done, is to misunderstand its value and its basis. The idea of natural rights was not finally discredited because

132

in eighteenth-century thought the natural was sometimes confused with the primitive and an *a priori* method of argument
commonly adopted. The introduction of the Golden Age and
the social contract as a makeshift support for natural rights was
unfortunate because, when the historical fallacy was knocked
away, the truth embodied in the idea of natural law was easily
overlooked.

The *philosophes* who talked of natural rights were relying
upon the sound assumption that men have everywhere certain
needs in common, and that these are spiritual as well as material.
They had too an historical basis for their claims. They might
profitably have put the matter thus. Society is made up of
individuals who have spiritual as well as economic needs. Now
it is of the very nature of a spiritual existence that it develops
from within, that no outside force can direct it and that its
development will be individual and unpredictable. There is,
therefore, a large part of the life of every man which must not
be regulated by any Government. Any society is self-condemned
which does not give opportunity for the spiritual life to develop,
and we have the long-record of history to show that men are
willing to suffer imprisonment and torture, to give up ease
and even life itself, in pursuit of religious freedom. When the
expression of thought is censored, and adherents to any religious creed proscribed, men demand the right of free speech
and religious toleration, just as they demand the right of private
property when the fruits of their labour are confiscated and
economic benefits unjustly distributed. Where justice is venal,
privilege flagrant, and government arbitrary, they demand
equal rights before the law and some form of political liberty.
A Government fails in so far as it omits to recognize and
give scope to these fundamental needs of human nature. In
this sense natural rights, as the *philosophes* argued, are anterior
to the State, since they arise out of the continuous demands of
men ; the preservation of rights remains a principal duty of
the Government, even though the substance of these demands
changes and becomes in part modified through the State's
action. It remains true that the State must be judged by its
capacity to secure the rights of man.

The mistakes of the *philosophes* were due to their failure to realize that natural law has a changing and developing content. When Montesquieu compared the customs of one country with those of another he distinguished permanent underlying principles from superficial differences due to local circumstances ; but he spoke as if the principles themselves were always constant, and as if geography and climate modified their application without any help from the development of social life itself. Voltaire, whose historical perspective was truer, though narrower, could write : " The empire of custom is vaster than that of nature : it extends over manners, over all usages : it covers the scene of the universe with variety : nature spreads unity there, establishing everywhere a small number of invariable principles : the foundations, therefore, are everywhere the same, and culture produces varying fruits." Even here the invariable principles seem static, and the idea that the needs of men in primitive society might not prove an adequate guide to those of modern civilization, totally absent. The Aristotelean conception of the natural as the full development of the potentialities rather than as the original constitution of the organism seldom makes its appearance in the eighteenth century.

In one direction the doctrine of natural law was more serviceable than the current form of Utilitarianism, which suffered equally from lack of historical perspective. The moral appeal in the doctrine of natural law was more immediately effective than an argument based on a balance of pleasure over pain. In the hands of a philosopher, no doubt, a principle established on utilitarian grounds was distinct enough from a temporary expedient. Liberty and justice were words which had meaning for the utilitarian as well as for the exponents of natural law. According to the utilitarian, justice is a principle founded on experience, more important than any passing advantage and always to be recognized by a government, even when the current balance of pains and pleasures would seem to favour its temporary neglect. No doubt this is a more scientific analysis than the conception of natural law, which bases rights on an intuitive apprehension by all men at all times. But in the hands of governments, utility and expediency are so easily interchangeable that men have clung to natural and inalienable rights, apprehending that, in the absence of a moral and absolute claim, their rulers could always find exceptional grounds for violating their liberty. So, when it came to founding a constitution and attempting to preserve the gains of the past from the passing wills of governments and the gusty passions of majorities, the basis of moral law seemed a more secure foundation than a utilitarian argument based on analysis and experience. Natural law was at least a method of forcing authority to recognize principles which transcend immediate expediency.

As employed by its more fervent adherents, the law of nature supports a comprehensive Protestantism. To the Protestant it is intolerable that any authority should stand between the individual and the conclusions of his own reason. Sixteenth-century Protestantism began in this spirit, but failed in courage and set up the Bible in place of the Pope. Only Anabaptists and Quakers accepted the whole faith of Protestantism. In the eighteenth century the arguments which Protestants applied to religion were applied generally to all departments of thought. The methods of science were the only guide to truth : authority could order but it could not prove. Occasionally, therefore, a *philosophe* could speak like a Quaker, though Diderot talked of "natural reason" where George Fox would have spoken of "inner light." But it was left to Paine and a more revolutionary school of thought to declare that the very word " toleration " was an insult, since it implied that any power might possess the right to grant or withhold liberty of conscience.[1]

When the Revolution came, Paine rushed to the defence of the new French Constitution, on the ground that it was "natural." A generation earlier when Voltaire wished to stress the contrast with French government he idealized England as the country where nature was obeyed and the rights of man effectively guaranteed. "Here is the point which English legislation has at last reached : it places every man again in

---

[1] "Toleration," Paine wrote, " is not the opposite of intolerance, it is the counterfeit of it. Both are despotisms. The one assumes to itself the right of withholding liberty of conscience, the other of granting it. The one is the Pope armed with fire and faggot, the other the Pope granting or selling indulgences."

possession of all those rights of nature of which men are robbed in almost all monarchies. These rights are : entire liberty of person and of property; the right to speak to the nation through the medium of the pen ; to be tried upon a criminal charge only by a jury of independent men ; not to be judged in any case except according to the precise terms of the law ; to profess peacefully what religion one wishes." An English radical might have pointed out to Voltaire that in fact only a portion of the population in England enjoyed the substance of these advantages. Liberty of person was not secure from the press-gang ; political comment could at times be sharply curtailed ; Quakers and Unitarians suffered civil disabilities, as well as Catholics ; the law was tortuous, antiquated and frequently administered in the interests of the rich against the poor. Even so, the contrast with France was sufficiently striking : the Church did not rule the State, the aristocracy was not wholly irresponsible nor parasitic, and a single legal code, theoretically at least applying to all classes, was some safeguard against tyranny.

The disabilities imposed on Catholics would certainly not have troubled Voltaire. Locke had argued that those whose creed necessarily made them intolerant were rightly excluded from exercising public authority. The French *philosophes* were naturally more Erastian, since their whole experience had taught them the danger of a powerful Church. They were not content with the principle that the State is a secular institution, whose policy should be divorced from religious considerations. Left alone, the Church would be too dangerous. " If," as Diderot remarked, " it is difficult to do without priests wherever there is a religion, it is easy to keep them quiet if they are paid by the State and threatened at the least fault with being hunted from their posts, deprived of their functions and their salaries, and thrown into poverty." Voltaire also advocated the strict subordination of the Church to the State. The State ought not to permit any of its citizens to be troubled with an allegiance to a rival authority. All religious observance should be supervised by the secular power. " If there are in a cult any formulas of prayer, canticles or ceremonies, they ought all to be submitted to the inspection of the magistrate. Ecclesiastics may compose these formulas, but it is for the Sovereign to examine them, approve them, and, if need be, reform them. We have seen bloody wars which would not have taken place if sovereigns had better known their rights." If the instruction of the young remained in the hands of the Church it was for the Government to inspect schools. Marriage, too, should be regarded as a contract, not a sacrament, and priests who performed the ceremony be servants of the State rather than of the Church. Where religion led to obvious abuses it was the duty of the State to restrict even the right of free speech : the Sovereign was justified in preventing the strife of Thomists and Molinists by " imposing silence on both parties and punishing the disobedient." [1]

Voltaire indeed never made any attempt to reconcile his doctrine of sovereignty with his theory of natural rights. Whenever it came to the test he supported the State against the individual and preferred order to freedom. He was even capable of wishing the State to ban an author of whom he disapproved, and was himself responsible for the imprisonment of an opponent. His general position, however, was clear enough. " It is a natural right to use the pen and tongue at one's own peril. I know many books which are boring : I do not know of one which has done real harm." Nevertheless, he could write that there were insulting books which ought to be burnt, because an insult is a civil offence ; whilst a book like *The Social Contract*, an " œuvre de raisonnement," being only illogical, not offensive, ought to be refuted, not suppressed.

Whatever his inconsistencies, Voltaire was successful in spreading the great principle he learnt from England, and from Beccaria, that it was the business of the law to punish criminals, not to supervise morals. It was better to prosecute for libel than to prevent free-thought by a system of spies and censorships.

---

[1] As an evil of clericalism which the State should certainly suppress Voltaire mentions the monastic vows taken by children. " How have governments come to be so much their own enemies, so stupid, as to authorize citizens to alienate their liberty at an age when to dispose of the least part of one's fortune is forbidden ? How can we permit the worst of all slavery in a country where slavery is forbidden ? "

He was nowhere more effective than in his work for the improvement of justice. He protested against the mediæval survivals which still passed as judicial procedure, exposed the barbarity and futility of the *question*—a torture which tried endurance, not innocence, and enabled the guilty to escape, provided they were strong enough, and condemned the weak, whether innocent or not. Bentham's analytic logic had not yet exposed the absurdities of judicial process in England, but, in any case, Voltaire would have been justified in citing English methods as an improvement on those of France, where the magistrate was accustomed "to conduct himself towards the accused as an opponent rather than as a judge," where the accused was not allowed his own counsel, was tried in secret, and not even permitted to confront the witnesses who testified against him.[1] Neither was it possible for anyone in France to know the law, although its endless complications and local variations kept lawyers fat. " Is it not an absurd and frightful thing," asks a litigant in one of his Dialogues, " that what is true in one village is found to be false in another? How strange a barbarism that fellow-countrymen should not live under the same law ! "[2]

The idea that punishment should be proportionate to crime and graded according to its deterrent effect was popularized by Montesquieu and Voltaire before Bentham had explained it to lawyers. Voltaire used the case of a young girl of eighteen, who had been hanged for stealing towels from her mistress (who had not paid her wages), as an example of legal inhumanity. What, he asks, is the effect of such punishment? " It is to multiply robbers. For what householder will dare to forswear every feeling of honour and pity so far as to deliver up a servant guilty of so slight an offence to be hanged at his door? He is

---

[1] The Calas case in itself provides an adequate example of judicial method in eighteenth-century France, or at least in Toulouse. A useful and readable account has been published in England, *The Case of Jean Calas*, by F. A. Maugham. Voltaire's work for Calas' wife and family was not only in the cause of toleration but also on behalf of a fairer method of trial.

[2] It has been estimated that there were four hundred different legal systems in pre-Revolutionary France.

satisfied by dismissing him ; the thief goes on to rob elsewhere, and often becomes a dangerous brigand." This was an early statement of the truth that, while certainty of punishment may prevent crime, severity may increase it. Further, Voltaire asked, was not the whole penal system founded upon a wrong basis? The main question to be considered was the public advantage ; not how to make punishment unpleasant, but how to make it " useful." Beccaria had suggested that the law itself encouraged crime : was it reasonable to expect to " teach men to detest homicide " by making magistrates also commit homicide with pomp and ceremony? Was there, Voltaire wondered, any argument at all for capital punishment, except in the case of a homicidal maniac whom one must kill for the purely utilitarian reason that there was no other means " of saving the life of the greater number "? In every other case the criminal should be condemned to live a useful life, to work " continually for his country because he has harmed his country. He must redress the harm he has done. Death redresses nothing."

Common sense was an excellent weapon for attacking existing French institutions. It enabled Voltaire to establish the principles of equality before the law, civil liberty and freedom of discussion. Beyond these immediate reforms, however, it solved nothing. Montesquieu and Rousseau were exceptions in their period in being seriously concerned with a political philosophy, in realizing that the form of government and the basis of political obedience were important as well as the passing of good laws and the efficiency of their administration. The Encyclopædists were sorry for the poor and hoped that the abolition of privilege and monopoly and the institution of a freer economic régime would bring them a higher standard of life. Diderot was the only Encyclopædist (unless Rousseau is included among their number) who had democratic sympathies or any realization of what poverty meant. The ideal of social equality was seldom taken seriously, though many agreed with Voltaire that something might be done to improve the lot of the indigent by the establishment of hospitals for the sick, the provision of work for the unemployed, and the reorganization of existing institutions like the Hôtel-Dieu in Paris.[1] The division between rich and poor, however, remained unalterable: " it is impossible on our happy globe that men living in society should not be divided into two classes, the rich one which commands, the poor which serves. These two classes, again, divide themselves into a thousand, and among these thousand there are still shades of difference."

By liberty the *philosophes* meant civil liberty, and it was only when men had come to doubt if it could ever be secure without popular government that liberty began to include democracy. It is true that on one occasion, carried away by enthusiasm for England, Voltaire spoke as if the element of democracy in her government was the real safeguard of civil liberty. England, a kind of disguised republic, was free because she taxed herself. The House of Commons was an epitome of the nation; " the King, who is the head, only acts for it and according to what is called his prerogative," while peers and bishops were there merely as their own representatives. " But the House of Commons is there for the people, since each member is deputed by the people. . . . In comparison with this institution the Republic of Plato is an empty dream." [2] It was, of course, a parliament of property-holders to which Voltaire referred. Even when he admitted that a republic might be a good form of government in a small country, he was careful to add that only holders of property could claim a share in legislation. As for the populace, he added, " when it mingles itself with reason all is lost. The populace are oxen, which need a yoke, a goad and hay." A monarchy, in any case, was preferable to democracy. He himself preferred " to obey a fine lion, much stronger than himself, than two hundred rats of his own species." [3]

Voltaire's attitude was not really inconsistent. England seemed a happy accident, a place where a measure of popular government proved compatible with enlightened administration. It was the enlightenment he cared about; whether the power was

---

[1] Vide *Dic. Phil. Charité.*
[2] *Dic. Phil. Gouvernement.*
[3] *Dic. Phil. Idées Républicaines.*

popular, aristocratic or despotic was of secondary importance. He held with Pope that it was for fools to contest about forms of government, "what's best administered is best." The best Government, he said, was that in which the rights of man were most securely recognized. On the whole, an enlightened despotism seemed more likely to preserve civil liberty than a popular or an aristocratic Government, in spite of the fact that a mixture of all three happened to have served the purpose well in England.

In France the reformer naturally centred his hopes in the King. The King might for the time be controlled by ecclesiastics, just as the mob which had hounded Calas to the wheel was incited by priests, but in the past only kings had ever been strong enough to check the power of the Church, to enforce toleration, and to keep order. The French Constitution had long been destroyed. The *Parlements*, its only remnants, were mainly busied with preserving their own privileges. In 1771, when Chancellor Maupeou exiled the *Parlement* of Paris and set up his own Council to take its place, Voltaire expressed his delight, remarking that the *Parlements* represented no other interests than their own, were useless as a reforming body, and could never, under any circumstances, justify the comparison of themselves with the British House of Commons. To enlighten a single powerful individual seemed comparatively easy, all the more since the *philosophes* found despots throughout Europe ready to buy their books, pay them pensions or compliments, and even on occasion to carry out some of the reforms they suggested. The *philosophes*, therefore, imitated the Jesuits and sought influence through the conversion of the powerful. "I am persuaded," wrote Voltaire to Frederick the Great, "that only a monarch can now crush the seeds of religious hatred and ecclesiastical discord in his kingdom. But he must be an honest man, not priest-ridden : for fools though they be, men know very well in their hearts that goodness is better than religious observance. Under a sanctimonious king, subjects are hypocrites : a king who is an honest man makes his people like himself."

In the thirty years preceding the Revolution the *philosophes* had considerable grounds for believing that European government was profiting by the enlightenment they offered. Frederick the Great, a genuine admirer even if a poor exponent of French literature, had disappointed their earlier hopes. But in spite of his wars and intrigues he had abolished serfdom in Prussia, he worked continuously to improve the honesty and efficiency of his administration, and he persecuted no one on the ground of religious opinion. Catherine of Russia, too, was scarcely as philosophic in practice as she appeared in conversation. She did not learn all the lessons which Diderot endeavoured to inculcate as he sat opposite her, thumping the Imperial knees in his exuberant exposition of Encyclopædist principles. Nevertheless it was much to have an Empress of Russia who patronized philosophy, who called Montesquieu's *L'Esprit des Lois* " her breviary," and who carried out his principles at least up to the point of formally abolishing the use of torture. If Catherine's reforms were often shams, like Potemkin's villages, Pombal in Portugal, Leopold in Tuscany, and, finally, Joseph in Austria, were all genuine reformers, whose inspiration came directly from Voltaire and his colleagues.

In spite of the fact that these remarkable rulers happened to be in power in Europe contemporaneously, enlightened monarchy failed. Its reforms did not make revolution unnecessary, nor prevent the triumph of democracy. Indeed, it was not in the power of the benevolent despot to do for his people all that the *philosophes* asked. A King cannot altogether break with the past traditions of monarchy, free himself from the hampering support of courts and aristocracies, nor suddenly enlighten a populace which has never previously been permitted any kind of education or share in government. The philosophic despots had no constitutional organization to which they could appeal for support in their struggle with feudal privilege and clerical hostility. When Joseph II. attempted, on his own initiative, to carry through reforms which were in advance of public opinion his benevolence led to revolution. The alternative method, attempted by Louis XVI., of appointing enlightened ministers might have been more successful if he had adequately supported them. As it was, the effect was merely to spread a full knowledge of social evils and administrative scandals amongst the populace, to create an impatience with the slowness of reform, and, finally, a demand that if the King could not reform his Government, and get rid of social misery, it was the business of the people themselves to take the matter in hand.

4. *ECRASEZ L'INFAME*—THE WORK OF VOLTAIRE

In *Candide*, Voltaire had given up not only the hope of explaining the universe but also that of reforming the world. His life, however, was a refutation of the doctrine of minding one's own business. Even when human nature seemed to him least worthy of respect, and the mystery of pain most incomprehensible, Voltaire could not lose the belief that there were some things worth doing, and some faith that was rational. "We may believe that industry will always progress more and more : that the useful arts will be improved : that of the evils which have afflicted men, prejudices, which are not their least scourge, will gradually disappear among all those who govern nations, and that philosophy, universally diffused, will give some consolation to human nature for the calamities which it must always experience."

If men were ever to be induced to turn their eyes from unpractical and superstitious beliefs, and choose the common-sense goods which life offered, they must begin by " doubting a little of their own infallibility," as Benjamin Franklin put it, and learn to realize that persecution was never justified by any benefits which it might be supposed to produce. Men have always admitted that the infliction of pain is an evil, but in every age they have believed in some end which seemed to justify it as a means. In Voltaire's day cruelty was justified, not on nationalistic grounds, but on religious ones. The first object of the humanitarian then was to overthrow popular superstitions, and so enable men to see cruelty as cruelty, not as sanctified and necessary suffering.

Voltaire once described how Reason and Truth travelled through Europe, and felt themselves at home only in such enlightened despotisms as Parma and Turin. In England they found that the worst stages of fanaticism and folly were past and a " unique " Government had been set up, in which the advantages of monarchy and the freedom of republicanism were combined. "My daughter," says Reason to Truth, " I think our reign may be just beginning, after our long imprisonment. , . . That will happen to us which has happened to Nature: she has been covered by an ugly veil and completely disfigured during countless centuries. At the end have come a Galileo, a Copernicus and a Newton, who have shown her nearly naked and who have made men almost amorous of her."

In France, however, men were scarcely ready to fall in love with Reason and Truth. When the Jesuit Order was abolished in 1764 Voltaire's prophecy seemed about to be fulfilled. But Jansenist *Parlements* and provincial mobs were as fanatical as Jesuit inquisitors. Already in 1762, Calas, a Protestant tradesman, was condemned by a Jansenist *Parlement* to be broken on the wheel, because of a rumour that his son, who had been found dead, had been killed by him in order to prevent his conversion to Catholicism. There was evidence that made it in the highest degree improbable that Calas had murdered his son : there was no fragment of evidence that he had. Sirven, similarly accused of murdering his daughter, escaped the wheel only by flying to Geneva ; while in a third case, La Barre, who was accused of insulting the Virgin Mary before the *Parlement* of Amiens, was condemned to have his tongue and right hand cut off and then be burnt alive. On appeal, however, the *Parlement* of Paris considered the Virgin's honour sufficiently vindicated by a mere decapitation, and in 1766 La Barre was beheaded.

It has been well said that, while the preacher tells us of our sins, and the magistrate punishes us for social delinquency, the greatest crimes can be dealt with only by ridicule. During the last sixteen years of Voltaire's life there could no longer be any doubt of the serious intention of his mockery. When Frederick wrote to him, taunting him with only coquetting with the " infamous monster," Voltaire replied : " No, I work only to extirpate it." To d'Alembert he wrote : " Here Calas

broken on the wheel, there Sirven condemned. . . . Is this a
country of philosophy and pleasure? It is rather the country
of the Massacre of St Bartholomew. Why, the Inquisition
would not have ventured to do what these Jansenist judges
have done. . . . Ah, my friend, is it a time for laughing? Did
men laugh when they saw the bull of Phalaris made red-hot?"

Putting aside his other work, his plays and history, his
epigrams and philosophy, Voltaire devoted himself to the
practical task of forcing the authorities to admit that Calas
had been unjustly condemned, to ridiculing Catholicism, and to
advocating free-thought and toleration. "Like Cato," he wrote,
"I always end my harangue by saying '*Deleatur Carthago.*'
It is only necessary for five or six *philosophes* to understand in
order to upset the Colossus. There is no question of stopping our
lackeys going to Mass; it is a question of snatching fathers of
families from the tyranny of impostors and inspiring them with
the spirit of tolerance." In scores of articles and pamphlets he
exposed the barbarities, the immoralities and artifices of papal
history, ransacked the works of Bayle and the more militant
English deists for examples of discrepancies of Biblical dates
and the improbabilities of miracles, described with all solemnity
the less savoury stories of Old Testament Fathers and Christian
saints, remarking that although according to ordinary standards
these would be subjects for incredulity, censure or ridicule,
with religious sanction they became matters of faith and inspiration. To doubt or criticize, in these circumstances, was,
of course, to deserve an eternity of future punishment, and
men who persecuted those who disagreed with them on such
matters were, after all, only emulating the vengeance which
an All-loving Father wreaked upon them when they did not
implicitly believe in His goodness.

In the long run, it was not argument which counted. It was
the whole outlook of men, historical, scientific and religious,
which Voltaire's appeal was designed to change. In his vindication of Calas he wrote: "Transport yourselves with me to the
day when all men shall be judged and when God will render to
each according to his works. Imagine all the dead of the past
ages and of our own appear in His presence. Are you quite

sure that our Creator and our Father will say to the wise and virtuous Confucius, to Solon the legislator, to Pythagoras, to Zaleucus, to Socrates, to Plato, to the divine Antonines, to the good Trajan, to Titus, to all the delights of the human spirit, to Epictetus, and to so many other men, the models of mankind : ' Go, wretches : go down to punishments infinite in their intensity and duration ; may your punishment be as eternal as I am ! And you, My beloved, Jean Châtel, Ravaillac, Damiens, Cartouches, you who have died with the prescribed formulas, you shall share for ever My Empire and My blessedness ' ? "

Perhaps, Voltaire suggested in his old age, the new outlook he was offering was not so very un-Christian : it might even be more akin to the New Testament gospel than the teaching of its orthodox interpreters. " Now I ask you if it is tolerance or intolerance which is the divine right ; if we wish to resemble Jesus Christ shall we be martyrs or executioners ? " In time, no doubt, reason would triumph, and men learn to distinguish Christianity from its counterfeits. " I shall not be a witness of this fine revolution," he wrote, " but I shall die with the three theological virtues which are my consolation : the faith which I have in human reason which is beginning to develop in the world ; the hope that ministers in their boldness and their wisdom will at length destroy customs which are as ridiculous as they are dangerous ; the charity which makes me grieve for my neighbour, complain of his bonds, and long for his deliverance. So with faith, hope and charity, I end my life a good Christian." [1]

---

[1] 13th February 1768, Voltaire to the Comte de Leninhaupt.

CHAPTER VI

THE BRITISH CONSTITUTION

AN enlightened and tolerant State, which guaranteed civil liberty to every individual : a State whose policy was entirely secular, and which was always on its guard against the encroachments of any Church : a State in which the only laws were reasonable applications of a single, universal and evideht law of nature—such was the political ideal of most of the *philosophes*. The task of a *philosophe*, therefore, was to enlighten those in authority everywhere, and to persuade them to carry out certain necessary reforms. This policy dominated French thought from the middle of the century, when the first volumes of the *Encyclopædia* appeared, until the downfall of Turgot, the revolt of the American colonies and the vision of Rousseau began to make men doubtful about the possibilities of enlightened monarchy and hopeful about the conception of democracy.

At the beginning of this period, in 1748, Montesquieu's *Esprit des Lois* had appeared. Its influence in stimulating social and political speculation was immediate, and the *philosophes* found many of its doctrines agreeable. Montesquieu's hatred of despotism and clericalism, his demand for toleration, his suggestions for reforming the system of taxation and of civil and criminal justice—all these were common to the philosophic outlook. The more far-sighted *philosophes*, however, recognized him as a dangerous ally, whose arguments might well be used on occasion by the enemy. His approach to politics was a combination of the conservative one usual with lawyers, property-holders and antiquarians and the radical one common amongst sceptics and humanitarians. It is natural to lawyers to hate innovation, but time and again lawyers have aided radicalism because despots are more liable to introduce innovations than revolutionaries. Moreover, the study of antiquity, which formed the basic study of every educated boy in the eighteenth century, exercised its peculiar influence over Montesquieu. His mind, like Rousseau's, was impregnated with an admiration for the

√ Sparta of Plutarch's *Lycurgus*, for ancient Athens and the Roman Republic. As a lawyer he instinctively shared the views of Fénelon and the later critics of the lawless despotism of Louis XIV., and ranged himself upon the side of the *Parlements* when they asserted their constitutional rights. As a student, d'Aguesseau's theory of divine right made no appeal to him, while he eagerly accepted Domat's interpretation of Roman jurisprudence, based upon the natural law of the Stoics.[1]

Montesquieu had early won a reputation as a radical, a sceptic and a wit by the *Persian Letters*, and he had appealed even more directly to the tastes of Madame de Tencin's *salon* by a fashionable study in polite pornography entitled *Le Temple de Gnide*. He was of the *petite noblesse*, had a sinecure post, a private fortune, and an equable, even a cold temperament[2] ; he had written scientific papers[3] and was something of an anti-quarian and historian ; he had been conventionally successful with women and after his election to the Academy in 1728 seemed well qualified to spend the rest of his life in society, after the manner of Duclos or Marmontel. He preferred, how-ever, to combine an enjoyment of his good fortune with serious work. The results were, first, a Roman history, and, secondly, *L'Esprit des Lois*.

He desired, as his friends desired, to find the simple rules which must surely govern social phenomena, as he had learned from science to believe they governed physical phenomena. But he differed from his contemporaries in several vital respects. It was his peculiar distinction to be alone in his generation in
√ perceiving that both the science and art of free government were difficult. Even so, he imagined them immeasurably easier

---

[1] Dedieu emphasizes the remarkable anticipation of Montesquieu's views in the *Vita Civile* of Doria. Montesquieu, however, does not seem to have been acquainted either with Doria or with Vico's *Scienza Nuova*, though Vico was a contemporary, and his work closely similar. *Vide* Vaughan's essay on Montesquieu in *Studies in the History of Political Philosophy*, vol. i.

[2] Montesquieu's own account of himself was that he had never " had any sorrows which an hour's reading did not dissipate."

[3] He had taken up experimental science just at the time when Fontenelle had begun to popularize it, and wrote papers upon physics, botany and natural history between 1717 and 1723.

than they have since proved. But from the beginning he could not confidently accept the easy universality of Lockean individualism. Unlike most of his contemporaries he was primarily an observer, and of that comparatively rare type of mind which is more interested in understanding things than in praising or deploring them. He was more detached and less subjective in approach than his friends. He set out to study social variations by the inductive method, convinced that in social as in physical phenomena the fashionable deductive method of Descartes led to premature " systems " and false simplification.

The division between natural law and actual law seemed to Montesquieu less definite and complete than the *philosophes* were accustomed to suppose. Actual law was admittedly defective since it sprang from the passing wills of individuals rather than from the permanent principles of justice. Yet even existing conventions and laws were not wholly arbitrary. There had been natural limitations upon the will of the legislator. Laws differed in different countries, not only because law-makers had willed variously, but also because the needs and conditions of countries had varied. Now, if this was true, a single uniform application of natural law would not everywhere produce the same result, and justice and liberty would be achieved only by a scientific adjustment of universal principles to special conditions. These special conditions included psychological as well as physical factors. The political thinker was forced to take into account the spirit as well as the substance of the law, and remember that the formal recognition of the rights of man did not in itself ensure individual liberty. New and complicated questions were thus introduced : the content and application of the law of nature might vary with varying material conditions and human opinions, and the reformer must begin to study, to classify and to compare the infinite variety of human habits and social institutions.

Montesquieu set about this task without appreciating its immensity. He believed that the results of a comparative study would be easy to classify and that final generalizations would be obtainable from the mass of facts he was collecting. " If serious people require some other work of me of a less frivolous nature," he wrote only a few years before his death, " I can easily satisfy them. I have been labouring thirty years at a work of twelve parts, which will contain all that we know of metaphysics, politics and morality : and all that the greatest authors have forgotten in the volumes which they have published on these sciences."

The claim was not very extravagant. *L'Esprit des Lois* was not frivolous though it contained passages that were, and, if it did not summarize all that was known of metaphysics, politics and morality in twelve parts, it at least added to that knowledge in thirty-one books. *L'Esprit des Lois* is the most formless of all masterpieces.[1] Its brilliant generalizations are scattered among countless ill-divided and ill-sorted chapters containing illustrations from ancient and modern history, contemporary observation and gossip, travellers' tales and spicy anecdotes, descriptive and analytic economics and politics. The natural assumption was that Montesquieu had not mastered his material but the material him. His friends in the *salons* were amused by the passages put there to amuse them and thought, like Madame du Deffand, that his book was really nothing but *de l'esprit sur les Lois*. Curiously enough, Madame du Deffand's *mot* is still quoted as though it were genuine criticism. Montesquieu may have weakened his argument by trivialities, but it was his critics who substituted wit for understanding. Voltaire, indeed, as Montesquieu himself remarked, had too much *esprit* to understand such a lengthy, formless and philosophic piece of work.[2] He was shrewd enough to see that

---

[1] Some of the confusion of *L'Esprit des Lois* is perhaps due to the fact that it was actually written over a period of seventeen years, the first ten books being written in 1731-1732 and the last five in 1747-1748. Montesquieu had travelled in Europe before he wrote the first ten books : his English visit came before the composition of the eleventh book, and all the remainder of his work was affected by his enthusiasm for England.

[2] " As for Voltaire," wrote Montesquieu, " he has too much wit to understand me. He reads no books but those he writes, and he then approves or censures his own progeny as the wind takes him." Voltaire's complaint, in his dialogue between A, B and C, that *L'Esprit des Lois* lacked arrangement, and that its gasconades were often irrelevant, nevertheless remained true. He was justified, too, in attacking Montesquieu for his easy acceptance of any contemporary or

the book undermined the current interpretation of Locke, and, though he once uttered a splendid panegyric on Montesquieu, he made two efforts to discredit his work and criticized isolated passages with customary shrewdness, but without attempting to appreciate Montesquieu's general intention or the book's significance. Helvétius, to whom Montesquieu submitted the MS. for criticism, joined with several friends in requesting him not to ruin his reputation by publishing it, though after its appearance he took the trouble to criticize it more intelligently. Most of the Encyclopædists failed altogether to understand its intention and contented themselves with incorporating undigested fragments from it in their own writings. Diderot, however, had an unlimited capacity for absorbing new ideas and new groups of facts, and finally reached political conclusions similar to those of Montesquieu.[1] Rousseau, already impatient with the standpoint of his Encyclopædist friends, attempted, at the price of some confusion, to bring his own views of the ideal to terms with Montesquieu's description of the actual. Between Montesquieu's conservative and concrete method and Rousseau's revolutionary and abstract one there could be little or nothing in common. At the Revolution, therefore, the legal and constitutional view of Montesquieu remained distinct, forming the basis of a third school which would not blend either with the declamatory egalitarianism of Rousseau or with the mathematical utilitarianism of Helvétius and Condorcet.

Montesquieu's immediate influence in France was chiefly exerted upon the *Parlements* and the antiquarians who sought on

---

historical anecdote which suited his argument. As an historian, Montesquieu was inferior to Voltaire in this respect at least : he paid less attention to Bayle's instruction as to care and accuracy in sifting historical evidence. For Voltaire's list of Montesquieu's inaccuracies *vide* his *Sur l'Esprit des Lois*.

Some of Voltaire's criticisms are obtuse, *cp.* his accusation that Montesquieu is Machiavellian in suggesting that the fear of attack by another nation is a justification for aggression. Montesquieu was surely ironic.

[1] Diderot was always too good an observer and too much a scientist to accept the abstract or "geometric" approach to politics. *Cp.* his attack in his *Pensées sur la Nature* and his insistence that a universal æsthetic is impossible in his article *Beau* in the *Encyclopædia*.

their behalf an historical basis for freedom. For Montesquieu revived the ancient French Constitution and transformed the struggle of the *Parlements* with the King from being a mere struggle to retain inherited privileges into a broader and more objective attempt to restore to the nation the ancient safeguards of its rights on which the seventeenth-century monarchy had trampled. It was this conception that inspired early leaders of the Revolution, like Mounier, in their efforts to make France a constitutional monarchy; had the royal family of France itself understood and been faithful to this conception it is at least possible that the Jacobins would not have had the chance to apply the idea of popular sovereignty which they had learned from Rousseau and Mably. The idea of popular sovereignty would then have played only the part it played in England—the people would have been regarded as ultimately sovereign, but the task of exercising their sovereignty would have been left to their representatives.

Outside France, Montesquieu's influence was equally great. The school of Blackstone and of Burke was directly inspired by him, while the Federalists modelled the American Constitution upon his interpretation of Locke and his observation of England. Nor was Montesquieu's influence exhausted in the eighteenth century. With his contemporary, Vico, he may fairly be called the founder of the comparative method of politics, and the whole study of historical jurisprudence dates from *L'Esprit des Lois*. Montesquieu changed the traditional outlook upon law; it became with him a concrete study, based on examination of facts rather than upon *a priori* principles. Moreover he made the discovery that whole groups of facts which had hitherto seemed to have no relevance to law were really essential to its understanding. He first showed that laws were not the arbitrary fiats of their makers, but were the formal recognition of customs which were themselves the results of economic and geographical facts. In maintaining that law is only the formal superstructure built upon a basis of tradition and economic and physical fact, Montesquieu was a forerunner of Marx, as well as of Savigny and Henry Maine.

2. THE COMPARATIVE METHOD OF MONTESQUIEU

Voltaire once remarked that Montesquieu was Montaigne turned legislator. The remark, meant merely as a jesting criticism of Montesquieu's irrelevant gasconades,[1] called attention to an important aspect of *L'Esprit des Lois*. Montesquieu did, indeed, share Montaigne's eager interest in the diversity of things; he enjoyed collecting and relating the various customs of men, and pointing the moral of understanding and tolerance in a world where good and bad were so mixed and our knowledge so fragmentary and imperfect. But Montesquieu, bitten by the scientific virus of his generation, could not remain an essayist or a sceptic: he was forced to attempt for the modern world the task which Aristotle had performed for the ancient. The facts of society had to be collected, not because they were curious or amusing, but in order that they might be classified and explained. Montesquieu sought to discover the basis of law and to trace the causes of social diversity.

He at once encountered a difficulty which has always haunted social philosophers—and which has led many altogether to deride the idea of a science of politics. He had learned that the physical world follows certain ascertainable and unchanging rules which by their joint action produce the variety of natural phenomena. If we look for similar rules behind social events, do we not imply that the movements of men, who believe themselves responsible for social institutions, laws and customs, are really just as much predetermined as those of material objects? How could one believe at the same time in free will and in the possibility of discovering all the causes of human behaviour and social institutions?[2] When *L'Esprit des Lois* appeared, Jesuit critics at once denounced its deterministic tendency and described him as a disciple of Spinoza and a

---

[1] Montaigne and Montesquieu were both born in Gascony.

[2] In one passage of his *Pensées*, Montesquieu admits that much appears to be purely accidental. If the Turks had conquered Europe and shut up all women in harems would it not have seemed obvious that such was the "natural" state of women? "It is not," he adds, "reason or nature that governs men, but pure chance."

materialist. Montesquieu, who had in fact dealt with this difficulty at the outset of his book, replied in a manner which satisfied the practical reader, if not the metaphysician.

In the first place, he had admitted the existence of God, and had argued that one of the causes of social phenomena was the moral intelligence of human beings. Materialism was antithetic to his whole outlook. " Can anything," he asked, " be more absurd than to pretend that a blind fatality could ever produce intelligent beings? " The world displayed a progressive manifestation of intelligence. The Creator had ordered that the material world should conform to certain invariable sequences. In the case of animals Montesquieu was doubtful how far they had been given the power to adjust themselves consciously to their environment. Men, on the other hand, clearly had the power to apprehend natural laws, and to control their adjustment, well or ill. In this scheme of things the word " law " is the difficulty and the key. A law is a relation ; God's relation to the universe is the law of His being. The laws of the material world are the invariable relationships between inanimate bodies. The laws of men are also " necessary relations," arising from their relationship to each other and the physical world. But, as they are " intelligent beings," they become conscious of this relationship and can modify it to suit their needs. They have in fact laws, or relationships, of their own making. Such adjustments were always possible ; when men had become conscious of a relationship they formulated it in deliberate laws. " Before laws were made there were relationships of possible justice. To say there is nothing just or unjust but what is commanded or forbidden by positive laws is the same as saying that before the describing of a circle all the radii are not equal." In other words, a law is a recognition of a relationship which had hitherto been unnoticed, not the arbitrary creation of a new relationship. All laws are, in Montesquieu's unsatisfactory definition, " the relations which necessarily flow from the nature of things."

The first book of *L'Esprit des Lois* was thus a reply to Hobbes and Spinoza. Hobbes had imagined that society was instituted by contract when the individuals who composed it found anarchy intolerable. Men, Montesquieu thought, had never been isolated creatures ; they were naturally related, bound together by common wants, common fears, sexual attraction and social consciousness.[1] This natural sociability in men has led them everywhere to unite their common force in political States and their common will in civil laws. Social life, being now more deliberate, brings a greater consciousness of common wants, and ideas of justice and morality, always innate in individuals, become recognized. Hobbes is therefore mistaken in identifying justice with the dictates of authority, in confounding sin with crime, and in speaking of laws as the arbitrary invention of kings, appointed to regulate the actions of men who would otherwise merely war against each other. Even savages, who ate their prisoners, had international and political regulations : their habits were founded on less true principles than those of civilized societies only because they had less knowledge of their true relationships with other peoples.

So far then Montesquieu had refuted Hobbes and Spinoza, and, at the same time, criticized and expanded Puffendorf and Locke. Law has a double origin : it is not purely the result of human will, but of reason acting upon causes which men cannot control. Now these external factors have varied in different places, and laws have therefore varied even though human nature has been essentially the same everywhere at all times. Montesquieu did not entertain the idea that natural man himself may have varied. Race was a complication introduced by later writers. "As men have in all ages been subject to the same passions," wrote Montesquieu, "the occasions which produce great changes may be different but the causes are always the same." If, then, human nature remains constant, two factors are left to account for varieties in social institutions : the first is environmental difference ; the second is the varying success and degree of understanding of legislators in adapting their laws to these different environments.

Montesquieu's task, therefore, was to examine past and present forms of government and political institutions, and to

---

[1] *L'Esprit des Lois*, Bk. I., chap. ii. Men in Montesquieu's state of nature are moved to form societies, not because they tyrannize over one another, but because they fear the unknown.

disentangle the permanent physical factors from the variable effects of human will. History was obviously one starting-point. Montesquieu, unlike almost all his contemporaries, thought of the Middle Ages not as a barbarous gap between the civilization of Rome and that of Louis XIV., but as the clue to existing French institutions. He brought, too, a new spirit into the fashionable study of Roman history. Machiavelli and numerous subsequent historians had been content to cull moral and political maxims from the story of Rome's growth, grandeur and decay. Bossuet's *Universal History* had indeed a more philosophic import. God ruled: the facts of history, Greek, Roman or French, must be arranged to support the axioms of Providential guidance. Montesquieu, however, wished to find the causes of development and decay by examination of the facts. " It is not chance," he wrote, " which rules the world There are general causes, some moral, some physical . . accidents are secondary to these causes. . . . In a word, the principal movement carries along with it all the particular accidents." From the history of Rome he developed one of his most famous generalizations. Rome, beginning with a small territory, attained strength as a republic founded upon the virtue of its citizens. When its territory had been everywhere extended, the old methods of government were no longer adequate, the spirit of the Republic was corrupted, and new vices accompanied the growth of Imperialism. Constitutional monarchy soon degenerated into despotism, relying no longer on virtue but on force and fear. It seemed then that certain fundamental characteristics of a country made a particular form of government suitable; if this government was to be successful it must adhere to its nature and principle—must maintain, that is, the essentials of its form and constitution, and keep alive the spirit which animated it. If, on the contrary, laws were passed or a policy was pursued which undermined this natural adjustment or changed the emotional bond which united Government and people, it must deteriorate and collapse.

In *L'Esprit des Lois* Montesquieu developed this idea in detail. European travel gave him many new illustrations and confirmed his belief that different forms of government might be suitable to different countries, and that their laws were not to be judged absolutely good or absolutely bad, but only in relation to their environment, history and traditions. The environmental factors which Montesquieu perceived were the climate of a country, the quality of its soil, its situation and extent [1]; these, in turn, occasioned the growth of certain occupations, religious beliefs, manners and customs among its inhabitants. A particular form of government was evolved, more or less suitable to these conditions. " From different wants in different climates have come different ways of living, and these different ways of living have resulted in different kinds of laws." Thus each country had its own variant of the law of nature : the purpose of the legislator should be to keep the positive laws consistent " with their origin " and, when making any change, to consider them in relation to all these factors.

So far, Montesquieu's sociological basis is clear. Two difficulties of application obscure many of his pages. Being completely unable to trace the relative importance of these factors in any country, he picked out any single factor which caught his attention and made it responsible for the whole. All sense of proportion and all sense of historical development disappear. In *Considérations sur les Romains* the material and psychological had been blended and presented in a complex and changing unity. In *L'Esprit des Lois*, climate and geographical situation are often spoken of as if they were immediate and sufficient causes operating in the eighteenth century, directly and obviously. He saw that what may be right in one place may be wrong in another, but he seems to have altogether forgotten that what may be right at one time may be wrong at another. For this reason his examples and arguments are often unreal : the uncivilized inhabitants of North America, the ancient Athenians, the eighteenth-century French and the sixteenth-century Russians are compared without allowance for variety of epoch, while the difference between the climates of Germany

---

[1] The importance of climatic and geographical factors in the formation of institutions was not a new idea. It is in Aristotle, and, among more modern writers, in Bodin.

and Spain is enough to excuse a custom in one country which is repudiated in another. He notes the fact that in the northern part of Europe, where the climate is comparatively cold, republics and Protestants flourish, while in southern and warmer parts of Europe kings rule over Catholic countries. He leaps to the conclusion that a spirit of liberty is the result of a cold climate. Voltaire found it easy to refute generalizations of so sweeping a character; any exception—Catholic Ireland, for instance—was a sufficient answer.

In the second place, Montesquieu does not make it clear when the legislator should conform to the existing characteristics of the nation and when he should attempt to modify them. If, for instance, drunkenness is the natural result of some climates, is the Government right in encouraging or discouraging alcohol? Montesquieu does not explain, but he apparently means that these natural predispositions are an important and ineradicable factor, always to be taken into account when making laws. Climate and geographical factors form the basis on which the political structure rests: if institutions do not conform to them and harmonize with them they will certainly fail. Peter the Great attempted too much —he could not change the eternal character of Russia: Solon was right when he gave the people " the best laws they could bear."

On this basis Montesquieu approaches the problem of government. Its form should be determined by the size of the nation. A small nation might, in Montesquieu's opinion, be republican, a large country could be ruled only by a single man, with or without constitutional checks. He was clearly influenced by Aristotle's analysis of the three types of government, each liable to degenerate by the loss of its moderating principle. The types in eighteenth-century Europe were a little different. Firstly there were monarchies which Montesquieu thought better described as despotisms. Here " a single person, without law or regulation, directs everything by his own will and caprice." Secondly, there were monarchies in which a single person governed " by fixed and established laws." Thirdly, there were republics, which might be either democratic or aristocratic. Each of these types of government, Montesquieu saw, demanded a different disposition on the part of the rulers and the ruled. A despotic government would survive only as long as its subjects were intimidated : fear must be its ruling principle. The despot's power depends upon the humiliation of his people : he begins by " making a bad subject in order to make a good slave." Thus education is contrary to the principle of despotism. "Everything must depend upon two or three ideas : therefore there is no need for any new notions to be added. When we want to break in a horse we take care not to let him change his master, his lesson or his pace. Thus an impression is made on his brain by two or three motives and no more." Despotism is, therefore, a crude, simple and destructive form of government : "when the savages of Louisiana want fruit, they cut down the tree to the root and gather the fruit. *Voilà le gouvernement despotique.*"

The principle of a republic, on the other hand, was far more difficult to attain : those who ruled, whether a few or the whole mass, must be imbued with " virtue," they must be filled with love of their country, and willing to subordinate their own interests to the public good. Successful democracies like those of ancient Greece and contemporary Paraguay were all small, based on economic equality, and animated by public spirit. Inequality bred class hatred and was fatal to virtue. The distinction between the propertied *noblesse* and the humble landless workmen is one that fits a country whose principle is one of status and function, but it is fatal where all are required equally to love the republic. Equality, therefore, is the necessary counterpart of political liberty. There may be advantages in a warring state of classes, where rivalry, honour and ambition lead men to great achievements, but they are incompatible with democracy. A repudiation of self-seeking and a real devotion to the public interest alone can make democracy a working institution. Thus frugality, encouraged by sumptuary laws and restriction of inheritance, is a good thing in a republic.[1] Private fortunes in trade, however, may even be good for morals, because they

---

[1] *L'Esprit des Lois*, Bk. V., chap. v.

are the result of frugality and hard work : they are dangerous because they may lead to the formation of an aristocratic class, and when " excessive wealth destroys the spirit of commerce the inconveniences of inequality begin to be felt." [1]

If despotism rests on fear and republicanism on virtue, monarchies are best supported by the motive of "honour." By honour Montesquieu means a rivalry for distinction and a jealousy of rank among the classes who make up the social hierarchy. Each class must be anxious to guard its privileges ; from this rather than from the highest motives it may be induced to perform its function. "Philosophically speaking, it is a false honour which moves all parts of the government." Nevertheless, "by this useful motive men can be induced to perform the most difficult actions, requiring a great degree of fortitude and spirit, without any other recompense than the fame and reputation arising from the actions themselves." France, Montesquieu seems to have believed, had once been such a monarchy : Louis XIV. had ruined his country by neglecting the nature and principle of its government. France is clearly referred to when he writes of " a certain country degenerating into despotism." The great kings of France ruled constitutionally, retaining the services of the aristocracy and the *Parlements*. They kept the affection of their people by a policy of moderation —a quality which is essential to a constitutional monarchy. In the first ten books of *L'Esprit des Lois*, Montesquieu is always thinking of France when he writes of monarchy.[2]

Montesquieu's interpretation of French history had an

---

[1] Montesquieu believed that luxury was good for trade ; in democracy, however, equality was more important than wealth. He approves the economics of Mandeville, but sees that luxury and *laissez-faire* are incompatible with public spirit.

[2] Montesquieu appears to have thought that France was too large to be a successful republic or democracy. It should have been a constitutional monarchy, but he feared that the essential principle of honour in the aristocracy as well as moderation in the government had been lost in the eighteenth century. He described the courtier as combining "ambition with idleness and baseness with pride, while wanting to be rich without work, hating truth and neglecting the duties and virtues which should characterize a citizen" ; and Louis XIV. had turned all the *noblesse* into courtiers.

immediate effect in France. The champions of the *noblesse* and the, *Parlements* had not altogether overlooked the value of an historical argument against the absolute pretensions of the King. Saint-Simon had complained that the King refused to recognize the right of the peerage to advise the Crown and Boulainvilliers had advanced a learned but untenable thesis that the *noblesse* of France were the descendants of the conquering Franks, and that the King was a usurper claiming autocratic powers which had never been accorded the tribal chieftain. Montesquieu also went back to Tacitus and championed the Teutonic against the Roman view of monarchy; the "beautiful system" of constitutional monarchy was, he said, invented in the forests of Germany. His argument was less extreme than Boulainvilliers', and based on a national rather than a class outlook. Even among the *noblesse* its effect was to stimulate the idea of service and function rather than that of rights and privileges. The contrast between the class-grumbling of Saint-Simon and the enlightened feudalism of Mirabeau in *L'Ami des Hommes* is, at least in part, to be explained by the publication of *L'Esprit des Lois*. But it was the lawyers rather than the *noblesse* who availed themselves of Montesquieu's championship of the rights of the ancient "orders" of France. From 1753 onwards, when the first ill-considered criticisms of Montesquieu had died down, numerous works by antiquarians and legalists appeared, giving documentary proof that mediæval kings had governed with the aid of the Estates, and that in France as well as England they had frequently respected a recognized constitution.[1] When, in 1770, the struggle reached its climax, when the King had exiled the *Parlements* and abolished the last remnants of the French Constitution, the lawyers and their supporters could bring forward a mass of evidence to prove that he was an innovator and that Maupeou's Government was illegal. That view was reinforced on the popular side by Mably, who also looked back to mediæval history, but argued that it was the States-General, and in particular the Third

---

[1] *Vide* Carcassonne, *op. cit.*, for an account of these legal and historical books. One of the most interesting is *Théorie des Lois politiques de la France* (1792), by Mademoiselle de Lézardière.

Estate, who should govern France. When the Revolution itself arrived, various interpretations of Montesquieu were in competition : the *noblesse* and the lawyers held that the Estates should vote separately—a provision which gave privilege the dominant voice ; while the Third Estate, protesting that numbers should outweigh rank, argued that the lower chamber, like the House of Commons, should have the decisive voice. For Montesquieu had not only championed the ancient Constitution of France, but also the whole idea of constitutional monarchy and, in particular, its English pattern. Until the advent of Republicanism, in 1792, it was Montesquieu who dominated the discussions of the Assembly. The nature and extent of his influence becomes clear only when his interpretation of the British Constitution is understood.

3. THE SEPARATION OF POWERS—THE INFLUENCE OF MONTESQUIEU

Montesquieu's visit to England in 1729-1730 probably occurred between the composition of his tenth and eleventh books. The discovery of the English Constitution had almost as great an effect upon him as the discovery of English philosophy had upon Voltaire. Many things in England disgusted him. He agreed with most visitors about the climate, and Voltaire's quip about the coincidence between the east wind and suicide assumed with Montesquieu the dignity of serious sociology. He found the English aloof and money-grubbing ; their roads too were execrable, although he admired their enthusiasm for landscape-gardening. English politics were at their meanest under Walpole ; each politician seemed to him anxious only to get the better of the others, and the whole country was endangered by the universal passion for making money. Religion, he saw, counted for little, though the Church was a great social institution to which all the respectable paid court. In nothing was he so far-sighted as in his observation of the characteristics of the aristocracy. The landowners were, he saw, the rulers of England, and their motive was "honour." What would happen if they turned increasingly to commerce and lost their sense of responsibility?

162

The monarchy would certainly decline and England become a nation of merchants and shopkeepers. Her natural resources, disposition and geographical position would then make her extraordinarily powerful. But her spirit would be transformed.[1]

In spite of jobbery and self-seeking, Montesquieu found in England what Voltaire had found—individual liberty. The rights of man were guaranteed by the Revolutionary settlement, by laws such as *Habeas Corpus* and by the common law, which made "outward acts" alone amenable to punishment. There was no sovereign except the law. The Government ruled according to a reasoned application of natural law, embodied in the positive laws of the country. This happy state of affairs was perpetuated by the nature of English government. The Government was mixed. In form England was a monarchy which retained the intermediary bodies, the aristocratic support and the legal checks which were proper to it. The aristocracy were still, in part at least, actuated by the ancient motive of honour. The Government was also in some degree democratic, and the common people were imbued with at least a portion of the republican virtue.[2]

The explanation of English liberty was now clear. The rule of law was maintained because authority was divided. No single authority could impose its will upon the whole, and each of the three functions of government was given just the requisite power to prevent the other functions from being abused. "When the legislative and executive powers are united in the same person," writes Montesquieu, "or in the same body of magistrates, there can be no liberty. . . . Again, there is no liberty if the power of judging be not separated from the legislative and executive powers." All liberty would be at an end if all three functions of government were concentrated in one person or body of persons. Here then was the secret of liberty—the separation of the powers or functions of government.

---

[1] For Montesquieu on England cp. *Pensées diverses*, *Œuvres*, vii. 167; *L'Esprit des Lois*, VI. vi. ; XIX. xxvii. Also *Lettres Persanes*, 104th letter.

[2] Montesquieu considered the liveliness of English politics a good sign. He contrasted the popular interest in England with the silence of France under Louis XIV.—the silence of a town which the enemy has just occupied.

The three functions of government were separated but not isolated, they were related by a nicely adjusted system of checks and balances. "England is the finest country in the world," wrote Montesquieu, "I do not except any of the republics. I call it free because the Prince has not the power to do any conceivable wrong; his power is curtailed and limited by statute. Similarly the legislature is harmless, being divided into two parts. One checks the other by the mutual privilege of veto. They are both checked by the executive power, as is the executive by the legislative." The whole therefore "naturally forms a state of repose or inaction. But as there is a necessity of movement in the course of human affairs, they are forced to move, but to do so in concert." [1]

It was not the Revolutionary settlement of 1689 which Montesquieu misunderstood, but its recent development. He could not perceive that the growth of the Cabinet system at the very time when he was in England was actually establishing the unity of authority which he feared. Liberty, he said, would be lost if "the same people shared in the legislative and executive power." The Constitution of 1689 was already gone; the ministers of George II. were, in fact, responsible less to him than to the House of Commons, and, in spite of the efforts of George III. to destroy this new Cabinet responsibility, sovereignty was becoming firmly established in a single authority, the "King in Parliament." Montesquieu had foreseen that the power of the House of Commons would increase at the expense of the King and the House of Lords,[2] though he had not understood the mechanism by which this

---

[1] Locke had already noted that the executive power (under which heading he included the judiciary) required different capacities from those needed by the legislator, and had argued that they ought not to be confounded in the same authority. When Locke wrote he was of course unable to foresee the future development of Cabinet government: everything pointed to a system in which the King would remain the executive power, to whom ministers were in fact responsible. If Sir William Temple's scheme had been carried into effect, or George III. had succeeded in establishing departmental government, the American Constitution would have been an accurate copy of the British.

[2] "If the Lower House [of the legislature] became mistress," he wrote, "its authority would be unlimited and dangerous, because it would have at the same time the executive power."

transference was to take place, and had imagined that the loss of an independent executive would be the end of civil liberty. Curiously enough, English constitutional lawyers, like Blackstone, accepted his description of the British Constitution without hesitation or inquiry, and indulged in unqualified panegyrics of a separation of powers which had ceased to exist.

Montesquieu's interpretation of the English Constitution had even more important results. The fathers of the American Constitution borrowed from him one of their central ideas. The fixed Constitution, enshrining the gains of the past, in a sacred document liable to interpretation only by an independent judiciary, was an effort to base the government of a newly-born nation upon the conception of a law of nature which no government was competent to abrogate. The provision which excludes Cabinet ministers from Congress was the work of the Federalists under the influence of Montesquieu. They were really not copying the British Constitution, but the " departmental system " which George III. strove to establish. When they made the President of the United States " a fossilized George III." they were carefully excluding the distinctive and most important feature of the British Constitution—the dependence of the executive on the legislature and the leadership of the legislature by the executive. As a result, the story of American constitutional development consists largely in a series of efforts to find some method of overcoming its central characteristic. No device was ever so hampering as the separation of powers ; no device has been so generally praised or so ingeniously evaded. It is a sober fact that Montesquieu's interpretation of the British Constitution resulted in constant antagonisms between Senate and President : he may be said to be ultimately responsible for the non-participation of the United States in the League of Nations.[1]

---

[1] The numerous constitutions inspired by the revolutionary movement in the late eighteenth and the first half of the nineteenth centuries were all haunted by the same fear of giving any one too much authority. The separation of powers, therefore, appeared in the French Constitution of 1791, the Prussian Code of 1792, the Spanish Constitution of 1812 and the various models of 1848. The best aspect of the separation of powers was the independence

Montesquieu's constitutional theory was based on Newtonian physics. In his early work he appears to have had a firmer grasp of the organic idea of the State than any other eighteenth-century writer, but his final political theory, in which each power is separate and related to the others only by a system of checks and balances, is entirely mechanical. The whole phraseology and conception is taken from mechanics : the State is a vast piece of engineering in which each joist is kept in place and made to do its work by an exact calculation of strains and stresses, held in place by a balance here, itself checking another joist, correctly attached and related to its neighbour. Since there is no animating principle, no directing head or organic life, the result would seem to be a motionless equilibrium. Sheridan might even have had it in mind when he constructed the scene in his play, *The Critic,* where each member of the cast desires to stab his neighbour, but is prevented by his neighbour's attempt to stab him, the whole remaining in tableau, each unable to act because the balance of forces is precise. A State in which no one has the chance to do harm will scarcely have much vitality.

Nineteenth-century Liberals naturally canonized Montesquieu. No writer had expressed a more fervent hatred of clericalism and despotism nor championed the cause of toleration more forcibly nor indicted slavery more splendidly. As an opponent of unified sovereignty and an advocate of the rule of law, Montesquieu could be invoked wherever individual liberty was threatened by irresponsible power. Yet Helvétius and Voltaire were right in fearing the conservative uses to which *L'Esprit des Lois* could be put, and the direct line of Montesquieu's influence runs from Burke to Maine. The com-

of the judiciary. Even here the effort to make it free from both legislative and executive interference has led in some cases to the adoption of popular election of judges. The belief that the separation of powers was a source of English freedom has never quite died, and the system of checks and balances is still praised both in England and America. This English model was already extinct in the eighteenth century, but some writers on political theory apparently imagine that it exists in England to-day. For a distressing example *vide* Sir John Marriott, *The Mechanism of the Modern State.* By way of contrast, *cp.* Robson, *Justice and Administrative Law.*

166

parative school of which he was the founder has been generally
conservative. His aim was descriptive, but, like other political
theorists, he found it beyond his capacity to keep distinct the
division between the real and the ideal, to avoid confusion
between his descriptions of what was and his views of what
ought to be. The confusion was easily made. If a law was the
recognition of a relationship which necessarily existed, it was
easy to assume that it was itself the only possible law. If institutions are based upon a traditional adjustment necessitated
by fundamental and unalterable conditions, then legal and social
change must certainly be dangerous. Unlike his contemporaries,
Montesquieu was always conscious of the complexity of society
and the interrelation of its parts, and he was therefore more
inclined than they to hesitate before advocating changes which
might have far-reaching and unexpected effects. He was almost
the only *philosophe* who regarded the fact that an institution
or law was *a priori* unreasonable as an insufficient reason for
abolishing it.[1]

For a Frenchman to champion the British Constitution in
the eighteenth century was to side with the party of reform.
To explain, however, that the perfection of British institutions
arose from the nice balance of forces and powers which they
had miraculously achieved was to give Burke the opportunity
of denouncing all reformers. Henceforward every suggestion of
change, every denunciation of corruption or declaration that a
rotten borough was in fact rotten, could be represented as an
effort to destroy the equilibrium of man's supreme architectural
achievement. When Burke led the reaction against the Revolution he based his championship of the British Constitution
upon the principles of Montesquieu. "Our Constitution,"
he wrote, "preserves an unity in so great a diversity of its
parts. We have an inheritable Crown ; an inheritable peerage ;
and a House of Commons and a people inheriting privileges,
franchises and liberties from a long line of ancestors. This

---

[1] Note Condorcet's criticism of Montesquieu's eulogy of "moderation" in
a monarchy such as the British : "By a spirit of moderation does not
M. Montesquieu mean that spirit of uncertainty which permits a hundred little
irrelevancies to modify the indispensable principles of justice ?"

policy appears to me to be the result of profound reflection; or rather the happy effect of following nature, which is wisdom without reflection, and above it. A spirit of innovation is generally the result of a selfish temper and confined views." The conclusion commonly drawn from such premises was that existing institutions had a sanctity necessarily containing an element of the mysterious, and that when the individual found himself in conflict with them it was his duty to " venerate where he was unable presently to comprehend."

These were not the conclusions of Montesquieu, who was attempting to form a science of politics and was not in search of a mystical justification for existing abuses. He would have agreed with Burke that " those people will not look forward to posterity who never look backward to their ancestors." He was even willing to argue that institutions like the Catholic Church, polygamy and slavery, though bad in themselves as he knew them, might have had, and might still have, some justification under certain conditions. The contemporary *philosophes* naturally feared any such concessions. They held the contrary view, at least equally justified by experience, that people who look backward to their ancestors frequently lose the capacity for looking forward to posterity. To the *philosophe* it seemed obvious that some things were bad and others were good, and that to discuss origins, past adjustments and balances of forces, was to seek an excuse for neglecting immediate duties. So Helvétius wrote to Montesquieu, complaining that the result of so much theorizing seemed likely to emphasize the difficulties and throw doubt upon the possibilities of desirable change. " I believe, nevertheless, in the possibility of a good government where the liberty and property of people will be respected, and where one may see the general good necessarily emerging without your balances of particular interests." To those who believed that men were reasonable and the path to happiness simple, Montesquieu seemed to be spreading darkness rather than light when he suggested that men were not altogether free to alter their institutions just as they liked, that there was no clear-cut issue between good and evil, but only a difficult problem of changing, with due circumspection and regard to circumstances, things which were in some respects bad and in others relatively good.[1]

---

[1] With regard to Christianity, Montesquieu explains that it is not of course to be judged rationally like other religions. Such remarks, which are frequent in his work, and may be considered partly as gibes for the benefit of his friends and partly as defences against the persecution of his enemies, did not prevent him from discussing Christianity as one religion among many, with good and bad points, mostly the latter, which needed analysis.

Montesquieu laid himself open to the charge of being an apologist for the *ancien régime* when he justified the use of patronage and purchase as methods for obtaining posts in his own profession. His own position as *Président à Mortier* was gained by the system of *venalité des charges*, and there was always personal bias in his outlook upon legal reform. *Cp.* Helvétius' *Lettre à Saurin* about Montesquieu : " He adhered to the prejudices of the lawyers and *noblesse*—this is the source of all his errors. . . . Deprived of his title of Wise Man, he will become no more than the lawyer, the nobleman, and the fine genius. I am distressed for him and for humanity."

CHAPTER VII

UTILITARIANISM: THE END OF THE COMPROMISE

I. THE PHILOSOPHY OF THE ENCYCLOPÆDISTS

THE bulky volumes of the *Encyclopædia* contained a large variety of doctrines. For the most part, however, it accepted both the principles and compromises of Voltaire. D'Alembert's *Discours préliminaire*, which introduced the first volume, was written while the Encyclopædists still hoped to avoid a clash with the authorities; it summed up the practical objects of the *Encyclopædia* and revealed its positive faith, even though it evaded the less obvious intellectual difficulties. It was to be a " reasoned " dictionary, designed to make what was known on every topic accessible to educated Frenchmen, to explain the relationship between one science and another and to serve as an introduction to current theory and philosophy.

D'Alembert was as willing as Voltaire to leave a sphere for the Church and to acknowledge a God who did not interfere with scientific research. The scientist's task was to investigate the nature of matter : metaphysics could be set on one side and the censorship kept quiet by what seemed harmless admissions. That done, d'Alembert could proceed to his main task. Firmly based on the Lockean principle that sensation is the only source of knowledge, he shows the scientist steadily advancing, confident, as Fontenelle had been, that all the sciences are ultimately one, and implicitly denying Pascal's proposition that there is " a domain set aside, which human intelligence may not penetrate."

At the outset all knowledge was classified, after the manner of Bacon, according to the mental faculty brought into play by its pursuit.[1] This method emphasized the purely sensational

---

[1] This method of classification, which places each branch of science under one of man's three faculties, instead of taking account of their subject-matter, led to most curious results. History, according to- the *Discours*, results from memory ; science, theology and gardening from reflection, and metaphysics and the *beaux arts* from imagination. In the same way, in the *Encyclopædia* itself the classification all turns upon the utility of the subject for human purposes.

Morley (*Diderot*, i. 203) selects some interesting examples of the resulting confusions.

origin of knowledge, even if it was not satisfactory in other respects. The tree of knowledge had grown amazingly since Bacon's outline more than a century earlier. Descartes, d'Alembert suggested, though useful because he had repudiated external authority, had on the whole delayed advance. His followers had been slow to learn the folly of system-making. " It is only within the last thirty years that people have begun to renounce Cartesianism," d'Alembert wrote; " our nation, singularly eager for novelties in all matters of taste, is in matters of science extremely attached to old opinions." Newton's splendid example, however, had now shown everyone the way; science was rapidly progressing, and man learning to understand Nature, to make her his ally and fellow-conqueror.

The preliminary discourse and the *Encyclopædia* itself were throughout imbued with a practical spirit. The Encyclopædists did not realize their own assumptions or the difficulties they left unsolved. They hid things from themselves as well as from the censor. Their metaphysics, ethics and politics were all more dangerous than they knew. If God was to be reduced to a First Cause someone was sure to point out that He was unnecessary, and indeed fatal, to clear thinking. The empiricism of the *Encyclopædia* led naturally, though not inevitably, to the rigid materialism of Holbach.[1] In the same way, in ethical matters the Encyclopædists found a belief in natural religion useful in saving the sceptic from the charge of undermining morals as well as religion. But natural religion was precariously allied to a psychology which made men's ideas depend entirely on experience. Morality, in that case, was a matter of convenience, a social code which could be changed if forbidden freedoms were found after all to be compatible with social happiness. Natural religion easily developed into utilitarianism. And, in politics, utilitarianism led to democracy. For if both ability and character were the result of experience, social distinctions were arbitrary or accidental. By nature one man was as good as another—a doctrine which undermined the established order

---

[1] Holbach's most extreme conclusions had been anticipated by La Mettrie, vide *Histoire naturelle de l'Ame* (1745) and *L'Homme Machine* (1748). For a vigorous vindication of La Mettrie *vide* Lange's *History of Materialism*.

and was promptly seized upon by those who claimed that all were equally entitled to happiness and power.

It was inevitable that someone should draw these logical conclusions. Men like Diderot and Condillac had already shown the dangerous implications of the fashionable physics and psychology. Helvétius and Holbach, however, went further. *De l'Esprit, Le Système de la Nature* and *La Politique naturelle* were systematic as well as bold, uncompromising as well as dangerous. Holbach is one of the few writers who can justly be called a "materialist." He left none of the loopholes and omitted all the modifications which usually make classification difficult. Helvétius was equally unafraid of a crude and complete utilitarianism, and both writers were prepared to accept representative government as the natural inference from sensationalist psychology.

2. MATERIALISM—LOGICAL PHYSICS—DIDEROT AND HOLBACH

Diderot's letters to Mademoiselle Voland have left a record of the conversations at Holbach's where the intellectual basis of these books was hammered out in the frankest discussion. Diderot describes the conversation that arose when someone declared that even " if a single supposition explained all phenomena it would not follow from this that it was true. For who knows whether the general order allows of only one reason?" God, they decided, was scarcely worth discussing; in any case it was impossible "to introduce him into nature or discussion without darkening them." Galiani indeed took up the cudgels on behalf of the Deity, asking how the *Iliad* or the physical universe could be accounted for by the chance throwing of dice. Considering the complexity of "that well-contrived piece of villainy, the world," did it not seem probable that nature's dice were "loaded, and that there is a big Rogue up there who takes delight in cheating you"? It was Diderot who replied that, if the number of throws were infinite, accidental combinations of molecules might account for the world or anything else, and went on to refute the current argument for God's existence, pointing out that to rely upon wonders of adapta-

ion and order in nature is to forget its failures, wastefulness
nd misadaptations. In his *Lettre sur les Aveugles*, published
s early as 1749, he applied the argument from natural
daptation in an unusual way, and suggested that the apparent
erfection of many existing organisms might be the result of
sifting process involving the destruction of numerous species
f badly adapted monsters so that an evolution had taken place;
" all the faulty combinations of matter had disappeared, and
hose only had survived whose mechanism implied no important
nisadaptation (*contradiction*) and which had the power of
upporting and perpetuating themselves." [1]

Diderot's promising approach to the theory of evolution by
atural selection bore no immediate fruit. Speculation was
nainly concerned with physics, not biology. The general prin-
iples of physics already familiar in Hobbes and Spinoza
vere now supported by scientific experiment rather than by
hilosophic speculation. The most plausible view seemed to be
hat put forward by La Mettrie, that men, animals and plants
vere all combinations of molecules, only quantitatively different,
ince thought and consciousness were themselves nothing
ut the movements of material particles. Diderot, it is true,
ad his doubts, arguing that the consciousness of a complex
rganism could not result from a mere conjunction of material
articles, even if the particles themselves were endowed with
potential capacity for receiving sensations.

In 1770 Holbach published *Le Système de la Nature*. The
torm it raised was comparable only with that which Helvétius'
De l'Esprit had produced twelve years earlier. Indeed the
vorks of Holbach and Helvétius are complementary to one
nother: taken together they form a single system of philosophy.
Holbach was primarily concerned with metaphysics, Helvétius
vith ethics and psychology, whilst both made incidental ap-
lications of their theories to politics. Holbach, too, dealt at
ome length with ethics, but his psychology differed from that of
Helvétius in emphasis rather than in substance. As writers, they
re in sharp contrast. Helvétius interlarded his psychological

---

[1] Translation taken from Morley's *Diderot*, i. 94.

analysis with anecdotal illustrations, which are successful as anecdotes rather than as illustrations. There is no trifling in Holbach. His temper at times is revolutionary, and an elaborate system of argument is capped with vehement declamation against every existing institution and current superstition. Justice has never been done to the political insight of Holbach or to his power as a social critic. Few writers of the century have either his force or his sincerity, and beside him Helvétius reads like a promising undergraduate with a theory. The theory, however, was a good one, and Bentham, who spent most of his life in developing and applying it, acknowledged his debt to Helvétius, while Holbach has been almost completely forgotten.[1]

Holbach's contemporaries were appalled by his temerity. He swept away all compromises; permitted no evasions; and included priests, kings and gods in a single majestic anathema. His system had no place for free will or immortality. Voltaire was horrified, and lost no time in composing a refutation. He feared atheism scarcely less than Rousseau did, but whereas Rousseau thought that it destroyed the spirit and denied the most sacred emotions, Voltaire was afraid that to deprive the poor and uneducated of the consolation of superstitions would endanger society. God as a Creator and Dispenser of rewards and punishments was surely an essential deterrent, an omniscient Policeman who must be invented should He happen not to exist.

Holbach cared for none of these things. Science seemed to him to reveal a closed universe composed of material particles which follow inevitable laws. Matter is the word we use for the condition of existence. Of its nature we are totally ignorant, though we discover its qualities, such as motion and extension, by observation. All phenomena, conscious and unconscious, are bound together in an unbreakable chain of causation: their diversity results from innumerable changes caused by the energy

---

[1] It should be remembered, however, that translations of Holbach's works sold widely in England in the early nineteenth century and were only less effective instruments of free-thought than Paine's *Age of Reason*. For the part they played in the battle for free speech waged by Richard Carlile *vide* Wickwar, *The Struggle for the Freedom of the Press*.

nherent in matter itself. There is no room for chance or final causes or free will. Man is but one combination of particles and thought a particular kind of molecular motion, a peculiar quality of the brain, hitherto unexplained.[1] The words which men have invented to cover their ignorance of these mysteries become actively harmful to the advance of knowledge. Scientific habits of mind grow so slowly that the civilized man, who has left off seeing hobgoblins in every bush, still finds comfort in superstitions such as deity, soul, immortality and free will. Unfortunately, such inventions, which offer no rational explanation themselves and hinder the progress of knowledge, are fostered by priests and despots who profit by them. Existing religion is nothing but "the fruit of a very deep and very interested theological policy. . . . If we go back to the beginning we can always find that ignorance and fear have created gods ; fancy, enthusiasm or deceit has adorned or disfigured them : weakness worships them, credulity keeps them alive, custom respects them and tyranny supports them in order to make the blindness of men serve its own ends."

The discovery that man is infinitely small, an ephemeral being, as much subject to unchanging law as any other creation, does not lessen the need or the value of knowledge. For knowledge itself may be the most powerful of the forces compelling him[2] : when he has learned that the spiritual and the material are one, and has come to rely on science and not on theories of the supernatural, he will be able to make use of his knowledge for his own happiness. He will be able, for instance, to cure what are now known as mental diseases by physical means. He will be able so to arrange political society that sympathy, understanding and affection become the dominant motives, and scientific knowledge

---

[1] Since all thoughts are only modifications of matter, and so many of them find place in one brain, La Mettrie had argued that thoughts must be very small in size.

[2] See *Système de la Nature*, i. 387 ff., for a striking passage dealing with the futility of hoping to change human nature by religious teaching rather than by knowledge. " To tell an ambitious man not to desire power and greatness is to order him to reverse at a blow the habitual system of his ideas ; it is to speak to a deaf man. To tell a lover of impetuous temperament to stifle his passion . . . is to combat realities with chimerical speculations."

of Nature be used to serve the purpose of human happiness. When men understand Nature they will adjust their lives to her laws. The contrast of that future society, the approach of which Holbach did not doubt, with the existing authoritarian State dominated by ancient superstitions, moved him to a generous apostrophe of Nature. For Nature had become personified ; in destroying the malevolent deity of the priests, Holbach had substituted a new one, whose purposes are good and wise but not past finding out. Holbach's materialism is a gospel of hope, not of despair. "Nature invites man to love himself, incessantly to augment the sum of his happiness : Religion orders him to love only a formidable God who is worthy of hatred ; to detest and despise himself, and to sacrifice to his terrible idol the sweetest and most lawful pleasures. Nature bids man consult his reason, and take it for his guide : Religion teaches him that this reason is corrupted, that it is a faithless, lying guide, implanted by a treacherous God to mislead His creatures. Nature tells man to seek light, to search for the truth : Religion enjoins upon him to examine nothing, to remain in ignorance. Nature says to man : 'Cherish glory, labour to win esteem, be active, courageous, industrious ': Religion says to him : 'Be humble, abject, pusillanimous, live in retreat, busy thyself with prayer, meditation, devout rites; be useless to thyself, and do nothing for others.' Nature proposes for her model, men endowed with noble, energetic, beneficent souls, who have usefully served their fellow-citizens : Religion makes a show and a boast of the abject spirits, the pious enthusiasts, the phrenetic penitents, the vile fanatics, who by their ridiculous opinions have troubled empires. . . . Nature says to man ' Thou art free and no power on earth can lawfully strip thee of thy rights ': Religion cries to him that he is a slave condemned by God to groan under the rod of God's representatives. Nature bids man love the country that gave him birth, serve it with all loyalty, bind his interest to hers against every hand that might be raised against her : Religion commands him to obey without a murmur the tyrants that oppress his country, to take their part against her, to chain his fellow-citizens under their lawless caprices. . . . If politics, which supernatural ideas have

so shamefully depraved, were to take account of the nature of man, it would contribute far more than all the religion in the world to make communities happy, powerful and prosperous under reasonable authority. . . . Nature herself would teach princes that they are men and not gods ; that they are citizens deputed by their fellow-citizens to watch over the safety of all. . . . Instead of attributing to the divine vengeance all the wars, the famines, the plagues that lay nations low, would it not have been more useful to show them that such calamities are due to the passions, the indolence, the tyranny of their princes, who sacrifice the nations to their hideous delirium? "

3. THE GREATEST-HAPPINESS PRINCIPLE—LOGICAL ETHICS—HELVÉTIUS

Bentham tells us that it was in the works of Helvétius that he first read that the " greatest happiness of the greatest number " was the criterion by which individual and governmental action should be judged. The idea of utility, the conception that actions are to be judged good or bad by their effect upon human happiness, had been of course implicit in the works of irreligious social theorists throughout the history of thought. In the eighteenth century almost all the *philosophes* may be considered utilitarians. Saint-Pierre had laid down the utilitarian principle in exact terms.[1] Hutchison, Hume and Priestley, and even the pious Paley, had all founded their systems of morals on utility, while the constant appeal to humanity in the works of Voltaire, Turgot, and other Encyclopædists, in itself constitutes a recognition of the utilitarian principle.[2] In Helvétius, however, it was explicitly laid down for the first time that if we would judge rightly of laws " it is indispensable to be able to refer them all to a single principle, such as that of the utility of the public—that is to say, of the greatest number of men submitted to the same form of government : a principle of which no one realizes the range and possibilities ; a principle that

---

[1] *Vide supra*, p. 61.
[2] For the sources of Helvétius' views *vide* Keim, *Helvétius*, p. 222 ff. *Cp.* also Halévy, *La Formation du Radicalisme philosophique* : i. *La Jeunesse de Bentham*.

contains all morality and legislation, which many people repeat without understanding it and of which even legislators have still but a superficial idea, if, that is, one may judge by the unhappiness of almost all the peoples of the earth." [1]

Helvétius desired to found ethics and politics on a scientific psychology. " If poetry, geometry, astronomy, and, in general, all the sciences advance more or less rapidly towards perfection, while morality seems scarcely to have left its cradle, it is because men, being forced to unite in society to give themselves laws, were obliged to form a system of morality before they had learned from observation its true principles." Montesquieu, who had investigated and classified various types of government, had begun at the wrong place, for he had neither established the principles which legislators ought to recognize in common nor tried to construct a science of human nature. He had succeeded in giving hints to the legislator, not in founding a sociology. His contribution was rather to the art than to the science of government. If, as he admitted, human nature was essentially the same everywhere, why discuss the accidental vagaries of men, born of prejudice and ignorance, before being in a position to understand them? Helvétius thought, as Chastellux put it, " that before examining systems of legislation and comparing them, man himself must be studied, and the structure of institutions to which he should be subject must be based on the nature of man himself. Such was the object of his book *De l'Esprit*, which, though later than *L'Esprit des Lois* in order of chronology, immediately preceded it in order of ideas." [2]

This difference in outlook between Montesquieu and Helvétius could scarcely be better illustrated than by contrasting their methods of dealing with religion. Ethical systems and religious cults differ in different countries for local reasons although human nature is substantially the same everywhere. This was common ground to both writers. Montesquieu, however, was interested mainly in the differences, Helvétius concerned with essential similarities. Montesquieu thought that local varieties

---

[1] *De l'Esprit*, Discourse 2.   [2] Quoted by Keim, *op. cit.*, 234.

would remain even though reforms might improve the natural adjustment in each case; Helvétius could not see why there should not be a universal religion deliberately constructed to suit everyone alike. "An universal religion," he wrote, "cannot be founded except on principles that are eternal and invariable, that are drawn from the nature of men and things, and that, like the propositions of geometry, are capable of the most rigorous demonstration." Are there such principles? "Yes, if they vary, it will be only in some of their applications to those different countries where chance has placed the different nations." [1]

The basis for a new psychology had already been laid down by Condillac and other disciples of Locke. At the very time that Hartley was developing the principles of mental association, La Mettrie was writing that development consisted in multiplying desires: the higher the organism the more sensations, and therefore the more cravings, it possessed. Helvétius began by assuming that man was a purely physical organism capable of receiving sensations and of forming ideas and mental habits, as a result of remembering and associating them. Descartes should have written "I feel, therefore I am," since our only certainty is the fact that we have sensations. Some of these are pleasant, some painful; we try to repeat the former and avoid the latter. "The simple recital of what I feel," he writes, "forms my judgment." Judgment, that is, is the memory that one sensation is preferable to another; this memory may in time become a mental habit and develop into a passion. Helvétius and Holbach were both explicit in asserting that there was only one possible spring of human action: "there is no other motive than the hope of a good or the fear of an evil." From this statement it would seem to follow that all affectionate conduct in private life, as well as public service and political obedience, is the result of a calculation that good conduct is rewarded and bad punished. It does not, of course,

---

[1] Helvétius insists that his method is the scientific one. *Cp.* preface to *De l'Esprit* : "It is by facts that I have ascended to causes. I imagined that morality ought to be treated like all other sciences and founded on experiment, as well as natural philosophy."

imply that every particular action is based upon such a calculation for, in adult life, habits and passions have been developed. Analysis nevertheless reveals a basis of self-interest in every action. We call our actions altruistic when they happen to benefit other people as well as satisfying ourselves. Sound virtue consists in finding one's own happiness in the happiness of the greatest number.[1]

In a civilized society it remains true, then, that men can only search for pleasure and avoid pain, but they may have learned to do so in indirect and surprising ways. The desire to gratify the senses, for instance, may lead to a passion for money in a society where money is the only channel through which so many gratifications may be obtained. Power, in the same way, is not a thing which men desire for its own sake, and in a society which provided men with more freedom and satisfaction without forcing them to fight for it the desire for power, as well as the craving for money, would cease to exist. The moral or altruistic passions prove on examination to have a similar indirect basis. Men want a just society because they fear the consequences to themselves of existing injustices, while a virtue like saintliness arises from a mistaken belief that asceticism will be rewarded in the next life—a form of selfishness far-sighted enough to look beyond the grave.[2] In any case, men can only search for pleasure, and everyone secretly knows that his kindness, generosity or self-sacrifice is really due to a hope that it will be repaid by similar favours from others, or that he will get a reputation for virtue, and so enjoy a more comfortable life.[3]

A virtuous action is one that promotes the greatest happiness, and truly virtuous men, like Lycurgus and Jesus Christ, have acquired "the habit of performing actions that are of use to their country." They have discovered that they are most happy when

---

[1] In all this Helvétius was almost certainly indebted to Mandeville. For a full account *vide* Kaye's introduction to his edition of *The Fable of the Bees*.

[2] "If a hermit or monk imposes on himself the law of silence, flogs himself every night, lives on pulse and water, sleeps on straw, offers to God his nastiness and ignorance, he thinks by virtue of emaciation to make a fortune in heaven" (*De l'Homme*, 1772).

[3] It was this that Madame du Deffand had in mind when she said that Helvétius "had told everybody's secret."

other people are happy, and that their pleasure lies in public service. The hero is a man who enjoys heroics, the saint one who finds asceticism pleasant, and the kind man one to whom benevolence is attractive. These statements seem to amount to a tautology. It is true that men prefer what they prefer, but the problem for the utilitarian moralist is to explain why some find pleasure in the gratification of the senses and others in the general welfare. The next stage was to give an account of the pains and pleasures actually at work in society, but the task of classifying human motives was one that Helvétius left to Bentham. It is conventional to say that the hedonist denies the altruistic impulses of men, offers no basis for social actions, and degrades all morality into enlightened self-seeking. Helvétius is, indeed, more open to this criticism than most utilitarians : he seems even to forget at times what he is at others at pains to emphasize—that in the course of education a desire which was originally purely selfish may have been transformed into a habit of social action. On occasion he writes as if man was a purely rational and calculating creature, who, before taking any action, considered whether the gratitude and public esteem which he would earn by kindness and generosity were, on balance, preferable to the immediate advantages to be won by brutality and fraud. Yet he argues that men need a universal religion, extols the Christianity of the gospels in contrast to current popery, and ends by asking why we should not " deify the public good."

Now how can a purely egoistic creature, who has, in some unexplained way, become part of an organized society, ever be inspired with a desire to serve the general good? To this question hedonists have given three main answers. Shaftesbury, followed for a time by Diderot, believed in a moral sense, a capacity for sympathy, the origin of which may be explained by the fact that it is unpleasant to watch other people suffering.[1] Bentham himself seemed to accept this view in several passages. In the second place, it was possible to rely on the

---

[1] Diderot later abandoned this doctrine, and he seemed often to hold that morality as we know it is simply a trick of the ruling classes to keep the common people in order.

theory of natural harmony ; " to do unto others as you would they should do unto you " is only common sense. Hartley had argued that Christianity itself needs no support except that of reason, since it always pays to do good to your neighbours. Though, as we have seen, there are traces of this doctrine in *De l'Esprit*, Helvétius is concerned mainly with the third solution, which was later to occupy Bentham's attention. In the absence of a natural harmony, it seemed possible to create an artificial harmony by the scientific development of education and by legislation designed to make honesty the best policy. It seemed wisest to assume that men would always behave selfishly and then so to weight the scales that enlightened selfishness would lead to the same results as genuine altruism. " Every man," said Hume, " should be held to be a knave," and Helvétius declared that it was " necessary to expect little from men in order to love them." Goodness, then, depends on the provision of the right incentive : men would be lovable only if taught to obey the Golden Rule from self-interest. Human beings are donkeys : if you hold the carrot in the right place they will walk the right path. The problem is to find the suitable carrot and present it so skilfully that from infancy onwards the child will be always lured into behaving nicely. And as all children are the same at birth the same carrots will do for everyone.

Helvétius was as contemptuous of Rousseau's theory that men are born good as he was of the clerical view that they were naturally wicked. They are not born, he said, with any " innate principle of virtue " or " natural compassion," but they may learn both, when they see the punishment that society inflicts on injustice and cruelty. Originally, their minds are blank sheets upon which the educationist can write whatever he thinks best, and " morality, law-making and pedagogy " are consequently a single science.

The differences between men are therefore due to variety of experience, of education, of physical and political environment. Some children, Helvétius admits, may be born with more energy than others, but in gifts all are identical. Nature, he says, " never made a dunce," while genius is the result of some accident which directs an individual's mind strongly and continuously to a particular subject. Under a good system of education and laws, therefore, creative ability can be manufactured. "It is certain," he writes, "that great men, who now appear haphazard, will in the future be produced by the legislature, and the abilities and virtues of the citizens in great empires need not be left so much to chance: by really good education they may be infinitely multiplied."

If character and ability are the product of education and law, Rousseau was wrong in suggesting that the child should be left alone to develop good habits. At times he had written as if all knowledge except that picked up in the course of daily life was actually harmful. Helvétius thought, on the contrary, that the more knowledge could be passed on to the child from the experience of the past the more virtuous he was likely to become. For virtue was intelligent self-interest, the result of knowing that honesty was the best policy. In a good State it would really be so: the child would see the solid advantages of goodness instead of hearing it extolled in a conventional manner and supported by supernatural sanctions, the unreality of which it soon discovered. It was no good to teach children the gospel of altruism if they soon learned that it actually paid to be avaricious, intolerant and cruel. The discrepancy between education and laws accounted, in Helvétius' view, for much of the misery as well as the hypocrisy of the world. "The majority of the people of Europe," he wrote, "honour virtue in theory; this is the effect of their education. They despise it in practice, which is the effect of their governments. . . . No one in any case has concurred in the public good to his own prejudice, so that the only method of forming virtuous citizens is to unite the interests of the individual with those of the public." If the laws were made with this object in view, that "nobility of soul" which is the habit of finding one's own happiness in the public welfare might become the rule, not the exception, among men.

4. REPRESENTATIVE GOVERNMENT—LOGICAL POLITICS

Helvétius' political system followed logically from this psychological basis. He laid down the utilitarian premise that no government ought to have "any other object than the happiness of the majority." Now happiness is a personal thing the result of the individual's own seeking. The business of the State is therefore to promote freedom. If the right penalties are attached to unsocial conduct, men will freely seek virtue The right laws will ensure both happiness and righteousness.

"Every country," wrote Helvétius, "always counts among the gifts of nature the virtues derived from the form of its government." Thus the Englishman who "thinks himself a being of superior nature and takes the French for a giddy brained trifling people" ought to recognize that "his fellow countrymen owe their spirit of patriotism" to the civil freedom of England.[1] In England the security of individual right makes men happy. The rights of man should be everywhere guaranteed, not because they are natural, except in the sense of arising from natural desires, but because they are useful and conducive to happiness.

The utilitarian reasons for granting men the rights they demand are clear enough. They should, for instance, be free to worship as they please. There is only one case, remark Helvétius, "in which toleration can be detrimental, and that is when it tolerates a religion which is intolerant, such as the Catholic, which causes universal destruction if it gets the upper hand." Liberty of thought and of expression, on the other hand, can be almost absolute. "To publish the truth can never be harmful," and truth, Helvétius argued, anticipating John Stuart Mill, could be discovered only by open discussion "Truth is a method of increasing happiness, the silence that

---

[1] Helvétius went as far as to admit that the insular situation of England might have in some measure contributed to her freedom, but he did not grant Montesquieu's thesis that climate could have been a serious factor. "The Englishman, who feeds on bread and meat and breathes a foggy air, is certainly not less intelligent than the lean Spaniard, who lives on garlic and onions in a very dry atmosphere."

s enforced by authority is the principal cause of the miseries
of nations."

Helvétius' principles seem naturally to lead to some form
of democracy. If ability and character are not the result of
inherited differences, but of artificial privileges, the usual justification of despotism or aristocracy disappears. What answer
could be given to those who claimed that all were equally
entitled to happiness and equally able to exercise power? If
men are born with substantially the same faculties, if their
ideas are the result of their education and environment, if they
must seek their own interest and are capable, with instruction,
of perceiving the right way of attaining it, the argument for
social and political equality is unanswerable. Any minority
group which rules must necessarily be swayed by what Bentham
termed " its sinister interest." It will find, that is, that its own
pleasure results from a partisan policy and not from pursuit of
the happiness of the greatest number. If the majority itself is
in control, however, it follows that the search for its own interest
will result in the greatest happiness for the greatest number.
Bentham was to reach this conclusion with reluctance, when
experience had taught him the strength of the " sinister interest "
of the aristocracy. Abstract argument sufficed for Helvétius.
Where a single individual or an aristocracy was in control " the
equilibrium of forces " resulting from democracy was disturbed,
and a struggle of group interests was inevitable. The worst of
all sinister interests was, of course, the Church, and Helvétius
remarks that " the real crime of the Jesuits was not the depravity
of their morals but their constitution, riches, power, ambition,
and the impossibility of reconciling their interests with those
of the nation."

Helvétius, then, was, within limits, a democrat, and in favour
of representative government. Amongst the greatest number who
were to rule he did not include the uneducated and the poor.
Without education or property a man could not be expected
to see any advantages in moral conduct; indeed Helvétius admitted that the poor were necessarily immoral, and argued that
private property was an essential without which a man " had
no country." " Have not the poor," he asks, " too many wants

to be virtuous?" The poor were haunted by jealousy of the rich, and mistakenly convinced that to possess riches was to be happy.[1] It seemed, then, that Montesquieu and d'Argenson had been right in thinking that a complete democracy was possible only where there was economic equality. Where riches or birth carried with them the privileges of idleness there would necessarily be divisions and unhappiness : " the labourers will die of happiness and the idlers will not be more happy."

Money, he agreed, was bad for virtue, and in a State governed by good laws men would not acquire a passion for wealth but would find "honour" a better substitute. Money, however, was a great source of happiness, and luxury, so far from being in itself an evil, was, as Montesquieu and Melon insisted, good for trade as well as pleasant. As a hedonist, Helvétius could scarcely take the ascetic view of the Utopian communists. The ostensibly economic argument for and against luxury in the eighteenth century is really only one aspect of the essential conflict between religious repression and austerity, on the one hand, and the Renaissance assertion of the right to happiness and freedom, on the other. While admitting therefore that wealth is a source of disharmony in society, Helvétius does not suggest the suppression of private property and money-making. Communism, he said, had always failed when it had been tried and private gain was a necessary incentive. He therefore came to an intermediate conclusion. The good State would " assign some property to each individual," would relieve the poor of the terror of penury and the rich from the misery of excessive wealth. Until such a redistribution of wealth was made, society would always live precariously. What, Helvétius asked, could prevent the poor some day realizing their strength and declaring themselves heirs to all the land and owners of all the wealth? He suggested that the wise course was to take the matter in hand in time, to tax the highest incomes out of existence for the benefit of all, and through legal means bring about sub-

---

[1] "O ye indigent, you are certainly not the most miserable of mortals! To alleviate your sufferings, behold the idly opulent, whose passions provide almost all their amusements, and who cannot divest themselves of discontent but by sensations which are too poignant to be frequent."

tantial equality. To combine private property with taxation of
the rich in the interests of the poor seemed the best solution.

Finally Helvétius took the usual eighteenth-century view
that large democracies become corrupt, and that the best sanc-
ion of social conduct, the fear of public disgrace, diminishes
proportionately with the size of the country. Internal federalism
was the solution. Men will search for the greatest happiness
of only a limited number of fellow-citizens. Internationally,
small republics should retain their own individuality, but form
themselves into a federal league, thus safeguarding themselves
against tyrannical neighbours. France would do well to divide
herself into thirty provinces or republics of about equal size.
Each provincial republic would have its own law, its own police
and elected magistrates, and would send its own deputies to a
superior council, whose business would be external relations, and
supervision of the provinces only when important changes were
under consideration by the constituent members of the federal
whole. Helvétius, like a number of other eighteenth-century
writers, was in revolt against the centralization of French administration and, like Rousseau and, to a lesser degree, Turgot,
an early apostle of regionalism.

Although not a federalist, Holbach reached political conclusions substantially similar to those of Helvétius. The political
theory of his *Politique naturelle* is like his metaphysics—bold
and systematic rather than original. In his treatment of the causes
of decay in states, there are traces of Montesquieu's theory
of the principles of governments; he speaks of the separate
interest of intermediary bodies and of the general will in a
manner faintly reminiscent of Rousseau.[1] He reproduces Locke's
theory of the basis of political obligation : a government was
legitimate only if it sought the public good, or, in his alternative
phraseology, legislated according to the guidance of nature.
Such a government would always keep the social compact : it
would legislate by consent, since the people would always desire
their own happiness. "Only the consent of the nation," he wrote,

---

[1] Holbach speaks throughout of the Sovereign as identical with the ruling
government, and thus avoids all the philosophic difficulties involved in the
conception of final and unlimited authority.

" makes the Sovereign legitimate," and he was less willing than Locke to assume that apathy denotes consent. The populace should not constantly interfere with the executive, but might demand that the government should be the kind they desired, and should revolt against arbitrary government. Consent constitutes "a supreme will, an indelible charter, an inalienable right, a right anterior to all other rights." Holbach constantly emphasizes the need for "public spirit," which he describes as a "reasoned attachment to the laws, the fatherland and the government." No State can be happy which is not animated by virtuous pursuit of the public interest on the part of its citizens, and this seems most likely to be obtained by a democratic system of government. Holbach fears, as Montesquieu had done, that popular government tends to degenerate, sectional interests to be formed, and the power to pass into the hands of demagogues.[1] The mass of the people he thought too ignorant for self-government. On the whole, he favoured a system of representative government, in which the right to vote would be confined to men of property, who are alone likely to feel their responsibility, since they alone have a stake in the country.

Holbach's use of natural law is not simply that of Locke. He accepts Helvétius' formula, and in fact tests every suggestion by referring it to "the greatest-happiness principle." He thus represents a half-way house between Locke and Bentham, and though he begins with Locke's phraseology his conclusions are substantially those of the "Constitutional Code." At first, indeed, he seems to anticipate nineteenth-century Benthamism with surprising completeness. He has the same belief in the State's power to influence the motives and behaviour of its citizens. Intelligent laws, education, and a peaceful and careful administrative system, can make men happy. On the political side the State may be a positive factor in producing the greatest happiness of the greatest number.

---

[1] It should always be remembered that eighteenth-century writers who speak of democracy are seldom thinking of representative government, but have Aristotle's warning in mind and associate democracy with the demagogy of Athens as described by the Greek writers of the fourth century.

In economic affairs, however, Holbach was not as optimistic as Bentham, and left it to Adam Smith and his disciples to develop the doctrine of the "invisible hand" which turns the selfishness of men into public beneficence. He was himself content to argue that free trade was obvious common sense, since nature had decreed that the surplus of one nation would supply the deficiency of another. Governments should repudiate the remnants of mercantilism, and seek prosperity and plenty instead of money and power. The less direct part the government attempted to play in trade the better. The government, he wrote, "could do nothing for the merchant, except leave him alone. No regulations can guide him in his enterprises so well as his own interest. . . . The State owes commerce nothing except its protection. Among commercial nations, those which allow their subjects most unlimited liberty may be sure of soon excelling all others."[1] Holbach, however, was aware of the dangers as well as the advantages of universal *laissez-faire*: the industrial revolution had not yet taught men to think commercial prosperity synonymous with happiness. He proved himself still a man of the eighteenth century when, like Montesquieu and d'Argenson, he uttered a warning against allowing the prosperity which may come from the abolition of privilege, monopoly and restraint of trade, to swamp real happiness, which depended on other factors in addition to economic welfare. He did not assume that for a man to be successful in business in itself constituted him a public benefactor, or that production was all-important, and that distribution would automatically prove perfect if left alone. He suggested that, "other things being equal," it is as well for a nation to live off its own soil, to retain some independence, and not to multiply its needs unnecessarily. Great wealth, he thought, was apt to create an unreal demand for the new and fantastic. Moreover the State should be concerned "to enrich its subjects as equally as possible." The labourer, the manufacturer, the sailor and even the savant play a part in production and distribution. A wise government would not

---

[1] *Pol. Nat.*, ii. 7, xxviii.

permit "wealth to be concentrated in the hands of a small number of citizens. . . . Governments seem to have altogether neglected this important truth. In almost all nations more than three-quarters of the subjects possess nothing. . . . Yet it is property which binds the individual to his country. . . . When all the citizens can procure themselves ease by moderate work the State can rely upon them for support, when a small number of men absorb all the property and wealth in a State they become the masters of that State, and it cannot without the greatest difficulty afterwards take away from them the wealth they have amassed." [1] There comes a point, too, when commerce ceases to be an advantage; luxury has caused the ruin of many empires, it leads to strife and rivalry : " the globe ceases to be large enough " for the merchant who, " in his delirium," finds " a desert island an object of importance " ; in time " nations are ready to cut each other's throats " for possession of " some heaps of sand " where greed already imagines treasure. " Entire nations," he continues, " are the dupes of the avarice of hungry business men, who beguile them with the hope of wealth, the fruit of which they gather for themselves only. States are depopulated, taxation piled up, and nations impoverished, in order to satisfy the avarice of a small group of citizens who enjoy themselves because of their fellow-citizens' folly. Thus wealth has become the signal for war between Powers. There is one people who in the transports of their greed seem to have formed the extravagant project of usurping the commerce of the world and making themselves owners of the seas—an iniquitous and mad project, whose execution, if it should be possible, would hastily bring the nation which is guided by this frenzy to certain ruin." [2]

Holbach's analysis of the evils of his own day led him at length to prophecies which are more likely to attract attention after a century of industrial development. The pursuit of riches, he argued, has a natural limit. " If one might read in the future the effects of this unbridled passion for trade which now divides the nations one would see, perhaps, that when they had destroyed

---

[1] *Pol. Nat.*, ii. 7, xxx.　　　　　[2] *Ibid.*, ii. 7, xxxii.-xxxiii.

each other under this pretext, the peoples would severally end by confining themselves to farming their own land, engaging only in that trade which proved essential for each. Governments more humane, just and sensible will perceive that money does not make the true happiness of society any more than of individuals. They will get to dislike sending armies of citizens to perish annually in scorching climates, in fighting and on the seas. At last, perhaps the day will come when Indians, having learned the art of war from Europeans, will hunt them from their shores, where their greed has inevitably made them odious."[1]

D'Alembert remarked that Holbach's system would be excellent if there were no such thing as history. And this, the orthodox plea of conservatism, contains an important if hackneyed truth. Helvétius and Holbach understood much of the needs of man : they saw that he could be rendered happier by a more reasonable social organization and that he would behave more reasonably under a happier one. But their temper was absolute and unhistorical. Just as they thought of each newborn child as a new slate to write upon, so they thought of society at any moment as a slate on which certain stupid things had been written which could be wiped off without leaving any permanent marks. Even Turgot, who recognized some of the power of inheritance and the inertia of accumulated tradition, could write to the King that the results of universal education would be that " in ten years your nation will be no longer recognizable." In that time every child would have become an enlightened citizen serving the public interest. Sensationalist psychology opened the way for an enormous optimism. The Encyclopædists never dreamed that if men were offered the truth they would not leap for it, that if they were told ugly facts they would prefer pleasant lies, that if reasonable ideals were offered them they would continue to act as their fathers had done ; they did not see that the follies of the past were not only imposed but ingrained, that men carried their history not only on their backs but in their heads.

---

[1] *Ibid.*, ii. 7, xxxiv.

CHAPTER VIII

DEMOCRACY

I. NATURAL RIGHTS AND POPULAR SOVEREIGNTY

UNTIL late in the eighteenth century the word "democracy" was still commonly used in its strict Aristotelean sense : it meant a form of government under which the assembled populace voted their own laws in the market-place and appointed their own administrative officers to enforce them. It was a system which the individualist feared, holding that mob rule was even more tyrannous than personal despotism. Democracy was objectionable as an alternative to the bureaucracy of Louis XV. for two reasons. First, believers in the rights of men disliked any system which located sovereignty in a single body ; the sovereignty of the people was repugnant because, like personal despotism, it put will above law and assumed that law proceeds from the transient wills of men, not from the eternal and irrevocable ordinances of God and nature. Secondly, it was not a system applicable to a modern State, and it was therefore discussed mainly for the sake of logical completeness and in deference to Aristotle. Rousseau declared that democracy was suitable only in the city-state, and added that in any case it was a system for gods, not for men. Yet it was he more than any other man who gave the idea of popular sovereignty its vogue : it was he who provided the slogans and the arguments which enabled the founders of nineteenth-century representative government to describe their system as democracy.

To most eighteenth-century French observers the British Constitution, as interpreted by Montesquieu, seemed the one practical alternative to despotism. In England, individual liberty was secured by institutional checks upon the abuse of executive power. Such a system had nothing to do with democracy : it was described as "republicanism"[1] or "mixed

---

[1] *Cp.* Kant's *Essay on Perpetual Peace.* He refers (in 1795) to "the common error of confusing the republican with the democratic constitution . . . the form of government is either republican or despotic. Republicanism is the political principle of severing the executive power of the government from

government," being aristocratic in substance, monarchical in form and popular only in so far as it permitted some plebeian persons to assist in electing its aristocratic House of Commons. Its essential feature was the separation of powers and the absence of sovereignty : it was " a government of laws, not of men." The *philosophes* knew the value of an independent judiciary and believed the English common law, based on nature and experience, to be secure from essential alteration by King, Parliament or people. They did not see that personal rights could be easily overridden in England when the landlords who dominated Parliament cared to exercise their effective sovereignty ; they did not grasp the significance of the Enclosure Acts, which in a few years swept away the ancient property rights of the English peasantry. Nor could they anticipate the repeal of the Habeas Corpus Act and the political persecutions which were soon to prove that the reputed separation of powers was but a frail protection for an unorthodox minority who insisted upon the right of free speech even in time of war.

The British Constitution, however, was a symbol of freedom on the Continent. It is an odd fact that when England and France went to war in 1792 both sides believed themselves to be fighting for the British Constitution. There was not a squire in England who would not have said that the cause of England against France was the cause of freedom and the British Constitution against French tyranny and revolutionary innovations. In France, meanwhile, revolutionaries were setting up a Constitution in direct imitation of the British. Paine was right in his answer to Burke : the principles of 1689 were at work in France, not in England.

When the era of revolutions, inaugurated by the revolt of the American Colonies, arrived, two sets of ideas and phrases were current : revolutionaries talked of the rights of man and thought them best guaranteed by the separation of powers

---

the legislature. . . . Democracy, in the proper sense of the word, is of necessity despotism . . . 'the whole people,' so-called, who carry their measure are really not all, but only a majority ; so that here the universal will is in contradiction with itself and with the principle of freedom" (Kant's *Perpetual Peace*, Miss Campbell Smith's translation, pp. 124-125).

and the British Constitution : they also acclaimed democracy and the sovereignty of the people. Now both these concepts—indefeasible rights and unlimited sovereignty—are legal fictions, not descriptions of reality, and the recognition of the one idea in absolute form would make the adoption of the other logically impossible. Constitutions and their makers, however, are not bound to adhere to any single logical system, and the numerous revolutionary constitutions of the later eighteenth and of the nineteenth centuries all show the marks of conflict between the two concepts. The new constitutions were therefore based on the sovereignty of the people, while they evaded its implications by the separation of powers ; they declare rights inalienable and indefeasible, and leave their practical limitation to the wills of peoples and parliaments. Sometimes there is more democracy and less stress upon rights ; sometimes Montesquieu and the separation of powers play a more prominent part than Rousseau and direct democracy.[1]

The type of government which was called democracy in the nineteenth century was therefore a mixture of two systems which the eighteenth century had kept distinct, and indeed regarded as antithetic. Even where, as was commonly the case, new institutions were based on the English pattern they were defended by phrases and arguments for which Rousseau, as well as Montesquieu, was responsible. Although Rousseau despised the British Constitution, and ridiculed the whole idea of representation, his followers could adapt his theory of democracy in support of both. In *The Social Contract* revolutionaries found that incompatibles could be combined and men

---

[1] It is to be noticed that the sovereignty of the people was open to a less exact interpretation than Rousseau's : Locke had avoided the phrase while justifying the Revolution of 1688 as a legitimate exercise of the ultimate rights of the people—a theory which conceded the whole principle of government by consent and therefore, by an unavoidable further step, of self-government. In the nineteenth century any form of government which included a form of popular election was described as democracy. It would have saved much confusion if the British system had been called representative government and democracy reserved for systems which at least attempted to approach Rousseau's ideal of direct government by providing for the popular election of executive officials and for plebiscites and referenda.

retain their natural and absolute rights while submitting to a sovereign authority. Rousseau's conception of the General Will turned what had hitherto seemed a contradiction into a truism. Popular government no longer appeared as the antithesis of individual freedom, but was assumed to be its necessary condition. This assumption was so general in the nineteenth century that men like de Tocqueville and John Stuart Mill were forced to explain at length to nineteenth-century democrats what everyone had taken for granted before the Revolution—that without safeguards democracy might be repressive to individuality. The voice of the people was no longer the untaught folly of the mob but the vehicle of divine revelation.

Crucial though Rousseau's argument was in the development of political thought, it was the spirit which infused his life and work which was the secret of his immense influence. The attack of Voltaire and the Encyclopædists was directed mainly against clericalism and scarcely tinged with democratic passion. The *philosophes* were critics : Rousseau spoke as one of the common people. He wrote not as a satirist or a humanitarian but as a man who himself suffered under an intolerable sense of injustice. His books were attempts to objectify his own conflicts—conflicts which commonly originated within himself but which always seemed to be, and sometimes in fact were, the outcome of social corruption and State intolerance. Thus the key to Rousseau's philosophy lies in the *Confessions*, where he portrays himself as a man of good instincts, good intentions and friendly disposition driven to knavery, buffoonery and misanthropy by the artificiality and falsehood of society. Each of his books is therefore an attempt to explain and resolve the miseries and humiliations of thwarted men—and Rousseau assumed that his own difficulties were typical—in an unjust and unequal society. His books contain numerous formal inconsistencies which are explicable only in the light of his emotional experiences. The clue to Rousseau's works is his own psychological history.

Each of Rousseau's attacks on the existing social system, each of the remedies he proposed for its transformation, sprang out of his own passionate misery and his consciousness of the miseries of others. And in every case he wrote with so much power and insight that he expressed the discontent and the aspirations of multitudes of men who had no other spokesman. Beginning as an anarchist in revolt against all social coercion, he came in time, as Plato had done, to a conclusion which made the State everything and the individual nothing. In the *Discourse on the Influence of the Arts and Sciences* he declared that social misery and individual depravity were the results of artificiality and sophistication. In the *Discourse on Inequality* he argued that the institution of private property was the curse of civilization. The first period of Rousseau's writing was thus devoted to denunciation of existing society; it ended spectacularly with his formal break from the *philosophes*, who attacked not society but religion. This rupture was signalized by two letters—one to Voltaire, defending God against the charge of injustice and indifference, and a second to d'Alembert, who had dared, in his article on Geneva, to praise Rousseau's birthplace for the wrong reasons, belittling its Puritanism and commending its theatre. Then came the great epoch of Rousseau's life, when he turned his face from Paris and sought in the peace of the country to objectify his personal revolt and to expound its real implications. In the *Nouvelle Héloise* he idealized the conception of friendship which he had always failed to realize in his own life and insisted that happiness is to be found in trusting to the instinctive goodness of men and women. In the *Emile* he explained that if human relationships were ever to be satisfactory the existing system of education would have to be transformed, and he pictured the happy results of a natural education which would give men mastery and freedom, save them from the miseries which he had himself undergone and which could alone serve as a basis for a natural society of free and happy men and women. Finally, long brooding over the problems of government led him to begin a full-length work upon the relation of the individual to the State. Of this only one part—known as *The Social Contract*—was completed. Its thesis was that although natural simplicity and economic equality had gone for ever, a strong State could still make men substantially equal, and could offer them that higher type of freedom and happiness which comes from voluntarily sacrificing self to the public good. In the last period of Rousseau's life, persecution, both real and imaginary, overthrew the precarious equilibrium in which he lived : in the *Letters from the Mountain*, however, he was able to vindicate himself against the authorities who persecuted him, and in his *Confessions, Dialogues* and *Reveries* to explain and justify his life against the attacks of the *philosophes*.

2. THE INDIVIDUALISM OF ROUSSEAU—THE EARLY DISCOURSES

Rousseau's first published work already foreshadowed his later rupture with the *philosophes*. It was a challenge to the main trend of the century, an attack upon the rationalism and sophistication which was its special pride. What, asked the Academy of Dijon, had been the moral effect of the rebirth of the arts and sciences? Had the Renaissance, and by implication every increase of knowledge and culture, had good or bad effects upon humanity? The question answered itself in Rousseau's mind. How happy and care-free he had been as a wanderer in Savoy, or when living an instinctive life in the society of Madame de Warens! How morose, how conscience-stricken he had become, and how suspicious of those who offered him friendship and hospitality in Paris ! If his life had been poisoned by contact with sophisticated persons, were not the *philosophes*, and all the brilliant society he met, in the same case? The form of his answer came to him as a sudden flash of illumination. "If ever anything resembled a sudden inspiration, it was the commotion which began in me as I read this. All at once I felt myself dazzled by a thousand sparkling lights ; crowds of vivid ideas thronged into my mind with a force and confusion that threw me into unspeakable agitation ; I felt my head whirling in a giddiness like that of intoxication. A violent palpitation oppressed me ; unable to walk for difficulty of breathing, I sank under one of the trees of the avenue, and passed half-an-hour there in such a condition of excitement that when I arose I saw that the front of my waistcoat was all wet with tears, though I was wholly unconscious of shedding them. Ah, if ever I could have written a quarter of what I saw and felt under that tree with what clearness should I have brought out all the contra dictions of our social system; with what simplicity I should have demonstrated that man is good naturally, and that by institutions only is he debased." [1]

The theme of Rousseau's essay was that of Genesis, a re statement of the Protestant doctrine of the Fall of Man in the speculative terms of eighteenth-century anthropology. Man born for goodness and innocence, had tasted the fruit of the Tree of Knowledge, had learned to think of interest rather than spontaneously to follow his natural instincts; Rousseau himself hitherto almost care-free and conscienceless, had been tempted if not by Eve at least by Madame d'Epinay, and lost both his innocence and his happiness.[2] Before art, knowledge and culture had corrupted man his "morals were rude, but natural." " In our day, now that more subtle study and a more refined taste have reduced the art of pleasing to a system, there prevails in modern manners a servile and deceptive conformity; so that one would think every mind had been cast in the same mould Politeness requires this thing, decorum that; ceremony has its forms and fashion its laws, and these we must always follow never the promptings of our own nature. We no longer dare seem what we really are, but lie under a perpetual restraint in the meantime the herd of men, which we call society, all act under the same circumstances exactly alike. . . . Ignorance is held in contempt, but a dangerous scepticism has succeeded it." Physical health as well as moral integrity had been sacrificed

---

[1] Second letter to M. de Malesherbes. Vide *Confessions*, Bk. VIII. *Cp* Morley, *Rousseau*, i. 134, note.

[2] In a note upon the influence of women, Rousseau remarks " we are no sufficiently sensible of what advantage it would be to society to give a bette education to that half of our species which governs the other. Men will alway be what women choose to make them." In his letter to d'Alembert, written in violent reaction against Madame d'Epinay and her circle, he says that the manners of the French are the opposite of those of the ancients: ". . . lâche ment devoués aux volontés du sexe que nous devrions protéger et non servir, il ont appris à le mépriser en lui obéissant, à l'outrager par leur soins railleurs chaque femme de Paris rassemble autour d'elle un sérail d'hommes plus femme qu'elles, qui savent rendre à la beauté toutes sortes d'hommages, hors celui du cœur dont elle est digne."

o artificial eloquence. " It is beneath the homespun of the labourer, and not beneath the gilt and tinsel of the courtier, that we should look for strength and vigour of body." Virtue had suffered as much as happiness and health ; the art of printing had merely perpetuated corrupt philosophies like those of Hobbes and Spinoza ; men had banished the gods (whom, in the days of innocence, they had kept in their huts) to magnificent temples where they could no longer witness the viciousness of their devotees ; a false education, which could not produce genius but which turned the man who would have been an excellent clothier into a bad versifier, had prevented men from recognizing the teaching of their hearts. " Virtue, sublime science of simple minds, are such industry and preparation needed if we are to know you? Are not your principles graven on every heart? Need we do more, to learn your laws, than examine ourselves, and listen to the voice of conscience, when the passions are silent? " [1]

D'Alembert's preliminary discourse was the answer of the *philosophes* to this declaration that virtue was more important than intellect, and that the character of individuals and society suffered from the progress of science. In 1753 Rousseau denounced civilization again in his *Origin of Inequality*.[2] The book has been generally described as too " abstract." Rousseau has been accused of a total disregard of facts and is supposed to have believed in the historical existence of a mythical " state of nature." In fact he explicitly denies the possibility of knowing the story of human development, though he did his best to get what hints he could from the accounts of primitive peoples which missionaries and explorers had recorded.[3] His use of the " state of nature " is, in the main, as he says, a hypothetical one, a way of illustrating his view of human nature and his diagnosis of society's ills. " Let us begin, then, by laying facts aside, as they do not affect the question." It was the basis of

---

[1] This and subsequent translations are taken from the Everyman Edition.

[2] A discourse, also written as a prize essay for the Academy of Dijon, and dedicated to Geneva. Unlike the first discourse it did not win the prize.

[3] *Cp.* the notes and references which he makes in *The Origin of Equality*, *vide* Vaughan's edition of the *Political Writings of J.-J. Rousseau.*

right in which he was interested, not the historical facts, and he exposed the fallacy shared by Hobbes and Locke of attributing social vices and virtues to men before the existence of organized society. He pictures man evolving through stages from an animal ancestry, and possessing two unique faculties —a capacity for learning by experience and an ability to sympathize—from which all his good qualities have sprung. After a long process, in which the pressure of population gradually drove men from their primitive isolation to a life of co-operation, family life began. Hunting, fishing, and then agriculture, took the place of promiscuous food-gathering. During this the happiest phase of human development men learned to co-operate in tilling the soil, and so learned the rudiments of morality. As long as there was ample produce for all there was no need for private property and no social difficulties. The time came, however, when the first man enclosed a piece of ground, "bethought himself of saying *this is mine* and found the people simple enough to believe him. This man was the real founder of civil society. . . . From how many crimes, wars and murders, from how many horrors and misfortunes might not someone have saved mankind, by pulling up the stakes, or filling up the ditch, and crying to his fellows, 'Beware of listening to this impostor; you are undone if you once forget that the fruits of the earth belong to us all, and the earth itself to nobody.'" From this original misfortune all other evils developed. Through private property the harmless inequalities which were the outcome of natural differences gave way to social inequalities. As a result of the inheritance of wealth one class was able to tyrannize over another. From private property moral evils sprang. "It now became the interest of men to appear what they really were not." On the one side insolent display and insatiable ambition, on the other servile trickery and corrupting jealousy. "In a word, there arose rivalry and competition on the one hand, and conflicting interests on the other, together with a secret desire on both of profiting at the expense of others." Men no longer worked to satisfy real wants, but to get more than others. There was permanent war between the rich and the poor, between those who were strongest by nature and those whose right was founded on the artificial institution of private property. In this society the natural inequalities of merit and capacity were subordinated to those of riches, which could be used "to purchase every other distinction." It was useless to say that there was a natural harmony of interests, " that every man gains by serving the rest." This, Rousseau saw, might be ultimately true. Unfortunately, as things were, men appeared to be able to gain still more by injuring others. " There is no legitimate profit so great that it cannot be greatly exceeded by what may be made illegitimately ; we always gain more by hurting our neighbours than by doing them good."

The Origin of Inequality ends with an invocation to the god of simplicity, but despairs of a return to simplicity after the corruption of civilization had done its work. If Rousseau had ceased writing at this point, he would have been rightly acclaimed an apostle of the simple life, and a pessimist who was certain of human degeneracy and of the impossibility of regaining natural happiness. His mind, however, was already at work upon a more constructive conclusion ; it appeared in an incomplete form two years after his second discourse, as an article on political economy in the *Encyclopædia*, and, after six years of brooding, he fully developed his ideas in *The Social Contract*.

3. THE COLLECTIVISM OF ROUSSEAU—*THE SOCIAL CONTRACT*

At the basis of the two discourses there is a complete individualism, a hatred of all authority and all institutions which prevent a man from freely following his instincts. Rousseau knew, however, that such an individualism was incompatible not only with the State but with society, and since it was impossible to desocialize man and revive a condition of amoral innocence it was now a question of finding a method of organization which would preserve moral and spiritual freedom, even at the expense of other forms of liberty. The social chains which restricted the development of man's instinctive freedom could not be altogether discarded. Yet the essence of freedom which lies in obedience only to oneself might be retained in

society. "The problem," he wrote, " is to find a form of association which will defend and protect with the whole common
force the person and goods of each associate, in which each,
while uniting himself with all, may still obey himself alone, and
remain as free as before."

Leaving aside the conception of an anarchic community as
a dream of the past, now for ever irretrievable, Rousseau sets
out to follow his master Plato and found a society based not
on instinctive freedom but on moral freedom and, therefore, on
justice. He begins with the explicit assurance that his object
is a philosophic, not a practical one; he is in search of the
principles of " political right," not of the methods by which
the best political compromise can be reached in any particular
instance. Natural law is mentioned only to be discarded, and
the social contract introduced merely as a method of informing
the reader that Rousseau is now dealing with the socialized
man we know, not with the abstract individual of *The Origin
of Inequality*.[1] Men had gained in society more than they had
lost from the state of nature. In primitive isolation " our whole
happiness would consist in not knowing our misery. There would
be neither kindness in our hearts nor morality in our acts. We
should never have tasted the sweetest feeling of which the soul
is capable—the love of virtue." [2] The moral self was more
important than animal freedom. Rousseau's own Puritan self-
analysis easily led him to the Pauline conclusion that there are
in every man two natures, a higher and a lower, and that to
abase the lower and surrender to the higher is to be free. In

---

[1] It was a misfortune, as Vaughan points out, that Rousseau did not decide
to call his work by its sub-title, *The Principles of Political Right*, instead of by
the highly misleading one which became so famous. The introduction of
social contract and of a " Legislator " are devices for getting over a logical
difficulty. In the absence of any evolutionary principle, Rousseau had to
explain how the amoral man of the state of nature (devoid as the latter was of
" reason, duty, justice and humanity ") could ever have come to set up a law
at all. This, as he remarked, implied a miracle. The miracle is the Legislator,
an idealized version of Lycurgus, a man who can force his fellows to accept the
society which they could not themselves perceive to be in accordance with
their own general will (*Social Contract*, Bk. II., chap. vii.).

[2] *Social Contract* (Geneva MSS.), quoted by Vaughan, vol. i. 27.

imself, he explained, there were two souls, that of the volup-
uary and that of the Puritan, which gained successive mastery
ver him for periods of about a fortnight. The one condition
as freedom, the other slavery: liberty is obedience to a law
hich we prescribe to ourselves. Thus the conclusion reached
n *The Origin of Inequality* is exactly reversed: the good society
s one in which men are virtuous and do not suffer from the
yranny of animal freedom.

Rousseau was now in a position to solve his problem. If
ndividual freedom consists in virtue, then social freedom is
present where men are subject only to those laws they have
mposed upon themselves. The legal system will then embody
he "general will"—that is, the altruistic, moral and rational
desire for the general good. The general will is not merely
he will of all but the sum of all the wills which make for the
common good: it is public spirit, not public opinion: the
spirit which Montesquieu called virtue, which subordinates
private interests to public ones, the spirit without which democracy cannot live. A society animated by this corporate spirit
gives every man his moral freedom, since the laws which restrain him represent his own moral triumph over the despotism
of his lower nature. The law coerces the selfish individual and
thereby gives him freedom, just as conscience coerced Rousseau
and gave him the sense of spiritual freedom in the reaction after
an unsuccessful struggle against his sexual appetite. A man
whose actual will conflicts with the law, which embodies the
general or moral will, may appear to be constrained, but is,
in fact, "forced to be free."

Where the general will is fully operative there will no longer
be conflicting units kept within bounds by an external force,
but a single corporate whole, composed of members each of
whom commands and each of whom obeys.[1] Each plays a part

---

[1] The organic theory of the State had been already stated by Rousseau in
his *Political Economy*. His debt to Hobbes was obvious: "The body politic,
taken individually, may be considered as an organized, living body, resembling
that of man. The sovereign power represents the head; the laws and customs
are the brain, the source of the nerves and seat of the understanding, will and
senses, of which the Judges and Magistrates are the organs; commerce, industry

in the activities of the body politic, and the whole society is a harmonious macrocosm of each individual. In such a State " we see at once that it can no longer be asked whose business it is to make laws, since they are acts of the general will; nor whether the Prince is above the law, since he is a member of the State; nor whether the law can be unjust, since no one is unjust to himself; nor how we can be both free and subject to the laws, since they are but registers of our wills."

Rousseau had now clearly established his basis of right. The only legitimate State is one in which the laws are made by the whole body of citizens, acting, not as units with particular desires and private passions, but as altruistic members of the body politic, solely concerned with the good of the community. In these circumstances every member of the community is free, but Rousseau's admission that there may be individuals who refuse " to obey the general will," and who must be " compelled to do so by the whole body," might seem to invalidate his argument. For, if the only legitimate rule is self-rule, what happens to the basis of right which has been established if some individuals are coerced? Is it not, in fact, a mere juggle of words to assume that an individual who differs from his fellows is being " forced to be free " when he is being compelled against his actual will? Is this anything but a muddled way of saying that the best compromise is to accept majority rule, and that this form of government will satisfy men's desire for a share in government as long as there is sufficient underlying agreement about fundamental issues to induce the minority to give way until their own opportunity of rule arrives?[1]

---

and agriculture are the mouth and stomach, which prepare the common subsistence; the public income is the blood, which a prudent economy, in performing the functions of the heart, causes to distribute through the whole body nutriment and life: the citizens are the body and the members which make the machine live, move and work; and no part of this machine can be damaged without the painful impression being at once conveyed to the brain, if the animal is in a state of health" (trans. Everyman Edition, p. 252).

[1] Contemporary critics seized upon this point. In plain language Rousseau's argument for sovereignty was a plea for the right of the majority to coerce the individual. *Vide*, e.g., *Anti-Contrat Social*, by Gerdil: "It is a dangerous maxim that the community cannot impose an inviolable law upon itself; it is to

Majority rule is the only practical application of *The Social Contract*. Rousseau makes no such admission. Since it is impossible that the body of citizens should not desire their own good it is clear that, even if they are sometimes mistaken in the methods by which they hope to achieve it, their decision is infallible in the sense that they alone have the right to make such a decision, and that no one can know their own will except themselves. If the fundamental condition of popular sovereignty be observed, the citizen may be assumed to give " his consent to all the laws, including those which are passed in spite of his opposition, and even those which punish him when he dares to break any of them." [1] In such circumstances to ask how a man can be both free and coerced is " to put the question wrongly."

The constant will of all the members of the State is the general will; by virtue of it they are citizens and free. When in the popular assembly a law is proposed, the people are not exactly asked whether they approve or reject the proposal, but whether it is in conformity with the general will, which is their will. Each man, in giving his vote, states his opinion on that point; and the general will is found by counting votes. When therefore the opinion that is contrary to my own prevails, this proves neither more nor less than that I was mistaken, and that what I thought to be the general will was not so. If my particular opinion had carried the day I should have achieved the opposite

---

submit public and fundamental law to variations and changes, often unjust and always pernicious. It is to excite revolutions in the heart of the country. . . . I read with pleasure that one may be free and coerced at the same time. I have long looked for a way of reconciling these two irreconcilables. I admit that I have never rightly understood how liberty can be the effect of constraint . . . being and not being, war and peace, the infinite and the finite will live under the same roof." Rousseau, says Gerdil, has really destroyed his whole basis of right. Government by consent has passed into government by force, and the morality, at first described as innate, has disappeared and become equivalent to such conduct as the existing government and public opinion approves.

[1] This argument leads to the position that in a democratic State a man who is hanged for breaking the law is hanged voluntarily. *Cp.* Vaughan, vol. i. 113, note, and *Social Contract*, Bk. II. v. : " his will is chained by his own permission, his past consent set off against his present refusal, and the obligation laid upon him to punish himself for having acted against his own deliberate intentions."

of what was my will; and it is in that case that I should not have been free." [1]

You cannot escape from a dilemma by a vehement denial of its existence, and Rousseau was forced to admit that his theory was applicable only to ideal conditions. He saw that wills would in fact conflict even in a democracy. Where public spirit is lacking, the transitory "will of all" may be confused with the permanent "general will," and private interests prove more influential than considerations of the public good. Particular associations within the State endanger the whole, since they have particular interests: they may, as Hobbes had put it, become parasitic, "like worms in the entrails" of the body politic. Such associations, indeed, may be general as regards their own members, but particular as regards the State: they may make a man "a devout priest or brave soldier," and yet prevent his being anything but "a bad citizen." "It is therefore essential, if the general will is to be able to express itself, that there shall be no partial society within the State, and that each citizen shall think only his own thoughts," without any intermediary associations to remind him of particular interests.

Even if these conditions are observed the perfect form of government in which the people would unite in themselves executive and legislative powers is an unrealizable ideal. In this strict sense, Rousseau remarks, "there never has been a real democracy and there never will be. . . . It is unimaginable that the people should remain continually assembled to devote their time to public affairs, and it is clear that they cannot set up commissions for that purpose without the form of administration being changed." Such a perfect form of government "is not for men. Were there a nation of gods their government would be democratic."

This being so, what remains? The people are still sovereign and must exercise their sovereignty. Rousseau exposes the error, made by Locke and earlier exponents of the "social contract," of imagining that there could be a contract between

---

[1] *Social Contract*, Bk. IV. ii.

people and government. The people cannot, even if they would, alienate their ultimate right to govern themselves; in imagining that they could do so, and thereby bind their successors to a future obedience, Hobbes was even more obviously wrong than Locke. The only contract admitted by Rousseau was the one made among all the original constituents of a society, the arrangement that they would co-operate in a single community. If it is, as a rule, impossible that everyone should take part in government, the people retain the right to appoint what executive they please, and to change its character and personnel as often as they like. When Rousseau discusses forms of government, therefore, he is merely comparing the merits of different forms of executive, which must in any case be directly responsible to the people, and should be so intimately controlled by them that it never has any opportunity of manifesting " a particular will " of its own in opposition to the general will of the community. An hereditary aristocracy is obviously the worst of all forms of executive, since it is certain to exercise its power in its own private interest : " an elected aristocracy," which is what writers often call a democracy, consisting of magistrates duly elected by the people and responsible to them, is commonly the best.

Elected persons may, then, perform executive duties satisfactorily as long as their authority is derived from and continuously exercised by the whole people. Legislative authority, however, can never be delegated or represented. Representation is no substitute for direct democracy. " The lukewarmness of patriotism, the activity of private interest, the vastness of States, conquest and the abuse of government, suggested the method of having deputies or representatives of the people in the national assemblies." Sovereignty, however, " cannot be represented ; it lies essentially in the general will, and will does not admit of representation ; it is either the same or other ; there is no intermediate possibility. . . . Every law the people has not ratified in person is null and void—is, in fact, not a law. The people of England regards itself as free ; but it is grossly mistaken ; it is free only during the election of members of Parliament. As soon as they are elected, slavery overtakes it, and it is nothing. The use it makes of the short moments of liberty it enjoys shows indeed that it deserves to lose them."

4. THE PRACTICAL POLITICS OF ROUSSEAU—FRANCE, POLAND AND CORSICA

So far, Rousseau's argument has been devoted to establishing the basis of political right. When he turned to the complex question of the art of government the result was surprising. Few writers in the eighteenth century had studied and grasped *L'Esprit des Lois* to such effect. The whole trend of Montesquieu's thought, with its Whig assumption that change is permissible only as a result of careful adjustment to historic tradition and unchangeable environment, with its stress on the relativity of good and evil, and its consequent acceptance of compromise—this whole method of thought seemed the antithesis of Rousseau's abstract philosophy and revolutionary Protestantism. Yet so imbued with Montesquieu's caution had Rousseau become that even in his *Social Contract* he applies his principles with an unexpected timidity. Rousseau was revolutionary only in theory, and when he was called upon to suggest practical reforms Burke himself could scarcely have considered his proposals extravagant.

In his political writings two strands lie side by side : on one page we are dealing with absolutes and on the next making compromises and exceptions which seemed to undermine his most cherished principles. What are we to say of a philosopher who opens his treatise by declaring that "the terms of the contract . . . are everywhere the same and everywhere tacitly admitted and recognized," and then proceeds to tell us that there are "unfriendly and barren lands" where all political society is impossible; that "liberty not being the fruit of all climates is not within the reach of all peoples," that Montesquieu was right in thinking that considerations of territory and climate sometimes justify a monarchy, that democracy suits only States that are small and poor and that no one can say "what sort of government is absolutely the best"? In the same way, when Rousseau, who had opened *The Social Contract* by saying,

" If I were a Prince or a Legislator, I should not waste time in saying what wants doing ; I should do it or hold my peace," was actually offered the opportunity of becoming a legislator, the main burden of his advice was to move cautiously and to practise moderation.

In *The Social Contract* he had admitted that the ideal conditions for which he sought were no longer attainable anywhere, and certainly not in most European countries. For " legislation is made difficult less by what it is necessary to build up than by what has to be destroyed ; and what makes success so rare is the impossibility of finding natural simplicity together with social requirements. All these conditions are indeed rarely found united, and therefore few States have good constitutions." In one country, however—Corsica—all the conditions for the foundation of a good society still existed. " The valour and persistency with which that brave people has regained and defended its liberty well deserves that some wise man should teach it how to preserve what it has won. I have a feeling that some day that little island will astonish Europe."

In 1764, Buttafuoco wrote to Rousseau reminding him of this passage, and suggesting that he himself was the wise man who could legislate for independent Corsica.[1] " Corsica has never yet borne the true yoke of the Law ; it has no fear of being crushed by a sudden invasion : it can do without the aid of other nations : it is neither rich nor poor ; it is sufficient to itself. Its prejudices will not be hard to overcome ; and I venture to say that the simplicity of nature will be found there to go hand in hand with the needs of social life." [2] Rousseau responded by a project of government which follows the principles of *The Social Contract* closely. Every citizen was to take an oath " in the name of Almighty God " to join himself, " body, goods, will and powers," to the Corsican nation, " granting to her full ownership of myself and all that depends upon me." In the

---

[1] In 1768 Choiseul annexed Corsica to France, and the hopes of creating a Utopia were thus destroyed.

[2] This is a summary of the conditions laid down by Rousseau which would render a people " a fit subject for legislation "—vide *Social Contract*, Bk. II. x., and *cp*. Vaughan, vol. ii. 296.

new State of Corsica there was to be social equality and a recognition of the "fundamental principles of prosperity." "No one should be rich," everyone should produce according to need, agriculture should remain the principal industry, and there should be no capital town, such as Paris, wealthy and corrupt, to undermine the simple happiness of a people who still spontaneously enjoyed their liberty and equality. When it came to more practical matters, however, Rousseau did not forget that the legislator should follow Montesquieu, and he requested Buttafuoco to provide him with all the facts—political, industrial and social—which could serve "to reveal the national character." He decided, consistently enough, that the island was too large to be an unmixed democracy, and suggested that the executive should be chosen, and changed frequently, by as many of the people as could effectively meet together in a congress at the same time. He was also cautious in his treatment of the Church, and, in spite of the anathemas he had pronounced upon "the religion of priests," did not advocate the abolition of church tithes, but only suggested the addition of a civic tithe to be paid to the State. As to the institution of private property, he held that the ideal would be State socialism. "So far from wishing the State to be poor I should wish on the contrary to see it the sole owner; the individual taking a share of the common property only in proportion to his services."[1] He was content, however, with the practical suggestion that the State should have the right to confiscate or bestow property when it desired to punish or reward.

In 1769 the Polish Convention resolved to ask the French *philosophes* to make suggestions for a new Constitution for Poland. In the next year Polish liberty was destroyed by the neighbouring despots, whose philosophic principles did not prevent them from dividing among themselves the territory of an independent people. Voltaire enthusiastically approved of this example of enlightenment. Rousseau and Mably, however, had already made suggestions for the reorganization of a free Poland. Rousseau decided at once that the situation and tradi-

---

[1] *Vide* Vaughan, vol. ii. 151-152.

tions of Poland made anything like an ideal Constitution out of the question. Montesquieu himself could not have been more statesmanlike. The most important thing was that Poland should be animated by the spirit of liberty, that every citizen should think only of his country, her independence and moral greatness. But the spirit of liberty was dangerous: "High-souled and holy liberty! If these poor men could only know thee, if they could only learn the price at which thou art won and guarded; if they could only be taught how far sterner are thy laws than the hard yoke of the tyrant; they would shrink from thee a hundred times more than from slavery, they would fly from thee in terror as from a burden made to crush them." Thus the Poles, and especially the serfs, should be moderate both in obtaining and using their liberty. "In thinking of what you would wish to acquire, do not forget what you may lose. Correct, if you can, the abuses of your Constitution, but never despise a Constitution which has made you what you are." Nevertheless, since "repose and liberty are incompatible . . . I will not say you ought to leave things as they are, but I will say that you must touch them with the greatest caution."

In accordance with these principles, Rousseau outlined a scheme of reforms. Poland, again, was too large for the democratic severity of ancient Sparta: "Your vast provinces will never admit the stern administration of a small State." Rousseau suggested, therefore, that the monarchy should become really elective; that taxation should be equitably administered and levied upon landed property; that the power should continue to reside in the aristocratic Senate. He offered the Third Estate no part in government and was opposed to anything more drastic than a very gradual scheme for freeing serfs, who might so easily misuse liberty when it was given them. He put his trust for the future of Poland in two things: education and the development of the principles of federalism. The education he recommended closely followed the precepts of *Emile*: it was not to proceed from books, not to aim at intellect, but to be a training for a useful life, rooted in virtue and inspired by patriotism. "Your citizens must learn to guide their tastes and opinions so that by inclination, by passion and by necessity they will be patriots." True patriotism and public spirit seemed to Rousseau to go only with a small State, where everyone could actively share in the duties of government. He pointed out to the Polish people that almost all the small States prospered because they were small, while " all the large nations, crushed by their own immensity, either grow like you into anarchy or sink beneath the petty oppressors whom their kings are compelled to give them." Poland, therefore, could hope to avoid the worst evils, though not to obtain the perfect society, by resolving herself into a Confederation consisting of Lithuania, Great and Little Poland. Each of the three would have its own Government, but would be united by a " legislative bond " and " subordinated to the Republic as a whole." " In one word, set yourselves to extend and perfect the system of federal government : the only one which unites the advantages of the large and the small State, and, for that very reason, the only one which is suited to your needs. If you disregard this advice I doubt whether your enterprise will ever come to good."

The apparent confusion between the absoluteness of Rousseau's principles and the caution with which he applied them is explicable by his doctrine of human nature. In both his early *Discours* he was certain that man, uncorrupted by human institutions, is naturally good. He could only hope that good institutions might redeem him from his actual wickedness. The doctrine of the social contract was an eighteenth-century reproduction of the sixteenth-century creed which he had first learned in Calvinist Geneva. Man, once innocent in the Garden, had been corrupted by the Fruit of the Tree of Knowledge, but a means of grace was offered him through which he could obtain regeneration and reach a far higher state than he ever could have attained before the Fall. Rousseau wrote *The Social Contract* to explain the social means of grace, by which civilized man could be saved. Redemption was possible, given the right political institutions. When, however, Rousseau was offered a repentant State clamouring for conversion, its heritage of sin seemed so overwhelming that an immediate attempt to find salvation in a wholehearted acceptance of the perfect life seemed out of the question. For Rousseau did not overlook the instinctive and passionate nature of man. Montesquieu had seen that there were environmental limitations, and these were fully appreciated and accepted by Rousseau. But he knew that they were less serious obstacles than human nature itself, since the men who suffered by the present institutions would have to work those which were substituted for them. Like the other *philosophes* he relied ultimately upon education ; but whereas they meant by education simply the destruction of existing superstition, and the teaching of scientific truths, Rousseau saw that the mind was not synonymous with the intellect, and that it was possible to use knowledge for bad as well as good purposes. Conscious of the strength of human passions, Rousseau could not attribute the same importance to institutions as did his contemporaries, and even in *The Social Contract* the essence of his teaching is not that any democracy we can institute can be perfect, but that it is the only form of government which can ever be good at all in the long run, since it is the only one that offers men and women freedom, and which may in time regenerate them, and lead to the formation of a truly social community.

It was therefore Rousseau who supplied the answer to the Physiocratic doctrine that there was a single natural system, the observation of which would solve all social problems. He wrote to Mirabeau : " It seems to me that compelling evidence is never to be found in natural and political laws, unless when we consider them in the abstract. In any given government, composed, as it must be, of very diverse elements, this evidence is necessarily wanting. For the science of government is a science purely of combinations, applications and exceptions, which are determined by time, place and circumstance. And the public will never detect with intuitive certainty the relations and workings of all that. . . . Moreover, even supposing this certainty of evidence . . . how can philosophers who know anything of human nature assign to it such influence upon the actions of men? Can they be ignorant that men guide themselves very seldom by the light of evidence and very often by their passions? My friends, allow me to tell you that you give too much weight to your calculations, and not enough to the promptings of the heart and the play of passion. Your system is excellent for Utopia. For the children of Adam it is worth nothing."

5. THE INTERPRETATION OF ROUSSEAU

This last aspect of Rousseau—the cautious reformer, the respectful disciple of Montesquieu, the revolutionary who even hesitated to abolish serfdom—has been usually forgotten, but other parts of his teaching have had long, complicated and surprising histories. No one can be as fairly quoted in support of opposite theories as Rousseau. His doctrines were capable of extension and elaboration in directions which would have astonished him. His influence was probably increased by the fact that some passages in his works were mystical and obscure : *The Social Contract* could be treated like the Bible and *Das Kapital*—it could be variously interpreted by enthusiasts, endlessly commented on by scholars, and triumphantly quoted by rival schools, each certain of possessing the true milk of the master's teaching.

To some, Rousseau is an extreme individualist, hating all forms of social coercion, and denying the right of State or Church to impose its will upon any individual. The ideal of both the early *Discours* was a simple life, in which property would be held in common, and each man would be able to live as he pleased, earning his own living by his labour under the coercion of hunger only, untroubled by governments and heedless of conventions. Rousseau's own life and expressed inclinations supported this interpretation of his main teaching, and the apostles of the simple life, as well as the philosophic anarchists and early Utopian communists, found inspiration in his work. Godwin's *Political Justice* is a logical continuation of *The Origin of Inequality*. *The Social Contract* was equally useful to the exponents of an opposite theory of government. For them the State, the result of the general wills of all the individuals who compose it, is everything, and the individual whose actual will is recalcitrant counts for nothing. He has

214

ceased to have rights of any sort against the State, he must be content with his opportunity to contribute to the general will. So far from being an exponent of natural rights, Rousseau is fairly quoted by authoritarians as a precursor of an extreme collectivism, in which neither private property nor religious liberty is free from the interference of government. Rousseau's division between the actual and real wills of individuals, the assumption that moral purposes can be fully developed only in the ideal State, led to nineteenth-century Idealism. Kant could base an individualist theory upon it, but the followers of Hegel easily used it to support a transcendental theory of the State, which, as the embodiment of the highest and best in the community, became valuable in itself and was alone able to give value to individual life. The confusion between the ideal democracy—in which the general will should give effect to the highest aspirations of individuals—and the actual dominance of class government in Prussia was the more easily made because the division between the ideal and the actual is never very clear in *The Social Contract* itself. The application of Rousseau to the more democratic conditions of England made by the Oxford idealists was more logical, but it resulted in a denial of individual rights as complete as that in the German followers of Hegel.

The truest interpretation of *The Social Contract* is some form of federalism : the Commune of 1870 is so far the nearest approach to a practical realization of Rousseau's theory. He had expressly said that the ideal freedom at which he aimed was attainable only in a small community, and had added that no freedom was possible in a large State unless it were divided into districts and given a federal constitution. The Girondists were attracted by this theory ; nineteenth-century communists based a revolutionary philosophy upon it ; syndicalists gave a new twist to its development by applying it to industrial groups instead of geographical areas. Exponents of mediæval federalism have found support in Rousseau's refusal to admit the validity of representation and have developed for their own purposes his argument that a social group other than the State may embody the will of its constituent members in relation only to the

purpose for which the particular association has been formed.[1]
Those who accept the corporation theory of the State are therefore indebted to Rousseau, as well as their bitterest opponents,
the idealist protagonists of unified sovereignty.[2]

In the Revolution itself much of Rousseau's theory was
inevitably misunderstood or neglected. For Rousseau had
solved the problem of reconciling liberty and authority by
postulating a State so small that the practical difficulties of
reconciliation scarcely arose. He had himself seen that his
argument applied only to the small community. He knew what
economists have often forgotten—that, while the consideration
of a simple case may sometimes elucidate the nature of a complex problem, it cannot provide a solution for it. The economic
problems of a million persons are not those of Robinson
Crusoe multiplied by a million, nor can the political problems
of a modern community of men be solved by a statement of
conditions which would be ideal for a small community of gods.
If you simplify both your people and your conditions the result
may be logical, suggestive, and even inspiring, but it cannot
serve the purposes of the legislator and administrator. So
much Rousseau had himself implicitly admitted when asked to
apply himself to the art of government. When his followers,

[1] It is worth while to notice that Mr G. D. H. Cole, the principal exponent
of guild socialism, began as an Oxford idealist, and wrote an introduction to
Rousseau's political works (Everyman Edition) on orthodox Hegelian lines
before he had developed his federalist theory. For his later use of Rousseau's
doctrine of representation, and the position of particular associations, *vide* his
Social Theory, p. 51. The argument that every modern State is really federal,
and draws its authority from the fact that particular associations and corporations all play their part in the composition of any genuine community, is not
of course confined to those whose federalism is mainly economic, but is equally
found in Maitland, Figgis and Laski. This position is really first stated in
Rousseau's *Political Economy*.

[2] The influence of Rousseau's remarks about particular associations in the
State provides a curious example of the elasticity of political terms and of the
ease with which the same theory can be utilized for opposite purposes by rival
parties. The Chapelier Law of 1791, which prohibited all professional organiza-
tions in France, was passed in accordance with Rousseau's doctrine : with
equal logic, modern theories of internal federalism appeal to Rousseau for
justification of the thesis that authority is rightly exercised only where every
member of the State is also organized in a professional association.

steeped in his phrases, tried to transform them into constitutions the only mechanism to their hand was that of representation. They could not stop to consider Rousseau's view, that the human will could not be represented and that representation really involved a different form of government. They did not consider the problem of how the " general will " could be made effective in a modern State : there is no hint in their writings or speeches of the need for organized parties or of an independent civil service.

Robespierre could not wait for a democratic meeting before taking action. He assumed, as naturally as Louis XIV. had assumed, that his own will represented the general will of the community. Rousseau's federalism, embodied in the Girondist proposal to give power to the communes of France, appeared political madness when foreign enemies were at the door. When the need for autocracy had passed away the only possible interpretation of *The Social Contract* seemed to be representative government and majority rule. Rousseau had supplied the populace with the cry of popular sovereignty, and in the French Revolution this could only mean the right to vote. Orators who quoted Rousseau were never tired of reminding their audiences that the people themselves were now sovereign, every common man exercising his share of the divine right of the French monarch. For the moment there seemed no difficulty. In the enthusiasm engendered by the struggle against the aristocrats and the Austrians, both the patriotism and the democratic virtue which Rousseau had acclaimed as the true basis of a political society seemed to be realized throughout France. Sebastian Mercier, a fervent disciple of Rousseau, expressed his astonishment, in 1791, that Rousseau could have imagined that democracy was only applicable to a State the size of Geneva, while the Abbé Sièyes popularized and gave effect to *The Social Contract* by his pamphlet *Qu'est-ce que le Tiers Etat?* He saw none of Rousseau's difficulties, had no objection to representation, no view that the only valid legislation is of a purely general character which affects everyone equally ; he was content to expound the doctrine of popular sovereignty in a form which people could understand. "What is the Third Estate?" the

first page of his pamphlet asks, and the reply is : " Everything.'
"What has it so far been in the political order ? " " Nothing.'
"What is its demand ? " " To be something." In the event, as
the result of revolutionary movements in many countries, the
Third Estate of Europe became something, and the arguments
which led to a middle-class franchise were available for a
later generation which urged that a property qualification was
inconsistent with democratic theory.

Rousseau's disciples were easily reconciled to the exclusion
of the working class from its theoretical share in government
They were also persuaded by utilitarian arguments to tolerate
representation. The elected representative would maintain his
constituents' liberty because his interest would lie in obeying
the will of his masters. Those who respected British practice
more than democratic theory were content that the representative should retain some independence and owe his constituents,
in Burke's phrase, "not his industry only, but his judgment."
Sterner democrats, who feared that representatives would
develop " sinister " or " particular " interests (here Bentham
and Rousseau meant the same thing), were anxious to make
them delegates liable to frequent re-election. Jeffersonian
democracy, directly inspired by Rousseau, had little influence
on the Federal Constitution ; it was more successful in the
case of some State constitutions which ensure administrative
inefficiency by providing for the annual or biennial elections
of their legislatures and officers. Further instalments of direct
democracy have been added in many parts of the world, and
Rousseau's influence is to be traced wherever civil servants
and judges [1] are directly elected and liable to recall, and
where referenda and plebiscites may override the authority
of parliaments.

These were later victories of the democratic principle. At the
Revolution itself the task of interpreting democratic doctrine
was in the hands of men of property. The peasantry and the

---

[1] The election of judges was tried during the French Revolution, and is still
the usage of some American States, which also elect many of their civil servants.
The institution of an independent civil service chosen by examination was
perhaps the most fortunate of all British contributions to the art of politics.

urban middle class, which controlled the Revolution except when the Parisian mob was out of hand, had long been burdened by an arbitrary executive which did not respect any rights of property, person or thought. They desired political power commensurate with their economic power; the practical method of obtaining it was the one which the great landowners of England had discovered in the seventeenth century. A Parliament elected by themselves should make the laws and see that they were enforced by a responsible executive. Thus European States in the nineteenth century were commonly governed by parliaments which represented the energetic and wealthy middle class : this class claimed to be " the people " ; its sovereignty was the sovereignty of the people and middle-class government was therefore democracy.

To mention the schools of thought that paid homage to Rousseau and to explain the developments of political practice which have been influenced by him is enough to show the varied possibilities of his teaching. But in truth Rousseau was a genius whose real influence cannot be traced with precision because it pervaded all the thought that followed him. Rousseau was the originator of a religious movement of which the Catholic revival was only one of the beneficiaries. He paved the way for men as various as Bernardin de Saint-Pierre, Chateaubriand, Victor Hugo and Lamennais. Everything anti-rational, whether it was religious, romantic or merely sentimental, profited by his teaching. Men will always be sharply divided about Rousseau ; for he released imagination as well as sentimentalism ; he increased men's desire for justice as well as confusing their minds, and he gave the poor hope even though the rich could make use of his arguments. In one direction at least Rousseau's influence was a steady one : he discredited force as a basis for the State, convinced men that authority was legitimate only when founded on rational consent and that no arguments from passing expediency could justify a government in disregarding the claims of individual freedom or in failing to promote social equality.

CHAPTER IX

EQUALITY AND PROPERTY

1. THE DEMAND FOR EQUALITY

EQUALITY, like other abstractions of political controversy, has been used as the standard and rallying cry of the battlefield, not as the measurable condition of a good life. There is no absolute equality, just as there is no single condition of liberty. Analysis shows that with each group and period the substance of the equality claimed has varied, though the emotions of the struggle always prevented any adequate analysis being made, either by those who claimed new rights or by those who defended old privileges. When men demand equality their desire for justice is stimulated by the hope of effecting concrete social changes, and it is only by examining the proposals which accompany the demand, and the use made of greater equality when it is obtained, that any light is thrown upon the political theory of the period.

In eighteenth-century France equality was the demand of the middle class, and eventually of the peasantry, for the abolition of privilege. They protested because the *noblesse* were not subject to the same courts, did not pay any share of the taxes which oppressed them, and added to their burdens an even greater toll of feudal dues. They asked for the unhampered right to work, the right to enjoy the fruits of their labour and the abolition of the powers which the idle possessed to levy toll upon it. Feudalism was a system of legalized inequality based on rank and function. When the functions were no longer performed the privileges stank. Equality, therefore, meant that nature gave no sanction for legal inequalities: that all men were entitled to the same rights, having equal needs and being able to perform the same functions.

A theoretical basis for this claim was evolved by moralists, psychologists and economists. Firstly, moralists of the school of Rousseau declared that men were naturally equal. They were once more expressing the Christian idea that men, being all children of God, were of the same intrinsic value. Secondly,

220

at the opportune moment, sensationalist psychology seemed to offer a scientific basis for what had hitherto been a religious doctrine intuitively apprehended. Starting from Condillac's elaboration of Locke, the politician was able to declare that men were by nature equal, not only in value but in intelligence, capacity and gifts. If the child's mind was a blank sheet at birth, and there was no original sin nor original merit, the presumption of hereditary superiority was merely a trick to support aristocratic privilege. If men were indeed all " perfectible " by the right education and environment, then there was no justification for social inequality.

Thirdly, the economists now produced arguments for abolishing privilege. The land, Locke taught, though originally " common to all men," became private property through individual work. "Whatsoever, then, a man removes out of the state that nature hath provided and left it in, he hath mixed his labour with it, and joined to it something that is his own, and thereby makes it his property." Men labour in order that they may enjoy the fruits of their labour : they are entitled to do so since " it is labour indeed that puts the difference of value on everything." "As much land as a man tills, plants, improves, cultivates, and can use the product of, so much is his property." Thus natural law and common sense seemed the same thing, and the peasant had a theoretical justification for claiming the ownership of the land which he tilled. The Physiocrats accepted Locke's basis of natural law as well as his argument for private property, though they emphasized the land itself rather than the labour expended upon it as the ultimate source of value. Providence, they believed, had so arranged society that the grant of equal property rights and trading opportunities would produce the greatest social well-being.

Avarice, for centuries repudiated by the Catholic Church as a sin, became in the new philosophy a virtue whereby the indulgence of each man's desire to do the best for himself proved also to be best for the public welfare. Even before the Revolution, however, there were some who thought this right to struggle on equal terms for private possessions an inadequate guarantee of social harmony. Locke's doctrine, moreover, was open to different interpretations. Like the Physiocrats, he had thought in terms of an agrarian community, and in the eighteenth century there were groups of town wage-earners whose claim to the whole product of their labour challenged middle-class employers rather than feudal landlords. Locke had assumed that Nature was beneficent and her gifts plenteous. A man's labour, he wrote, " being the unquestionable property of the labourer, no one but he can have a right to what that is once joined to, *at least where there is enough, and as good left in common for others.*" Men submitted to unequal distribution of land, "having, by consent, found out and agreed in a way how a man may, rightfully and without injury, possess more than he himself can make use of by receiving gold and silver." But what if this arrangement proved to be not "without injury," and "right and conveniency" failed to go together? What if a property owner, in spite of Locke's assurance, did not regard it as "useless, as well as dishonest, to carve himself too much, or take more than he needed"? What if the institution of private property actually led to inequality instead of making all men equal? Would not communism then be the fulfilment of the law of nature?

In the second half of the century, therefore, we may distinguish several distinct schools, united in attacking the social and legal inequalities of the *ancien régime*, but basing their opposition on widely different philosophies and looking forward to opposite alternatives. The Church and the *noblesse* defended their privileges against the King, whose financial needs tempted him to assert his sovereign right to tax all the orders equally. Driven by bankruptcy, the monarchy undermined the feudal structure and initiated the Revolution. Encyclopædists and economists took sides with Louis, appealing to him to recognize openly the iniquity of all privileges, to abolish economic restrictions and levy taxes, when necessary, only upon the land, which they thought was the sole source of wealth. Above all, the King should establish equal rights for all descriptions of property. Communists, on the other hand, planned Utopias in which private property had been altogether abandoned and a life of co-operative service substituted. More directly revolutionary writers were concerned less with the moral degradation of society than with the physical miseries of the Fourth Estate, and suggested Liberal reforms which would produce greater equality, though they shrank from the practical results of advocating a socialist revolution. Two men are especially interesting here: Linguet, because he alone submitted society to a purely class analysis and prophesied a future revolution of the poor against the rich; and Babeuf, because, unlike his fellow-theorists, he was unsatisfied with limited political democracy as a substitute for the economic equality he had preached and was willing to put his socialistic faith to the test of action. When the Revolution came, the grievances of the town worker and the communistic visions of theorists were alike unheeded. Babeuf's socialist rising was quickly suppressed; the peasants had gained the free ownership of their land and the middle classes had destroyed the social superiority of the *noblesse* and won the right to trade freely without the restrictions of the *ancien régime*. But political equality as well as economic equality was refused to the town worker and the nineteenth-century State was a middle-class affair, governed by men of property. Even equality of opportunity was but partially established, since inheritance of wealth remained to form the basis of a new aristocracy.

2. PRIVILEGE—THE SURVIVAL OF FEUDAL THEORY

The establishment of a Liberal economic régime in France meant, as the Physiocrats well knew, sweeping away the privileges of all the ancient corporations. It meant attacking not only the *jurandes* and *maîtrises*, but also the aristocracy and the Church. Turgot confronted these vested interests with arguments ultimately derived from Locke. " I do not think," he wrote, after describing the reforms which he hoped the King would bring about, " that such useful plans would be opposed on the great principle of the respect due to property." Such opposition would indeed be " a very strange contradiction," since corporation property was, in its origin, " almost all founded on usurpations." Yet those who possessed it were

" permitted, on the pretext of a very badly understood right, to steal the property which is most sacred of all, that which can alone be the basis of all other property "—a man's right " to the fruit of his labour." [1]

Ancient corporations, however, become habituated to the possession of property, and seldom see the necessity of justifying their title-deeds. When Turgot was at length given his short opportunity of reform, all the corporations opposed him. His edict suppressing the *corvée* which fell exclusively on the poor, carried with it the threat of more equable taxation. In its remonstrance on behalf of the privileged orders, the *Parlement* of Paris reminded the King that all his subjects were " obliged to contribute to the needs of State," but " by this very contribution order and harmony will always be maintained. The personal service of the clergy is to fulfil all functions relating to education and religious observance and to contribute to the relief of the unfortunate by alms. The noble consecrates his blood to the defence of the State and assists the Sovereign by advice. The last class of the nation, which cannot render such distinguished services to the State, contributes industry and manual labour. . . . By freeing the last class of citizens from the *corvée*, to which it has hitherto been subjected, the edict transfers this charge to the two orders of the State which have never been subjected to it. The difference between your subjects disappears, the noble and the ecclesiastic become liable to the *corvée*, or, what is the same thing, they become liable to contribute to the tax which must take the place of the *corvée*. This is not, as people have tried to persuade you, Sire, a battle of the rich against the poor. It is a question of State and one of the most important ; for it is a question of knowing if all your subjects can and ought to be treated in the same way ; if there must be an end of admitting different conditions, ranks, titles and pre-eminences amongst them."

Certainly the case for class as an institution could scarcely have been more clearly expressed ; it would have been a stronger case, however, if the Church had, in fact, organized any general

---

[1] *Collection des Economistes*, t. iii. 253.

system of education or poor relief, or if the *noblesse* had really been the principal sufferers in Louis XV.'s numerous wars. Indeed, the defence of feudalism on the ground that privilege was the reward of service was out of date in an age when feudal services had long ceased to be performed.

After the Revolution, de Maistre attacked the *philosophes* on the ground that they had undermined that spiritual authority without which society is merely a chaos of conflicting groups and individuals seeking their own advantage, heedless of social outlook or Christian purpose. This is a sound line of defence for the mediæval Church : it seems scarcely applicable to the eighteenth century, when a resident bishop was a rarity, a large part of the clergy were free-thinkers and the struggle between Jansenist and Jesuit filled France with discord. The seventeenth century had produced ecclesiastics like Claude Joly, who were not afraid to speak freely, and during the age of Louis XIV. Fénelon, Massillon and Bossuet had at least reminded the rich of their Christian duty to the poor and warned the King of the dangers of misrule and arbitrary government. But in the eighteenth century the clergy left social criticism and public instruction to the *philosophes*. Marmontel describes a conversation between a *philosophe* and de Broglie, Bishop of Noyon, in which the Bishop complained of the impudence of the *philosophes*.

" ' It is true, Monseigneur,' I replied, ' that they take it upon themselves to usurp some of your noblest functions, but only when you fail to fulfil them.' 'What functions?' he asked. ' Those of preaching from the roof-tops the truths that are too rarely told to sovereigns or their Ministers or to the flatterers who surround them. Since the exile of Fénelon, or perhaps since the touching little course of moral instruction given by Massillon to Louis XIV. as a child, useless because premature, have the clergy once protested boldly against public crimes and vices ? ' " [1]

There were, however, some clerical protests against social evils in the century.[2] Poucet de la Rivière declared that " all men are

---

[1] Quoted by Roustan, English trans., p. 262.
[2] For these *vide* Lichtenberger, *Le Socialisme au XVIIIe Siècle*, 349 ff.

only depositories and administrators of those goods of which God, who has put them into their hands, always remains proprietor and master," and approved the maxim of Saint Ambrose that to give alms to a poor man is only to give him back part of that which is already rightly his; in any case, the poor man possesses spiritual riches, while the rich man obtains earthly possessions instead and runs the risk of suffering the fate of Dives hereafter. Popular orators like the Abbé Poulle and the Abbé de Cambacérès reflect current sentiment in insisting on the right to happiness rather than the duty of mortifying the flesh; and Father Griffet warned rich men that they owed their wealth to the accident of birth, and should share it with the poor. God might not hold the rich guiltless if poor men were driven to blasphemy and wickedness by the injustice of their lot. Some preachers even praised the ideal of Christian communism. The wickedness of usury still formed an occasional theme for clerics, one of whom, Père de Gasquet, went so far as to assert that interest is " a tax imposed by the idle or unintelligent owner upon the industrious cultivator and hard-working merchant. . . . Moneylenders gnaw and devour the best citizens, as insects fasten upon the best fruit; hidden under a mysterious veil of bills drawn upon the borrower they amass criminal wealth without giving him the sad satisfaction of knowing whose is the unjust hand which gathers the fruits of labour." This section of society, consisting of all the useless persons in the State, lives on the cultivator's knowledge and the business man's toil, but contributes least to the taxation levied on the nation because it occupies all the privileged positions. " The rich never pay in the same proportion as the poor," because their wealth can be carried in a pocket-book and so cannot be assessed.

An occasional churchman might still remember that Saint Thomas had denounced trade for mere gain, saying that " it is justly scorned since in itself it serves the lust for wealth "; and the early years of the Revolution were to show that Rousseau's picture of the Savoyard vicar, beloved of his flock and teaching the gospel of Christ rather than the doctrines of Catholicism, was not an imaginary one.

The greater clergy, however, had become indistinguishable from the rest of the higher *noblesse*. Bossuet had been of middle-class origin, but the great churchmen of Louis XV.'s reign usually owed their position to their families, as in the case of a Rohan or a Montmorency, or alternatively to intrigue, as in the case of a Dubois or a de Tencin. The general view presented by the eighteenth-century Church is that of a feudal corporation grasping a great inheritance, free from recognized obligations or service, absorbed in a struggle nominally due to dogmatic differences, but actually concerned with temporal power, and willing at every opportunity to crush with violence and cruelty any rival faction, heretic or critic.[1]

The clergy were not, therefore, a popular body, and when the Clerical Assembly protested against the King's demand for a twentieth the royal lawyers found immediate public support.[2] They declared that the sovereignty of the Monarch was not restricted by past immunities and that all property was held at the King's pleasure. Pamphleteers supported the theory of absolute sovereignty, making *raison d'état* the final test and denying all rights against the State. The churchmen were reminded that even in the original feudal contract, by which they had gained their immunity, the Crown was " the first proprietor of all goods," that they, like other men, were subject to the social obligations that arose from the existence of the State and the facts of sovereignty. The entire goods of the State belonged to the Sovereign, one writer declared; individuals had only the usufruct of them. "Property," he wrote, " ought to be respected; yes, certainly : but only in this sense, that one ought not to alienate it unnecessarily, and without a necessity arising from the actual condition of public affairs." The safety of the State is the final law. " All means are good, according to the circumstances in which a State finds itself." Even taxation

---

[1] The landed property of the clergy is estimated at five to six per cent. of the whole territory of France. The annual revenue of the Church was some 80 to 100 millions livres in rent and about 123 millions in tithes. For all this *vide* the summary in Sée, *La France économique et sociale au XVIIIe Siecle*, 55-57.

[2] For this controversy *vide* Lichtenberger, *op. cit.*, 383 ff.

which would break up the property of families would be justified on occasion, but obviously the goods of the clergy can be confiscated with less dislocation to society. In this controversy the revolutionary struggle is already foreshadowed; the clergy were soon to find themselves attacked by the Jacobins in the name of the sovereign people who sat crowned upon Louis' throne. Popular support of despotism has always arisen where it alone is sufficiently strong to check greedy and powerful corporations.

3. LIBERAL ECONOMICS AND NATURAL HARMONY—THE PHYSIOCRATS AND THE BOURGEOISIE

Conditions were in every way favourable to the rise of a Liberal school of economists. The King's financial embarrassment, the burden of oppressive and arbitrary taxation, the restraint of trade and the absurdity of surviving feudalism, the agricultural depression and miserable condition of the peasantry, all added point to criticism and led to the growth of a group of economic thinkers who expanded and systematized the views already expressed by Vauban and Boulainvilliers in the reign of Louis XIV. It was natural that this school should have been primarily concerned with attacking Colbertism and emphasizing the importance of agriculture as the source of wealth.[1] The form which this doctrine took, however, was greatly influenced by current philosophy, and its most important generalizations applied not only to France but to all States which adopted a basis of free contract and private property.

In the thirty years which followed the death of Louis XIV. there was frequent but spasmodic discussion of economic theory. Controversy raged around John Law's luckless scheme of inflation; Cantillon's *Essai du Commerce* (1715) did for economics

---

[1] Holding that land was the only source of wealth, the Physiocrats believed that the only just tax was a land tax. Unlike any other kind of property, land yielded a rent, a net product. The landlord could pay a tax on this without the right of private property being infringed and without the productivity of the land being impaired. The State would always leave the landlord as much revenue as he could have acquired in any other kind of business, and by the *impôt unique* the State and the landowner would become partners.

what Voltaire's *Letters on the English* did for "philosophy," ✓ summarizing English political economy and introducing Locke's economics to a wider audience. Melon's *Essai politique* (1734) and Dupin's *Mémoires sur les Blés* (1742) both struck at mercantilism and advocated the removal of restrictions upon the transport of corn in France, though neither Melon nor Dupin reached the point of suggesting complete freedom of trade. Montesquieu's *Esprit des Lois* (1748) was the signal for a great outburst of economic discussion, and by 1760 a group of economists had been formed, holding a common doctrine and advocating a common policy. Quesnay was safely installed at Versailles as Madame de Pompadour's doctor; the official *Gazette du Commerce* was converted to the new economic doctrines in 1765, and the hitherto hostile *Ephémérides* became the organ of the Physiocrats two years later. The publication of the *Tableau économique* signalized the unity of the new group whose abilities were openly pitted against the royal policy. The Government indeed played into the hands of its critics, sometimes admitting its conversion by passing reforming edicts and then advertising its weakness by new surrenders to private interests. In 1754 it passed an edict to facilitate the transmission of corn from one province to another, but neglected to remove the feudal rights which actually prevented its passage. Physiocratic influence reached its height when Turgot, who, as *intendant*, had already attempted to apply Physiocratic principles in his own province, became Controller-General of France. His dismissal eighteen months later was an admission that though the King might be Liberal in sentiment he was not powerful enough to carry reforms in the teeth of the aristocracy. Disappointment was increased when, after Turgot's dismissal, the *Parlements*, once more secure from attack, initiated an obviously reactionary policy. Instead of edicts designed to promote free trade and social equality, Turgot's successors passed decrees excluding all who had not four degrees of nobility from holding military commissions, forbidding anyone to cut grass or corn with a scythe, and demanding that in future all pocket-handkerchiefs should be exactly as broad as they were long. The Commercial Treaty with England in

1786, though believed to be unfavourable to France, seeme
to be a further vindication of the Physiocrats, and reinforce
their view that it was bad government, not natural poverty
which made the State bankrupt. But the direct influence o
the Physiocrats really ends with Turgot's dismissal, and whe
Liberal economics revived with J. B. Say, Adam Smith ha
taken Quesnay's place as the patron saint of economists.

The starting-point of the Physiocrats was that of eighteenth
century philosophy in general. The scientific notion that th
material world was not subject to the arbitrary caprice of
personal deity, but was governed by fixed and ascertainable law:
was applied by them to the organization of society. Quesnay'
conviction that a natural order of society lay within our reach
if the Creator's ordinances were followed, was built, just a
Locke's had been, upon his training and experience as a doctor
He believed, as one of his disciples put it, that " natural law
extended far beyond the bounds hitherto assigned to them,
and applied to the circulation of money just as they did to th
circulation of the blood. The order of nature was merely th
physical constitution which God Himself had given the universe
" its laws," said Mercier, another disciple, " are irrevocable
pertaining as they do to the essence of matter and the soul o
humanity ; they are simply the expression of the will of God.
In the organization of society, therefore, just as in the physic
order, there are unalterable processes, the understanding an
observation of which lead to salvation, the neglect to destruc
tion. Thus the art of government is not to make or administe
new laws but to maintain a condition in which the laws of natur
freely operate. Social life must follow nature—that is, must b
regulated by an intelligent adherence to divine law. Therefor
in Dupont's words, " there is a natural judge of all ordinance
even of the sovereign's." This judge, who recognizes n
exceptions, is simply the evidence of their conformity with, o
opposition to, natural laws. The Chinese, the Physiocrats be
lieved, had so far been alone in appreciating this truth, " for,
said Baudeau, they speak of " the order or voice of heaven an
reduce all government to a single law to conform to the voic
of heaven."

The Physiocrats were therefore left with the task of discovering the law of nature and persuading the rulers of France to conform not to their own wishes but to the dictates of Heaven. Fortunately the natural laws of society were much easier to discover than their counterparts in the physical world. Newton had established the truth of a natural law only after many years of arduous calculation, but the formulæ of social gravitation were believed by the Physiocrats to be immediately "evident," since the supply of apples and other commodities always came in response to men's demands. "The order," said Mercier, "obviously most advantageous to each nation only needs to be known to be observed." Man had only "to examine himself, to find within him an articulate conception of these laws." A simple process of introspection was conclusive, though an empirical investigation might be necessary for scientific demonstration.

Descartes and Locke together offered the psychological basis for this confident conclusion. "Evidence," declared Mercier, "is a clear and distinct discernment of sentiments which we have and of all perceptions which depend on them." The "evidence" here is Cartesian : the "rational intuition" which is corroborated by "the witness of the senses." "It would be a great enterprise," wrote Thomas, in an *éloge* on Descartes in 1765, "only to judge of all customs, usages and laws after the great maxim of Descartes, according to the evidence. . . truth exists by itself and is in nature, and the act of judging is nothing else than the talent of opening the eyes." The influence of Locke was in the same direction. The social truth became more certain when innate ideas were abolished. Condillac, himself a notable economist, had already argued that the child's only instinctive tendency was to repeat some sensations called pleasures, and to avoid others called pains. "Love of pleasure and aversion from pain are the two great springs of humanity," said Mercier, long before Bentham had arrived at the same formula. Unhampered by the false teachings of morality, men would soon find that this simple tendency led them to happiness ; being endowed with a capacity for reflection, they would quickly discover their dependence on one another, would avoid giving offence to those who could inflict

pain in return, and realize that their own happiness lay in th
welfare of others. Christian ethics could easily be deduced fror
self-interest, since, as Mercier put it, " not to do to others wha
we should not wish them to do to us is an invariable law c
reason."

The task of the economist, therefore, is to work out th
detailed application of principles which are evident to ever
reasonable human being who cares to reflect upon his experienc
Since these principles are part of the law of nature, and every
where valid and invariable, economics must cease to be a matte
of opinion, of probabilities and surmises, and become a scienc
whose conclusions are as reliable as those of the physicist. Onc
the information is obtained and the laws known, the calculu
can do the rest. Economics then becomes a question o
mathematics. The amount of taxation, for instance, which th
Sovereign is right in demanding can be discovered by simpl
" addition and subtraction." His calculation may be wrong
if so, his error is easily demonstrable, for, with the *Tablea*
économique as a basis, anyone may check him, and his conclusio
must, like a proposition in Euclid, be either right or wrong.

By an easy transition the whole service of government seeme
to the Physiocrats capable of the same mathematical treatment
The warning of Montesquieu that the application and develop
ment of natural law vary with place and circumstance wa
altogether neglected. The *a priori* habits of classical though
were reinforced by a mathematical approach, and political anc
economic problems were all capable of simple and final solutions
" It will suffice to have that amount of capacity and patienc
which a child who is good at arithmetic employs, to becom
a good politician or a truly good citizen," wrote anothe
economist.[1] Mirabeau declared that politics, on the basis o
natural law, was more exact than any of the physical sciences
To collect particular facts and deduce principles from them
might be a " very good or even the only method " in othe
sciences, such as chemistry or physics, but it was quite un
necessary to establish the truths of politics and economics,

---

[1] *Vide* Weulersse, *Le Mouvement physiocratique*, vol. ii., p. 123.

which were " everywhere susceptible of decisive demonstration."
The Physiocrats, believing in the universality of natural law,
could cast all caution to the winds. Bentham, who repudiated
the whole conception of natural law, was scarcely less optimistic
about the possibility of founding an exact science of politics.
Bentham saw, however, that such a science was possible only
—even theoretically—if the pleasures and pains which moved
men to action could be classified. The " felicific calculus " was
an indispensable supplement to the " *tableau économique*." But
Dupont anticipated James Mill's arithmetical political science
without the least attempt at psychological analysis. " If the
different powers [in the State]," he wrote, " are equal, there is no
authority ; if one among them is superior, that is the authority,
the others are nothing." Historical considerations seemed as
futile to the Physiocrats as to the early utilitarians. The past
is to be remembered only to be condemned. " All human legislation has been only the institution of legal disorder, excited
by the particular interest and excused on the ground of the
public interest."

The task of the enlightened ruler in the eighteenth century
was, therefore, a godlike one ; as " a living image of the most
high " he could harmonize all things by simply substituting
natural order for existing chaos. The first and most evident
teaching of natural law was the mutual interdependence of men.
In a natural society men and nations would freely exchange
their superfluous products, and all would gain, since some were
rich in one thing, some in another. Particular interests would
then automatically serve the public well-being. This would
always be the result if the natural right to private property
were recognized. A man who worked had the best title to the
fruits of his industry, and would hardly work well unless pricked
by the incentive of personal gain. The first duty of the State,
therefore, was to abolish all hampering restrictions and feudal
contracts which kept men from enjoying the property which
was naturally theirs. If men were to benefit by their mutual
interdependence, private property must be coupled with freedom of contract and equality of opportunity. Both production
and distribution were best served by freedom of the market,

in which supply and demand swing upon their eternal balance.
Though it was left to Adam Smith to make the full deduction
from the theories of division of labour and natural inter
dependence, the need for international peace and its connection
with international free trade finds a prominent place in Physio
cratic writing. If it is desirable for individual men to exchange
freely, it is equally important that there should be no barrier
between provinces, and, since " each nation is only a province
of the great Kingdom of Nations," universal free trade will
result in universal prosperity.

The prospect was certainly bright. Mercier wrote : " Each
of us, by favour of this full and entire liberty, and pricked by
desire of enjoyment, is occupied, according to his state, in vary
ing, multiplying, perfecting the objects of enjoyment which
must be shared amongst us, and thus increases the sum of
the common happiness by increasing his private happiness.
And so each in the sum total of the common happiness would
take a particular sum which ought to belong to him. We must
admire the way in which every man becomes an instrument of
the happiness of others, and the manner in which this happiness
seems to communicate itself to the whole. Speaking literally,
of course, I do not know if in this State we shall see a few un
happy people, but if there are any, they will be so few in number
and the number of the happy will be so great that we need not
be much concerned about helping them. All our interests and
wills will be linked to the interest and will of the Sovereign,
creating for our common good an harmony, which can only be
regarded as the work of a kind Providence that wishes the land
to be full of happy men."

This is the very apotheosis of optimistic Liberalism. In an
age of feudal privilege, dynastic war and arbitrary taxation,
the removal of legal and customary barriers appeared to be all
that was required for happiness and prosperity. It was easy to
believe in the existence of a natural harmony when so much
misery was obviously caused by artificial maladjustment;
freedom and *laissez-faire* seemed the same thing to a generation
fettered and choked by unreasonable methods of interference.
Agriculture and trade could never prosper while the feudal

perior, the monarch and the tax-gatherer took from the
easant and the merchant the best fruits of their industry.
ngland seemed to the Physiocrats a model only less to be
nitated than China : they praised the system of peasant pro-
rietorship in England just at the time when England was in
ct ceasing to have peasant proprietors and when the land
as being absorbed by great landowners who had often as little
terest in agriculture as the French *noblesse*. But the com-
arison served for the time. The demand for freedom of contract
d for private property involved the reversal of the whole
cial system in France ; and the Revolution itself gave the land
the peasants, who, having won it at the expense of the private
ghts of their feudal superiors, have adhered steadfastly to a
lief in the absolute rights of property ever since.

4. SOCIALISM AND UTOPIA—MESLIER, MABLY AND MORELLY

In an agricultural society property and equality are naturally
sociated. To the French peasant they were coincident. In
community of small farmers, all who own are equal, and,
here there are no differences of rank, degrees of prosperity
 not give rise to social problems. The freeholding peasant
 not directly in the power of any capitalist, and feels himself
e superior, rather than the inferior, of the merchant, while the
ews of the landless labourer are seldom expressed and almost
ways unheeded. In an urban civilization, on the other hand,
here land and inheritance play a smaller part, property and
quality seem contradictory conceptions. Distinction depends on
oney, not on land, and in an industrialized community money
eans power and carries with it social superiority. When the
wn worker demanded equality, therefore, he was not asking
r a change of legal status, but for a different distribution of
e product of industry. Socialist theory has always suffered,
d still suffers to-day, from a failure to distinguish between
o contradictory views of what this new distribution should be.
he worker might claim his right to a just share in the product
f industry : in this case he was using the orthodox argument
at since every man is entitled to the reward of his own labour

a system which gives the capitalist and the shareholder the first claim on profits is inequitable. But since it was in fact impossible to apportion exactly what was produced by labour and what by capital in an industrial society, the worker might demand that the whole product of industry should be vested in the State and then equally divided among producers. Even before the Revolution some writers declared that all profits were the result of labour, and one, Simon-Henri Linguet, anticipated the theory of "surplus value" and the "iron law of wages." Communism, however, does not depend on the Marxian argument, and consistent egalitarians, alike innocent of dialectic or of economic science, demanded that the social product should be divided according to need, not according to productive capacity.

France was a land of peasants, not of industrial workers, and the main current of revolutionary economics was therefore in the direction of equal rights of ownership, and not of equal distribution. The demand for property and equality meant quite simply that all should have the legal right to free economic activity—a claim that would have been fairly described as "equality of opportunity" only if there had been a universal system of free education and if all rights of inheritance had been abolished. This theory assumed the existence of a natural harmony. But even in the eighteenth century some observers were unfavourably impressed by the effects of the growing capitalist organization, and doubted whether the interests of employers and employed were identical. And before the rise of these early urban socialists there were moralists who, being moved to pity by the misery of the poor, and haunted by the precepts of the gospels, recalled the canons of the mediæval Church and the ideal republic of Plato. They denied the right of the individual to act without consciousness of social obligation, and described enlightened self-interest as the sin of avarice. Eighteenth-century socialism sprang from a moral objection to the theory that luxury is socially beneficial. It was in origin a Puritan attack on economic hedonism.

Thus, although the results of *laissez-faire* economics could be only dimly foreseen in the eighteenth century, a number of writers, who joined with the Physiocrats in criticizing the *ancien régime*, repudiated the remedy they offered. They denounced the existing order because rights were divorced from service : it seemed to them no remedy formally to recognize a practical evil and to substitute irresponsible competition for irresponsible privilege. The search for money and for possessions was in itself bad. Private vices, they declared, could never be public benefits : no moral, communal nor happy life was possible upon the basis of individual self-seeking. A community implied a common effort. The individual ownership of property in an unorganized society would lead merely to an aristocracy of wealth founded on the destruction of an aristocracy of birth : a new struggle between rich and poor would take the place of the existing one between the privileged and the Third Estate.

Socialism in the eighteenth century was primarily moral, and only incidentally economic. It found its inspiration in the conception of a natural state of communism, and supported it by accounts of the primitive virtues of the American Indians whom Jesuit missionaries described. It looked to Plato and to Stoicism for its theory and the Sparta of Lycurgus became its stock example of an egalitarian society. The Christian Church, too, though in the main ready enough to find the usual moral justification for institutions condemned in the New Testament, gave birth to occasional priests who contrasted the political Church of the eighteenth century with the simple life of the early Christians.

The moralist believed that the love of money was the root of social evil : it was bad that some should live as parasites on the labour of others, worse that most people should want to do so. As long as men based their society on self-interest, struggle and chaos were inevitable. Socialists agreed with Physiocrats that in a natural society men would help one another without pain or effort, but were sure that this desirable result would not automatically follow from the encouragement of selfishness and the removal of State regulation. Harmony would take the place of chaos only if society were deliberately organized on a moral basis. It was absurd to expect a harmony from the absence of order, or a guiding hand to bring universal peace and prosperity to men engaged in cutting one another's throats.

Even in the first half of the century, men like Montesquieu and d'Argenson agreed that democracy implied socialism. Montesquieu had argued that a democracy must be inspired by civic virtue, and it was rare "for there to be much virtue where men's fortunes were unequal." D'Argenson also treated property, not as a natural right, but as a matter of utility, and criticized Montesquieu for thinking that economic inequality was ever desirable, even in a monarchy. He held, on the contrary, that "a legislator, like a doctor, ought to aim at banishing inequality and luxury," and declared that the extravagance of private individuals in France was one of the usual signs of decadence. He complained of monopolists, compared great financiers to drones in a hive, and proceeded, in a remarkable passage, to attack the whole theory of capitalism. Why, he asks, this elaborate method of enabling a few to accumulate all the power and money? Are big merchants really good for the country? Would it not be better if the State lent money to small cultivators rather than to merchants who made themselves monopolists? "The question comes down to this: does the well-being of a pond demand the existence of huge pike which grow fat on all the little and moderate-sized fish?"[1]

This was an isolated view. The main stream of eighteenth-century socialism begins in 1755 with Rousseau's attack upon private property in the essay on *The Origin of Inequality*. The simple and carefree state of nature had been destroyed by the introduction of private property, and from this fatal departure from natural (that is, primitive as well as ideal) conditions came all the crop of social evils and unjust laws which the usurpers of the common stock of property imposed on the others. The present institution of private property could not be defended by Locke's argument that it was the natural result of labour. When there ceased to be enough land for everyone ownership changed its character: the owner used his strategic advantage to make others do the work for him. Thus Rousseau's

---

[1] The whole passage is quoted by Lichtenberger, *op. cit.*, 98-99.

whole attack on wealth could be deduced from a mere hint in the *Essay on Civil Government*. The wealthy, Rousseau argued, not having either good arguments or superior physical strength, conceived " the profoundest plan that ever entered the human mind." They made allies of their adversaries, persuading them to institute rules of justice, to stabilize the *status quo*, and thus safeguard their ill-gotten gains. So did the rich persuade the poor to run " headlong to their chains in the hope of securing their liberty." Society is therefore founded on fraud, and a revolution, followed by a return to primitive communism, seems the natural conclusion of Rousseau's argument. Rousseau, however, explicitly repudiated this inference. "What then is to be done?" he writes. "Must society be totally abolished, must *meum* and *tuum* be annihilated, and must we return again to live among bears?" No, that was impossible, unless for any fortunate individuals whose passions were still uncorrupted and who could subsist on plants or acorns and live without laws and magistrates. Those who had once learned the moral law " will respect the sacred bonds of their respective communities, they will love their fellow-citizens, scrupulously obey the laws, although they will never lose their contempt for a constitution which is only rendered tolerable by so much good government."[1]

Other more logical writers held that, if private property had been unjustly acquired and was upheld by class legislation, it must be abolished.[2] Among those who reached this position the Curé Meslier was the least compromising. He was an obscure country vicar, who, after forty years' labour in his parish, struggling, as it seemed in vain, on behalf of his flock against the extortions of their overlords, is said to have starved himself

---

[1] *Vide* Appendix II. of *The Origin of Inequality*.

[2] One learned Benedictine, Dom Deschamps, tried to escape from the dilemma by the same idealistic device as Rousseau. Indeed his conclusions were more extreme than those of *The Social Contract*, and in many particulars he anticipated Hegel. In his *Letters on the Spirit of the Age* (1769), and later, in *The Voice of Reason against the Reason of the Time*, he looked forward to a society in which individual personality is absorbed in that of the State. He built a Utopia akin to that of Plato, but founded on the doctrines of Catholicism : the Church had been originally right in regarding individual property as the result of original sin.

to death, only taking the precaution of ensuring that several manuscript copies of three bulky volumes in which his real convictions were stated should reach the hands of the sceptical *philosophes* in Paris. He preferred, as he said, to be roasted after than before his death. His attack was primarily directed against organized religion, which in practice upheld private property and other social evils which theoretically it condemned. He ridicules the conception of a personal or spiritual deity, is convinced that there can be no life after death, and regards French institutions, including the Church and the monarchy, as a single fraud perpetuated by the propaganda of religious and political superstition.

In his sixth book he deals especially with the social failure of the Church, which " suffered and authorized the abuses, vexations and tyranny of the great," and made no protest against the un-Christian condition of society. For the social order was morally evil, and at its root was private property. Instead of a society of Christian parishes, where men and women co-operated as brothers and sisters, one actually saw the workers starving because their produce was devoured by the idle and the useless. The rich were proud, ambitious and arrogant. What could the poor feel but hatred, envy and lust of revenge? How hardly could either rich or poor enter into the kingdom of heaven, where love and mutual service reigned! How could Christianity and social inequality co-exist? Christ had taught that blessedness was service : the religion which adopted His name supported conditions of privilege and class hatred.

The ruling class based their power upon successful robbery, and secured their stolen property by unjust laws. They lived as vermin preying on the lives of those who worked. The greatest of all vermin were kings. Samuel had vainly warned the people against setting up a monarchy, and from Saul down to Louis XIV. kings always used their subjects as chattels, stealing their goods and calling it taxation, laying waste their homes and driving them to slaughter in the name of the Prince of Peace. *Le Grand Monarque* was the perfect type of ruler, living in luxury, flaunting his concubines, "great at least in love." Indeed, adds Meslier, he was certainly not surnamed the Great " for great and praise-

worthy actions . . . but for great injustices, robberies, usurpations, desolations, ravages and massacres of men on all sides."

While the aristocratic vermin thrive under his protection the
priests of the Christian Church frighten the people with stories
of an imaginary Devil to prevent their revolting against the
ladylike and gentlemanly devils who live upon them. Worst of
all are the great clergy themselves, who dwell in palaces, and
the religious orders, who wear ridiculous costumes to prove
that they have taken sacred vows which they have not the least
intention of keeping. Finally, to complete their hypocrisy, they
lead the people to church, and there, in " lugubrious tones,"
ask God " not to deal with them according to their infirmities
nor remember their iniquities . . . but to help them to slaughter
their enemies with success, thanking Him for their prosperity,
and ending the whole ceremony with a pious *Te Deum*."

Such a world, Meslier declares, cannot be the work of an
all-powerful God, unless, indeed, God and the Devil are one.
If there is a good God the malice of men must have thwarted
His intentions. On the one side the rich in paradise, on the other
the poor in hell ; between them is a great gulf fixed—a social
gulf which cannot be passed until there is community of goods
and equality of service. The myth of religion, the political
myth and the myth of property are all part of the same fraud.
Even the social institution of the family is evil.

In a natural society men and women would live together and
part again on inclination. The miseries of domestic life would
disappear and children would be brought up together in communal schools. No one would fear poverty ; " equal sharing
of moderate work for all " would take the place of idleness on
the one side and excessive toil on the other. Social hatred, class
contempt and the cries which arose from them would cease.
The true doctrines of Christ would at length be practised ; men
would once more return to the ideals set them by the early
Church, when " all things were in common " and distribution
was regulated by the needs of the weakest, not the might of
the strongest.

Who could wonder if the poor attempted to overthrow such
a system by force ? When the people were told the truth would

it not be a reproach to them if they did not entirely destroy "the odious yoke of their tyrannical Government"? "Where are the Jacques Clément and the Ravaillac of our France? Are there none still alive in our days to stun and to stab all these detestable monsters, enemies of the human race, and by this means to deliver the people from tyranny?" When the great political and religious fraud was discovered, would not injustice and iniquity be quickly overthrown and the equal and free communities of the ancient world be re-established? Would not the people make all goods common in every parish and all share equally in the fruits of their common labours? "Dear people, your safety is in your own hands, your deliverance would depend only on yourselves if you could but understand."

Meslier indicted the economic and social order on the ground that it was fundamentally immoral and un-Christian : he suggested that communism was the natural order to be established after the probable revolution. The future society was described in more detail by Meslier's younger contemporaries, Morelly and the Abbé Mably. Morelly described the communist society in both prose and verse,[1] while Mably preached a similar gospel of equality in his *Entretiens de Phocion*, his *Doutes proposées aux Philosophes*, his *De la Legislation* and his *Du Gouvernment de Politique*. Morelly and Mably completely rejected the current individualism and declared that happiness is to be found only in an organized society where individual satisfaction is deliberately subordinated to the public good. Voltaire's irreligious Deism, the natural order of the Physiocrats, the pleasure-pain psychology of Helvétius and Holbach—all these would alike lead to anarchy. Did not the advocates of natural harmony really admit this themselves? They did not altogether trust to Providence. They argued that to serve one's own economic pleasure automatically secured the public welfare ; but they had not the courage of their convictions and made constant calls upon the legislator to supplement the work of the Deity. Sometimes they seemed to hope that men would

---

[1] Morelly's principal works are the *Basiliade* and the *Code de la Nature*. The latter has recently been admirably re-edited with a fine introduction by Gilbert Chinard. (Paris 1950).

realize that unselfishness was the true path to happiness, but even Holbach admitted the need of laws to restrain the unenlightened. Reason, Mably thought, might indeed show that nature "unites and confounds the general happiness of society and the particular happiness of each citizen," but reason alone was certainly not powerful enough to curb the passions of individuals to whom chance desire would often seem more important than ultimate happiness. The Encyclopædists' mistake was to emphasize happiness rather than virtue. Happiness was only the incidental result of virtue, and it was virtue which laws should foster. "Is it not certain," Mably wrote, "that the polity ought to make us love virtue and that virtue is the only object which legislators, laws and magistrates ought to have in view?"[1]

Morelly took the trouble to describe in detail the polity which could make us live virtuously. His true pattern of natural legislation is remarkable in many respects and closely anticipates the proposals of Fourier. Three fundamental and sacred laws will make all the familiar social evils impossible, and under their protection it will be "impossible to be depraved." Firstly, no private possessions beyond those which are necessary for the individual's daily comfort will be permitted; secondly, every citizen will be a public servant and his needs supplied by the State; thirdly, he will himself contribute to the general welfare in accordance with his powers, talents and age, performing his duties under a strict and elaborate economic code.

The nation will be divided into families, tribes and garden-cities of the same size; each city will have a public square, round which "uniform and agreeable" shops and assembly halls will be grouped. Beyond these will begin the residential quarters of the city, of the same size and shape, regularly divided by parallel streets. Each tribe will occupy one quarter, and each family a spacious, convenient and uniform building. On the outskirts of the city, beyond the workshops and special houses in which the agricultural workers will live, there will be a public hospital, a workhouse and a prison, in which any citizen who is unfortunate enough to be ill, decrepit or criminal

---

[1] *Entretiens de Phocion : Œuvres*, t. x. 511.

in these ideal circumstances will be looked after. Still further off will be the "burial field," a strongly fortified place for the perpetual imprisonment of anyone who has deserved to be " civilly dead."

All buying and selling will be communal, durable goods housed in public stores will be rationed and distributed daily to the public. The citizens may, however, exchange their surplus agricultural produce in the market square. The city will be surrounded by cultivated land sufficient for the needs of the inhabitants, and all the youths of the city from twenty-one to twenty-five years of age will be obliged to help in farming.

In every profession one master will watch over ten workmen, each master taking turns to be head of the whole profession for one year. The chief of the profession will direct all the labour and, in consultation with fathers of the families, see that the standard dress of each trade is worn "without any superfluous adornment" by each worker during his hours of labour, though every citizen will have a different holiday dress of a "modest and serviceable kind." "All vanity" will be suppressed by the ruling fathers. At the age of ten every child will learn a profession which appeals to him, at fifteen or eighteen he will be married, and after his agricultural period take his turn as a master. At the age of forty, having satisfactorily passed through these various stages, he will retire, doing only voluntary work, happy in the knowledge that in the event of becoming old and infirm "convenient lodging," nourishment and entertainment will be provided.

The nation will be divided into multiples of ten, and composed of federations of families in tribes, cities and provinces, and will be governed by a senate, composed of fathers who have reached the age of fifty. Each subdivision of the nation has its own council of fathers, who will send representatives to its superior council. The supreme senate is to guard the constitution and to prevent the city senators ever contravening the fundamental laws. Within this limit the councils of fathers have absolute power. Any individual loss of liberty will be atoned for by the formula which begins every public order : " Reason wishes, the law orders."

Every kind of excess will be prevented by education, marriage
laws and the penal code. No celibacy is permitted after forty
and marriage will usually be early. A marriage ceremony will
take place in public at the beginning of each year, when each
eligible young man, in the presence of the senators and public,
will choose the girl who pleases him, and after obtaining her
consent take her for his wife. Marriage is indissoluble for ten
years, after which divorce is permitted on adequate grounds,
but made absolute only after a period of six months, during
which the partners may not meet. This last provision appears
to be the only proposal of Morelly which the modern world
has adopted.

Mothers will tend their own children up to the age of five,
after which the city will take care of them and provide them
with all they need, including an exact uniform education. Parents
who have special interest in education will look after them,
all the boys in one building and the girls in another, where
they will learn the laws of the community and be introduced
gradually to their future occupation. They are then passed on
to the care of a professional master until they are old enough
to enter their agricultural period. The whole process is to be
most carefully supervised by the fathers, lest any suspicion of
the spirit of property should corrupt the young and " any
fables, stories or ridiculous fictions " should warp their natural
love of truth.

Morelly recognizes that there may be individuals who will
not immediately approve of such a system. Like Plato he
feared the critical habits of the young, who may be ignorant
of the laws of nature. He is especially anxious to encourage
scientific research and to give studious children every opportunity of indulging their curiosity and improving the resources
of the State, but no one may be allowed to question the
simple tenets of the prescribed religion. The existence of a
just Creator, the natural operation of His laws, the working
of His intelligence in the world, must be accepted, and the
hopelessness of attempting any further inquiry into the eternal
mysteries acknowledged. The sacred laws are to be engraved
on columns in the public square, where every child may read

them : he will also learn to celebrate the simple, happy an
unheroic story of his nation and its distinguished citizens i
eloquence, poetry and painting.

If, in spite of this education, any citizen should be so ur
natural as to kill his fellow, plot against the sacred constitution
or introduce " detestable property," after conviction by th
supreme senate he would be shut up for the rest of his life i
a specially constructed cell in the place of public burial. Othe
crimes—adultery, lack of respect to elders or assaults in
volving " outrageous epithets or blows "—would be punishe
with shorter periods of imprisonment.

Both Morelly and Mably assumed that a very modera
amount of labour would produce sufficient for human want
If nature were more bountiful men would have less reason fo
association, and the value of co-operation might never have bee
discovered. "The world is a table amply furnished for ever
guest." No one has the right to assume control or to tal
more than his share : all are hungry and all may be satisfied. Bi
Mably knew that chaos, not harmony, would reign at the tabl
however well stocked, unless men learnt to curb their appetite
Quarrels might arise in the distribution of plenty just as
the sharing of a little, unless virtue had supplanted greed
men's minds.

Happiness can never come from libertinism, nor from a
excessive asceticism, but only from virtue, which is ment
harmony, "the peace of the soul, which is often troubled by th
revolt of the senses. Virtue ought to fly excess and all hum;
morality to consist in a wise moderation which can reconci
the sublimity of reason and the folly of passion. In a wor
morality, if it is to open the way to virtue and happiness, mu
begin by diminishing needs, since it is in these needs that th
passions of men find their source and their nourishment."

The most destructive of all the passions is " avarice." T
other vices are its offspring. " It is the Proteus, the mercur
the basis, the vehicle of all vices. Analyse vanity, pride, ambitio
knavery, hypocrisy, villainy ; all resolves itself into this subt
and pernicious element which you will find in the very hear
of disinterested people." Avarice is not a necessary part

man nature, but is developed by an immoral society. Men
e naturally affectionate and full of compassion, and reason co-
erates with natural goodness in showing men the "happy
cessity of being beneficent." The question then arises how
en ever came to behave as they do. Mably thinks that no
e can explain the origin of evil, but Morelly gives a similar
swer to that of Rousseau.

When the growth of population made land scarce, new
cieties took the place of the primitive family. Individuals
re allowed to "usurp possessions which ought to belong to
manity." When Mercier de la Rivière talks of just laws and
en defends the private ownership of land and capital he has
stroyed the basis of the natural order which would admit
ly personal property. Where a man may add to his posses-
ons at the expense of another, avarice triumphs, and the very
art of the community is corrupted.

In his *De la Législation* (which appeared in the same year as
he Wealth of Nations) Mably stages a debate upon the ethics
private property between an Englishman and a Swede. The
nglishman is aglow with the new Liberal doctrines. He has
doubt that freedom makes England the greatest country in
e world : its glory, strength and wealth are the direct result of
flourishing trade. When mistakes occur (as in the recent case
the American Colonies) it is because the principles of free
ade and international unity have been imperfectly grasped.
n the whole, however, he is sure that there can be nothing
riously wrong with a country whose wealth is so great and
10se Constitution is so wonderful. But he is more open-minded
an most patriots. In the course of two volumes of argument
e Swede is gradually able to convince him that Sweden is
better country than England. In Sweden, it seems, there is
longer a search for glory (Charles XII. is happily forgotten),
d no preoccupation with money-making. Contentment and
scipline are the rule—the effect of a moderate prosperity,
sufficiency of work and a comparative equality of wealth.
appiness is found to arise from virtue of manners, not from
undance of material goods. In Sweden character comes before
nown and contentment before property. " In our poverty,"

says the Swede, "we can still hope to make citizens: you by increasing your riches will make only mercenaries."

England has been led by the search for wealth to forget the true ends of life. Happiness, however, comes from restricting needs, not from multiplying possessions. This is why sumptuary laws are wise, why Lycurgus was the greatest of legislators and Plato of political thinkers. It is a mistake too to believe that money means liberty. England is wealthy, but liberty lives only in the hearts of such of her poor as have not learned to want to be rich. For the most part rich and poor are alike corrupted: the rich grow arrogant and grasping through success; the poor envious and rebellious through failure. The boasted perfection of the Constitution offers no remedy: Magna Charta may have destroyed political tyranny, but it did not make England as happy as North America, where primitive communism was still to be found.

Montesquieu had been right in saying that an aristocracy would govern well only if it were animated by a sense of honour and in prophesying that the British aristocracy would degenerate if it took part in commerce. Avarice would increase and the disasters attendant upon private property grow and overwhelm the nation. "As for us," says the Swede, "who see the infinite evils which have come from this fatal Pandora's Box, ought we not, if the least ray of hope gleams upon us, to aspire to that happy communism which the poets have so much praised and so much regretted: a state which was established by Lycurgus at Sparta, one whose revival Plato hoped for in his Republic, and which, thanks to the degradation of manners, can be only a chimera in the world?"

Mably easily dismisses the objections usually raised to communistic proposals. The Englishman, though at length convinced that a communist society is theoretically the best, argues that the motive of acquisition is so deeply engrained in society that it cannot now be discounted. Existing society is held together by the hope of reward and the fear of punishment; men no longer want equality and are spurred to industry by self-interest and ambition. The Swede replies by recommending the study of history, quotes the example of Sparta and mentions

hat primitive peoples are untroubled by avarice, which is the
offspring, not the progenitor, of the institution of private
property. " I think," he says, magnificently begging the
question, " that no one will contest the obviousness of this
proposition, that where no property existed there could not
be any of its pernicious consequences."

Men need no such spur to industry. In a natural society their
necessities force them to work until their simple wants are
satisfied. The corruption of civilization is nowhere better illustrated than by the fact that men are constantly induced to desire
new luxuries and to put a fictitious value upon the artificial
distinctions which money brings. Communism, not competition,
is the way of nature. " In place of the essential order of nature,"
writes Mably, in replying to the Physiocrats, " I am much
afraid that we are given the natural order only for avarice,
greed and folly." The only test of a good law is whether it adds
to the substance of equality : everyone should be ensured a
subsistence wage and laws should be passed prohibiting luxury
and guarding against avarice. How absurd " to ruin everyone
on the plea of enriching property owners. . . . What man could
be so unreasonable as to claim that a sane policy should not lay
down for the rich the conditions under which they may enjoy
their fortune and prevent them from oppressing the poor?"

Mably is scarcely more hopeful than Rousseau of a return
to a natural society, and is almost as cautious as Rousseau
when the practical question of rebellion is mooted. " Perhaps,"
he says, " men are now too depraved ever to be able to have a
wise polity," though he elsewhere admits that the people are
sovereign and have the right to rebel if they wish. " Choose,"
he cries in one passage, " between revolution and slavery, there
is no half-way house."

Mably, in fact, agreed with Rousseau in thinking reason a weak
bulwark against passion. If the corporate feeling which alone
would support his communistic society should ever come, it
would be the result, not of self-interest, but of a fervent religion.
He argues that men have an intuitive knowledge of God and a
consciousness of right and wrong, and that atheism and Voltairean
deism are only " fashionable cults," natural reactions from the

superstitions of Catholicism. Materialism is as fatal to humanit
as "war, famine or plague." The true legislator will stimula
the innate religious feeling in man by insisting on a simpl
religious ceremony, emphasizing the lesson of God's con
demnation of the wicked and reward of the good. Moreove
Mably differs from Rousseau because the community he im
agines is not national but world-wide. Patriotism must be
subordinate virtue : only a universal sentiment of brotherhoo
will prevent jealousy between States destroying the harmon
resulting from economic communism. Three things are essenti
if men are to live the good life : internal equality within th
State, political organization of States into a world federatio
and, lastly, a religion to reinforce the teaching of reason an
to keep private and group passions at bay. Mably was an inter
national socialist, and he remained an abbé and a Christian i
spite of his free-thinking.

5. THE FOURTH ESTATE—REVOLUTIONARY THEORY—LINGUET T
BABEUF

The communist theory of men like Morelly and Mabl
had little practical application to eighteenth-century conditions
They were moralists, content to praise a natural order remotel
staged in the past or the future. During the last ten years of th
ancien régime, however, the condition of the landless proletaria
was the subject of numerous pamphlets, and many reformers
among whom Necker is perhaps the best known, at least talke
as if they were socialists. They were not content to attack th
Government and to demand an equal system of taxation, bu
went on to repudiate the whole institution of private property
When the time came to make definite suggestions, however
the majority of them were satisfied with demanding a guarantee
living wage. Babeuf was alone in making any serious attemp
to establish socialism when the middle-class character of th
Revolution had disappointed the hopes of his party.

The Fourth Estate stormed the Bastille, but it had few spokes
men in the States-General and but little voice in its election
An occasional pamphlet, like that of Devérité, was significant o

uch submerged feeling.[1] As " a working man " he complained
at he would have no chance of expressing his views in the
tates-General. He recounts the " grievances of a poor devil "
ho can only play the part of an " army mule " bent beneath
e weight of the baggage, while the battle between the privi-
ged classes and the bourgeoisie raged about the rights of
roperty. "How will laws of property help a poor labourer? "
lis limbs are his only capital. Out of his precarious earnings
e pays away a large share in taxes to the rich. Under a wise
overnment great fortunes would be limited and " taxes would
e increased in geometric proportion as fortunes increased."
Under the existing system the more luxury the less taxation.
he effect of agricultural and industrial machinery was to leave
ie labourer at the mercy of the rich : those who laboured
eceived an ever smaller share in the product of industry. The
estruction of machinery as a whole would perhaps be too drastic
step, but its operation should certainly be stopped where it
aused distress and unemployment. Other spokesmen of the
ourth Estate declared that the demands of the peasants failed
o meet the needs of those without land, that mere reform of
he iniquitous system of taxation and the abolition of feudalism
vere inadequate. One of the clauses of the civil compact is that
o one should be condemend to die of hunger.

Many of the later leaders of the Revolution went far in the
ame direction before they obtained power. Carra, the future
Girondist, remarked, some years before the Revolution, that
here were limits to the patience of the poor : they had strong
arms, and if they could not look after themselves by cultivating
part of the land as their property they could do so " by purging
t of the monsters who devoured it." [2] His practical advice, however, was that they should claim their natural rights, including
hat of an adequate livelihood. A number of other writers,
equally violent against the injustice of poverty and equally
willing to argue that democracy might ultimately involve a
more equal division of wealth, still agreed that, as things were,

---

[1] *La vie et les doléances d'un pauvre diable pour servir de ce qu'on voudra aux
prochains Etats-Généraux* (1789).
[2] *Vide* Lichtenberger, *op. cit.*, 394-395.

the existing institution of private property was useful and unalterable.[1] Distributivism seemed a more hopeful doctrine than communism.

There were others less easily contented. Gosselin declared that the happiness of man does not demand the sacrifice of wealth or the repudiation of the pleasures of social life or the neglect of agriculture. And what then does it demand? Simply an organization which guarantees to those who work a sure means of subsistence. "Land belongs to the whole community" and should be taken, though not without compensation, from the big proprietors and shared out until France is " filled with happy people who will ever bless the bold mortal who carries out such a revolution, and becomes the artisan of their happiness and the author of their prosperity."[2]

In the same spirit Boissel, after the usual commendation of Rousseau's analysis of economic inequality, points to the weakness of his political solution. "He only considered the origin of evil and did not trouble to look for any remedy or for the origin of good."[3] He deplored the first theft of communal property, but accepted its disastrous results as inevitable. Yet a remedy must be found. Violent revolution could still be avoided, Boissel argued, if communist schools were established and industry nationalized. A sound and moral revolution might then be peacefully accomplished.

Brissot de Warville's *Philosophic Researches on the Right of Property and on Theft in their Relations to Nature and Society* appeared in 1780.[4] His main argument is that, since property is a social not a natural institution, theft is not a crime against natural law, and should not be punished by death. Property is justified by nature only in so far as it fulfils essential needs. Thus, as Proudhon was later to urge, where property is unjustly divided it is not the thief who breaks the moral law but the man who has seized more than his share. There is no " sacred right of property to travel by carriage while we have legs, or to eat the food of twenty men when one man's share is enough." In a

---

[1] Lichtenberger, 426-427.　　　　　　　　　　[2] *Ibid.*, p. 438.
[3] *Ibid.*, pp. 448-449.　　　　　　　　　　　　[4] *Ibid.*, p. 413 ff.

subsequent book [1] Brissot spoke of the laws " as a conspiracy of the stronger against the weaker, the rich against the poor, authority against humanity." Yet his conclusions were only mildly revolutionary. He felt, as Rousseau had, that though the institution of private property had originated in injustice it could not be overthrown—theft might be morally justified but it could not be tolerated : it should be considered a minor offence, not a crime punishable by death. During the Revolution itself Brissot was attacked by Morellet for having defended robbery : he replied by pointing out the moderation of his programme, and pleaded that in any case his writings of twelve years earlier had been only schoolboy essays, not to be taken seriously.

All these writers advocated economic change before the Revolution, and were satisfied with political democracy when they found themselves in power. Linguet is a unique and neglected figure. He was a barrister, who was early disbarred as a result of an attack upon law and property, published as early as 1763. During the final decade before the Revolution he poured into the journal of which he was editor a constant stream of brilliant social analysis mingled with invective. His position was unusual, but logical. He was a conservative who saw through the shams of society and exposed them, who stated the Ricardian theory of the iron law of wages and anticipated Marx in declaring that there was a class war, and that it would be fought out on the issue of private property. He argued, however, that since property rights were now the basis of the whole social system, the struggle would destroy society itself : it was therefore best to keep things as they were as long as possible. His unflinching analysis of social injustice, however, was scarcely likely to aid conservatism. The most sincere of pessimists, he saw no remedy for fundamental social abuses except a communist revolution. Yet he hoped nothing from such a revolution : it would destroy existing injustice, but not make human happiness. He therefore stuck to analysis and eschewed advice. Nevertheless he was imprisoned in the Bastille

---

[1] *Théorie des Lois criminelles*, 1781.

and exiled to London : after the Revolution itself had broken
out he returned to France and spoke before the Assembly
on behalf of the insurgent blacks of San Domingo. He was
guillotined in 1794.

Law, he declared, was the chief instrument by which those
who had won their possessions by force or by fraud retained
their spoils and their power. The institution of private
property "was not set up to hinder the poor from losing
anything," but to safeguard the rich man. "Laws are destined
above all, to safeguard property. Now as one can take away
much more from the man who has than from him who has not
they are clearly a guarantee accorded to the rich against the
poor. It is difficult to believe, and yet clearly demonstrable
that the laws are in some respects a conspiracy against the
majority of the human race." Property turns society into a
vast prison, where a few warders control the mass of prisoners
who "groan in the disgusting rags which are the livery of
poverty. They never have any share in the plenty which
their labour creates." In these conditions, was the suppression
of slavery a benefit to the slaves ? " I say it entailed as much
suffering as liberty : all that they have gained is to be constantly tormented by the fear of starvation, a misfortune
from which their predecessors in this lowest rank of humanity
were at least exempt." Slaves, after all, were worth keeping
alive and feeding all the year round ; the modern labourer
whose work was only seasonal, had to find his own fodder. If
he begged for food it was a crime : "the crime of having a
stomach and no money."

Linguet proceeded to state the main tenets of Marxian
theory—the class war, the doctrine of surplus value and the
inevitable communist revolution. " Society is divided into two
parts : the one consists of the rich, owners of money who, since
they are consequently owners of commodities, also claim for
themselves the exclusive right to tax the reward of the industry by which the commodities are produced ; the other is
composed of isolated labourers. Since they are no longer
anyone's property, and no longer have masters, they no longer
have guardians with an interest in protecting them or relieving

hem; they are helplessly delivered over to the mercy of
ivarice itself. "The rich are even saved the pain of hearing
he cries of the poor, who die silently in their huts." Linguet
regarded the Liberal programme of the Physiocrats with con-
empt.[1] There is no natural harmony between the interests of
vorker and employer : when profits are increased wages do not
ise simultaneously, nor is the price of food proportionately
owered.[2] There is always a "lag" period, terrible to the
abourer. Any benefits he may ultimately reap from general
prosperity are but part of the capitalist's surplus—a surplus
created by the work of the labourer. It is an error to think the
rich benefit the poor by providing them with employment. On
he contrary "it is the life of the hireling which builds up the
rich man's wealth." Streams maintain the river, not the river
he streams.

The economic system gives rise to a competition between
the right to life and the right to private property. Where the
latter involves the destruction of the former, where the wealth
and power of the few are destroying the vitality of the State
and the happiness—the lives even—of the mass of citizens,
individual property rights would justly be subordinated to the
general welfare. He compared a rich man denouncing slavery
to a bird of prey screaming "while it rends a pigeon in its
talons." To speak of progress and liberty in such circumstances
was hypocrisy. A philosopher might counsel patience on the
ground that a destruction of all organization and return to
natural anarchy would be even worse, or he might encourage
revolt, but if he were honest he could not preach the usual optimistic doctrine of the Physiocrats. For his part, Linguet leaves
little doubt as to his own view—the poor have the right to revolt,
and some day will have the power, though he could not counsel
them to attempt it. They could console themselves, however,
with the thought that their rights had been stolen, and that
"if they or their posterity had the courage one day to seize
upon them again, nothing could prevent them." Providentially,

---

[1] *Réponse aux Doctrines modernes.*
[2] *Ibid.*, vol. ii., pp. 83-84.

Linguet remarks, despair seems to make men inert, not violent. Yet inertia could not last for ever. "Never," he wrote, "has want been more universal, more murderous for the class which is condemned to it : never, perhaps, amidst apparent prosperity has Europe been nearer to a complete upheaval. . . . We have reached, by a directly opposite route, precisely the point which Italy had reached when the Slave War inundated it with blood and carried fire and slaughter to the very gates of the mistress of the world." [1] Perhaps, he suggested, Spartacus was already preparing for a war of liberation.

When the Revolution arrived it was a middle-class affair. The Third Estate was represented mainly by lawyers : there were also some merchants and even a few peasants. The Fourth Estate was scarcely represented, and the revolutionary politicians were generally and enthusiastically agreed, first, that all existing feudal property rights should be abolished, and, secondly, that all private property was sacred and inalienable. Property was even considered a necessary qualification for the vote, and proposals for social equality never went further than attempts to regulate food prices and relieve urgent distress. Confronted with the disappointment of the Fourth Estate, and challenged to make good the promise of equality to the poor, both Danton and Robespierre deliberately appealed for the support of the peasant and the tradesman. "It seems to have been thought," said Danton, in 1792, "excellent citizens have held, that friends of liberty may do harm to the social order by exaggerating their principles. Well, let us now eschew all exaggeration : let us declare that all territorial, individual and industrial property shall be for ever maintained." In the following year Robespierre put the matter more argumentatively but equally definitely. "Certainly a Revolution is not necessary to convince us that the extremes of wealth and poverty are the source of many evils and many crimes, yet we are nevertheless convinced that equality of wealth is a chimera. For myself, I think it even less necessary for private good than for public happiness. It is much more important to make poverty honour-

---

[1] *Annales*, t. i. 345.

ble than to proscribe riches. The cottage of Fabricius need
not envy the palace of Crassus. . . . Let us therefore honestly
declare the principle of the rights of property." [1]

Babeuf's communist rising of 1796 was a reply to Robespierre. Sylvain Maréchal had written, before the Revolution
itself, that society was a huge slave market, where men were
daily bought and sold. "The chaos which preceded the Creation
was certainly nothing in comparison with that which reigns
on the surface of this earth now that it has been created, and
hell, with which I am threatened after death, cannot be worse
than the life one leads in a society where the individuals are all
free and equal and where, however, three-quarters are slaves
and the rest master." What if the servile class should refuse to
continue to serve their rulers and answer : "We are three to
one. Our intention is to re-establish for ever things on their
ancient footing, in their primitive state—that is, upon the basis
of the most perfect and legitimate equality. Let us divide the
earth once more among all its inhabitants. If any of you is
found to have two mouths and four arms, it is quite fair : let
us assign him a double portion. But if we are all made on the
same pattern, let us share the cake equally."

Maréchal's draft for the "Manifesto of Equals" elaborated
the same principle. "Since civilized society began, this finest
possession of humanity has been unanimously recognized, yet
not once realized ; equality was only a fair and sterile fiction of
the law. To-day, when it is more loudly demanded, we are
answered : Silence, wretches ! real equality is but a chimera :
be content with constitutional equality ; you are all equal before
the law. *Canaille*, what more do you want?"

The time had come for open recognition of the principle
that "the earth belongs to nobody, while its fruits are everybody's." The French Revolution, Maréchal wrote, "is but the
precursor of another revolution, far greater, far more solemn,
which will be the last. . . . Let there be no difference now
between human beings except in age and sex ! Since all have
the same needs and the same faculties, let there be one education

---

[1] Quoted. Postgate, *Revolution*, 1789-1906, pp. 41-44.

and one standard of life for all. . . . On the morrow of this true revolution men will say 'What! Was the common good so easy to achieve! We had but to will it!' "[1]

Unlike most of his contemporaries, who were revolutionary before the Revolution and quickly frightened by its development, Babeuf began with a careful social analysis and with cautious recommendations, and pushed his theory of equality to its logical conclusion only when he saw that France was becoming a land of peasant proprietors and that economic equality was not part of their programme. He pushed it to the point of abortive revolt and his own execution. His principles were clear enough. Land should be divided equally for the purposes of occupation, but ownership should be national. No one, he wrote in 1796, " can, without committing a crime, appropriate for his exclusive use the goods of the earth or of industry." His full programme included the abolition of all inheritance and the nationalization of the land. He declared that the Revolution was not at an end, because the rich absorb all valuable products and exclusively command while the poor toil like real slaves, pine in misery and count for nothing in the State. Babeuf's own attempt to establish communism failed but both he and Maréchal were more far-sighted than their contemporaries when they declared that the Revolution was not ended and that the poor were not likely to be satisfied nor society rendered harmonious, by the establishment of legal equality without the further bestowal of the substance of economic and social equality. If the Commune of 1870 was on its political side, the logical development of Rousseau' philosophy, on its economic side it was a fulfilment of the prophecies of Linguet, Maréchal and Babeuf.

---

[1] Postgate, *op. cit.*, 54-56.

CHAPTER X

PEACE, FRATERNITY AND NATIONALISM

I. INTERNATIONAL ANARCHY IN THEORY——MACHIAVELLI AND GROTIUS

"Hugo Grotius, Puffendorff, Vattel and others—Job's comforters all of them—are always quoted in good faith to justify an attack although their codes, whether couched in philosophic or diplomatic terms, have not—nor can have—the slightest legal force, because States, as such, are under no common external authority" (KANT's *Essay on Perpetual Peace*).

INTERNATIONAL as well as social peace seemed to be the natural result of the Revolution. Just as the destruction of privilege and the victory of the middle class removed the immediate causes of social conflicts in the eighteenth century, so the downfall of the divine monarchy and the establishment of popular government abolished the type of warfare which had devastated Europe for two centuries. At the end of an age of religious and dynastic wars it was easy to assume that wars would cease when States became secular and popular.

In 1648 the Treaty of Westphalia gave a legal sanction to international anarchy. The Pope's claim to rule over a united Christendom had ceased to have any meaning in the sixteenth century : the modern State was established as the recognized and final Sovereign, subject to no moral law, without obligations or responsibilities to its neighbours. Machiavelli had exposed the practices of mediæval diplomacy, and advised the Renaissance Prince to adopt similar methods on behalf of the nation-state, undeceived and undeterred by the religious maxims and moral purposes professed by the rulers of Christendom. Perhaps this advice was unnecessary ; in any case, kings and ministers pursued a policy of war and aggrandizement, of intrigue and faithlessness, exactly in accordance with his suggestions.

With the Reformation the theory of the modern State became complete. Bodin evolved the doctrine of royal sovereignty, while Sully's *grand dessein* was based on a conception of European States legally equal as juristic persons, entitled to enter into a permanent alliance if they wished without consideration of religious differences. Richelieu's domestic and foreign policy

259

was founded on the same principles : the State was a territorial unit ruled by a Monarch, absolute at home and abroad. The objects of the Sovereign's policy were internal unity and foreign aggrandizement, resulting from war or from alliances which he was as free to make with Protestants or Turks as with Catholics. But the most striking assertion of juristic sovereignty was not made by a despotic Monarch but by the rebellious Dutch. William the Silent appealed to Europe against Philip II. on the ground that he too was a sovereign Prince : when the rebellion succeeded, Holland became a fully fledged nation, claiming a Sovereign's right to make alliances and wars and to oppress her own minorities and conquered people just as Spain had oppressed her. By the end of the sixteenth century the new moral disorder of Europe was complete.

To assert one's own sovereignty, however, does not in fact make one independent of extra-territorial obligations, and to declare that one's own interest is the final criterion does not get rid of the consciousness of a moral relationship. It was this fact that Hugo Grotius perceived, and which is the basis of his *De Jure Belli*. Machiavelli assumed that individuals are amoral units, kept together only by fear of their rulers : similarly he regarded States as amoral units which had no external authority and which were therefore in perpetual conflict with one another. As a generalization about sixteenth-century Europe this account of the relationship of States was roughly true. But just as Machiavelli neglected the fact that men were bound together, not only by force but also by a sense of moral obligation, so he overlooked the existence of a rudimentary desire for an international morality. The opponents of the Machiavellian view that society rests only on force have commonly founded their case on the Stoic doctrine of natural law and of the contract implicit between fellow-members of a society. Grotius transferred this doctrine from the national to the international sphere, and founded international law upon the law of nature. Ultimately national States were the outcome of the individual's consciousness of moral obligation. An analogous development between States should some day lead to international government.

Grotius of course was far from reaching such a conclusion. He accepted the facts of his age. He assumes the territorial sovereignty of nations and the international anarchy which is its consequence. Every State, whatever its size, religion or form of government, is an equal juristic personality, and Europe, if united at all, even in the manner suggested by Sully, would be held together only by treaty obligations voluntarily incurred. So much Grotius takes for granted. He argues, however, that these facts do not destroy the law of nature : that moral obligations exist even between persons juristically separate. Thus there is no external sanction to coerce a State which breaks a voluntarily made treaty on grounds of *raison d'état*. But there is a moral obligation, universally binding, to keep faith. The natural law which forbids treachery and cruelty also imposes an obligation not to break one's pledged word, even in dealing with an enemy, and not to make war on non-combatants. International law, therefore, begins with Grotius as a system of rules which nations are morally bound to obey. It is concerned with laws of humanity and decency whose public recognition would mitigate somewhat the horrors of international anarchy.

2. INTERNATIONAL ANARCHY IN PRACTICE—THE DENUNCIATION OF WAR IN THE EIGHTEENTH CENTURY

This tentative beginning of international law did not materially modify the behaviour of kings in the seventeenth and eighteenth centuries. Yet in days of mercenary armies it was valuable to have rules for the protection of non-combatants, even if they were only occasionally observed. Civilian populations which had experienced every kind of abomination during the Wars of Religion did find some slight measure of protection from these rules in the eighteenth and nineteenth centuries. It was only in the twentieth century that the rules of war ceased to have any significance. Yet the main effect of the attempt to institute rules of international behaviour was to change the excuses made in breaking them. Phraseology changed, if practice did not. The policies of Henry VIII. in the sixteenth century, of Louis XIV. in the seventeenth, and of Frederick the Great in the eighteenth, were in essentials similar: all were obedient disciples of Machiavelli and all showed their obedience most faithfully when they publicly denounced his precepts. The only important difference was that whereas Henry and his contemporaries were close to the Middle Ages, and found it best to justify their policy and their wars on religious grounds, Louis XIV. based his claims on legal fictions and broke rules of international law, supported by his pledged word, on high grounds of national honour. International law became itself an excuse for war: an alleged infraction by your enemy of a rule you did not expect him to keep and did not keep yourself would serve as a *casus belli*. Frederick the Great used the same subterfuges on occasion, but could more easily dispense with hypocrisy and boast that national expansion was the justification of his policy and force its sufficient sanction. Both the ends pursued by States and the means of pursuing them remained in any case the same.[1]

National aggrandizement, the increase of power, prestige and territory at the expense of neighbours, was the object of State policy. Every statesman from Louis XIV. to Talleyrand would have agreed with Catherine the Great that "he who wins nothing, loses." It was a competition for power, which involved stealthy annexations of territory, constant wars and general plunder and destruction. The practice of diplomacy was aggrandizement by any means at the disposal of the diplomat, however contrary to the ethics of ordinary human intercourse.

---

[1] The right of self-defence provided an excuse for aggressive war in the eighteenth century as well as later. Montesquieu raised the problem of defining aggression when he wrote that the natural right of self-defence sometimes carried with it the right to attack, since, if a people fear that another Power intends to attack them, their only means of saving themselves from destruction may be to strike the first blow. Voltaire's comment (article *Guerre*, in *Dic. Phil.*) is always valid against this argument. You could not, he remarks, find a more obviously unjust reason for war. It would be impossible for you to attack your neighbour on the excuse that he intended to attack you unless you were yourself prepared to attack him—which meant, on your own argument, that you had given him the right to attack you. "This is to kill your neighbour (who is not attacking you) for fear that he should be in a condition to attack you: you must, that is, risk ruining your country in the hope of ruining another's country without any reason."

The pursuit of power through alliances which might lead to increases of territory and prestige without war was commonly known as the "Balance of Power." In practice, however, it led to war. For, since the object of each party was always to weight the balance in its own favour, the equilibrium could scarcely be permanent, and constant war was necessary to preserve a balance which had been invented in order to maintain peace. By the balance of power, Mercier remarked, "people arm against each other and cut each other's throats according to a system invented to prevent throat-cutting." Throat-cutting was continually resorted to when diplomacy failed to gain its end by chicane.

Much of Europe and most of Germany had been devastated by the Wars of Religion. A generation after Westphalia, Louis XIV.'s dynastic ambition carried the work of destruction further. Under Louis XV. matters were little better, and the moral, economic and political criticism of writers like Fénelon, Boulainvilliers and Saint-Pierre was renewed and repeated in many of the philosophic writings of the eighteenth century. From 1740 onwards Europe was an armed camp. Montesquieu speaks of the international competition of armaments as "the new malady" which "has spread itself over Europe; it has infected our Princes and induces them to keep up an exorbitant number of troops. The disease increases in virulence and of necessity becomes contagious. For as soon as one Prince increases his troops the rest of course do the same; so that nothing is effected thereby but the public ruin. Each Monarch keeps as many armies on foot as if his people were in danger of being exterminated; and they give the name of peace to this general effort of all against all. Thus Europe is brought to such a pass, that were private people to be in the same situation as the three most opulent Powers of this part of the world, they would be below subsistence level. We are poor, while we possess the riches and commerce of the whole universe; and if we continue to increase our troops at this rate, we shall soon have nothing but soldiers, and be reduced to the very same situation as the Tartars."

This was the philosophic view of eighteenth-century war. Seen from the council-chamber it looked very much the same to a sensitive statesman. Bernis had become Foreign Minister in France after his successful negotiation of the Franco-Austrian Alliance. He had embarked on the struggle with Frederick the Great willingly enough, but in his letters to Choiseul at Vienna he made a gradual repentance as disillusionment came upon him. He was a man of exceptional honesty, genuine humanity and only fluctuating ambition. Not many months after the commencement of the war he told Kaunitz that there was no hope of success. It was not, he explained, a question of good or bad luck next year or the year after, since success would always be impossible "without generals or well-disciplined troops." As to the generals, their chief motives were avarice and ambition. They thought only of "what will be said at Versailles," and were always willing, if they thought they could hide their incompetence from the King, to run away from the battlefield, leaving behind them, as they actually did on one occasion, half the artillery and 20,000 wounded or sick men. As to the troops, how could discipline prevail when the officers had " the manner of *grisettes*," and the men themselves neither pay nor food?

"The misery of the soldier," wrote Bernis, " is so great that it makes one's heart bleed. . . . The army has neither food nor shoes, half of it is without clothes, part of the cavalry is without boots. The troops have plundered terribly and done great mischief. The reason for all this is the excess of misery in which the officers find themselves, so that they send the soldiers out to pillage or buy bread and meat for them as cheaply as possible."

Bernis found that he could neither stop the war nor reform the Administration. The Government was controlled by the King's latest mistress. "The King is not at all upset by our anxieties nor embarrassed by our embarrassments." Empire, trade and prestige were vanishing under an indolent routine administered by " little spirits and narrow heads." "We live like children : we shake our ears when the weather is bad and we laugh at the first ray of sunshine." "We expect money like dew from heaven . . . every day we are on the eve of bankruptcy." Every week Bernis had " to spend a day coaxing Montmartel, the financier, to lend the King money," and was

so dependent upon him that " he could always force our hand."
" It is not," wrote Bernis, " the state of affairs which frightens
me ; it is the incapacity of those who conduct them : it is not
the misfortunes which crush me ; it is the certainty that the
right means of remedying them will never be employed. The
only remedy is a better Government. Give me this condition
and I will advise the continuance of the war, but it is precisely
that which we lack, and that which no one can give me—I mean
a Government." " God keep us," he wrote, " from light heads
in the management of grave affairs." Bernis knew that the
populace hated him, believing him responsible for a disastrous
war, which he was only too anxious to bring to an end. His situation became intolerable : he begged Madame de Pompadour
to accept his resignation. " She tells me sometimes," he
wrote, " to enjoy myself, and not to look gloomy. It is as if
a man with a burning fever were told not to be thirsty."
Finally, after urging " peace at any price," Bernis persuaded
the Pompadour to submit a letter to the King giving a full
account of his own illness, weakness and inefficiency, and suggesting that his friend Choiseul would be a more energetic and
capable Minister. The King regretted to hear that State affairs
had proved too great a strain for his Minister's health, accepted
his resignation, made Choiseul a Duke and appointed him
Bernis' successor. Bernis was made a Cardinal, and, after a vain
attempt to remain without portfolio in the Cabinet from which
he had resigned, retired to the country, in order, as he said,
" to cultivate cabbages."

At the very time that Bernis was taking this decision Voltaire
was composing *Candide*. The horrors of war and misgovernment in Europe brought him to the same conclusion, that in a
world so terrible, so inexplicable and so fortuitous, the only
course for a sensible man was to cultivate his garden.

Yet he could at least tell people what war was like, and
expose the sophistries by which despots excused themselves
when their ambition ruined their subjects.[1] Voltaire could pay

---

[1] For a detailed example of a case in point *vide* the account of the war
between Frederick II. and Joseph in *Frederick the Great and Kaiser Joseph*, by
Temperley and Reddaway.

equivocal compliments to Frederick the Great on his victories, but he left Frederick in no real doubt about his views upon his foreign policy. In his *Philosophical Dictionary* he described with unpleasant accuracy the origin of a dynastic war: "A genealogist proves to a Prince that he is the direct descendant of a Count whose parents had made a family compact three or four hundred years before with a House whose very memory is now forgotten. This House had distant claims on a province whose last possessor had died of apoplexy. The Prince and his council see his unmistakable right. This province, which is some hundreds of leagues away from him, in vain protests that it does not know him, that it is not at all anxious to be governed by him, that a people cannot be given laws without at least consenting to them: this talk never gets beyond the ears of the Prince whose right is incontestable. He straightway finds a large number of men who have nothing to lose; he dresses them in a coarse blue cloth at a hundred and ten sous the ell, trims their hats with a coarse white ribbon, turns them to the right and to the left and marches to glory.

"The other Princes get wind of this preparation, they all take part according to their strength, and cover a section of the country with more mercenary murderers than Gengis Khan, Tamerlaine or Bajazat trailed behind them. . . . These multitudes rage against each other, not only without any interest in the proceedings, but without even knowing what it is all about. . . . The marvellous part of this infernal enterprise is that each leader of murderers has his flags blessed and solemnly invokes God before going out to exterminate his neighbour. If a chief is only lucky enough to get two or three thousand men's throats cut he does not thank God for it: but when he has got ten thousand of them exterminated by fire and sword, and as a crowning mercy has completely destroyed some city, then a pretty long part-song is sung, written in a language unknown to all those who fought and quite full of barbarisms. The same song serves for marriages and births—as well as murders—which is unpardonable, especially in a nation greatly renowned for new songs. . . .

"A certain number of spouters are paid to celebrate these

days of murder . . . they all talk for a long time, quoting what was once done in Palestine.

"During the remainder of the year these people denounce vices. They prove by three points and antitheses that women who lightly spread a little carmine on their fresh cheeks will be the eternal objects of the eternal wrath of the Eternal . . . that a man who has two hundred crowns' worth of fish on his table one day in Lent is assured of salvation, while a poor man who eats mutton worth two and a half sous is going for ever to all the devils. . . . The wretched spouters unceasingly talk against love, which is the only consolation of humanity and the only way of improving it ; they say nothing of these abominable efforts which we make to destroy it."

3. THE IDEA OF PEACE——SAINT-PIERRE——ROUSSEAU AND KANT

Voltaire made no constructive suggestions for the abolition of war. Indeed he remarked that it was unfortunately inevitable. His hope lay only in the enlightenment of monarchs, who might in time realize the claims of justice and humanity. He was always a practical man, and it was only men who did not fear ridicule who seriously considered schemes for attacking the institution of war and substituting law for anarchy between States. And the politician could afford to tolerate the dreamer : the statesman, as Kant remarked at the end of his *Perpetual Peace*, " looks down upon the theorist as a mere pedant whose empty ideas can threaten no danger to the State." Why, then, should the philosopher not be permitted " to knock down his eleven skittles at once without the worldly-wise statesman needing to disturb himself "? In any case, philosophers can never be kings, and they can do no harm amusing themselves with schemes for social improvement.

Some philosophers actually did address themselves to the problem of war. They relied for the most part on the operation of natural law, upon the results of free trade and upon the dissipation of ignorance.

According to the doctrine of natural harmony the removal

of artificial restrictions would show men that their real interests were the same, and that all war was really civil war, and ruinous to the victor as well as to the vanquished.[1] If men could see that the world was becoming economically united, that the gain of one man was also another's gain and not his loss, self-interest would dictate a policy of free trade, peace and plenty, instead of protection, war and power. Kings, Mercier pointed out, already addressed one another as brothers, an excellent recognition of the law of nature, which meant States to be fraternally useful to each other. The very kings, however, who thus paid a ceremonial tribute to their common fatherhood proceeded to organize their people into robber bands in order to spoil one another's property and destroy one another's subjects. The natural order was clearly a general confederation of all States. In this idea there was nothing chimerical, since each State had what another lacked and all would gain by mutual service. To think of enriching oneself at another's expense was the most obvious fallacy of international economics "This false policy has cost us very dear: its supposed advantages occasion wars which threaten the safety of the State. These advantages vanish; as soon as one understands them they are found to be losses. . . . After all, each nation is only a province in the great Kingdom of Nature."

According to the doctrine of natural harmony international peace would follow inevitably from the advance of knowledge. If it could be demonstrated that men's interests were not

---

[1] That free trade would in itself bring peace was a natural assumption for a rationalist who had realized the economic advantages of free interchange of commodities between nations. After the publication of *The Wealth of Nations* this view became a regular part of Liberalism, and was the centre of Cobden's political philosophy. Bentham stated it in classical form in his *Universal Peace* (*Works*, vol. ii., pp. 557-558) : "Conquer the whole world, impossible you should increase your trade a halfpenny ; it is impossible you should do otherwise than diminish it. Conquer little or much and you pay for it in taxes." When popular ignorance is dispelled by publicity, peace, free trade and prosperity would be the choice of everyone. In the twentieth century Norman Angell still found it necessary to prove that war and conquest did not pay, though, with the history of the later nineteenth century behind him, he was too intelligent to imagine that considerations of self-interest would be sufficient to prevent men from fighting.

antagonistic but reciprocal, war would be swiftly outlawed by the operation of self-interest. The majority of philosophers who accepted the current rationalistic philosophy were therefore ready to assume that the growth of international commerce, the discovery that it was more advantageous to trade than to fight and the gradual linking up of the world as an economic unit would shortly abolish war. They hoped that the enlightened despot would soon see that it was to his interest to lead his subjects in the way of peace.

Rousseau could be relied upon to oppose any view which assumed that reason was more powerful than passion or that despots could be enlightened. His hatred of war was as intense as Voltaire's or Holbach's, and he was equally convinced that bad government and the false ambitions of Princes were its cause. But whereas Voltaire and the other *philosophes* hoped to convert the Princes to a peaceful policy, Rousseau thought that peace would come only through democracy. He had met the Abbé de Saint-Pierre in his old age, and knowing that his work was neglected because of its length and heaviness of style he undertook the task of editing and abridging it. His short edition of *La Paix perpétuelle* appeared in 1761. Nowhere is Rousseau more surprising—here are all the unromantic qualities which he is supposed to lack. No book of the century is more logical, definite or persuasive, and none has a stronger grip upon reality.

The fundamental cause of war, Rousseau pointed out, was international anarchy: men had learned to co-operate within the State while they remained " in the state of nature with the rest of the world " : " we have prevented private feuds, only to fan the flames of public wars, which are a thousand times more terrible ; in short, mankind, by gathering itself into groups, has become its own enemy. If there is any means of getting rid of these dangerous contradictions it can be only by a confederative form of government, which, uniting nations by bonds similar to those which unite individuals, submits them all equally to the authority of the laws." Such a government is preferable to all others, since " it comprehends at one and the same time the advantages of both large and small States " ; its basis already exists in European culture. Christianity had been a social bond sufficient to keep alive an underlying unity in Europe after the last traces of Roman organization had disappeared. Every part of Europe was necessary to every other, so that Europe was not merely a collection of peoples, with nothing but a name in common, like Asia and Africa, but a real community with its own religion, its manners, its customs, and even its laws. Nevertheless the nations remained in a state of war, and their partial treaties could be no more than truces, " either because these treaties had generally no other guarantee than that of the contracting parties, or because the rights of the two parties were never thoroughly settled. These unextinguished rights . . . would infallibly become sources of new wars as soon as the trend of circumstances gave new strength to the claimants."

A Confederation of Europe is the only possible solution ; no single ruler can ever be strong enough to impose his own peace on all the other Powers, and if two or three States attempted to combine for the permanent subjection of the others they would only quarrel amongst themselves when it came to dividing the spoils. A Confederation, however, of so general a character "that no considerable Power would refuse to join it," with its own judicial tribunal and rules for enforcing its will on a recalcitrant member by the common forces of the rest would have a considerable chance of permanence. As a basis the *status quo* in Europe, however unjust to those who had been despoiled in the past, would have to be accepted ; any Power which attempted to alter it would be declared a common enemy. The Presidency of the new Confederation would fall in rotation between the different Powers, and all disputes would be submitted to arbitration.

Once established, Rousseau believed all parties would find such a Confederation to their advantage, and there would be no fear of revolt. The only obstacle was the nature of the sovereigns themselves. The Abbé de Saint-Pierre had relied on the fact that " the true glory of Princes consists in securing the public good and the happiness of their people "; Rousseau pointed out that this was small comfort if they were actually in the habit of disregarding their true glory and preferring the false splendour of conquest and self-aggrandizement. How could you take away from sovereigns " the precious right of being unjust when they please "? There was the alternative possibility that Princes who would not consider the public good might be convinced that peace would pay them better than war. Would they never realize that after a war the victor himself is weaker than he was before it, and that " he has only the consolation of seeing the vanquished more enfeebled than himself"? A list of the advantages of peace to the Prince, drawn up by the Abbé de Saint-Pierre, seemed to establish beyond question that if Princes consulted their true interests his project would be adopted. " The only thing we assume on their behalf is enough intelligence to see what is useful to themselves, and enough courage to achieve their own happiness. If, in spite of all this, the project is not carried into execution, it is not because it is chimerical; it is because men are crazy, and because to be sane in the midst of madmen is a sort of folly."

Saint-Pierre's project of perpetual peace, Rousseau declared, was no vain speculation, but " a solid sensible book." If Princes did not adopt its conclusions that was not the fault of the project, but of the Princes. They valued war, not only in order to extend their rule abroad, but because it alone enabled them to preserve their tyranny at home. " Any other view is either subservient to one of these objects, or a mere pretext for obtaining them. Such are the ' public good,' ' the welfare of the people,' or the ' glory of the nation,' words always banished from the King's closet, and so clumsily used in public edicts that they seem to be warnings of approaching misery; and the people groan in advance when their masters speak to them of their paternal care."

Saint-Pierre, therefore, was a little simple-minded in thinking to persuade tyrants to abandon their tyranny. As long as monarchies lasted, the Confederation could be set up only at a time when there happened to be a number of kings as wise and enlightened as Henry IV., every one of whom had learned " to see in the good of all the greatest good he can hope for himself. Now this demands a concurrence of wisdom in so many heads and a fortuitous concurrence of so many interests, such as chance can hardly be expected to bring about." Finally, therefore, Rousseau concludes, there is no prospect of an international Confederation being established except by general revolution. Even a bold man would hesitate to say whether a European League is more to be desired or feared at such a price. The immediate destruction might outweigh any good that it could produce in the course of centuries to come.

The Revolution came, and with it a new type of warfare, in which the mercenary armies of the Allies were continually worsted by an enthusiastic nation in arms. During the armistice of 1795 Kant wrote his *Essay on Perpetual Peace*. He laid down as one of the positive rules for preventing war that every State must have a republican form of government. Under popular constitutions he thought war unlikely. "And the reason is this. If, as must be so in a Republic, the consent of the subjects is required to determine whether there shall be war or not, nothing is more natural than that they should weigh the matter well before undertaking such a bad business. For, in decreeing war, they would of necessity be resolving to bring down the miseries of war upon their country. This implies that they must fight themselves ; that they must hand over the cost of the war out of their property ; that they must do their poor best to make good the devastation which it leaves behind. On the other hand, in a country where the subject is not a citizen holding a vote, plunging into war is the least serious thing in the world. For the ruler is not a citizen but the owner of the State, and does not lose a whit by the war, while he goes on enjoying the delights of his table or sport, or of his pleasure palaces and gala days. He can, therefore, decide on war for the most trifling reasons, as if it were a kind of pleasure party. Any justification of it that is necessary for the sake of decency he can leave without concern to the diplomatic corps, who are always only too ready with their services."

Men who attack an existing evil naturally assume that it will cease when the circumstances with which they have always seen it associated are changed. Rousseau and Kant saw that the wars

of the eighteenth century were made by politicians to the ruin
of common people : give the power to the people and war would
cease. Experience, indeed, proved them right in part : under
popular governments, elected rulers do not declare war as if it
were a game ; they have to persuade the people that war is both
necessary and right. This, however, has proved surprisingly
easy, and the very same moral reasons by which eighteenth-
century diplomats excused themselves have served to justify
the wars of a more democratic Europe.

For the Revolution did not change the nature of States though
it changed their rulers. Kant argued that there were certain
preliminary principles which must be observed if war was to
cease. These preliminaries included the abolition of standing
armies and the provision that when peace was signed it should
be real peace, not merely a temporary armistice in which each
country made a " secret reservation " to fight again when a
favourable opportunity arrived. Such preliminaries would have
been carried out only if the advent of democracy had meant a
change in the objects of State policy as well as in its institutions.
States still remained armed and sovereign, and the same causes
of war therefore remained in operation.

With the Revolution the sovereignty of the State formally
passed from the King to the people, but its character changed
little in the transference. The King, as Kant protested, treated
the land as his private *patrimonium*, an estate for which the
common people were obliged to fight as the feudal serf had
once fought for his lord's fief. In the nineteenth century the
State still remained an estate, sacred territory whose defence
was a supreme duty and whose extension was always desirable.
Patriotism was not weakened but reinforced by the Revolution :
the people, now sovereign lord of their own territory, volun-
teered to overthrow the invader, and were ready enough to
become invaders themselves if they could believe the old excuses
that they were fighting in self-defence, for the balance of power
or for the integrity of international law.

Thus a new patriotism was born. The aristocracy had never
been patriotic in the modern sense, though, as owners of the soil
and the State, they had been willing to fight or hire mercenaries

in its defence.[1] At the Revolution the soil of France became the private property of the peasantry, and every property holder learned to regard himself as exercising part of the sovereign power. Even in countries where the number of patriots and property holders has been smaller than in France democracy has had the same result—the bestowal of power and property on a new class and therefore an enormous extension of patriotism. For patriotism is the sentiment of ownership extended to the nation : its virtues and vices are those of private ownership. Its virtues are affection for the countryside and desire for the welfare of its inhabitants, its vices the pursuit of imagined greatness and the vulgarity which enjoys size, show, and a cheap superiority over others.

Those who believed that international hatreds would end with the *ancien régime* were deluded by a psychology which neglected the whole of man's instinctive nature. They thought that a change of rulers, and a clear exposition of the economic advantages of peace and of the moral evils of war, would suffice to change human behaviour. In fact the occasions rather than the causes of war were changed. Greed, ignorance and the lust for power were potent in the era of democracy and industrialism as they were in the days of despotism and mercantilist economics. Rousseau and Kant, however, were not mistaken in thinking that democracy had released new forces making for peace. Vice has had to pay more extravagant homage to virtue : the nineteenth-century citizen was an easy victim of propaganda, but it was at least necessary to persuade him that he was acting rightly when he did all those things which his usual code of ethics forbade. The strength of this reluctance to settle disputes by force has grown in the nineteenth century, and the number of

---

[1] Voltaire had commented (*Dic. Phil.*, art. *Patrie*) on the value of their patriotism, and on the mockery of expecting patriotism from the dispossessed As for the luxurious Parisian who had never journeyed farther than "to Dieppe to eat fresh fish, who only knew his smart town house, his pretty country villa, the champagne that came to him from Rheims, and his rents"— of course he loved his country. No doubt financiers, officers and soldiers who preyed on it had the tenderest love for the peasants they ruined, but you could hardly expect the worker, a slave to a superior's orders, without any property or share in government, to be an enthusiastic patriot.

persons who hold that national ends can no more justify war than personal ones justify murder has steadily increased. Kant stated an essential truth when he based his hope of a European Federation upon the growing desire for moral relations in international affairs : the moral revolt against the European anarchy grows side by side with and reinforces the repulsion against the horror, waste and futility of war.

" In all these twistings and turnings of an immoral doctrine of expediency," says Kant, " which aims at substituting a state of peace for the warlike conditions in which men are placed by nature, so much at least is clear—that men cannot get away from the idea of right in their private any more than in their public relations ; and that they do not dare (this is indeed most strikingly seen in the concept of an International Law) to base politics merely on the manipulations of expediency and therefore to refuse all obedience to the idea of a public right. On the contrary, they pay all fitting honour to the idea of right in itself, even though, at the same time, they devise a hundred subterfuges and excuses to avoid it in practice and regard force, backed up by cunning, as having the authority which comes from being the source and unifying principle of all right. It will be well to put an end to this sophistry, if not to the injustice it extenuates, and to bring the false advocates of the mighty of the earth to confess that it is not right but might in whose interest they speak, and that it is the worship of might from which they take their cue, as if in this matter they had a right to command."

Kant saw that there could be no solution to any problems of social justice while nations continued to claim their own sovereignty. If their own interest was the final good, morality and politics must necessarily be divorced. Every representative of the nation was confronted with an insoluble problem ; he was appointed to further the ends of his State, whether they were, viewed from outside, moral ones or not. He was therefore constantly in the dilemma of having to act immorally or disloyally. The only solution was an international federation which would create an ethical relationship between States and thus release the statesman, and indeed every individual, from the necessity of repudiating his moral code and his sense of decency in his dealings with foreign nations. Kant believed that an international government might be realized in the future after a long evolution—it was an " idea of reason " which accorded with the trend of evolutionary forces and which could be accomplished when men saw the need for it and willed its realization.

CHAPTER XI

PROGRESS

I. THE NEW RELIGION

THE distinctive feature of European thought since the French Revolution has been its attitude towards time. Liberty, equality and fraternity, nationalism and internationalism, democracy and toleration had been the subject-matter of political discussion in earlier periods of history. Neither were the *philosophes* on unexplored ground in substituting a secular for a religious outlook. Anti-clerical writers had always urged that the object of life was terrestrial happiness, not eternal salvation. But the *philosophes* made a new and surprising synthesis when they combined a belief in the goods of this life with a doctrine that they were to be judged good only if they contributed to a better future. This was to join the advantages of hedonism with those of Christianity. The creed of the *libertins* had the practical advantage that it concentrated upon actual human satisfactions rather than upon conventional obligations to act morally and believe unreasonable doctrines. It was unsatisfactory as a religion because it was almost wholly individualist : however much its best thinkers might urge that the highest happiness came from altruism, it provided no spur to social conduct. It saw the value of human development and of individual freedom in contrast with the Church's insistence on abnegation and obedience. Hedonism was usually sterile because it treated men as separate units whose nature was to find pleasure ; it forgot that society existed because men were naturally social beings. The mediæval Church had built a wall round human life in the belief that men would be lost if left to find their own way : the hedonists assumed that, if the wall were broken down, men would need no guidance except their own desires. Hedonism emphasized the value of the moment : Christianity, the vanity of temporal happiness. At its best, mediæval Catholicism had put before men an ideal of service and had attempted to inspire every part and aspect of common life with social purpose. The new doctrine of progress, soon to be christened " the religion of humanity," accepted the terrestrial values of the hedonist : it stressed the importance of individual happiness, the practical satisfaction of human desires, the solution of earthly problems and the utility of increased knowledge. But, like mediæval Christianity, it subordinated these to social ends, and judged them valuable only in relation to an ultimate standard. This social and religious aspect had almost wholly disappeared from eighteenth-century Catholicism and the *philosophes* were the true religious teachers of their generation. The French Revolution was a religious revival : the articles of its creed were liberty, equality and fraternity, its ideal was social happiness and its deity was the future of the race. Like most religions, progress could be defended by reason and was considered the very embodiment of reason. Comte took from Condorcet the motto : " Live for others : it is only then one lives for oneself " ; and this recommendation to lose your life in order to find it was sound utilitarianism as well as sound Christianity. But the most competent utilitarian philosopher could show no reasonable grounds for including the unborn as well as the born among those for whom one was to live. The generation for whose welfare the present was to be lived might never be born, and could not in any case repay the consideration of its ancestors. In the event, indeed, it might prove that their forethought had been misdirected and their sacrifice futile. Progress was a religion because it offered men a vision which they could follow irrespective of utilitarian considerations, an ideal in whose service they were prepared to do most unreasonable things.

All religions decay, and the sceptic is quick to profit by the widening gap between profession and practice. Indeed, there is nothing more worthy of ridicule than the religious attitude which remains after the inspiration has gone : the conventional phrases and reverent posturings which accompany commonplace conduct. It was not long before the religion of progress had degenerated into a gospel of acceleration : before ends were often confused with means, and change of any sort welcomed as advance. Rapid movement was exhilarating and men forgot, in the midst of scientific discovery and industrial change, to ask in what direction they were hurrying. The philosophy of progress is a serviceable one as long as the better future it assumes is clearly imagined and deliberately willed. It is essentially a moral philosophy, continuously concerned with the effects of action —the creation and enjoyment of beauty fits only with effort into its scheme and programme. The artist has naturally objected to this emphasis on the future : time and moral preoccupations are alike his enemies. In his view the men of the nineteenth century spent their time and energy pouring out the wine of the present as a libation to the future.

The habit of judging the past and the present by their contribution to the hypothetical future is the child of modern science. A few scientists in the ancient world had approached the modern attitude, and Lucretius had emancipated himself from the legend of the Golden Age, but his scientific evolutionary theory was not a regular ingredient of classical thought or literature. The Middle Ages were almost wholly free from the notion of progress. Knowledge of essentials was complete ; time and space were both fixed and defined in Catholic cosmogony. The boundaries of Christendom were limited and the date of the millennium known, at least to the best authorities. In any case, it was no business of the ordinary man to hasten or retard the Second Coming. Secular improvement was of only secondary importance in the estimation of the Church, and the structure of society, based on social orders with appropriate functions, seemed not fluid and wilful, but static, divinely ordained and final. The mediævalist might concern himself with his own and his neighbours' salvation, but time and space and the future of the world were God's mysteries, not man's. Most moderns, with an endless vista of time ahead and an unalterable assumption that human wills are important in shaping future history, appreciate with difficulty a literature and a philosophy which were indifferent to the temporal effects of actions, and judged them by their contribution to the glory of God. A charmed circle surrounds the Middle Ages : none may enter it who are preoccupied with the religion of progress.

With the advance of scientific habits of mind after the Middle Ages, the past began to seem absurd, the present hopeful and the future glorious. If uniform and unalterable laws of nature

279

could be everywhere discovered, man could adjust himself to them for his own advantage : knowledge gave him the power to control his own destiny. This view could be fully effective only when it had replaced Catholic cosmogony in the minds of ordinary men and women. Scepticism of past dogmas and religions was an inevitable stage towards the new faith. Above all, the doctrine that men came into the world already burdened with an unalterable inheritance of sin was repugnant to a progressive theory. If progress is to be effective as a religion, man's fate must be, at least to some extent, in his own hands, and knowledge his sufficient means of grace. By the end of the seventeenth century the new psychology combined with the rapid advance of scientific discovery had enabled Saint-Pierre to preach a doctrine of human perfectibility.

At first sight the doctrine of progress seems complete in Saint-Pierre. He believed in the indefinite possibilities of human improvement (which is the accurate translation of *perfectibilité*) through the power of reason applied by governments and scientists. His faith was so pure as to be completely uncontagious. He wrote infelicitously and at enormous length, and it was only after a period of administrative breakdown, religious struggle and philosophic propaganda that men were ready to listen to the new religion. When Saint-Pierre boasted of man's perfectibility the facts seemed to contradict him. Things seemed to get worse rather than better. Men were unlikely to believe in progress unless they could see it. History was still commonly presented as a decadence, not an advance. The Renaissance had assumed without question that the world of classical antiquity was a peak from which men had permanently descended. Without any conception of historical evolution, Saint-Pierre and his contemporaries had the material for generous speculation and philosophic hope: they could still argue that science and reason might one day triumph, but they could not convince the sceptic or excite the enthusiasm of the common man. The driving force of religion in the West has usually been the conviction that the ideal is already in process of development and that its arrival can be hastened by human agency. The believer needs a God who is omnipotent and yet in need of his help.

Saint-Pierre offered men a religion without a God : a century
later philosophers had discovered a teleology in natural development and learned to regard man as the climax of a divine
purpose which utilized human effort for the attainment of an
ultimate perfection.

2. HISTORICAL INTERPRETATION——VOLTAIRE, TURGOT AND CONDORCET

The doctrine of historical progress means, when strictly used,
first, that there has been in history an increase of things considered good at the expense of those considered bad ; secondly,
that this desirable trend may be expected to continue indefinitely.
If such a belief is to stand criticism the historian must provide
a philosophy and interpretation of the past, he must be able to
generalize about what has happened and to explain why it has
happened, to state laws of development and show what forces,
physical and psychological, have been and are at work. Without
a doctrine of historical causation there can be no confidence
that an increase in the good, even if evident one day, will continue. The historical philosophy which best suits the religion
of progress is one which suggests that advance is inevitable
and yet dependent upon human will.

The idea that the historical process might be a record of
improvement rather than of degeneration was first clearly
conceived in the seventeenth century ; the effort to explain this
development, to apply the intellect to the record of the past as
a whole, did not begin until the eighteenth. The humanists of
the Renaissance, inspired by the writings of classical antiquity,
assumed that the age which had produced Seneca was an un-
assailable summit of civilization. Bacon struck one of the first
blows at this conception when he suggested in his *Novum
Organum* that the title of antiquity was properly used not of
ancient Greece, when civilization was young, but of "the time
in which we live." Knowledge and experience belong to the
present : we stand on the shoulders of the past and can see
farther. Pascal, in an almost equally famous passage, wrote
that those whom we call "*anciens*" were in fact "*nouveaux*."

"The whole succession of human beings through the whole course of the ages may be regarded as a single man, ever living and ever learning." Fontenelle pushed this conception even further. He successfully transformed the literary battle between the ancients and moderns from a sterile conflict of pedantries into a serious discussion of an intelligible question. Did historical evidence support a theory of degeneration? If the trees of antiquity were no larger than those of the eighteenth century neither were the men : the sap of nature had not run dry, but remained precisely the same. Knowledge, however, had increased, and we might therefore look forward to improvement. Fontenelle contributed to the doctrine of progress the idea of an indefinite advance, resulting not from a change in human nature but from the accumulation of knowledge and experience.[1] The world, he said, would never degenerate because the "best minds" would always contribute to each other's wisdom.

The problem for the eighteenth-century historian was to show this improvement at work. How did men pass on their social heritage from one generation to another? What, in other words, was the mechanism of historical change? There were several possibilities. Was the sequence of events the result of an external Providential plan, as Bossuet declared? Were historical forces purely material or did human reason and organization play a part? The eighteenth century did not discuss these factors scientifically or realize their possible combinations, but it stated this central problem of history and provided a variety of answers.

Most history Voltaire regarded as a "parcel of tricks we play on the dead." For his part, historical writing served two purposes. It was primarily a method of propaganda and a reply to Bossuet. Bossuet's *Universal History* was not, as Voltaire urged, either universal or very good history ; it was, however,

---

[1] In *Dialogues of the Dead* Fontenelle seems to express just the opposite view—that of the sceptics—that men behave instinctively, not rationally, and never learn from experience. Montaigne is made say to Socrates : "Little silly birds, they suffer themselves to be taken in the same nets that have caught a hundred thousand of their kind already : the follies of the fathers are lost upon the children, and do not seem to instruct them at all."

an effort to apply the intellect to history, to interpret, not to list, events. Bossuet's doctrine of Providence marked a clear stage towards a philosophy of secular progress. It set events in a time-sequence, and pictured the march of man, under the guiding Hand, towards a future goal. It enabled men to accept doctrines which seemed at first contrary to Christian conceptions and still to remain believers : it prepared the way for the creed of natural harmony and reconciled many of the orthodox to scientific discoveries. God ruled by law, and man might legitimately inquire into His mysteries and thus serve as a more efficient instrument in His hand.

Voltaire pictured the amazement of a Chinaman who bought the *Universal History* and found no mention of the great civilization of the Chinese, while the Jews, " an ignorant and barbarous people "—" a race of pedlars "—were represented as the pivot of history. Voltaire found this an excellent starting-point for an account of historical evolution which put the Jews in their proper place, which justified the persecutions of Diocletian on political grounds, which found natural causes where orthodoxy sought for miraculous ones, which praised the statesmanship of Julian the Apostate, which exploded the sanctity of saints and the heroism of heroes, and which suggested unflattering parallels between ancient abuses and modern methods of government.

Voltaire's history attempted more than this. He made a genuine effort to envisage the pageant of history, to see the story of man as a unity. He was no mere chronicler, recording picturesque details of wars and courts, but an historian selecting his facts in obedience to a conscious philosophy. " Laws, manners, arts,—these," he writes, " have been my principal concern ; paltry facts shall not enter into this work except where they have produced important results." Art, literature and philosophy were the only important social products, and they had flourished in four great epochs of good government and enlightened opinion. History was the story of man's long martyrdom, occasionally relieved by wise rule and favourable circumstances. War and religion were the two principal enemies of mankind ; when they were destroyed by the onslaught of reason an age of greater happiness and culture might arrive. Voltaire's sociology stopped at this point. His interpretation of history was more rational than Bossuet's, but equally partial. He saw only political causes where Bossuet saw only Providential ones, and when politics seemed not to explain everything he fell back on Chance. The great epochs of which he writes remain unexplained : they hang so precariously upon personal genius or accidental circumstance that there seems no security for their continuance or recurrence. He saw that there were natural tendencies usually outside human control, but that a genius at the right moment could do much to utilize them.[1] " Almost all laws," he wrote, " have been instituted to meet passing needs like remedies applied fortuitously they have cured one patient and killed others." Voltaire resembled Gibbon not only in his ironic treatment of Christianity but also in his lack of all sociological interpretation, his contentment with political events and ostensible motives. Like Gibbon again, his treatment is flat : he judges all institutions good or bad irrespective of place or period. All religions are equally harmful at all times ; he admits no contribution to civilization in any period when science was not dominant. Voltaire admitted improvement and hoped for progress : he believed that reason was valuable but saw nothing to ensure its triumph.

Montesquieu was in point of accuracy and method Voltaire's inferior as a historian, and he had none of Voltaire's sense of the pageantry of the past. But from Aristotle, Harrington, and perhaps from Bodin, he had learned that political explanations are usually inadequate, and he had too scientific a bent to fall back upon Chance when knowledge was lacking. In the *Décadence des Romains* he had shown an admirable sense of historical perspective, and even in *L'Esprit des Lois*, when he wrote as if all constitutions and institutions were to be judged and explained by a few invariable physical factors, he was over-emphasizing and misapplying a truth, not stating a falsehood. He at least saw that the record of external politics is intelligible only against an economic and social background.

---

[1] *Cp.* his article, *Chaîne des Evènements*, in the *Dic. Phil.*

Two years after the publication of *L'Esprit des Lois* Turgot
gave the first of his remarkable discourses on history at the
Sorbonne. He was only twenty-three years of age, and his essays
were rather suggestions for others to work out than finished
products. He combined Montesquieu's idea of underlying
causes with a conception of human will and social evolution.
He begins by comparing the futility of mere animal and vege-
table change with the fruitful development of man's history.
Natural phenomena are " enclosed in a circle of revolutions
that remains the same for ever " ; successive generations of
vegetables and animals perpetuate themselves and " time does
nothing more than continually produce replicas of that which
it has just thrown aside." Humanity, unlike the rest of
nature, acquires knowledge and transmits experience : it steps
outside the circle to which all other forms of life are condemned, and consciously improves itself. Physical phenomena
may be precisely explained if we know the preceding events
and the laws which apply to them : an historical event depends
on mental and social factors as well as physical ones. The
historian must trace a succession of social states causally connected but explicable only on the assumption that mechanical
factors play a diminishing part and the intelligent control of
man an increasing one. The growth of knowledge is the key
to progress.

The whole human race moves slowly forward. Unlike his
contemporaries, Turgot felt that even the Middle Ages had
not been altogether retrogressive—something was learned, even
if only the fact that religious domination was evil. There is no
real retrogression though there may be periods of maladjustment : the suffering involved forces men to new efforts, acts as
a stimulus to better government, and proves, in the long run,
progress too. Humanity is a baby tumbling upstairs. " I search
for a progress of the human mind and I find almost nothing
but the history of error." Nevertheless, the evidence of anthropology (and Turgot naturally assumed a lineal and similar
development of man everywhere), showing at the same moment
all the shades of advance from barbarism to civilization, dis-
closes to us in a single glance " the footprints of all the steps

of humanity, the measure of the whole track along which it has passed, the history of all the ages."

How could it be otherwise? Natural laws are invariable; man controls his life by experience and knowledge. When knowledge is complete man will be able to make an exact adjustment to natural forces, his tumblings and strivings will cease and a static Utopia be achieved. The day of the scientific Utopia had begun. The imagination of men dimly saw that mechanical power would transform the face of the world: they ceased to dream of a Platonic Republic built neither in space nor time and proposed to establish a modern Utopia in Paris itself, renewed, reorganized and scientifically managed. In the future State the scientist, not the philosopher, is King.

When, in his second *Discours* on universal history, Turgot came to trace the epochs of past development and to account for human institutions, he anticipated Comte's famous division of intellectual evolution into three stages. Man gradually passed from primitive animism and anthropomorphism into the stage of philosophical guesswork—from the religious to the metaphysical stages, in Comte's phraseology. Each of these earlier stages continued, unfortunately, in some degree to retard the growth of the scientific age which had superseded them.

During the forty years that elapsed between Turgot's essay and Condorcet's elaboration of a similar thesis in the *Prospectus for an Outline of the Progress of the Human Race*, the idea of historical evolution from a barbaric past to a scientific and perfect future was expressed in numerous books. In his *Public Felicity* published in 1772, Chastellux contrasted different historical epochs, with the object of discovering in which men had been most happy. He concluded that even ancient Greece, the one period not dominated by the priest and the despot, was made wretched by the existence of slavery. In the modern world there was hope: war, superstition and tyranny were at least dying before the attack of science. Other Utopias of the later part of the century are influenced by the same hope. Such predictions as Mercier's *Year 2440*, Volney's *Ruins*, and Restif de la Bretonne's play *The Year 2000* are new in the history of Utopia making, not because the worlds they suggest are more attractive than those of earlier ideal republics, but because they assume that moral and political improvement are necessary by-products of mechanical science.

When during the Revolution itself Condorcet wrote a fuller outline of the history of human progress, his perspective and interpretation were substantially those of Turgot. His *Tableau* is one of a long series of refutations of Rousseau's early essays. He aims at showing that knowledge, not simplicity, is the key to happiness and morality, that society moves not from primitive excellence to sophisticated misery, but from bondage and superstition towards an ultimate perfection of freedom and reason. Condorcet began, as his predecessors, Turgot, d'Alembert and Chastellux had done, with a dogmatic explanation of sensationalist psychology. And if the individual formed his ideas and regulated his conduct as a result of knowledge and experience, so did the race as a whole. The general laws which are to be observed in the development of an individual's faculties govern the progress of the race. For the race advances only because a great number of individuals develop together. The process is cumulative, each period knowing more than the last, and passing on that knowledge and also a wider power to utilize it. Indeed, had not the time come when there might be a science of society itself, when it would be possible " to foresee the progress of humanity, to direct it, to hasten it "? If so, we must begin by understanding the part and discovering the mechanism by which error and superstition had been induced to give way to truth and science. When this was accomplished, and the strength of the directing forces better appreciated, a provisional answer might be given to the further question—whether there were obstacles which still barred the way to ultimate perfection.

Condorcet divides the past of the human race into nine epochs, stretching from the dawn of history up to the Revolution itself, through long ages when men first learned to hunt and then to plough, to write and at last to print and so to spread and pass on the knowledge they had gained. In Condorcet's as in Turgot's treatment the story of progress is identical with that of knowledge ; it is a long struggle with error and with the priests and despots who opposed truth for interested reasons. In early periods the progress of knowledge was slow; men had "a natural attachment to opinions acquired in infancy and to the customs of their country"; ignorance and superstition made men averse from every kind of novelty; laziness of body, and even more of mind, prevailed over their early curiosity, and often kept primitive society almost stagnant. To these natural obstacles must be added "greed, cruelty, corruption and the prejudices of civilized peoples." The vice and unhappiness of the powerful, the educated and the cultured, "with their eternally restless passions, always active and always unsatisfied," had not been due to the growth of knowledge itself, but to its struggle with ancient errors and prejudices which it had not yet been able to overcome. Enlightenment had been confined to the few: its power to promote happiness depended on its extension over the whole society where superstition still reigned. Rousseau had misunderstood the symptoms: knowledge was not a sign of decadence nor misery its result, but humanity was in the course of "a struggle and painful passage from a rude society to a state of civilization . . . a necessary crisis in the gradual advance of the human species towards absolute perfection."[1]

In spite of hindrances, however, man had gradually acquired the art of civilization, and the beginnings of science had appeared in the ancient world. Unfortunately, Rome had failed to stem the invasions of the barbarians, on the one hand, and of mystical religions, on the other. Many warring sects from the East were gradually merged in a common worship of "a Christ, a messenger sent by God to redeem the human race. . . . The time, the place of his appearance, his human name were all matters of dispute, but the claims of a prophet said to have appeared in Palestine under Tiberius eclipsed all the others, and the new fanatics rallied to the standard of the son of Mary." The spirit of the new sect suited the conditions of the decaying Empire so well, and it learned so effectively to organize itself as a political force, that it triumphed in spite of the wise and courageous efforts of Julian the Apostate to deliver the Empire from the religious plague he saw settling down upon her.

---

[1] *Deuxième Epoque.*

Every religion demands the acceptance of miracles and other absurdities from its adherents, but the particular characteristic of Christianity was its contempt for the humane sciences. "Thus the triumph of Christianity was the signal for the total decadence of the sciences and of philosophy." Without printing there was no way of preserving knowledge : the barbarians and the Christians had their own way, and the Dark and Middle Ages began, when men could not distinguish between authority based on knowledge and self-constituted authority which exists only because none dare contradict. Condorcet, summarily dismissing a thousand years of history, reverted to the theory of Voltaire. Unlike Turgot he did not think progress continuous : it began again at the Renaissance. The eighteenth century did not define knowledge widely enough to include mediæval contributions to art and literature, to moral perception and to political ideas. The Middle Ages were a period of "slavery of the mind," harmful not only directly but still more "by reason of its corruption of the method of studying"—a period in which men learned to adopt "a proposition not because it was true but because it was written in a particular book and had been accepted in a particular country or since a particular period."

The discovery of printing, at the close of the mediæval period created a new tribunal of public opinion. The authority of the priesthood was undermined and men were able to accumulate knowledge and profit by experience. The revival of classical literature and the discovery of America completed the foundations of the new era. The Reformation, instead of leading to the general destruction of Christianity, was seized upon by kings for their own advantage and a new form of State tyranny instituted. Science, however, made great strides in spite of persecution. Religious toleration and freedom of thought were granted, if at all, "not to men but to Christians." Consequently the history of this period was marked by "little real progress towards liberty but more order and strength in governments and in the nations a stronger and, further, a more just consciousness of their rights. Laws were better put together : they seemed less often the shapeless work of circumstance and caprice : they were made by *savants* if not yet by *philosophes*."

Moral, political and economic sciences were in process of formation : International Law came into existence, founded, unhappily, "not on reason and nature," but "on established customs and the opinions of the ancients." Science, reason and humanity grew in isolated places where "pure and strong souls, of fine character, united to unusual gifts, appeared here and there amidst scenes of fanaticism, hypocrisy, corruption and bloodshed. . . . The human race is still disgusting to the philosopher who contemplates the scene it presents : but it no longer humiliates him and it offers him hope not so far distant."

In the ninth epoch, opened by Descartes' *Discourse on Method* and ending with the Fall of the Bastille, political liberty advanced side by side with scientific discovery. The slavery of the old world had disappeared even if the liberty of the most advanced countries was still imperfect. Under enlightened despots the illumination of science spread and "the practice of governments followed slowly and as if regretfully the march of opinion and of philosophy." The ideas of equality, rights and democracy, the discovery of economic laws and the universal dissemination of the new philosophy with "its battle-cry, reason, liberation and humanity," were the work of the epoch leading to the Revolution itself. Thought had become international as well as humane and free. "Animated by a universal philanthropy, the *philosophes* fought injustice wherever they saw it at home or abroad, both Englishmen and Frenchmen calling themselves friends of the negroes whom stupid tyrants scorned to count among the number of men." Russians and Swedes were taught by the French to praise toleration, while Beccaria, the Italian, exposed the barbarity of French jurisprudence. "Frenchmen sought to cure the Englishman of his commercial prejudices, of his superstitious respect for the evil of his Constitution and laws," while English philanthropists, like Howard, applied the new philosophy to the task of social reform. Philosophy, letters, art and science all advanced, and with the success, first of the American Revolution and then of the French, the influence of the new doctrines was spread far and wide. Even after the Declaration of Rights, however, only a small proportion of the world was enlightened : most of it was still "vegetating in the infancy of the early epochs." The number of men with real understanding appears almost nothing "in comparison with the mass of mankind, still bound by prejudice and ignorance." "We see that the labours of these last periods have done much for the progress of the human mind, but little for the improvement of the race: much for the glory of man, something for his liberty, but almost nothing yet for his happiness."

3. THE FUTURE—THE TENTH EPOCH AND THE ASCENT OF MAN

By the end of the eighteenth century men, Condorcet thought, had discovered how to acquire knowledge, how to learn nature's secrets, and therefore how to be happy. That they were not generally happy was because this knowledge was confined to a few. Progress, the increase of knowledge, and therefore the beginnings of happiness, had been due to the almost accidental adoption of useful inventions and discoveries made by occasional men of genius who had contrived to survive in a society inimical to new ideas. Now however that men knew that the laws both of external nature and of the human mind were constant, a science of society was possible and men could learn consciously to co-operate and control their future. Man's happiness was within his grasp: he could destroy traditional barriers and set up institutions which would give his capacities full scope. Nature set no limit to progress.

Condorcet based his hopes on three main lines of advance. First, he could see no reason why all nations should not reach "the same point of civilization at which the most enlightened, free and emancipated nations, such as the French and Anglo-Americans," had arrived. He could see no reason to think that any people were congenitally incapable of learning to reason. In the second place, he asked, was it not possible to remove most of the inequalities which existed within each nation? The differences of education, opportunity and wealth which had hitherto divided society into classes were mainly the result of the "*imperfections actuelles de l'art social.*" The aim of the *art social* should be to remove all unnecessary and harmful inequalities. Thirdly, Condorcet hoped for the indefinite improvement of man himself: "May it not be expected that the human race will be improved by new discoveries in the sciences and arts and, as an unavoidable consequence, in the means of individual and general prosperity?" It could scarcely be doubted: there would be "progress in the principles of conduct and in practical morality" and a continuous improvement in "the intellectual, moral and physical faculties," as well as in "the instruments which increase the intensity and direct the use of these faculties." The thought that general prosperity might not be an "unavoidable consequence" of scientific advance scarcely occurred to him. That men would know and still act as if they were ignorant, that they might be creatures of heredity even more than of environment and might disregard the clear teaching of science and follow instinct even to disaster, that their values might be wrong when their knowledge was accurate—these did not seem real difficulties in the eighteenth century. As long as freedom and knowledge spread everywhere, all was well: they could be extended by democracy, economic reform and education.

"The principles of the French Constitution are already those of all enlightened men": now that democracy had destroyed the power of despots and priests in France, truth must soon find its way even "into the hovels of slaves." Released from their long humiliation even the slave would respond to the call. So far the white colonist, with his "commercial monopolies, treacheries, bloodthirsty contempt for men of another colour or another faith, his insolent plundering and religious fanaticism, had not made a good impression, and had destroyed the natural respect of the black man for the white's superior intelligence and the benefits of his commerce." Democracy has changed all this: some English "friends of humanity" had already begun to attack slavery, and now that the advantages of free trade were known, tariffs and monopolies would cease. Colonization would proceed peaceably and white men, "too enlightened about their own rights to trifle with those of others, would respect the independence of backward peoples and instead of sending monks to spread shameful superstitions among them would themselves become colonists, anxious to teach them the truths useful to their

happiness." Eventually, it might be after a period of misery
and distrust, natives everywhere would learn to look to their
"brothers among the Europeans" and to become their friends
and disciples. Their progress could be swifter and more certain
than ours had been because they could benefit by our experience.
"It will come at last, this moment when the sun will shine
upon a world in which all men are free and recognize no master
save reason; when the tyrants and the slaves, the priests and
their stupid or hypocritical tools will no longer exist except in
history or on the stage"; when men will know how to "recognize
and stifle with the force of reason the first germs of tyranny
and superstition, should they ever dare to reappear!"

The backward peoples then offered no permanent barrier to
progress. What of the struggle between classes, the social and
economic inequalities within each nation? One may summarize
Condorcet's economic aspirations by saying that he was not a
socialist but that he was a somewhat advanced twentieth-century
Liberal. He accepted the Physiocratic theory of natural harmony
with reservations and admitted the necessity of government
regulation on behalf of the weak: he thought that "nature's
inevitable evils" might be lessened by public foresight and wise
State action. Like the Physiocrats, therefore, he emphasized the
injurious effects of trade monopolies and tariff barriers which
interfered with the free flow of commodities and the formation
of the world into a single economic unit. But he went further.
If the market was to be really free, he saw that the small man
must be protected against the big capitalist, whose monopoly
might be none the less injurious because it was the result of
his own efforts and not of a royal gift. Condorcet had all the
economist's belief that most evils may be remedied by statistics
and scientific forethought: "the application of the calculus"
should enable men to devise social safeguards against the greed
of rich men and to discover ways of releasing industrial and
commercial progress from its dependence upon great capitalists.

Some of the worst miseries of poverty might, he thought,
be provided against by an increase of every form of insurance.
All those who were unable to compete on fair terms—the sick,
the old, women and children—should be protected not only

by private insurance but also "by social authority." He had certainly departed from any principle of *laissez-faire* when he remarked that under good institutions " riches would no longer be the means of satisfying vanity and ambition," and that men would cease to work mainly for money and be content with a more moderate and equable distribution. Condorcet looked forward to a distributivist State in which there was no proletariat and little luxury, and in which government guarded the interests of small property holders of every type, commercial as well as agricultural. Some natural inequalities would remain, but their evil social effects could be abolished.

Together with democracy and economic reform must go education. The State could ensure that " the entire mass of the people are instructed in what each man needs to know for the management of his private affairs, the free development of his industry and talents. He need not be a stranger to any of those lofty sentiments and delicate feelings which are mankind's distinction : he can know his rights and defend and make use of them." Thus education was the way to substantial equality, since men feel injured not by inequality of talent but by inequality of opportunity. Class distinctions were based on the contrast between refined and uneducated speech and on similar social distinctions ; they resulted from a system of education which increased natural inequalities instead of correcting them. And every argument for male education was equally one for female, just as every claim for the rights of man was also one for the rights of woman. Condorcet, as the friend of Mary Wollstonecraft and Thomas Paine, was not likely to suffer from the usual inconsistency and imagine that democracy could exist without equality of the sexes.

Condorcet had a practical opportunity of advancing the cause of education. He opposed the communist proposal in the Convention to educate all children, boys and girls, at the public expense, taking them from their parents and providing them with " the same clothes, the same food, the same teaching and the same care." But his own proposal, so effective in nineteenth-century France in obliterating class divisions of speech and outlook and in cultivating a specific French culture, could scarcely be termed an individualist solution. Every child should be "*un élève de la patrie,*" provided with a sound grounding of elementary knowledge and enough teaching about religion, politics and economics to make him safe against the wiles of charlatans and demagogues.

Condorcet believed that education should aim at diminishing rather than encouraging the spirit of rivalry: "the habit of wishing to be first is a ridiculous one, a misfortune for those who have acquired it and a real calamity for those whom fortune condemns to live near it." A school should teach practical co-operation as well as the principles of commercial, political and moral science. Both pupils and masters should, however, be encouraged to form and expound their own opinions, and the only views proscribed should be the dogmas of religious cults. In the same way, the teaching of political science would not aim at making men admire a complete legislative system or form of government, but at "making them able to appraise its value." Even the French Constitution and the Declaration of Rights, he said, should not be taught as if they were "tables come down from heaven which must be adored and believed." Fearful of State propaganda, he devised an educational hierarchy to secure the independence of teachers and, above all, to guarantee complete freedom of opinion in higher education. In the event, the Convention accepted the bulk of Condorcet's educational proposals—his division of education into primary, secondary and superior, the provision of free elementary education for both sexes and the opportunity of comparatively cheap higher education. And though the Revolutionary system of education did mean that during the nineteenth century class distinctions in France have depended less on differences of speech and culture than elsewhere, French teachers and professors have not been altogether free from State interference or owed their position entirely to non-political considerations.

Good laws and a free educational system could altogether end the social inequalities which destroyed men's happiness and could provide against natural and inevitable inequalities in such a way that they were humiliating to none and advantageous to all. The only final authority would be that of science, an authority based not on arbitrary power but upon reason, one whose claims could be rationally examined and rationally supported. As scientific precision grew it would be increasingly possible to order society for the general good : men themselves may or may not improve in their innate capacity, but the same effect must result from the improvement of scientific instruments, and the growth of accurate and perfect machinery will release men from most of the labour which now occupies their time, exhausts their energy and retards their progress.[1] If we remember that, " even in enlightened countries, scarcely a fiftieth part of those to whom nature has given talents receive the necessary training to develop them," the possibilities of future improvement in all the arts and sciences seem unlimited. The production and distribution of commodities will be scientifically controlled, each country producing what best fits its soil and receiving what its populations most need. Population will increase, enabling more to be produced and the needs of all to be more fully satisfied.

At this point Condorcet was confronted with the objection which seemed to Malthus and his followers a complete refutation of his hopes. Will there come a time, he asks, when the increase in the number of men will be too great, when the well-being of the population will commence to deteriorate— " a retrograde movement, at least a kind of oscillation between good and evil "? Will such a period " mark the point past which all improvement becomes impossible, the limit to human perfectibility which it will reach in the vastness of the ages, without being able to overcome it "?

Condorcet's answer has been commonly misunderstood. It is true that he brushed aside the fundamental and ever-present difficulty of adjusting food supply to population as a distant and scarcely relevant speculation. " It is equally impossible," he wrote, " to pronounce for or against the future reality of an event which would be realized only in an enlightened age—an epoch when the human species had acquired intelligence almost

---

[1] Both Helvétius and Condorcet emphasized the dependence of a real social science on the possibility of finding a language in which one word would mean one thing.

beyond our powers of imagination." In any case, if over-population did ever become an actuality, men would have learned by that time that their obligation to their children was not to " give them existence but happiness . . . they would have lost the childish notion of filling the earth with useless and unhappy beings." Indeed Condorcet's view was sound enough on the assumption that the society of the future would be scientifically regulated and public morality rationally guided. " Is not a wrong understanding of interest the most frequent cause of actions that are contrary to the general good? Would not a consciousness of dignity—which belongs to free men—and an education based on a deeper knowledge of our moral constitution, inevitably fertilize in almost all men the principles of a rigorous and pure justice : would it not lead men to act habitually from the motives of a lively and enlightened benevolence, of a delicate and generous sensitiveness? The germ of all these things has been placed in our hearts by nature : it awaits only the sweet influence of knowledge and liberty to develop." The reason for unsocial actions will disappear when institutions based on science make the common interest also the individual one. " Is not the aim of politics to destroy their apparent opposition? Man is capable of indefinite improvement because he changes with his environment and may change that too as his knowledge grows. Nature therefore has made a chain of which truth, happiness and virtue are all inseparable links." In particular we may hope for the entire destruction of the prejudices which hinder equality between the sexes. The effect of the emancipation of women will be to transform family life, and its effect on men will be scarcely less great than upon the women themselves. War, the most fatal scourge and the greatest of crimes, will be known for what it is, conquest will be thought futile and unprofitable, and a permanent confederation of nations will cease to be the dream of a few philosophers and become the natural way of organizing the world. A simple universal language will make knowledge accessible to all and overcome national divisions. Art and science will be seen to be only in their infancy and political science, now the monopoly of a few, will be generally understood.

Finally there is good reason to think that the natural capacity of men will improve. All species either improve or decay, and with the improvement in medicine, with saner methods of living, and the destruction of the two most active causes of degradation—poverty and riches—better bodily and mental health will be assured. The length of life will be increased, and, though immortality may be impossible, man's life may be lengthened to a degree which we cannot conjecture. We do not yet know enough science to be sure whether there is any limit to the possible duration of human life. Intellectual and moral improvement is equally within our reach. Parents transmit physical traits and perhaps "they may transmit also that part of the physical structure which is responsible for intelligence, strength of mind, energy of spirit and moral feelings." And if education can improve these qualities, will it not modify and improve the inheritance we pass on?

Condorcet was not far from the scaffold when he wrote the concluding words of his *Tableau*. The philosopher, however, could take courage amidst present misery, not in the thought of a personal paradise but in the imaginative conception of future human happiness. "*Cette contemplation,*" he concluded, "*est pour lui un asile, ou le souvenir de ses persécuteurs ne peut le poursuivre: ou, vivant par la pensée avec l'homme rétabli dans les droits comme dans la dignité de sa nature, il oublie celui que l'avidité, la crainte ou l'envie tourmentent et corrompent: c'est là qu'il existe véritablement avec ses semblables, dans un élysée que sa raison a su se créer, et que son amour pour l'humanité embellit des plus pures jouissances.*"

CONCLUSION

Progress was the religion of the nineteenth century, just as Catholicism was of the Middle Ages. In both a great gulf was fixed between practice and precept. But if men confused progress with magnification and acceleration it was no more the fault of Condorcet and his allies than the degeneration of the mediæval Church was the fault of Augustine. The *philosophes* gave men a creed whose phraseology has been readily adopted even when its social implications have been ignored.

The *philosophes* taught that by reason man may be the master of things, that he can imagine a society in which all men enjoy freedom and happiness, and that he can deliberately create the society he has imagined. They directed their most powerful blows against the traditional and clerical view that " our times are in His hands," that man is a creature fallen and perverse, who cannot be saved from self-destruction except through the gift of grace and must bow his individual reason before the sublime authority of Church and State.

Ultimately no doubt a question of values is involved. One phase of a perpetual conflict was heroically staged at the Revolution. For the moment victory appeared to belong to the party which preferred reason to dogma, liberty to authority and the individual to the State. But in this conflict there is no permanent victory. The serviceable doctrines which reason offered have in their turn become dogmas. Those who demanded liberty have set themselves in the seats of authority. The nation-state which seemed under democratic rule the complete guarantee of free individual development is now almost as great a barrier to the realization of the ideals of the Revolution as it was when men toppled kings from their thrones in the name of humanity.

The religion of the Revolution may be rejected for a variety of reasons. It must be opposed at every point by those who believe that truth is revealed, not to be discovered, and who regard temporal happiness as trivial in comparison with eternal salvation. But even those who approve its philosophic and social ends—who accept individual development as the justification

of political organization, who believe in liberty and hope for a
future in which a world-order takes the place of an international
anarchy—even these may fairly dissociate themselves from the
presumptuous enthusiasms of the Revolution. For the contemporaries of Condorcet attributed the same universal validity
to the institutions they founded, and to the scientific and social
theories they formulated, as their opponents had to the atrophied
convention which passed for religious observance in the
eighteenth century. They understood none of the difficulties:
their all-absorbing task was one of clearance, and the fact that the
decaying lumber they condemned to the fire was the remains of
what had once been a stately building did not concern them. The
Catholic Church as they knew it was an instrument of tyranny
and a purveyor of lies: it must be destroyed. Man had been
denounced as the victim of his passions: he was extolled as the
embodiment of reason. They had been told that the poor were
always with us: they declared that the total abolition of poverty
was immediately at hand. They had found privilege and monopoly everywhere hampering men's energies and corrupting their
relationships: they acclaimed that economic freedom and the
absolute rights of property would lead to universal harmony.
Absolute kings had ruled and inefficiency and cruelty had stalked
the land: the people should be absolute and political problems
would be solved. It was a generous and fighting creed, not the
elaboration of a programme of social organization.

This faith had been built up during a century of struggle.
At every stage in the battle and in every aspect of thought,
theological, ethical, economic and political, the *philosophes* had
taken advantage of the breakdown of government and the conflict of classes to substitute reasonable and practical theories
for traditional and moribund ones. Under the influence of
seventeenth-century science a god who conformed to universal
law took the place of the providential and personal deity of
the Old Testament. Deism then passed by easy stages into
materialism, which should logically have been a deadening creed
but which was actually in practical matters an invigorating one.
Ardent materialists, like Holbach, were apt to reintroduce
teleology in the guise of a personified Nature, a beneficent

Cp. Carl
Becker.

300

guide who intended our interests and activities to be harmonized and mutually advantageous. The doctrine of Natural
Harmony was a support, though not a necessary one, for the
new religion of Progress.

Ethical theory underwent a parallel development. The
libertins had long protested against the clerical doctrine of
sin and asserted the right to happiness : hedonism, the protest
of the individual against clerical domination, developed into
the positive creed of " humanism," which makes the full development of human faculties the only goal worthy of pursuit. Natural
religion was its immediate outcome : men of all races and colours
had the same needs and capacities and could therefore be rendered happy by the same rights and the same instruction. As a
sensationalist psychology was substituted for an intuitional one,
humanism developed into scientific Utilitarianism. In its completed form Utilitarianism threw off its individualist inheritance
and declared that men should find happiness not in the search
for pleasure but in the improvement of society and of human
nature itself.

In social and economic questions the critics of atrophied
feudalism and of inefficient mercantilism began by demanding
that governmental policy should aim at popular welfare and
economic freedom, not at State power and private monopoly.
The demand for specific administrative reforms gradually took
a more general aspect and led to the theory that if artificial
restrictions were removed, and the rights of property fully
recognized, natural harmony would ensure peace and prosperity
both internationally and within the State. Economic laws were
easy to formulate from the axioms of human nature : it seemed,
curiously enough, that if men followed their selfish impulses
the result would be exactly the same as if they were actuated
by Christian principles. This dominant theory was challenged
by a school of thinkers whose analysis was more realistic, even
if their constructive proposals were no less Utopian. These
early socialists held that the right of property must be strictly
limited if social happiness was to be diffused among the population, and that *laissez-faire* would bring a renewal of strife not an
era of peace. The battle between the privileged and unprivileged

would be succeeded by the even more bitter contest between the rich and the poor.

Finally political theory passed through a similar development. The first stage was the declaration that the monarch should not rule arbitrarily but in accordance with the traditional Constitution of France and with the fundamental laws of nature. The king might be absolute, but he must also be enlightened and tolerant and promote the happiness of his people. The subject, however, had no security unless the power of the Crown was limited, and its responsibility enforced. The British Constitution offered a model of responsible government and the separation of powers was a practical method of safeguarding rights against the sovereign's claim to irresponsibility. The British Constitution appeared to be the best practical expression of the social contract between government and people : it guaranteed by an ingenious mechanism the eternal superiority of the moral law to the wills of governments. Rousseau, however, unable to contemplate a divided State, hoped to solve the problem of liberty by transferring the sovereignty of the monarch to the people themselves : the difficulty of making the State responsible to the subject was thus evaded by the facile assurance that in the ideal community they would be identical, every citizen being at the same time sovereign and subject. Faced, however, with the practical difficulties of applying such a doctrine in the modern nation-state, Rousseau and the more far-sighted of his contemporaries learned to look to Federalism for a solution. Indeed their ideal of complete individual development was compatible only with a more complex society than they had imagined—one in which men were not only members of a self-governing State but associates of many groups, both national and international.

Thus the temple of liberty, equality and fraternity was supported by an elaborate structure of doctrine. If its framers had not so loudly declared that their work was final and indestructible a later generation might have watched its collapse without so much ironical satisfaction. For the physics, biology and psychology of the eighteenth century have been largely superseded, and in so far as they still form a background for twentieth-century thought they serve mainly to impede

inquiry and to increase the difficulties of those who are attempting to construct a social philosophy out of the accumulating
fragments of more modern science. Moreover, it did not occur
to the men of the Revolution that liberty as they understood
it—meaning the security of private rights—might not be easy
to pursue at the same time as equality as they understood it
—meaning the same opportunity of self-development and of
happiness for all. They were too thick in the fray to pause :
they dealt in absolutes and knew nothing of quantitative
thinking. To the modern critic the *philosophes* seem somewhat
naïve : they were quite unconscious of being moved by any
but disinterested motives though it has subsequently become
clear that many of the theories they thought final were dis-
torted by the violence of their revolt against the conditions
in which they lived. Physiocrats and utilitarians, for instance,
desired a strong political State to put an end to privilege :
they also constructed elaborate philosophic arguments to show
that State interference in economic matters—in all that touched
on property rights—would necessarily be harmful to the general
welfare. Indeed the eighteenth-century State was so inefficient,
and its control of trade and industry was so hampering, that
laissez-faire seemed to be an immediate corollary of the
principle of utility. The connection however was historical,
not logical, and even at the Revolution itself men like Paine
and Condorcet saw that the State must engage in positive
social and economic activity if equality and liberty were not to
be the sole perquisites of the propertied class. In the event,
however, the original argument for private property that the
peasant who tilled the land had a natural right to the product
of his industry was forgotten and the industrial *rentier* often
defended profits which were no more the natural result of
social service than those of the landed *rentier* whom he had so
vehemently denounced. Indeed, though the " accident of birth "
was less powerful in the nineteenth century than it had been in
the eighteenth it remained the most striking proof that the
ideal of equality, like that of liberty, had been given a partial
and a class interpretation at the Revolution. Yet liberty and
equality remained ideals to which society had formally pledged

itself: property has made many subsequent concessions to them, and the conflicts of the twentieth century turn upon the acceptance of their fuller implications.

But there is a more serious charge made against the men of the Revolution. It is said that the history of the nineteenth century is a sad commentary upon their individualism: that they stressed the rights of the individual instead of emphasizing his social duties, and by their negative view of the State they led men to lose sight of its organic unity.

It is of course true that in the struggle with Leviathan and *l'infâme* it was individual liberty, not social organization, which seemed of overwhelming importance, and that the growth of the "Great Society" has necessarily involved an ever-increasing degree of State activity and an ever more closely knit and elaborate effort of social organization. The *philosophes*, moreover, were led in part at least by mechanical analogies of contemporary physics to regard society as a machine rather than as an organism and the individual as an isolated unit related to his fellows not by common purposes and sympathies but by the automatic propulsion of self-interest. From the theories of the *philosophes* agrarian categories of property and contract passed into an industrial age whose need was not so much a statement of individual rights as a conception of purpose and a principle of social organization. But it was not the men of the Revolution who were responsible for the commercial selfishness which actuated the drab era of early industrialism: they could not anticipate its arrival nor know that their championship of individual liberty against Church and State would be used to justify the commercially powerful in oppressing the weak. It was not the *philosophes* who substituted a mechanical for a purposeful State: they found a society which had no informing principle of justice; in which there was no longer any relation between function and position; which was, in fact, nakedly a class domination even if its forces and its religious phraseology bore witness to a time when the aristocracy served as well as owned, and the Church taught as well as persecuted. They made no vain effort to recall the dead. Even had they desired, they could not have revived the Church. It had once given mediæval society significance as a microcosm of a universal whole and informed a social order with purpose by relating men's activities to their functions in the corporate unity. The *philosophes* were attempting to offer that spiritual leadership of which the Church was no longer capable. They told men of their great inheritance and opportunity: they emphasized their unity and their progressive development towards perfection and urged them deliberately to hasten the advance towards a happier, freer and more equal society. Without this conception " the march of science" was a meaningless accumulation of the less interesting kinds of knowledge. This religion of humanity—the development of the individual within and through the developing social organism—has, in spite of its misinterpretations, inspired the most fruitful work which has been done since the Revolution.

BIBLIOGRAPHY

Editor's Foreword:

The following works are important for an understanding of the 18th century in its many aspects: P. Hazard, *La Pensée Européenne au XVIIIème Siècle. De Montesquieu à Lessing*, 3 vols., Paris 1946; see particularly the volume *Notes et Références*. The same author's *La Crise de la Conscience Européenne (1680-1715)*, also in three vols., Paris 1935, is equally an invaluable study. E. Cassirer, *Die Philosophie der Aufklaerung*, Tuebingen 1932, American edition under the title: *The Philosophy of the Enlightenment*, Princeton 1951, is probably the best work on the philosophy of this epoch. Carl L. Becker, *The Heavenly City of the Eighteenth Century Philosophers*, New Haven 1932, is a short but brilliant book. Basil Willey, *The Eighteenth Century Background*, London 1949, is indispensable. Cf. also L. Gershoy, *From Despotism to Revolution*, 1763-1789, New York 1944, with valuable annotated bibliography. A. Chérel, *De Télémaque à Candide*, Paris 1933 is immensely suggestive.

FRENCH LIBERAL THOUGHT IN THE EIGHTEENTH CENTURY.

General orientation:

Manuel Bibliographique de la Littérature française. III. Dix-Huitième Siècle, Paris 1911. Jeanne Giraud, *Manuel de Bibliographie littéraire pour les XVIème et XVIIIème siècles français*, Paris 1939, brings Lanson up to date. See also the volumes VII, 1, 2 and 3 of the series *Clio*; *Le XVIIème Siècle* par Edmond Préclin et Victor L. Tapié, Paris 1949 and *Le XVIIIème Siècle* by the same authors, Paris 1952. Henri Sée's *Histoire économique de la France*, Paris 1948, edited by Robert Schnerb is fundamental. See also the same author's: *La France économique et sociale au XVIIIème Siècle*, Paris 1925; *L'Evolution Commerciale et Industrielle de la France sous l'Ancien Régime*, Paris s.a.; *Les Idées politiques en France au XVIIème Siècle*, Paris 1923; *Les Idées politiques en France au XVIIIème Siècle: L'Evolution de la Pensée Politique en*

France au XVIIIème Siècle, Paris 1925. Cf. the important work by Fr. Olivier-Martin, *Histoire du Droit français des origines à la Révolution*, Paris 1948; D. Mornet, *La Pensée française au XVIIIème Siècle*, Paris 1932, is a useful summary. M. Leroy, *Histoire des Idées sociales en France de Montesquieu à Robespierre*, Paris 1946; H. J. Laski, *The Rise of European Liberalism*, London 1936. Philippe Sagnac's two volumes: *La Formation de la Société française moderne*, Paris 1945-1946, are masterly. The recent volume by R. Mousnier and R. Labrousse, *Le XVIIIème Siècle*, Paris 1953, is a suggestive synthetic effort. Cf. also Bernard Fay, *La Franc-Maçonnerie et la Révolution intellectuelle du XVIIIe Siècle*, Paris 1935.

Chapter I.

Georges Lefevbre's *La Révolution française*, vol. XIII in the series *Peuples et Civilisations*, Paris 1951, is a veritable Summa of the work done until now on the French Revolution. Its rich bibliographical indications should prove of great value to the student. See also my edition of Tocqueville's *Ancien Régime et la Rèvolution* in two volumes, Paris 1952 and 1953. (In vol. I, pp. 354-355, of this edition, I have given a short summary bibliography of more recent studies on the pre-revolutionary and early phase of the French Revolution.) *Les Origines intellectuelles de la Révolution française. 1715-1787*, by Daniel Mornet, Paris 1947, though somewhat pedestrian, contain very rich material.

Chapter II.

Cf. G. Lacour-Gayet, *l'Education politique de Louis XIV*, Paris 1923; R. von Albertini, *Das politische Denken in Frankreich zur Zeit Richelieus*, Marburg 1951. Rébelliau's *Bossuet*, Paris 1900, is still a standard-work. See also: Gustave Lanson, *Bossuet*, Paris 1894; and J. Calvet, *Bossuet. L'homme et l'oeuvre*, Paris 1941, with valuable bibliographical indications. For Fénelon, see A. Chérel, *Fénelon au XVIIIème Siècle en France. Son Prestige, son influence*, Paris 1917; see also the same author's edition of Fénelon's *Oeuvres choisies*, Paris 1930. E. Carcassonne's small volume *Fénelon. L'Homme et l'Oeuvre*, Paris 1946, is admirable and contains instructive bibliographical material. On Vauban, see Daniel Halévy's *Vauban*,

Paris 1923. Vauban's *Projet d'une Dîme Royale* has been edited by E. Coornaert, Paris 1933 (with important bibliography). See also Ch. W. Cole, *French Mercantilism. 1683-1700*, New-York 1943. On Bayle: Cf. A. Cazes, *Pierre Bayle*, Paris 1905; E. Faguet, *Pierre Bayle* in *Dix-Huitième Siècle. Etudes Littéraires*, Paris s.a.; Jean Delvolvé, *Religion, critique et philosophie positive chez Pierre Bayle*, Paris 1906. On Fontenelle, see *La Philosophie de Fontenelle*, by J. R. Carré, Paris 1932.

Chapter III.

Cf. the bibliographical indications given in my edition of Tocqueville's *Ancien Régime I*.

Chapter IV.

See Barckhausen's and Carcassonne annotated editions of Montesquieu's *Lettres Persanes*. On the *salons*, there is now the suggestive volume by Roger Picard: *Les Salons littéraires et la Société française. 1610-1789*, New-York 1943.

Chapter V.

Leslie Stephen, *English Thought in the Eighteenth Century*, two vols., London 1881. A classic. Cf. also Ch. Bastide, *John Locke*, Paris 1907. On Voltaire: Cf. G. Lanson, *Voltaire*, Paris 1919; see H. N. Brailsford: *Voltaire*, London 1935, and Raymond Naves, *Voltaire. L'Homme et l'Oeuvre*, Paris 1942. The latter volume gives precious bibliographical indications. Cf. also: René Hubert, *Les Sciences sociales dans l'Encyclopédie*, Paris 1923. See also *Origines de l'Esprit encyclopédique*, in Brunetières' suggestive volume *Etudes sur le XVIIIème Siècle*, Paris 1911. Voltaire's *Lettres Philosophiques* should be studied in Lanson's fine edition or in H. Labroue's more recent one.

Chapter VI.

On Montesquieu: the best book so far is probably Joseph Dedieu, *Montesquieu. L'Homme et l'Oeuvre*, Paris 1943. Dedieu gives also a short and admirable bibliography. *De l'Esprit des Lois* has recently been edited in an American edition by Franz Neumann who has added to the old translation by Thomas Nugent a well-informed introduction: Montesquieu, *The Spirit of the Laws*, Hafner Classics, New-

York 1949. See also the recent French edition *De l'Esprit des Lois*, edited by Jean Brethe de la Gressaye, *Les Textes français*, Paris 1950. Amongst the older studies on Montesquieu the following are still indispensable: Albert Sorel, *Montesquieu*, Paris 1887; H. Barckhausen, *Montesquieu. Ses Idées et ses Oeuvres d'après les papiers de La Brède*, Paris 1907; *Montesquieu*, by Joseph Dedieu, Paris 1913; *Montesquieu*, by Victor Klemperer, Heidelberg 1914-1915. Meinecke's *Die Entstehung des Historismus*, Munich and Berlin 1936, contains a fascinating chapter on Montesquieu. Cf. also Dedieu, *Montesquieu et la tradition politique anglaise en France*, Paris 1909, which ought to be read in conjunction with G. Bonno, *La Constitution britannique devant l'Opinion française. De Montesquieu à Bonaparte*, Paris 1932. Important with invaluable bibliography. E. Carcassonne, *Montesquieu et le problème de la Constitution française au XVIIIème Siècle* is indispensable. See also F. T. H. Fletcher, *Montesquieu and English Politics. 1750-1800*, London 1939. The most convenient recent edition of Montesquieu is the one done by Roger Caillois in Gallimard's admirable series *La Pléiade* in two volumes. Caillois' introduction is brilliant. Emile Durkheim's famous thesis has recently been re-edited: *Montesquieu et Rousseau, Précurseurs de la Sociologie*, Note introductive par G. Davy, Paris 1953. A fine and scholarly complete edition of Montesquieu's works is in progress, edited by André Masson. Vol. I and II have already been published (Paris 1950 and 1953). See also D. C. Cabeen, *Montesquieu; A Bibliography*, New York 1947.

Chapter VII.

Elie Halévy, *The Growth of Philosophic Radicalism*, London 1938, a classic study. (With invaluable bibliography.) W. H. Wickwar, *Helvétius and Holbach* in *The Social and Political Ideas of some great French thinkers of the Age of Reason*, edited F. J. C. Hearnshaw, London 1930; cf. A. Keim, *Helvétius, Sa Vie et son Oeuvre*, Paris 1907; on Holbach see Pierre Naville, *D'Holbach*, Paris 1943.

On Diderot: Jean Pommier, *Diderot avant Vincennes*, Paris 1939; Daniel Mornet, *Diderot. L'Homme et l'Oeuvre*, Paris

1941; Henri Lefèbvre, *Diderot*, Paris 1949; John Morley's *Diderot and the Encyclopaedists*, London 1878, 2 vols. is still useful.

Chapter VIII.

For a recent interpretation of Rousseau's totalitarian democracy, see the important volume by J. L. Talmon, *The Origins of totalitarian Democracy*, London 1952. (With valuable notes.) On Rousseau see Albert Schinz, *La Pensée de Jean-Jacques Rousseau*, Paris 1929; Alfred Cobban, *Rousseau and the Modern State*, London 1934, an important book. Cf. also Robert Derathé, *Jean-Jacques Rousseau et la Science politique de son temps*, Paris 1950, an admirable study; see the same author's *Le Rationalisme de Rousseau*. There are two suggestive essays by Ernst Cassirer in *Rousseau, Kant, Goethe*, Princeton 1945. Amongst older studies two should be mentioned: E. Champion, *J. J. Rousseau et la Révolution française*, Paris 1909; and Richard Fester's important work: *Rousseau und die deutsche Geschichtsphilosophie*, Leipsic 1890. Vaughan's edition of the *Political Writings of Rousseau* in two vols. is still not superseded. Cf. also Bertrand de Jouvenel's edition of the *Contrat Social*, Geneva 1947.

Chapter IX.

André Lichtenberger, *Le Socialisme au XVIIIème Siècle*, Paris 1895, is still fundamental. On Mably and Morelly, see *Morelly and Mably* by C. H. Driver in *The Social and Political Ideas of some great French thinkers of the Age of Reason*, with bibliography.

On Physiocrats, see the classic work by G. Weulersse, *Le Mouvement physiocratique en France de 1756 à 1770*, two vols., Paris 1910; and by the same author *La Physiocratie sous les ministères de Turgot et de Necker (1774-1781)*, Paris 1950 (with important bibliographical references). Cf. also M. Beer, *An Inquiry into Physiocracy*, London 1939. On Babeuf see the valuable little book by David Thomson: *The Babeuf Plot*, London 1949.

Chapter X.

On Saint-Pierre see P. Vaucher, *The Abbé de Saint-Pierre* in *The Social and Political Ideas of some great French Thinkers of the Age of Reason:* J. Drouet, *L'Abbé de Saint-Pierre*, Paris 1912. See also Albert Duchène, *Les Reveries de Bernardin de Saint-Pierre*, Paris 1935. On Kant cf. K. Vorlaender, *Immanuel Kant. Der Mann und das Werk*, two vols., Leipsic 1924. Cf. also E. Hoffmann-Linke, *Zwischen Nationalismus und Demokratie. Gestalten der franzoesischen Vorrevolution*, Munich 1927. Meinecke, *Die Idee der Staatsraeson*, Munich and Berlin 1929. Chapter XI.

J. B. Bury, *The Idea of Progress. An Inquiry into its origin and growth*, London 1928. On Condorcet, see L. Cahen, *Condorcet et La Révolution française*, Paris 1904; the best edition of the *Esquisse d'un tableau historique des progrès de l'esprit humain* is by O. H. Prior; with bibliography. See also John Morley, *Condorcet* in *Critical Miscellanies*, vol. II, London 1892 and J. S. Schapiro, *Cordorcet and the Rise of Liberalism*, New York 1934.

Conclusion.

Cf. Léon Brunchvicg's great work: *Le Progrès de la Conscience dans la Philosophie occidentale*, 2 vols., Paris 1927.

These bibliographical references do not aim at completion. They merely intend to give some guidance for further study.

J.P.M.

INDEX

ACADEMY of France, influence on the *philosophes*, 61, 104-5
Aguesseau, d', 83, 88, 148
Aiguillon, d', 81
Alembert, d', 93, 97, 102, 104, 105, 107, 108, 144, 170-1, 191, 196, 198, 199, 287
Althusius, 12
Ambrose, St, 226
Anabaptists, 12, 135
Angell, Norman, 268, n.
Aquinas, 1, 226
Argenson, d', 68, 76, 79, 80, 94, 105, 186, 189, 238
Aristotle, 1, 10, 118, 128, 153, 157, 188, 192, 284
Arnauld, author of *La fréquente Communion* (1643), 36-7
Arnould, author of *De la Balance du Commerce* (1788), 75
Atkinson, G., 120, n.
Aubertin, 67
Augustine, St, 36, 299
Aulard, 77, n.

BABBITT, Professor, 66
Babeuf, 223, 250, 257-8
Bachaumont, 79, 94, 100
Bacon, 13, 170-1, 281
Balzac, 37
Barbier, 79, 81-2, 94-5
Barre, La, 144
Barry, Madame du, 78
Baudeau, 230
Bayle, 35, 44, 47-54, 67, 98, 119, 122, 124, 145, 151
Beaumarchais, 71, 93
Beccaria, 137, 139, 290
Benedict XIV., 106
Bentham, 7-8, 61, 127, 132, 138, 174, 177, 181-2, 185, 188, 189, 218, 231, 233, 268
Bernis, 76, 265
Blackstone, 127, 152, 165
Bodin, 29, 83, 120, 157, 259, 284
Boisguillebert, 58-61
Poissel, 252
bonald, 66
Bonhours, 28
Bonneau, 35
Bossuet, theory of absolutism, 26, 29, 34-5; theory of Providence, 42-4, 156, 282-4; mentioned, 31, 39, 52, 55, 56, 121, 225, 227
Boulainvilliers, 57-8, 61, 161, 228, 263

Bourdaloue, 54, 55, n.
Bretonne, Restif de la, 286
Brissot de Warville, 252-3
Broglie, de, 225
Brosses, de, 120, n.
Brunetière, 39, n., 43-4, n.
Bruyère, La, 14
Buffon, 99, 100, 104-5, 121, 127
Burgundy, Duke of, 55, 57, 63
Burke, 96, 152, 166-8, 208, 218
Butler, Bishop, 125
Buttafuoco, 209-10
Buvat, 94

CALAS, execution of, 138, 144-5
Calonne, 89
Calvin, 50
Cambacérès, de, 226
Cantillon, 228
Carcassonne, 83, n., 161, n.
Caribs, 121
Carlile, Richard, 174, n.
Carra, 251
Catherine the Great, 104, 142, 262
Chaise, La, 38, n.
Champion, 67
Chapelier Law, the, 216
Chastellux, 178, 286-7
Chateaubriand, 219
Châtelet, the, 82, 87, 95
Cherel, 55, n.
Chesterfield, Lord, 89
Chillingworth, 125
China, as Utopia, 98, 230
Choiseul, 81, 209, 265
Churchill, 120
Clarke, 47
Claude, 32
Clement XI., 38
Cobden, 268, n.
Coke, 23, 83
Colbert, 28, 58-9
Cole, G. D. H., 216, n.
Comte, 278, 286
Condillac, 121-2, 172, 179, 221, 231
Condorcet, his theory of progress discussed, 286-99; referred to, 16, 21, 62, 66, 88, 108, 123, 151, 167, 278, 303
Copernicus, 13, 144
Corsica, 209-10
Cours des Aides, 82, 87

DAMIENS, 77, 100
Dante, 42, n.
Danton, 256

312

INDEX

Darwinism, influence of, 4, 122
Dedieu, 148, n.
Deffand, Madame du, 16, 103, 105, 115, 150, 188
Delaisi, 27, n.
Descartes, 13 ff., 36, 40, 45, 48, 117-8, 128, 148, 171, 179, 231, 290
Deschamps, Dom, 239, n.
Déverité, 250
Dickinson, G. Lowes, 61, n.
Diderot, 42, 81, 92-4, 97, 102, 104-5, 108-10, 119, 127, 129, 135, 136, 139, 142, 151, 172-3, 181, 242
Diggers, the, 12
Domat, 83, 148
Doria, 148, n.
Dubois, 227
Du Bosc, 32
Dupin, 108, 229
Dupont, 230, 233

EDUCATION, theories of, 56, 182-3, 191, 196, 211, 213
Encyclopædia, 46, 94, 97, 98, 100, 102, 147, 170-1, 201
England, its influence on French thought, 23-4, 32-3, 123-7, 135-8, 140-1, 152, 162-9, 177, 181-2, 188-9, 192-5, 206-8, 214-5, 233-5, 247-8
Entresol club, 94
Epinay, Madame d', 96, 110, 198
Escobar, 31, 37
Everett, C. W., 227, n.

FAGUET, E., 67
Federalists, the, 152, 165
Fénelon, 39-40, 55-7, 61, 63, 148, 225, 263
Figaro, 75, 95
Figgis, N., 216, n.
Filmer, 34, 120
Flammermont, cited, 83-5
Fleury, 76, 94
Fontenelle, 44-6, 103, 170, 281
Fourier, 243
Fox, George, 135
Francis I., 95
Franklin, 50, 108, 143
Frederick the Great, 104, 141-2, 144, 261-2, 266
Fréron, 96
Freud, influence of, 4
Fronde, the, 24-5, 31

GALIANI, 106, 172
Galileo, 13, 144
Gallicanism, 31, 35 ff.
Garrick, 108
Gasquet, de, 226
Geoffrin, Madame, 103, 105, 109

George II., 164
George III., 164-5
Gerdil, 204, n.
Gibbon, 131, 284
Girondists, 215, 251
Godwin, 214
Gosselin, 252
Griffet, 226
Grimm, 96, 107, 112
Grotius, 259-261

HALÉVY, E., 177, n.
Haller, 112
Harrington, 284
Hartley, 179, 182
Hegel, 215, 239
Heine, 18
Helvétius, his philosophy, 172-4, 177-188; mentioned, 7, 61, 102, 109, 151, 166, 168-9, 242, 296
Henry IV., 23, 30-2, 51, 62, 271
Henry VIII., 261-2
Herbert of Cherbury, 125
Hobbes, 23, 34-5, 120, 121, 154, 155, 173, 199, 200, 203, 206, 207
Höffding, 124, n.
Holbach, his salon, 103, 108-110, 115; his philosophy, 131, 171-7, 179, 187-191; mentioned, 101, 242, 243, 269, 300
Houdetot, Madame d', 110
Howard, 290
Hugo, Victor, 219
Hume, 14, 108, 177, 182
Hurons, 120-1
Hutchison, 177

IROQUOIS, 120-1

JACOBINS, 152
James II., 33
Jansen, 36
Jansenism, 36 ff., 69, 79, 94, 100, 144-5, 225
Jefferson, 8
Jesuits, 11, 35-8, 69, 79 ff., 94, 100, 102, 144, 153, 185, 225, 237
Johnson, Dr, 128
Joly, Claude, 24, 225
Joseph of Austria, 142
Julian the Apostate, 283, 288
Jurieu, 33-4, 50
Jus gentium, 10

KANT, his *Perpetual Peace*, 272-6; mentioned, 21, 192-3, 215, 259, 267
Kaye, 180, n.
Keim, cited, 177, n.

313

INDEX

INDEX

Plato, 10, 98, 128, 140, 196, 202, 236, 237, 239, 245, 248
Plutarch, 148
Poland, 210-12
Politiques, the, 49
Pombal, 142
Pompadour, Madame de, 78, 81, 102, 229, 265
Pope, 120, 129, 130, 141
Port Royal, 36-7
Postgate, 257, n., 258, n.
Potemkin, 142
Poucet de la Rivière, 225
Poulle, Abbé, 226
Poupelinière, 74, 108
Protestants, French, 1, 30 ff., 47-9; relief of, 88-9
Puaux, 27, n., 32, n.
Puffendorf, 155, 259

Quakers, 129, 133
Quesnay, 97, 229-30
Quesnel, 37-8

Rabelais, 1, 90
Racine, 16, 105
Rambouillet, Hôtel de, 103
Ramsay, Abbé, 94
Rapin, Father, 52
Reddaway, 265, n.
Retz, Cardinal de, 23, 25
Ricardo, 253
Richelieu, 30, 51, 259
Richelieu, Marshal, 66
Robespierre, 217, 256-7
Robinson Crusoe, 120, 216
Robson, W. A., 166, n.
Rochefoucauld, de la, 14, 103
Rocquain, 67
Rousseau, character and social relations of, 96, 108, 113, n.; philosophy of, 192-219; views on property, 238-9; views on perpetual peace, 269-73; other references, 12, 19, 21, 62, 66, 74, 88, 89, 93, 101, 121, 127, 130, 139, 147, 151-2, 174, 182-3, 187, 220, 226, 247, 250, 253, 258, 287, 302
Roustan, 68, 74, n., 225, n.

Saint-Cyran, 36
Saint-Evrémond, 39-40
Saint-Pierre, Abbé de, 61-3, 94, 122, 177, 263, 269-71, 280-1
Saint-Pierre, Bernardin, 219
Saint-Simon, 57, 63, 161
San Domingo, 254
Saurin, 169

Savigny, 152
Say, J. B., 230
Sée, H., 57, n., 84, n., 89, n., 227, n.
Seneca, 281
Servetus, 50
Shaftesbury, 47, 126, 181
Shelburne, 108
Sheridan, 166
Sièyes, Abbé, 8, 217
Simon, Richard, 47
Sirven, 144-5
Slavery, abolition of, 292-3
Smith, Adam, 59, 189, 234
Sorbonne, 38, 95
Sorel, Albert, 86
Sparta as a Utopia, 10, 121, 148, 211, 237, 249
Spartacus, 256
Spinoza, 14, 40, 128, 153, 154-5, 173, 198
Staël, Madame de, 29
States-General, 2, 24, 30, 71, 76, 82, 84, 87-9
Stephen, Leslie, 124
Sully, 259, 261
Sweden as a Utopia, 247-8

Tellier, Le, 38, n.
Temperley, H. W. V., 265, n.
Temple, Sir William, 164, n.
Tencin, Madame de, 91, 103-4, 148, 227
Terray, Abbé, 87
Theresa, Rousseau's mistress, 113
Thomas, 231
Tindal, 47, 125
Tocqueville, de, 24, 195
Toland, 47, 125
Turgot, 72, 76, 86-8, 97, 108, 115, 147, 177, 187, 191, 229-30; views on property, 223-4; view of history, 285-7

Unigenitus, Bull, 37 ff., 79, 82
Utilitarianism, 7-8, 23, 61, 132 ff.

Vallière, Mademoiselle de la, 28
Vattel, 259
Vauban, 58-9, 61, 87, 228
Vaughan, 148, 199, 202, 205, n.
Vauvenargues, 15, n., 108
Vico, 148, 152
Voland, Mademoiselle, 172
Volney, 286
Voltaire, his philosophy, 20, 117, 123, 146, 174; on war, 63, 262, 265-7, 269; view of history, 282-4, 289; other references, 45, 46, 47, 49, 66, 74, 79, 81, 88, 93, 94, 97, 99, 101, 104, 108, 109, 112, 115, 122, 151, 153, 162, 163, 170, 177, 195, 229, 274

315

INDEX